NUMBER ONE
FAN

HELEN AITCHISON

Published by Write on the Tyne

Printed and bound in Great Britain by Clays Ltd, Elcograf S.p.A

Paperback ISBN: 978-1-0682274-1-7

Cover image & design: Jarmila Takac (Instagram: @jarmila.covers)

Published by Write on the Tyne
www.writeonthetyne.com

For Paul, my number one fan.

Chapter 1

'Barney!' the woman shouted, as the leaves made a satisfying crunch under her feet. She whistled to the Labrador, who ignored her, immersed in ecstasy from his freedom. A flash of yellow shot past the corner of her left eye as he darted around the woods with joy, before turning to her momentarily, tongue hanging out in glorious pant. Giggling, she jangled his lead as she continued walking – observing the caramel-coloured leaves, the odd ruby red one dotted amongst them, like gems on a crispy carpet.

'Barney,' she called, glancing around to locate her dog amongst the plethora of trees. 'Come on, son.' There was no bounding back to her for a pat on the head or treat before sprinting off again. *Where are you?* the woman thought, whistling and shouting his name once more.

The woods of Ashmouth were vast. Ancient oaks and silver birch trees stood like sentinels across the endless green area. Dog walkers usually kept to the track but Barney had surplus energy, bouncier than a tennis ball at Wimbledon, and loved nothing more than to torpedo through the dense trees and chase rabbits.

Eventually she saw his golden coat ahead. 'Hey, come on.' She tapped her thigh for her usually obedient dog.

The hound's head remained down in the ground, nuzzling and digging. Tutting, the woman headed towards him. No doubt he was sniffing for something he shouldn't, she absentmindedly pondered. Traipsing over, her walking boots cracked on fallen branches and stuck lightly in muddy earth. She let out a groan as she travelled the slight incline to her pet.

Getting closer, she saw Barney still hadn't looked up from snuffling the ground, his paws stomping on the mud below them. As his owner approached, he barked loudly, tilted his head, then turned his gaze back to the ground.

'What you found, nosey boy?' she said playfully.

The dog barked again, louder and fiercer as his eyes remained on the ground. The woman was five metres away, then four, three… Barney released a tiny whimper.

I hope it's not a dead rabbit, she thought, reaching her beloved dog to discover his source of interest. Next to him lay a pile of leaves. To the side, a heap of earth that he had dug up. Her vision moved from the pile of soil to the left. Time paused as the woman's eyes picked up the image and her brain registered the horrifying sight. A tip of an exposed nose and upper lip popped out of the earth as if revealed through an advent calendar door. She dropped Barney's lead and screamed so loudly the trees shook.

Chapter 2

It was the end of September and the air in North East England held an autumn coolness. Detective Sergeant Polly McCardle stood with Detective Constable Claire Boyd, as CSI, in their ghostly uniforms of PPE, examined the area where a body had been found. Uniformed police stood at the entrances of Ashmouth woods, advising dog walkers and runners that the green space was closed. The witness who made the grim discovery was at Crosley Police Station, giving a statement.

'What do we know so far, boss?' DC Boyd asked her superior, as they stood side by side, watching the officers perform their methodical routine.

'Male, Caucasian, young. Little signs of decomposition so likely it's a very recent death. Hopefully, pathology can give us a speedy update on the cause and we can obtain a positive ID.' DS McCardle tucked her blonde bobbed hair behind her ear then placed her hand on her chin.

Both officers remained facing forward, studying their colleagues' rituals in silent contemplation. Polly McCardle had been a police officer for ten years and at thirty-five years old, had been a DS for the past eleven months, following the retirement of her superior, DS Ronnie Ericson, and then subsequently filling the vacant position. She loved being part of the Murder Investigation Team, but she doubted she would ever get used to the disposability of humans and the unnerving way that life could be extinguished so quickly and brutally.

It wasn't a job for everyone, and harder than ever in a world of constant crime. Where stabbings seemed to happen daily in parts of the UK, and jarringly, no one seemed shocked anymore. Prisons were full and the criminal justice system had as many holes as a colander. McCardle knew that she and all of her colleagues across the force were essential, and made a difference. However, they were still human.

The pair returned to Polly's car, leaving the CSIs to gather much-needed evidence, and the deceased would be transported to the mortuary at North Tyneside General Hospital. Arriving at the station, McCardle nodded and took her vape out of her black wool coat pocket.

Boyd sniggered. 'I'll put the kettle on.'

She walked into the building leaving Polly to stroll to the smokers' yard. The air was cold but the sky blue, the sun trying to push its way through thick, heavy clouds. Closing her eyes momentarily, she recalled that beautiful warmth of summer sun on her face from the few months prior. Autumn and winter were long in North East England. Of course, nothing like other places in the world such as Canada, but they seemed to go on forever. Inhaling her cherry-flavoured vape, Polly exhaled deeply. It was better than the cigarettes, that was for sure, and it had been one of her New Year goals to give up smoking tobacco. She'd mainly stuck to it so far.

After a few minutes' respite in what would undoubtedly be a long shift, McCardle clicked her neck from side to side as she entered the police station. Walking the corridor and stairs, she rang the coroner's officer to request a Home-Office registered pathologist. Entering the MIT office, she announced there would be a team briefing in twenty minutes – then she would head to the hospital to meet the pathologist and the CSI manager for the post-mortem of the discovered body.

Boyd slid a cup of tea onto her desk with a smile.

'Thanks.' McCardle returned the smile.

Holding the cup in her cold hands, she pressed her lips

together and glanced at the photo attached to the unattractive blue privacy board on her desk. It was from a holiday last year to New York with her wife Lisa. Brooklyn Bridge on the second day of their break; when jet lag and being a copper meant that Polly was awake at 5am, and the pair were strolling across the iconic bridge an hour later. She smiled at the photo: a selfie with happy faces, eyes squinting in the sun that was beginning to heat the day like lightly toasted bread. Smiles of love, relaxation, excitement, and adventure. The smile that her wife told her she only ever really wore when she was off work, detached from the all-consuming job that was a detective sergeant.

Sipping her tea, McCardle checked her emails in case of anything from the CSI manager, following the removal of the body two hours ago. The usual checks would be run through the system to try to identify the deceased: fingerprint and DNA database search, immigration check, facial recognition from the national police database, and missing persons check.

She placed her cup down on the grey slate coaster, embossed with 'DS McCardle', a gift from DS Ericson when he retired a year ago. Even though they only worked together for eighteen months, he had left an imprint on her that was more than a boss. He was a role model, a life-long friend and in many ways, a father figure to Polly. Being at his old desk strangely made McCardle feel close to him, as if his wisdom remained in the plastic-coated grain of the desk top and the runners of the desk drawers.

It was five minutes until the briefing, and her colleagues began going to the toilet or to make a hot drink. Rising from her seat, she walked to the small office space used for briefings. Even with her ankle-boot heel, at five foot two inches in height and of slim build, McCardle found her colleagues often towered above her. Despite her petite size, she took no prisoners, in and out of work. Soon her small team were all in the room, sipping hot drinks, clicking pens, and chatting. She sat at the front, facing her colleagues, glancing at her notepad before there became a natural silence and she spoke.

'Team, just after 8.40 this morning, the body of a young, white male was discovered in Ashmouth Woods. A civilian found the deceased, thanks to her dog. We haven't got a positive ID or a cause of death but I'm heading to the hospital after this.' McCardle scanned the room, meeting the eyes of her team, who listened intently. 'The deceased hadn't been there long, and given the way the body was found, we are treating it as suspicious. CSIs remain on site. Chief Inspector Richardson is issuing a statement for the press...' she glanced at her watch, 'within the next hour or two with anything we have up to date. The witness has been interviewed. DC Birdy, DC Lucas, can one of you please check on her this afternoon?'

Both officers nodded to their superior. 'There are no CCTV cameras in and around the area.' She rolled her eyes. 'The rest of you, await further instructions and keep communication open with the teams, especially any possible leads from front desk and call-handlers.' The team rose and returned to their desks while Polly remained in the room to call Chief Inspector Richardson – not that there was much information she could provide until she returned from the hospital.

Arriving at North Tyneside General Hospital, Polly found an empty bay. Cutting the engine and leaving her vehicle, she dashed across the car park and into the main entrance of the busy hospital. Smiling to the receptionist, she nodded and kept walking briskly to her destination. Opting for the stairs rather than the lift, McCardle walked down the clinical corridors. Walls decorated with framed photos and artwork tried to bring colour and comfort into the sterile, white environment. Distant beeping, the rushing past of medical staff, and faces of patients or visitors, more solemn than jolly, accompanied her for a minute or so, before she opened a door and travelled down two flights of stairs to the double doors that led to the mortuary. As she flashed her access pass, the door unlocked.

A strong stomach was needed to visit the mortuary and it still baffled Polly how someone could actually do the job of a pathologist. Surely, they could never see the human body through the same eyes as everyone else? And undoubtedly, they had nightmares. She shook her head. Polly and her team, her predecessors and future colleagues had and would continue to witness trauma during their work practice. The painful, the tragic, the heart-breaking, the shocking, the indescribable – they all left a catalogue of images imprinted on the mind. However, these were mainly sporadic and not a daily event. Unlike pathology, whose role was studying and dissecting corpses, regardless of the upmost respect and precision they did it with. Sculptures and jigsaws of the dead to find critical clues.

She shuddered, walking the few steps to the next set of doors, and pressed the intercom, seeing into the office where Home-Office registered Doctor Harris stood, notes in hand. Doctor Harris's eyes lifted from her notes and she waved with one hand before lowering it and pressing the door release. McCardle pushed open the door.

'Ah, Polly, hi. How are you?'

'Good, thanks, Marie. And yourself?'

Doctor Harris smiled. 'Great, and better for seeing you. Although, I'd prefer we were having a cup of tea and talking about the latest book releases than this.' She glanced to the main room of the mortuary, the examination room, where stainless-steel tables lay, almost sparkling in the harsh strip lighting and white painted walls.

McCardle nodded. 'Only a young lad by the looks of it.'

They walked to another room where Crime Scene Manager Malcolm sat, who would take photographs. The three covered the information gathered at the scene of crime. Photos showed the young man, and Polly swallowed, feeling sadness creep up her throat. There was always something about the young victims that got to her. Those around twenty-five and under, who had their lives ahead of them. Perhaps just discovering who they were, enjoying the lightness that youth often provided. Adventure, new relationships, careers, and travel.

They made her think of her own twenties, when she struggled with her sexuality before coming out as a gay woman and felt like the ice she had been frozen in for so many years was melting. Touching her collarbone over her grey jumper, she pressed her lips together. No one deserved to be murdered, regardless of who they were or how old they were. McCardle and CSI Manager Malcolm looked through the existing photographs and discussed notes for ten minutes, before both followed Doctor Harris into the changing room to get ready.

Entering the examination room, she felt the temperature drop as they walked across the hard flooring to meet Doctor Harris's assistant at a table occupied by the victim, a range of surgical apparatuses by the side. Polly cleared her throat under her facemask. The body bag was opened, revealing the young male's body, and the procedure began with Doctor Harris explaining each thought and action.

'You'll see here, DS McCardle, trauma to the back of the cranium. Blunt force from an object such as a brick or spade.'

McCardle observed as Malcolm remained silent, taking photographs. The shape of the deceased's head had changed with the impact of the head trauma.

'Ready?' Doctor Harris asked gently, knowing that her nine-to-five, and then some more, was no longer shocking or squeamish for her, but it likely was for detectives, who were exposed to such procedures infrequently.

She nodded. Of course, she wasn't ready for what her colleague was about to do, but it was essential and Polly needed to know everything in order to give it her all in solving the crime. Doctor Harris's eyes curled up slightly, indicating a smile behind her face mask. She began operating on the deceased's head, cutting around the back and side of the skull at the hairline. Done with precision and respect; Doctor Harris was methodical.

Swallowing and taking a deep breath, Polly puffed out her cheeks, knowing all colour had drained from her already pale complexion. There was a sound that resembled Velcro being pulled apart as Doctor Harris peeled the incised part of the skull back and exposed the brain where head trauma could be identified. After highlighting and discussing the blunt force impact, Malcolm took photos as McCardle asked questions.

'There are no other signs of injury, no puncture wounds, no visible bruising around areas of concern such as the neck, and no broken bones. I can conclude the head injury was likely the cause of death.' She glanced, nodding, to McCardle. 'Of course, we do need toxicology to assess whether there is any substance of concern in the deceased. That may change my thinking. But as it stands, with the head trauma, it is likely the victim died due to subdural hematoma.' Doctor Harris moved away from the table and turned her body to Polly.

'We don't have a positive ID as yet, hopefully this will be forthcoming from medical records or family coming forward,' McCardle said, moving on the spot. 'I've put in a Home Office urgent request for toxicology, so hopefully that will come back in twenty-four hours or so,' she added.

Thanking Doctor Harris and CSI Manager Malcolm, she left the hospital and drove back to Crosley Police Station, the only audio being her thoughts in her mind.

Within twelve hours of attending the autopsy, the police had a positive ID of the body, confirmed by the deceased's next of kin. Oliver Thornton, a twenty-one-year-old Northumbria University student. Originally from York, he had lived in Newcastle for two years. After his flatmates raised the alarm due to him not returning home for over a day, his mother subsequently travelled the ninety-minute drive from York to confirm the deceased was her son. Something no parent should have to do, but something that McCardle and her colleagues across the force had to instigate daily.

Samples had been sent to toxicology by pathology, and the team were awaiting the results. For now, it was looking like Oliver Thornton had been killed by a blunt force blow to the head, likely something such as a bat, brick, or spade. Any substances in his body may or may not have played a part but that head injury was certainly inflicted by another person. There was limited further damage to his body meaning, for example, that he had not fallen from a height.

Pathology informed McCardle that they estimated that Thornton had been dead around thirty hours before his body was discovered. As a positive ID had been conducted and Oliver Thornton died in suspicious circumstances, a murder hunt would be launched and updates and actions would be disseminated by DS McCardle at the 8am team briefing the following morning.

Chapter 3

Polly arrived back home fourteen hours after leaving for work that morning. Her wife greeted her at the front door, a warm smile on her olive-skinned face that soothed Polly immediately. Home was a feeling, not a place, and Lisa was definitely her home. Half an hour later, she was showered and sitting on the sofa, legs tucked under her bum, a bowl of rice and chicken on her lap, and Lisa by her side.

'A kid, Lees. His whole life ahead of him. Wiped out, just like that.' She clicked her fingers and shook her head.

Lisa squeezed her wife's knee. 'I don't know how you do it.' She took an intake of breath. 'I mean, the things you see, have to deal with. I know I say it all the time but jeez, you and your team, you're all some kind of superheroes.'

Polly made a hmph noise. 'With no useful superpower!'

They both released a sad laugh. Lisa leant in and kissed her cheek. 'I'll make us a cuppa.' She rose from the green velvet sofa and left Polly staring into her half-eaten bowl of food, wondering what tomorrow would bring.

The wind kept Polly awake half of the night. Well, that, and the grim discovery of Oliver Thornton's body. She was an experienced detective and had seen a lot in her decade-long police career, but it never got any easier, and the day Polly stopped caring, would be the day she was in the wrong career. Ronnie Ericson had repeated that to her, and in over thirty years in the force, he still had that compassion and drive, even on his final shift.

Polly smiled to herself on her way into work, thinking about Ronnie and their time working as a team. Their unbreakable friendship that developed from working on their first case together: a murder case. Luckily, after his retirement a year ago, he had kept in touch and Polly saw him frequently, as well as popping by the Cake Station each week – a bakery and café run by Ronnie and his wife Caroline.

Arriving at the station, she grabbed her handbag and the tote bag containing her lunch from the passenger seat. Walking across the carpark, she scrunched her shoulders to her neck and winced slightly – her weekly session of Pilates couldn't come quick enough. But first, she had a few more shifts to make progress with the team on the Thornton murder.

The team briefing commenced at 8am. Reiterating the discovery of Oliver Thornton yesterday and the circumstances surrounding the death, McCardle rose from her chair and moved to the next photo, her pen pointing towards it.

'Thornton was killed late on the evening of 29th September or the early hours of 30th September. A blunt instrument was used with force on the victim's skull.' She pointed to a photograph on the incident board, showing the injury on the right-hand side of the deceased's head. 'Likely an object such as a brick or a spade that caused a subdural hematoma. The fact that the body had been hidden tells us this is suspicious. Toxicology results came in half an hour ago. Alcohol in the deceased's system, nothing else. Any update from the witness?' She glanced at DC Lucas and DC Birdy.

Lucas nodded to Birdy, who began talking. 'No update from the initial statement but to reiterate, the witness was walking her dog on a regular route. The dog ran off into the woods and wasn't responding to her calls. She approached the dog who was nuzzling into the ground and barking. His buried treasure was some poor young bloke. She didn't recognise the deceased, although I'm sure his face will unfortunately be etched on her mind for a long time.'

McCardle lifted her chin. 'Thanks. At this stage, team, we have no more updates. No doubt the next twenty-four hours will prove critical. So, the plans for today: Myers, Lucas, Birdy, if you can lead on talking to Thornton's housemates, university friends, and colleagues, please. Boyd and I will visit his family and once we know of his movements in the days leading up to his murder, we can retrace.'

With that the briefing was over and all officers had a role. Now that the formal ID of the body had been completed, there would be a press conference. The story would be released to the world, likely bringing in lots of calls to the station, both useful and a waste of time, but officers would be available to deal with enquiries and make notes of any potential leads.

McCardle and Boyd travelled to Corbridge, where Oliver Thornton's parents were staying in a rented cottage to help police with enquiries, until his funeral back home in York. On the way, the pair chatted about work and life. Polly had a calmness and empathy to her personality. She was a listener by nature, more than a speaker, which came in handy for police work: observant and reflective. And she was one of those women about whom, even in 2025, people still commented would make a great mother. Boyd had children herself and had previously worked with disabled kids before joining the police. She had a warmth about her that worked well with McCardle.

'How's the kids doing, Claire?' Polly asked as her eyes remained on the motorway.

'Getting bigger and cheekier each day,' she replied, laughing at the end of her sentence.

Polly smiled. Lisa was keen to start their family, but she was less convinced than her wife. There was a pressure for women to procreate that almost still felt as strong and debated as it was seventy years ago – as if motherhood were the only identity a woman could hold. When McCardle first came out as a gay woman fifteen years ago, she remembered the initial reaction of her usually supportive mother.

'Does that mean you'll never give me grandchildren?' Her mother had clasped her hands to her head, bereft at the thought of no babies from her daughter.

It was ignorant and offensive, although her mother just didn't get it, any of it. And her mother was like many people who thought parenthood was the be-all and end-all of life. But it was for life, being a parent, and despite the responsibility that weighed more than an elephant on her shoulders daily at work, Polly wasn't 100% sure she wanted the responsibility of being a parent. And days like yesterday, with young adults being murdered, made her waver even further.

They soon arrived at their destination, a quaint holiday let that would have been an idyllic break under very different circumstances. As they walked up the cobblestone path, decorated either side by plants and bushes, a weary-looking Mrs Thornton opened the door. Her bobbed, curly, grey-infused hair framed her face, and small round glasses covered her heavy eyes. She greeted them and the officers entered the cottage, to a tall, thin Mr Thornton standing in the hallway, leaning against the thick oak bannister.

'How are you?' McCardle asked with a sad smile, knowing the parents would never recover from such horrendous tragedy.

They answered, with words expected. Then the four people moved into the lounge so the police could update Oliver's parents and try to answer the questions that were haunting their every moment.

Chapter 4

It had been spontaneous yet instinctual for David Creighton to attack Oliver Thornton. The need to protect, like a wild animal defends its young from predators. The requirement to prove to himself that he could protect her, do anything for her; Emily Robinson's own superhero. Had he wanted to kill Oliver Thornton? David wasn't sure. But if he hadn't ended his life, he would have surely been caught. The drive in him, his love for her – it took over. David was defending the woman he adored. The woman he would do anything for, including kill. And that smug little bastard had it coming. Three times in the last six months he had witnessed Oliver embarrassing her by asking those questions in his annoying drawl.

'I'm a criminology student and I'm just wondering…' the smug, pompous shit would say. He had to listen, watch with fury erupting in him, as she moved nervously in her chair. Yet she smiled, attempting to placate his insistent probing, clearly embarrassed and uncomfortable with his relentless showing off and interrogating. That voice, his lack of accent that just made him seem like an imposter to the area. His demeanour as he crossed and uncrossed his legs, as if he were a lord, sent to show the underdogs how important he was. Asking questions to try to impress others but to intimidate, belittle, and degrade her creativity. He was stupid and young. What the hell did he know about life? About the world and working hard?

That night at Crosley Library the student had sat there, clearing his throat and making overemphasised noises the full hour then asking the author question after question. His friend, silently beside him, cheeks flushing now and then as she witnessed her companion blabbing on about things he knew nothing about. David had wanted to drag him out there and then, tell him he was never allowed back. Instead, he had to listen further, rage building until the session ended. He almost saw the relief in Emily as she rose from the chair, taking a gulp of water, and thanking the room. Watching her sigh, feeling the heavy weight from his scathing questions. An attack from an egotistical, clueless kid. David wanted to embrace her, reassure her, and deal with the problem. Even with arseholes like Oliver Thornton, she was still humble, graceful, beautiful.

Observing his idol, he watched her glide like a swan from person to person, grateful to each of them. Her smile illuminating the room. Her eyes like a burst of evergreen on the coldest winter day. Her slender fingers shaking hands and gently touching arms. Chunks of her golden hair slipping forward as she signed books. Emily Robinson was magnetic, mesmerising, magnificent. He couldn't stand for her to feel intimidated, challenged, or embarrassed. Anger wailed inside him like a screaming baby as he pushed his fists into his trouser pockets to try to contain the urge to lash out. This wasn't the first time Oliver had done this to her, but it would be his last.

As the event finished, it was closing time and the large group dispersed onto the street. He was on fire inside thinking about what he wanted to do to the whiny student. Heading into a nearby local bar, David thought alcohol might help him calm down. Ordering a pint, he saw Oliver's friend exit the female toilets. Eyes following her, he spotted the idiot in a booth, four drinks at their table. He hmphed, gritting his teeth.

Forty minutes later, David ordered another pint. Having moved closer to the pair, but not within earshot, he sat supping his beer, wondering why young people had no respect. Oliver walked past him to the bar, not looking. Although, he wouldn't recognise him – these arrogant, self-important, pompous types saw nobody they didn't want to. And David blended in – he had done all his life. As Oliver returned with a further four drinks on a tray, he sneered, watching the cockiness of the self-important shit, strutting to his seat.

Anger filled him as he thought of Emily. She was probably at home, feeling the book event was tarnished by the smug student's unrelenting questioning and quoting, referring to himself and his thoughts about criminology – despite no one asking for them or wanting to hear them! Yet here he was, having the time of his life. Selfish, self-important prick. Clasping his hand around the beer glass, he wanted to shatter it across Oliver's head for upsetting her. For upsetting him.

Inhaling deeply, he would deal with him. David knew he'd be with Emily Robinson soon; looking after her, protecting her. She was his destiny. They'd grown closer, spoken, and she'd remembered his name from that first meeting. Now, they would chat, her telling him how supportive he was. And he was convinced that each time they met, Emily was flirting with him. So polite and friendly, she was always grateful for everything, and this was why people like Oliver made him seethe. She didn't deserve anyone questioning, criticising, or being nasty to her. He wouldn't stand for it. He would look after his woman and Emily would love him like he loved her.

Despite his long day and rumbling stomach, David didn't want to leave the bar or let the idiot out of his sight, feeling compelled to watch and wait. Wanting to say something, challenge him. It was 10.30pm before Oliver's friend left, hugging him as she said goodbye. The student remained, sipping his drink as he stared at his phone.

Oliver stumbled out of the bar ten minutes later. It was raining, cold, and dark. Putting his hood up, David followed, looking around the quiet streets as he left the building. He hung back, strolling behind the student. Heading round the rear of the bar, the student was taking the short cut to the bus station, down the back alleys of takeaways, newsagents, and houses of multiple occupancy. David shadowed, wanting to confront him but not sure how to. Oliver was in his own self-absorbed world on his phone as he strolled absentmindedly in the rain, tipsy from his drinks.

The lane was dark and empty of people. Oliver passed a house of multiple occupancy, David creeping behind. Some renovation work must have been going on as there was rubble in a skip outside of the back gates. A large boulder lay on a pile of broken paving stones and scraps of wood. Lifting it up, David made an almost inaudible groan. Although slightly under average height for a man, he was strong and lean, swimming and cycling frequently. He held the boulder with his left hand, the heavy concrete cradled into his lower inner arm. He gained speed, reducing the distance between the two. With no street lighting, the odd light from a property illuminated the back alley, like a torch in an almost pitch-black garden.

Suddenly, Oliver turned, eyes wide, and looked at him. Taken aback, he twitched his head slightly then a smile curled on his face as if he were mocking David. The student's brow furrowed and he opened his sneering mouth to speak but before he could talk, he spotted the boulder nesting in the dimly lit frame of David's body. His expression changed to a flash of fear as David remained silent, inhaled deeply, and swung the rock, landing it on Oliver's right temple. Mouth open and eyes bulging, he fell to the wet ground as a streak of blood trickled from his head into the glistening road.

David's hand shook and his mouth felt like a sand box. Pushing his lips together, he swallowed, gaze fixed on the body slumped on the ground. The student's eyes were open, glaring at him. Dropping the boulder, he bent down, leaning over the motionless body, close to his mouth to see if he could feel breath. He couldn't. Standing quickly and moving back, he rubbed his hands on his scalp, fingers interlaced with his brown hair.

'Fuck,' he said quietly before letting out a slightly nervous laugh. The scene was shocking yet comical and euphoric to him. *Little bastard deserved it,* was his next thought, followed by a speedy glance around. Panic ignited in him and he shuffled his feet on the spot. As he looked backed down at Oliver's body, bile travelled up his throat and he turned, rushing to the side of the alley to be sick against a tall back wall. Shit, he couldn't leave him here.

'Aggh,' he said, his back clammy, the reality of what he had just done whirling around him. David had no gloves, his fingerprints would be on the rock. Picking up the murder weapon, he dashed back to the skip, feeling breathless and pushed it under some plywood. Taking his coat off, he glanced around, wrapped his hands and arms in the material and began pulling the body along the ground. It was almost impossible to grip him as David's arms shook, made harder by the panic producing stars in his eyes. Slowly, he dragged the body ten metres back to the house with the skip, and left his victim by the side of it.

Running to where his car was parked, several streets away, David gasped for air. His hands trembled as he started the engine, hoping no one would walk down the back lane where Oliver lay until he returned in his vehicle. A few minutes later, he was back in the lane, his car lights off. Anxiety coated him as his vehicle crept down the alley and he wondered if the body would be gone. Perhaps he was fine – had gotten up and walked off. Oliver wasn't fine and his lifeless body remained slumped by the skip, like a tatty old ragdoll.

Grabbing some driving gloves from the car's glovebox, he stuffed his hands into them, eyes darting around the alley. Getting out, David looked around again. Feeling nauseous, he also felt a buzz of being a protector, a superhero, disposing of the villain. There was no one in sight and only a few windows were illuminated behind closed blinds and curtains. Opening the back door of his Ford Focus, David grabbed his victim's lifeless body, groaning as he hooked his hands under the armpits of the corpse and dragged it once more, before reaching his car and lifting Oliver's body into it, his top half slumped on the back seat. He cursed, his heart thumping in his ears as he pushed the rest of the lifeless body into the car.

Even though David was strong, it wasn't easy and Oliver was tall. Feeling faint and sweaty, despite the cold night, he managed. Shutting the car door, he jumped into the driver's seat, legs shaking like a pneumatic drill. He took three deep breaths then drove out of the alley, turning his headlights back on at the bottom of the lane before making the four-mile journey home, his thoughts accelerating.

Pulling up at the block of flats where he lived alone, he cut the engine and breathed out as his hands shook, gripping the stationary steering wheel, thoughts exploding in his mind as he tried to absorb what had just happened. What David Creighton, an unremarkable, unnoticeable man, had just done. Sniffing up, he looked at his knuckles, encased in leather gloves as he gripped the steering wheel. Letting out a small yelp, he released his grip, pulled off the gloves, and rubbed his hands over his eyes. It was still raining outside and he watched the drizzle gather on the windscreen, tapping his feet in the footwell of the car, anxious about what to do next.

This was his first kill. He'd thought about it before, but hadn't most people fantasised about doing away with someone they loathed? Someone who had wronged them? He had wanted to kill his abusive stepdad, Keith, many times, but luckily a heart attack took care of him when David was eighteen. A shitty husband to his mother, who was now in a local care home with progressive dementia – after years of sacrifice by her only son, who looked after her as her health deteriorated.

Growing up, there was no father on the scene until his stepdad came along when he was seven years old. Ex-military and a bully, he would impose unachievable regimes and punish the youngster when the unobtainable wasn't complete. The punishments became more severe as he grew older. Physical punishments, things taken away from him if David didn't get A grades, or didn't make the fastest time in the swim team. He was mocked by his stepdad when his first girlfriend dumped him and told to 'man up' when his grandfather died.

An endless catalogue of bullying, Keith was no kinder to his mother, but she was one of those women who was desperate for love and even an unhealthy love was better than none. So yes, he had wanted to kill before, and not just his cruel bastard of a stepfather. However, David was also loyal to those he loved, still visiting his mother twice a week, even if on some days she wasn't lucid enough to recognise him.

Yes, he was loyal, and he was loyal to author Emily Robinson, his goddess – and that was why he killed Oliver Thornton and he would hurt anyone who got in their way. David had played the game all his life and still hadn't secured the prize. Forty-five years old, waiting for love. Waiting for his life to truly begin. Now, Emily was within his reach and he was changing the rules, creating his own game – one he would be the champion of.

Zoning out, he thought about his beloved and the way their relationship had developed over the last ten months. Stumbling across her by accident, he had only become aware of Emily when she attended an event at the library. It was love at first sight and he couldn't believe that he hadn't seen her before, as she was simply created for him. With several books already out, she was releasing another. Listening to her that day, he was mesmerised, besotted, and made it his mission to adore her, patiently waiting for her. David had fallen fast, and she felt like his reason for living at times. He had been patient, learning about her, studying her, until the time was right and he knew that they could be each other's everything.

Closing his brown eyes, he could see her. Golden hair, thick and in natural waves. Her green eyes, shining like precious emeralds. Her slender frame and perfectly-sized breasts. She could be a beauty queen. But she wasn't just beautiful to look at, Emily Robinson had the most attractive personality, and a magnificent mind. Pulling the fingers of his left hand with his right, he pondered for a moment, his anxiety soothed by thoughts of the woman he loved. Over that last year, he'd watched her, studied her: her body language, her mind, and imagination. And this shithead in the back of his car was part of his commitment to her and her profession.

Oliver Thornton got what he deserved and what she deserved, also. He'd had enough of bullies, intimidators, people making a mockery of him, her, the establishment. Instead, he would advocate on her behalf, on the behalf of others like her who work hard, bringing joy to the world. The trolls wouldn't win, well not when he was around, anyway. If he couldn't protect the woman he loved, who could he protect?

Getting out of the car, he opened the boot and retrieved a tatty blanket, left in the vehicle for emergencies. And this fitted the bill. Throwing the blanket over the lifeless body, he sneered before shutting the back door, locking the car and rushing to his flat for the solution of what he would do with the body of the man he had just killed.

David bit his bottom lip, shaking his head furiously as he drove to work the following morning, still seething from the atmosphere Oliver Thornton had created the previous night with his whiney voice, patronising comments, and ignorant questions. Well, he got what he deserved and wouldn't be hassling Emily or anyone else again. Chuckling, he then pressed his lips together. He hadn't slept more than an hour last night. Despite that, in his heart, he knew he had done the right thing: for Emily, for *them*. But he felt a sickness that covered him like a layer of frost – chilling him, turning his blood cold and his mind fearful.

Leaving home earlier than usual, he drove via the car valeting garage. Having already scrubbed the seat where that pompous shit had been, as a precaution, he would get the Poles or whoever they were to scrub inside his car, muttering in their mother tongue, as they removed all traces of death. He had to cover his back, just in case. In the early hours, he'd gone to Ashmouth woods. Driving with a fuel in his body, it had been a perfect solution. A homage to her really, as in her most recent book, a body was discovered in the woods. David had replicated her imagination, her vision, her creation. She was his muse. He grinned, former fear replaced by adrenaline and achievement.

Burying the body in the woods, he had dug a swallow grave in the chilled darkness, only the nocturnal animals as his companions. Even then, the crackling of leaves and earth noises had made him shiver with fear, as opposed to the falling temperature. Covering his victim's slim carcass in earth and leaves, he had bit back the foul taste of guilt. David was sure the body wouldn't even get discovered, well, not for a long time. People didn't go deep into the woods, unless they were up to no good themselves. And so what if it was found, no one would trace Oliver back to him. There was no link. But it was another link to her. Another way to get closer and protect her, removing obstacles to be with her. He had done it for her.

Grimacing a little, he felt like his body had been overtaken, possessed – as if the act, the whole night, had been led by another entity. However, his victim had it coming. How could he sit back and let the ignorant young know-it-all embarrass Emily like that? He was no fan. He was no friend of hers. Instead, he was a foe and needed disposing of. She would want it herself. Until she realised, until she could see that he was the one for her, he would protect her from harm. David would be his favourite author's very own hero!

Logging on to Emily Robinson's Facebook fan page, David scrolled through each post from the last twenty-four hours to analyse any new posts or comments. Just like he did almost daily, keeping up with everything and ensuring no one was getting away with trolling her, or getting too close. Some of these 'fans' thought that they knew her, were her friends, and deserved to be in her life. Oliver Thornton was one, and look what happened to him! Sniggering, David leant back in his cream, cracked leather armchair and groaned. No one knew her like he did. No one had studied her, her words, her imagination. He was her number one fan, and wouldn't let anyone else claim to be.

Running a hand through his brown hair, he took a deep breath. Perhaps he could write to her again? It had been six months since he had first written to her. Signed with his middle name, William, it had taken hours to perfect the letter. Much like the routine he was sure she did with her bestselling books. It had to be right, respectful and reflective, and he was certain it was, after much editing. She hadn't acknowledged it through the new email address he had jotted down on the letter, or even put a post on her social media. At first, he had felt deflated, rejected, angry. Perhaps she hadn't received it? Her gate-keeper agent might still have it on a pile of fan letters. She had liked and replied to his comments on her Facebook page, through his fake account in the name of Jen Bradley. So surely, she appreciated his commitment to her? He would soon find out as he got closer to his prize.

At the events – when he had the courage to speak to Emily without feeling like an embarrassed young teen about to embark on their first kiss – she had responded, smiling, thanking him. He'd composed himself, kept his cool. David didn't want to be like those others, the fans who were pathetic. He wanted to show her he was a man. That he could look after her, and it had led to their relationship developing.

Emily had remembered his name, thanked him for his help and support. Smiled at him in a way he was certain she hadn't smiled at anyone else. A look, exclusively for him. It was only a matter of time before they would get closer. He nodded, convincing himself it would be okay to write another carefully constructed letter. Thoughts back to the Facebook monitoring, he looked at a thread about fans' favourite novels in the series. Reading through the comments, he shook his head.

'I've read them at least five times each. Emily and the DCI McCoy books would be my Mastermind subject.'

Rolling his eyes, he sipped from his bottle of beer.

'Well, I think they are all rubbish and she's exhausted this storyline.'

His eyes widened. Placing the beer bottle on his side table, he furiously typed under his fake account, Jen Bradley.

'Stupid comment from a bitter person.'

The comment had come from an account he had been made aware of recently. A Chloe Logan. Clicking on her profile, it was locked but he made a mental note of her and the comment. Certain she hadn't been to any of Emily's book events, he would remember that face covered in falseness: lips, eyelashes, and layers of greasy make-up that made her look like a clown that got dressed in the dark. Sneering, David swigged the rest of his beer, then burped loudly. He kept scrolling, noting that Emily had liked his three comments from two days before, all under Jen Bradley. Smiling, he leant back in his tatty chair, stretching his legs along the carpeted floor. Feeling warm inside, he truly believed that they would be together soon and that she would love him just as much as he loved her.

Chapter 5

It was time for the afternoon briefing. McCardle and the team had focused on gathering intelligence about the last known movements of Oliver Thornton and collecting information about his life, that might lead to some clues as to why he ended up buried in a shallow grave in local woodland.

'Any updates on the interviews with his friends?' McCardle asked, glancing at Myers, Lucas, and Birdy.

DC Myers scanned the page, then began talking. 'I talked to his university tutor who described him as a diligent, likeable student. He spent time in the library, enjoyed research and studying.' She held her hand out, palm up.

Polly pressed her lips together. 'And the housemates?'

Birdy side-glanced to Lucas, who began their update. 'We spoke to Thornton's two housemates. One hadn't seen him since Monday morning, before she went to university. She returned at 9pm, showered, and went to bed. The other housemate saw Oliver on campus at lunchtime on Monday, then was at home early evening as Oliver got ready to go to an event with a friend in Crosley.'

Lucas rubbed a finger over his ginger beard as his eyes scanned his notepad then returned to his boss. 'The housemate said he couldn't remember where or what the event was. Both housemates said Oliver was a friend, but none of them lived in each other's pocket.' He sat back in his chair and DC Birdy sipped water then chipped in.

'The housemates gave us the number of the friend Oliver went to Crosley with on the night of his death, but the phone has been off. We've left messages.'

'Great, thanks. DC Boyd has an update on the event and his last movements.' McCardle ran a hand over her blonde, bobbed hair and turned to her. 'Can you share, please, Boyd?'

Uncrossing her feet at her ankles, she cleared her throat. 'Yeah, boss. Crosley Library rang in and stated Thornton was at an event the night he died. He was there until the library closed at 9pm. His phone data will be able to confirm this once obtained, and hopefully his friend who could have been the last person to see him alive, will corroborate.' She glanced at Birdy and Lucas who nodded.

Putting her hands together in a pray movement, Polly brought them to her face, the tips of her fingers tapped her lips. 'Brilliant work, team.' She smiled to the room before continuing. 'Boyd and I spoke with Thornton's parents to try and establish any possible enemies or any information he may have given them about being scared, followed etc. They couldn't think of anything. He was single and hadn't had a long-term relationship for over a year, that they were aware of.'

Birdy raised his hand slightly and she nodded for him to speak. 'Yeah, his housemates said the same – no significant other or flings that would cause alarm.'

Taking a sip of tea, Polly kept her cup in her hand. 'So, next steps are to visit the library, continue trying to establish contact with Thornton's friend and last known movements, and once we have phone data, the analysts can search for any intel.' Placing her cup down, she clapped her hands together. 'Great work so far, all. Thanks.'

Her colleagues rose from their seats, exiting the room, leaving Polly in the small space alone, staring at the photographs on the incident board of Oliver Thornton. Her team were amazing, skilled, thorough, and worked cohesively with a wide range of expertise complementing one another.

However, she couldn't help but think of Ericson and what he would do. Murder wasn't common in the rural county of Northumberland. Vast and with a population of around 325,000, there was crime, without doubt. Organised crime gangs, due to the access to ports, rail network, border of Scotland, and rural villages and towns, was a frequent occurrence. Murder cases were usually a single homicide from someone the victim knew. Stranger killing, less common, and serial killing, thankfully, even less.

Since DS Ronnie Ericson had retired a year ago, there had been one domestic homicide in the area and the offender had been arrested within the critical twenty-four-hour evidence period. McCardle had learnt so much from the local killings of two homeless men, working alongside Ericson, as well as two domestic homicides that had happened in the county after that. Her thoughts were broken by her mobile phone ringing. It was Chief Inspector Richardson, who would want the latest update.

There was a media appeal in the Oliver Thornton case, requesting the public's assistance. It was a move that would promote as much concern and useless information as perhaps nuggets of potentially precious leads – but after over a week of CCTV scrolling, speaking with friends and family, and retracing Thornton's last movements, McCardle and the team had limited further intelligence. When resources were stretched and with crimes occurring more frequently than she had lunch, progress was essential to stop cases going cold.

That morning, Polly sat at the breakfast bar in her kitchen, her backside hugged by a foam-padded blue stool as she sipped a cup of coffee and scrolled on her mobile phone. It was 7am, and she had been up half an hour. As she contemplated moving from the cosy spot, her short legs dangling like a child's, Lisa came into the kitchen.

'Morning,' she said as she passed, kissing Polly on the cheek, her long brown hair falling in her face. Walking to the countertop, she mechanically began the process of making a cup of tea. 'Sleep well?' She turned and instinctively took her wife's almost finished cup, to make her another coffee.

Polly moved slightly on her seat. 'Not bad. You?' She lied, and wasn't sure why. Lisa knew all about sleepless nights as a newly qualified social worker.

Lisa tilted her head, popping wholemeal bread into the toaster. 'So-so. You want some?' She gestured to the bread.

Polly nodded. 'Thanks.'

The pair ate side by side at the breakfast bar, enjoying the peace before work. Their home, a sanctuary and the opposite of their work environments. Their stressful, often demoralising but most of the time, rewarding roles, meant that their three-bedroomed Victorian terraced home really was their haven. Despite Polly only being thirty-five, and Lisa five years younger, their party days were behind them and they lived in quiet harmony, often without even the TV or music on – simply the sound of their chatting or the noises of the house as their audio.

An hour later, Polly pulled up at work. After saying good morning to her colleagues, checking emails, and returning phone calls, she read over the latest on the Oliver Thornton case. It had been over a week since the discovery of his body and information had almost stopped trickling in. Most of her team being allocated to other cases, including another OCG suspected drugs ring in Ashmouth. Soon, it was lunchtime, a luxury in the force that often never happened. McCardle glanced at her watch and tapped her finger to her lip. She needed a boost and knew exactly where to go. Grabbing her long black coat, she left the office.

Ten minutes later she opened the door to the Cake Station. Ronnie stood behind the counter, serving a customer. As the bell on the door chimed, he glanced up, flashing a smile. The customer exited the shop, and he came around from the counter to hug her.

'And where the hell have you been, Poll? I nearly sent a missing person report in,' he said, letting go of her.

Blushing slightly, she held her palms up. 'Sorry. Work.'

Ronnie narrowed his eyes slightly. He knew when she wasn't quite right. When perhaps she was work-fatigued.

'Hmmm,' he said tilting his chin up. 'Scone?' He waved a hand over the array of baked goods on display.

'That's the only reason I'm here.' She winked. 'Where's your better half?'

'At the wholesalers. Probably buying more stuff for the house. She can't stop!'

Polly smiled and moved across the wooden flooring towards the glass cabinets displaying the taste-bud tantalisers. Ronnie took a scone with a pair of metal tongs, placing it on a plate, along with jam.

'Clotted cream?' He raised an eyebrow.

'Not today.' She tapped her stomach then got her bank card out to pay.

Ronnie held a hand up, wafting her card away. 'You pay in your duty to the community. You know that.'

Polly smiled, swallowing a slight lump of emotion. He said it every time and even though it made her feel proud, it also made her miss him. There was no one to look after her at work now. Although she had always been independent; growing up just her and her mother on a council estate, she took no shit. Never had. But doesn't everyone like to be looked after now and then? Or have someone at work who you can offload too?

Polly loved her colleagues, but she was the boss, the protector, the role model. Sometimes, she just needed that care, that boost. And Ronnie, well, he always provided it – alongside the tastiest cakes in Crosley.

The pair had a quick catch-up, Polly commenting a little on the case but not in the detail that she wanted to. Although the Cake Station was quiet, two customers came in and Polly was always aware of confidentiality. Alongside this, within her there was often an inability to ask for help. Pride, stubbornness, fear of failure and rejection, or all of them combined, she wasn't sure. Nevertheless, Polly received some reassurance that she needed that day, along with a decent cuppa, a scone, and a few chuckles with Ronnie.

Checking her watch, she half-smiled. 'Back to the grind.' Rising from the seat at one of the gingham-table-cloth-covered kitsch tables, she sighed lightly.

Ronnie and his tuned instinct knew she had wanted to say more and embraced her. Shoulders dropping, her body softened, and she allowed herself to be vulnerable. Polly swallowed and closed her eyes, permitting herself a few comforting seconds to receive a hug from the friend and fatherly figure, before pulling away, slightly embarrassed.

'Thanks, Ron,' she said quietly, her blue eyes on him as a smile flashed on her face.

'Anytime, pet,' he said, nodding, eyes widening, as if to reiterate the message.

'Same time next week, hopefully.'

'Aye. Never be a stranger, Polly.'

Pressing her lips together, she nodded, not sure if she could speak as she swam in emotion. Instead, she walked the few steps towards the exit, opened it, turned briefly and raised her hand in a goodbye gesture to Ronnie.

Chapter 6

The letter had been written and posted to Emily. It was complimentary and respectful, and David had signed it off with his middle name, William. The aliases on social media were fine, to monitor and get closer. However, it wasn't a way their real relationship could develop and blossom. For that, he had to be himself, and the middle name felt the safest way. Just like last time, he had signed it off with the same email address, hoping that she would reply. It might take time, she was a busy woman, but he had the events and the closeness that he knew was developing. Love was a slow game and he was patient, as long as no one got in his way.

There had been little in the media about Oliver Thorton the days following the murder and a week later, it was even quieter. David had fluctuated between euphoria and dark dread – but his overriding feeling was love for Emily. He felt for the woman who discovered the body, who was mentioned on the news. Never had he wanted to drag innocent civilians into his plan, but shit happens. David was her protector. He had done the ultimate, passed the hardest test, and after killing, there were no lengths he wouldn't go to ensure she wasn't hurt and to get closer to his treasure. It had gone quiet about Thorton, and David was looking forward to the next time he would be with his beloved.

There was a book signing at the local indie bookshop in a few days, scheduled as part of the launch of her fourth book in the series, that had been discussed briefly at the library event where smug Oliver Thornton had attempted to humiliate her. Look what happened to him! David rubbed his trim beard with his thumb and index finger, speckles of auburn hairs dotted amongst the brown.

Plus, he would be there at the library a week later, for another launch event for Emily. He knew he was getting closer to her, that she was gravitating towards him, growing fonder of him. Surely, she could see his dedication to her? He wouldn't miss any of her events and he knew she appreciated loyalty. And no one was more loyal than him. As well as dedicating his heart to Emily Robinson, David was loyal to his job, and to his mother – despite her recognising him less and less.

His mother, in her deteriorating state, often forgot who he was. But some visits she was alert, bright. She focused on their past and would talk about him as a teenager and young adult. It was as if that's what she saw when she looked at her son, her eyes tricking her alongside her mind. She would ask how her own parents were and if he had been helping his grandfather at the allotment. Of course David hadn't, as his grandfather had been dead for twenty years, but the allotment was now his sanctuary, so he was able to talk about it with her.

Those times were nice, nostalgic, albeit sad. Then anger would take over as his mother never seemed to forget his abusive stepfather. She would talk about Keith, ask if he was visiting. He too had been dead over two decades, yet the bastard still dominated. That cruel prick had abused him throughout his childhood. Made him feel inferior, inadequate, and unwelcome in his own home for so long. And she had always taken his side, scared to disagree with her husband in case he would leave her and she would be alone again, despite her ever-loving child. She might not have inflicted the punches, slaps, and kicks, but David's mother had assaulted his heart, his head, and those wounds hadn't healed until he had met Emily and his world had changed, at last.

However, David never gave up on his mother. She was the only family he had, caring for her to the detriment of his own life, until her staying in the flat was no longer an option. She was a risk and he had to work, had to pay the bills. And now, he continued to visit and care for his mother, even with the knife being twisted further into him each time she mentioned that bastard's name.

Emily's event at the local indie bookshop was wonderful. Intimate, cosy, personal, and David had glowed the whole time. Even more so when she touched his forearm and thanked him for being so supportive. The local media team from the *Northumberland Herald* had been there to celebrate her book launch, along with the newspaper's reviewer, who had promised to read and review her new release in his weekly column.

Emily had looked breathtaking, her golden honey hair framing her soft, warm face. White teeth surrounded by full lips, painted with the softest pink lipstick. She always looked so elegant, so beautiful, without the need to look trashy and false. He couldn't fathom how her marriage had ended – if she were his wife, he would cross the Earth barefoot to make her happy. Her ex-husband was obviously insane or ungrateful. Either way, it made room for him.

Watching her prepare for the talk at the bookshop, he pressed his lips together, his eyes following her, unblinking. She hadn't yet answered the letter. However, she wouldn't have known it was from him. If she did, perhaps it would be different. He flared his nostrils and shook his head lightly before folding one arm over the other and glancing at his brown wool sweatshirt. He had to be more patient.

His mother always said, 'Good things come to those who wait.' A smile flashed across his face, as his eyes remained on his jumper sleeves, oblivious to the noise around him. She was right and he was making all the necessary steps to get to his love, as if gently navigating over a rickety wooden bridge, that threatened to give way if not trodden on carefully. All the right movements in the right direction.

Luckily, smug Oliver Thornton wasn't at this event. *I wonder why?* he thought to himself, chuckling lightly as someone passed him, nudging his elbow without apologising. He flashed the back of them a dirty look. He couldn't stand bad manners. Working with the public, he witnessed some shocking states of decorum. However, he also saw some excellent interpersonal skills and professionalism, and none more than those displayed by Emily Robinson.

The night had gone so well. He had been hypnotised by her elegance, grace, and expression of her muse for writing. Of course, he had already purchased her latest book in the series: *Persuasion*. Having read it cover to cover, he decided it was another masterpiece by his favourite author. Emily had signed it for him, looking into his eyes as she handed it back. He had felt heat in his cheeks as she held his gaze, her plump lips smiling, her eyes sparkling. The few wrinkles crinkling around the sides of them from such a wide, genuine smile but also from growing older.

She was thirty-four, a wonderful, assertive, sexy age where she knew what she wanted from life but still had time for marriage again and children. Hopefully, with him. He might be over a decade older, but he didn't look it, keeping in shape and fit. David felt aroused as he stood so close to her, inhaling her light floral perfume with a hint of vanilla. He would have to find out what her signature scent was, having smelt it on her before.

'See you next week at the library,' he said, tilting his head.

Placing her hands together, she held them on her torso, resting lightly on her floral dress that made her look like a beautiful summer day. 'Indeed, you will. Thanks so much again, David.'

He bit his lower lip as another reader coughed next to him and he snapped out of his Emily trance, glancing to the person and trying not to show his rage. Moving to the side, he nodded to her as he stood out of the path of fans. Back in the shadows, he continued watching his true love, his heart beating fast with joy and anticipation of their future.

The book reviewer from the local rag was flirting with her and he saw Emily run a hand over her thick, wavy hair. David's nostrils flared and he narrowed his eyes. Who did that slimy prick think he was? Making a mental note of his name, he vowed to keep an eye on the pervert and continue to protect his beloved.

The next week, Emily still hadn't responded to his letter. Pushing it to the back of his mind, David continued monitoring her Facebook page and making plans for their future. Plus, it was the library event that evening, so he would get his Emily fix.

'I've met someone, Mam,' he said to his mother when he visited the care home that afternoon.

Sitting in the pink, padded hospital chair, she glanced to the window of the small bedroom, gazing off to somewhere he could never reach.

'I met someone once. Keith. He was a tough man but a good man. I miss him.'

Her stare remained out the window as he seethed, feeling hotter than a boiling kettle. 'He was a bastard, Mam. And you let him be a bastard to me.'

He stood from the hard plastic chair, hands transformed into fists by the side of his dark blue jeans as spittle gathered around his mouth. His mother turned her head slowly and looked at him, eyebrows furrowed.

'Whatever is the matter, David?' she said, shaking her head as if he had come home from school with grazed knees.

He closed his eyes. She would always be stuck in the past and only seeing what she wanted to see – blind to his torment and the impact of Keith's abuse. Then the subsequent caring for her once the bastard died. He loved and loathed his mother in equal measures. A knock at the ajar door popped his bubble of fury. It was one of the carers checking if they wanted a cup of tea, and for him, his cue to leave. Saying goodbye to his mother, he kissed her gently on her forehead, as she weakly clasped his hand in hers. Paper-tissue-thin skin that was still soft against his.

He put his bottle-green fleece on and left, emotions battling as always after visiting. His mother wasn't even old, not by today's standards. But her life had been unhealthy, in more ways than physically, and he often wondered if it had contributed to an-earlier-than-average onset of dementia. His chukka boots click-clacked on the lino of the corridor as he made his way out of the care home, nodding to the receptionist as the exit doors opened.

Not wanting to dwell on his negative thoughts, David flipped the switch in his mind and contemplated that evening: the library event for Emily. She was becoming like a drug for him and he craved seeing her, touching her. Compelled to be around her, it was as if his soul came alive when he was in the same room as her. No woman had ever had that impact on him.

He'd had a few flings, and had a relationship of two years when he was in his mid-twenties which had been ruined by his mother's needs and David's co-dependency. His mother had almost sabotaged his youth – not wanting him to leave her alone in the flat. Saying she was unwell, claiming it would be better just the two of them. Keith had turned her into a savage as well as an emotional wreck and he resented that he let her control his destiny. Well, no more. She was in the care home and his obligation to visit was enough. It was time for David Creighton to live and his life had to involve love: the love of Emily Robinson.

Three hours later, David was at the library. He was off work that day, but still dressed smartly for the event. Pride in his appearance was something he could control. Wearing dark blue chinos and a striped blue and white shirt, David looked casual yet stylishly smart. Saying hello as he entered the building, he looked around, making sure everything was set up the way it should be and nodding to the odd person.

Emily was accommodating, grateful, with no diva demands. Still, the place should be nice and welcoming for her – bad experiences might make her less likely to do such events and that would be devastating to him and others. She soon arrived, like a beautiful sea breeze entering the building. Noticing him, she smiled and said hello, her face illuminated. Magnetic green eyes, soft lips coated in the lightest shimmer of lipstick and her cheeks, a rosy innocence like a princess from a fairy-tale. She was David's fairy-tale, his happy-ever-after. He knew it, he just had to be patient.

Crowds soon gathered and David said hello to some of the regulars. Refreshments were neatly displayed on a table with white cups and glasses. Rows of slightly padded chairs stood uniform, like lines of cadets. Then there were two chairs set up at the front, a hula-hoop-sized round table in between them. He smiled; she deserved to be centre stage and the library made a good effort to make her feel admired. David took some photos, to keep in the scrapbook of their love story.

Half an hour later, it was time to start. He stared at Emily in a pretty turquoise and black dress, its hem reaching her mid-calf and the material cinching in between her bust and waist, highlighting her svelte body. She was more beautiful than a Mediterranean sunset. David noticed the book reviewer, Ryan Mortimer, from the local newspaper. He hadn't forgotten about the sickening flirting he had witnessed the sleazeball push onto his beloved. However, he had not remembered to check if the review of Emily's latest book, *Persuasion*, had been published. Clenching his fists, he was angry, promising himself he would work harder for her.

The author did her usual of talking about the new book release and the ideas behind it as well as the others in the series. Then she opened the floor to questions and comments. A few people asked questions before Ryan Mortimer spoke.

'*Persuasion* had some gripping subplots and a strong protagonist, but like my review in the *Northumberland Herald*…' He paused and David noticed a grin flash across his face.

Was he flirting with her or being insulting? He felt his heart begin to beat faster. He needed to read the book review of *Persuasion* by Ryan Mortimer and he needed to read it now. Trying to keep alert to Ryan and Emily's body language and discussion, he tapped on his iPhone and typed into Google to search.

Ryan continued, 'It felt that this book was rushed and lacked the attention to detail of the others.' He tilted his head.

David's eyes grew wide, appalled, as he tried to find the bloody review.

Emily took a sip of water. 'Well, of course, it's important you and other readers have their opinion. We can't always all think everything is flawless, because, well, it isn't.' She smiled and locked her hands together, placing them on her lap.

Ryan tilted his head, raising an eyebrow slightly and crossed a denim-covered leg over his other, knee out, in an alpha-male pose. David's brow furrowed. *Absolute prick*, he thought, biting back rage. Another question began as David continued to scroll on the *Northumberland Herald's* website. It was littered with adverts as he tried to scroll through articles.

'For fuck's sake,' he whispered under his breath.

The elderly lady beside him glanced over, a nervous half-smile on her lips. He smiled back quickly as his knees bounced. He zoned out from the conversation happening with the audience and Emily as he found Ryan Mortimer's article, featuring the review of *Persuasion*. With his index finger to his mouth, he held his phone with his other hand and began to use his thumb to scroll the article.

The third in the current series by Robinson. With a continued robust protagonist in DCI McCoy, the book started off strong. However, this instalment of the series felt rushed at times and lacked the attention to detail in Robinson's previous novels. Average, but nothing exceptional.

David flared his nostrils. Who the hell did Ryan Mortimer think he was? How dare he slate Emily's work. His comments were simply untrue, considering all the members of the audience that evening and at the recent book shop event. Plus, all the fans on her Facebook page, and the bloody fact that *Persuasion* had reached number one in the book charts, showed it was a phenomenal read. Emily was exceptional. And if this shitbag thought it was so bad, why the hell was he here?

He could see the profile of Ryan Mortimer. His thin, slightly crooked nose and a splattering of brown facial hair around his jaw and chin. His body language stank of an attempt to dominate. His left brown suede boot moved a little as his foot balanced off the end of his right knee. Ryan's gaze kept on Emily. He shouldn't be there; he clearly wasn't a fan in the slightest.

Confused and angry, David couldn't concentrate on the remainder of the Q&A, bewildered as to why the journalist was actually there. Half an hour later, it became perfectly clear. The patrons began to leave after getting their copies of *Persuasion* signed and taking photos with Emily, who smiled and chatted encouragingly with readers. He watched her, mesmerised. She was kind, sociable, brilliant. She conducted the room. He moved some cups and glasses off the floor, returning them to the table and tutting at the fact people so seldom tidied up after themselves. It would make it easier for the cleaner.

The crowds thinned out, only a few people remaining. David approached Emily. 'Thank you. Another inspiring talk.' He placed his hands together, his brown eyes looking into hers.

'You're so kind, David, thank you. It's lovely to see you.'

He swallowed and pressed his lips together, feeling a grin spread across his mouth. He loved it when she used his name. When she appreciated him. It felt like part of their courtship.

She smoothed a hand over her hair. 'And thank you, for you know, clearing up.' She turned towards the table where he had placed the empty cups and glasses. 'Always the professional.'

Feeling a glow of pride, he responded, 'I hope you can come back soon. Your events are always my favourite, everyone's favourite – a sell-out!' Swallowing, he moved on the spot slightly, wanting to embrace her and kiss her full lips.

'Yes, I'd love to. Anytime.' She gently tapped his arm, then looked at the table, where she began to collect her spare books.

David felt he would explode with lust. It was happening, it was all coming together. She was interested, he could tell. 'Let me help.'

He started picking up the books and helping Emily place them in a large canvas bag. The remaining people left and he was about to offer to assist her to her car. Perhaps he could instigate a conversation about hobbies, or where she drank or exercised.

'Would you like…'

'Oh, we're the only ones left.'

He spun around to Ryan Mortimer approaching from the toilets, grinning. He had been watching Emily so intensely that he hadn't noticed Ryan head to the bathroom. Narrowing his eyes, he observed the confident journalist stroll over. Tall, with chiselled cheekbones and floppy hair, he ran a hand over his beard as he walked towards Emily. David immediately felt inferior.

Without acknowledging David, he spoke. 'Emily, let me help you to your car with this bag and I can talk to you about a possible interview.'

She glanced at David and he was unsure as to whether it was for help. He coughed but the journalist had already picked up the bag and was using his head to gesture in the direction of the door. Emily moved and he followed behind. Ryan seemed oblivious to him being there, as if he were a ghost only she could see. His jaw clenched. What was it with this pushy, creepy prick? His review was scathing, yet here he was flirting with Emily. His Emily!

They travelled down the escalator of the library, David a few seconds behind after saying an abrupt goodnight to the staff member on shift. Trying to catch up to them, as he stepped onto the escalator, he witnessed Ryan turn to Emily, stroking her cheek with the back of his hand.

'Emily,' he shouted to the ten steps or so below as he began rushing down them.

She shot her head around, hair bouncing with the jolt.

'Are you okay?' he said, eyes wide.

Her mouth was slightly ajar as she shook her head quickly, as if to shake out of a trance. 'Erm yes, yes, I'm fine, thanks, David.' Placing a hand on the side of her neck, she stepped off the escalator. David rushed down the last few steps to her.

'What the hell is wrong with you?' the journalist asked, shaking his head and making an amused hmph noise.

Feeling his cheeks redden from anger and embarrassment, David spoke, fury in his voice. 'You. Groping her!'

Throwing his head back, Ryan laughed loudly.

David's nostrils flared and he moved his jaw from side to side.

'Honest, it's fine. Thank you.' Emily looked at him, eyes soft, and tapped the back of his hand with her palm.

Rolling his eyes. Ryan shook his head, out of Emily's vision.

Raising his eyebrows, David kept his gaze on her. 'Are you sure?' he asked with pleading eyes. Surely, she didn't want this creepy prick touching her. Surely, she couldn't like him? Fancy him?

She nodded. 'Yes, everything is okay, thank you. I've had a lovely night and appreciate your support.' Smiling again, the dimple in her left cheek was just visible.

Raising an eyebrow, the journalist walked towards the entrance of the library with the bag of Emily's books.

'Have a lovely night, David.' She turned and headed out the entrance after Ryan.

Alone, he felt he could set the building alight with the fury in his heart, having witnessed the slimy hands of Ryan Mortimer groping his beloved. Following along the terraced street from the library, he hung back behind the pair, who never glanced around once. He knew that it wasn't because Emily didn't care, more likely that she was trying to escape the self-absorbed conversation from that prick, and was simply too nice to be rude to him. He followed them for a few minutes until they slowed. Stopping part way down the street at a bus stop, he hoped that he was out of view, and sat straining to see the pair. Their dark outlines were visible where Emily was parked. Watching the journalist place the bag of books into her boot, David squinted and fizzed inside, witnessing his peacock display of vulgar flirtation.

After five minutes, but what felt like forever, Emily got into her car. Shutting the door for her, Ryan waved as she drove off. He bolted up, dashing after him, watching as he walked further down the street, getting into a red VW that was parked beside a lamppost. Making a note on his phone of the part of the registration plate that he could see, he hung back, fist clenched and nostrils flaring as he observed the journalist drive away. Arriving home soon after, David showered then lay on his sofa and scrolled through photos on his phone of Emily for almost two hours – lost in his love for her and vowing that no one would get in his way to be with her.

The following day, David drove to the site of the *Northumberland Herald*. Scanning the car park, he was lucky enough to see what he thought was Ryan Mortimer's car. After four hours, he was dozing off and jerked, hearing laughter and goodbyes. Ryan stood ten metres away, putting something on the back seat before entering his vehicle, starting the engine, and slowly pulling out of the parking bay.

Promptly, David began to drive behind. As they hit a busier main road, a car went in between them at a junction making it perfect for him to see but to still remain undercover. He made a hmph noise to himself: he had always been undercover. Never bright enough to shine above the average. Never successful enough to obtain the promotion. Never attractive enough to get the second glances. Never getting the girl. Although this time he would make sure he got the girl, and nothing and no one would stand in his way.

In his forgettable black Ford Focus, he cruised along a few cars behind, shadowing the journalist, unsure where he was going or how long it would take. It transpired that Ryan Mortimer lived in Crosley, only a few miles from the library, next to an entrance of Crosley Country Park. Squeezing his car into a spot, David pulled up on the end of the terraced street, shutting down his lights and engine immediately to avoid extra attention.

Ryan exited his car, casually trotting onto the pavement and opening a low gate, before walking up a driveway out of David's view. After waiting a minute, he got out of his car and slowly strolled down the road. Reaching Ryan's VW car, he sneered and looked at the gate then the house the journalist had walked into. He was unable to see anything going on inside, horizontal wooden blinds obscuring his view. Inhaling, he puffed his chest out and turned, walking back to his car, a plan already beginning to formulate in his mind.

Chapter 7

It had been several weeks since the murder of Oliver Thornton and the case was growing colder by the day. The team had collected all possible evidence from the days leading up to, the day of his murder and the following days, but had ironically met a dead end. CCTV from outside the library, grainy footage from the bar that didn't identify him leaving and even CCTV recordings from the university campus had been collected and viewed with no leads. McCardle and her team had followed all possible avenues, even the ones that came in through the call-handlers, that they knew were bullshit. Polly hated loose ends and not being able to solve a crime. After all, it was one of the main reasons she had entered the force as a twenty-four-year-old. Well, that and being the victim of an assault.

Sitting at her desk, she shuddered, running her forefinger over her mouth, recalling the assault on a night out by a sleazy octopus-handed bloke who thought it was okay to grope her, despite her saying no. He'd followed her after she left the club, her friend rushing ahead to the takeaway shop as Polly struggled in new heels. Appearing from nowhere, the predator had towered over her, as if on stilts next to her petite frame.

Sneering and slurring, he'd grabbed her. She'd pulled away and walked quicker. Following, he had pulled her arm, grasped it and shoved her into a shop doorway, where he pushed his hand down her skinny jeans and into her underwear. She'd frozen, eyes wide as he snarled in her face, breath stinking of lager. Over in ten seconds, he'd said her body was gross. The sexual assault from a stranger, that she never reported, had eroded her self-image and confidence further but gave her the drive to help prevent crime and catch criminals.

'Here's the file, boss.' DC Boyd halted McCardle's thoughts by dropping documents onto her desk.

It was the file on a recent sexual assault victim, one of two in the last week, that were undoubtedly linked – and what had evoked McCardle's reflections of her past.

'Thanks, Claire.'

Boyd nodded and took her boss's empty cup from her desk, indicating she would make a fresh cup of tea for them both. The rest of the shift was spent catching up on admin and scrutinising the recent sexual assault cases before the team briefing and allocation of tasks.

Leaving the station early evening, Polly drove the eight miles home to her terraced house in Whitley Bay, following the coastal route. The beach was such a soothing place for so many, and their award-winning coastline was often filled with walkers, exercise groups, families, and swimmers – even on the coldest North East days, with the Boxing Day Dip being a local tradition. Polly smiled as she drove; she couldn't think of anything worse than swimming in the freezing North Sea, even on the warmest day of the year in North Tyneside. But still, she appreciated its mesmerising beauty and was proud of her locality.

After a quiet night with Lisa, Polly had a restless sleep, her slumber interrupted by the nightmare of her assault almost fifteen years ago. She woke, coated in a film of sweat, mouth dry, and her top lip cracked in the middle. Her tongue instinctively went to it and she winced slightly at the sting. Groaning, she rolled over and lay awake for ten minutes, before checking her watch, and admitting defeat at 5.35.

As she went downstairs the world was quiet, only the creaking and clicking of the old terraced house as her audio.

Alone in her own thoughts, she boiled the kettle and pulled her cream fleece dressing gown tighter around her chest. Two cups of tea and a scan through social media later, it was 6.20 and Polly went upstairs. Getting out of the shower fifteen minutes later, she grabbed her mobile phone and noticed a missed call from DI Richardson.

'Sir? You rang?' she said when he answered, as she put moisturiser onto her face with her spare hand, looking at her reflection in the 1960s-style dressing table mirror of their spare room.

'Hi, Polly. Sorry to call early. I thought you would want to know before you get into headquarters...'

Swallowing, her eyes fixed on her reflection, hair wrapped in a towel as she smoothed cream onto a round cheek.

'There's been a body of a male found. A hit and run by the looks of it. Police were alerted by a delivery driver on a lane leading to one of the entrances to Crosley Park. CSI are there now. You may want to head over with one of the team.' He spoke calmly in monotone. Years of controlling emotions, focusing on procedure and organisation made him sound almost robotic. But he was a good guy, respected force-wide and beyond – something that wasn't always the case in the police.

'Understood, boss. Thanks. I'll head over in the next half hour and update you accordingly.'

'Thank you, DS McCardle.'

And with that, the call ended and Polly got ready for another day with Northumbria Police.

Chapter 8

Seven days ago, David Creighton followed Ryan Mortimer home. He had observed him most days since, fitting it around his shifts at work with military precision. Revenge was cooking in the pot and it was about to bubble over. He had done his research, he was nothing if not thorough. Discovering that the journalist lived with one male housemate, he had monitored their routines. The housemate, a chubby guy with glasses, appeared to work night shift. It meant that Ryan was home alone most nights and David had observed him coming and going, getting home from work, having parcels and takeaways delivered, and leaving to exercise.

He was a jogger and seemed to go for a 9pm jog every other night. Having worked late on two nights, David hadn't been able to get to Ryan's house each night to be certain of his leave and return times. However, the journalist's property was only a seven-minute drive from his own flat, which meant he had caught the prick on his return from his jog, at around 9.45pm. A few times, he had watched him come out of his house, stretch his legs up against his low wall, like a dog taking a piss, then swing his arms from side to side, before pushing his headphones into his ears.

Following him, Ryan hadn't heard the car tailing him, headphones in, listening to whatever rubbish was his music or podcast of choice. He might have even been listening to Emily's novels as audiobooks – no doubt criticising them in his head whilst plotting ways to get her into bed. He disgusted David, whose malice towards him had accelerated after viewing his social media, noticing he had been liking Emily's posts, putting winking emojis and hearts as comments. It was unprofessional at the least, and rage-inducing. Ryan wouldn't give up on his pursuit of Emily, despite his criticism of her art, so David would stop him in his tracks, permanently.

After discovering the journalist jogged to Crosley Park, up a country lane leading to one of the entrances to the vast green area, David needed to manage any risks. His plan would be executed that evening. Methodically going over the detail, he reiterated his approach that day at work. The country lane to the entrance of the park was short. No houses were situated on the path, only houses in the street leading up to it, terraced houses with off-street parking. Cars parked close, like tins on a supermarket shelf, with lampposts scattered thinly. That night, he had slid his vehicle in inconspicuously. It was dark, chilly, with dampness in the air. People wouldn't be out unless walking their dog or on a late-night exercise route themselves. It would reduce his risk of being seen.

Thinking ahead, he'd purchased fake registration plates from a dodgy shop on eBay. He wouldn't put them on until he was a few streets away and even then, they would be quickly attached with cable ties and would be on and off within thirty minutes. The small chance of any sightings would have a fake plate and his car wasn't exactly unique, with many people choosing a mid-range vehicle like his. David had been methodical and felt certain that all risks were minimized. He had the comfort of the Oliver Thornton case going cold as a security blanket – feeling confident that if nothing was picked up there, nothing would be here.

The dark early November evening and heavily-parked street meant that he could get close and sit, watching in the shadows, observing the journalist's moves. Saying that, he thought he could be standing at that prick's front door, dressed as a clown with a flashing light above his head and Ryan still wouldn't see him. Types like Ryan Mortimer never saw anything they didn't want to see, their own perceived reflection always more important. Those self-absorbed bastards with main character syndrome. He clenched his jaw as he thought about Ryan-types, Oliver Thornton-types, Keith-types, who had always made him feel inferior and unworthy.

No more. He would no longer feel silenced, unimportant, insignificant. He had proven he could do it by delivering to Oliver Thornton exactly what that smug bastard had deserved. And nothing had happened as a repercussion. No comeback, no care. He was, after all, protecting his true love. And he would sacrifice the world if it meant that he could get closer to Emily, his destiny. Pressing his lips together, he smiled whilst returning some of the stock to its place at work. He knew they would be together soon.

David's shift ended and he gathered his belongings, tidied his workstation, and said goodnight to his colleagues. He was respected at work, liked, and knew he was good at his job, despite not getting promoted last year. He wasn't bitter; it had all worked out for the best and meant he was more front of house than he would have been, had he secured a promotion. Less money, of course, but more access to what was important to him, and for that, he was grateful.

Leaving work, he walked the short distance to his car and got inside, placing his blue backpack in the footwell of the passenger side. Taking several minutes, he inhaled and closed his eyes, replaying his plans for the next few hours. Even today, during his shift, quiet periods in between customer enquiries, tidying, and admin, David thought through the process again that he had perfected for a week. It hadn't been rushed, that was when mistakes happened. He had been impulsive with

Oliver Thornton, as if to prove something to himself. But the murder, the process, the spontaneity of it all, that had been out of character. It could have resulted in a messy end of him being discovered as the criminal.

He had been lucky. And luck often runs out. David had planned, detailed, gone over each possible scenario, until it felt failsafe, perfected like a work of art. Humming, he tapped his fingers on the steering wheel and started the engine. While he pulled out of the parking space, his smile remained as he headed towards the journalist's home and began his journey closer to Emily. And now he felt confident that Ryan would be dealt with in the right way and his path to Emily Robinson would have one less obstruction in it.

Within ten minutes, he was parked in the residential street at the bottom of the country lane, leading to an entrance of Crosley Park. It was 8.30pm, and as he sat in his Ford Focus, the fake registration plates on, it remained quiet for the next twenty minutes. Not seeing a soul helped calm his nerves. There was no doubt in his mind that he had to destroy Ryan Mortimer. The scathing review of Emily's book, *Persuasion,* was enough of a reason but added to that was the pursuit in his obvious affections towards her. The journalist was pestering and perving on her in person, online, and no doubt behind the scenes. He sneered in disgust.

Not prepared to compete, David would simply eliminate any competition permanently. He shook his head, lips curling. It was likely this bastard just wanted another notch on the bedpost and couldn't give a damn about Emily, only wanting the credibility that goes alongside bedding a minor celeb. However, to him, she was his world and he would not let someone use, exploit, or hurt her in any way. His purpose, his unyielding role to protect her and then look after her forever in blissful love, gave him the adrenaline and strength to know it was necessary.

Taking deep breaths, he ran a hand through his brown hair. Glancing at his mobile phone, he saw the screensaver lit up – an image of his beloved. *Perfection in a photo,* he thought, as he placed his hand on his heart and exhaled. His mindset was an accumulation of years of feeling invisible and his life being consumed by his mother and her needs. Now it was his time. It was time for David to live and love, and he had to remember that this was part of obtaining his goal.

It was 8.45pm and he sat in the car, engine cut. Like a sniper waiting to attack, his eyes were wide, his focus sharp as he watched the direction Ryan would come from, hopefully in the next fifteen minutes. Doubt had danced around David all week. It didn't have time with Oliver Thornton – his murder was less premeditated and more in the moment, perhaps like an unexpected fight on a night out. But with Ryan, it had been researched and meticulously planned. Flaring his nostrils, he inhaled, wondering for a moment, what was the turning point when he became 'this' person.

Years of belittling, bullying, feeling insignificant. Well, he had more power than anyone would have thought and would have the last laugh. His degradation had birthed a resentment, fuelled by revenge and it wasn't just about Oliver, or Ryan. Not even Emily. It was payback for Keith, for the bullies at school who picked up on the fact his home life wasn't great, and in some way, for his mother who he continued to feel responsible for – a burden he had carried like a boulder all his life.

David shook his head to take his mind away from his self-pity and focus on the task in hand. Gripping the steering wheel, he grimaced, the pervy journalist was just like those bully boys at school, always thinking they were better than him. Well, no more, and certainly not when it came to him getting his girl.

The clock crept closer to 9pm, as his mind travelled to what would soon happen. Rubbing his mouth, he felt a pang of guilt for the person that might find his victim, and he still thought about the person who discovered his last. It wasn't nice, of course it wasn't, but it was a necessary evil. He made a hmph noise, then saw movement. Someone coming towards the lane, and that someone was most definitely jogging.

Watching from where he was parked in darkness, David remained camouflaged by the other sleeping cars in the street. Once Ryan ran past, in his own exercise bubble, he started the engine, lights off to not alert his prey, and crept forward in his car. Heading slowly towards the entrance of the country park, he trailed the target on his regular route. There was no one around, the area dark with a drizzly rain that probably made jogging a relief. David had to assume, hope, that Ryan had his headphones in as usual. Tailing him, he let the journalist get far enough up the country park lane to feel almost certain that no one would see – unless they were dodging around the bushes!

He jogged, without a care in the world, unaware of what was about to happen. It gave David a thrill, a flash of just deserts that helped solidify his plan. Ryan was strong, muscular, and lean from his exercise regime. He would have to put some extra force into the act. Licking his dry lips, he swallowed before glancing around the quiet lane one more time. It was clear, a perfect opportunity. One hundred metres in front, David was behind, doing less than 20 mph, his lights off. But as he got closer, he felt a suffocating panic encase him. Could he do it? Was he strong enough?

Hands shaking, he clutched the wheel. His knees began to bounce and he clenched his jaw. 'Get a fucking grip,' he said aloud. This wasn't about David, it was about them: him and Emily. It was about love, and nothing and no one stood in the way of love. Needing to accelerate rapidly, he could do it and it would be over quickly. Inhaling aggressively, he pushed his foot down on the accelerator with all his force. The car made a small squeal, not wanting to speed up so quickly, but as David gripped the steering wheel and his eyes bored into his target, the car complied and soon he reached over 40 mph. Time seemed to freeze, only the car moving, as the murder weapon approached its goal.

He was less than thirty metres away, the speed increasing again. Right in the bullseye, David would surely wipe Ryan out, like a strike on a pin by a hefty bowling ball. And all he could think was that it would get him closer to Emily. The speed meant he reached the journalist within seconds. Before his black Ford Focus struck the unsuspecting jogger, Ryan turned around at the last second, perhaps hearing the car over his music, or the vibrations on the gravel path. Maybe it was survival instinct kicking in, warning him. He jerked around rapidly, his eyes widened in fear, his mouth contorted into an expression of horror. David held his breath, and it was as if a TV turned off in his head. No longer a programme, a work of fiction, he was there, it was real and he felt the jolt of his body from his car seat as he ploughed into his target.

Ryan Mortimer would not have seen the person in the car, even though, in that split second, he seemed to glare straight into the eyes of David Creighton. Then he was lifted, propelled into the air as if a toy thrown by a playful pup. The metal menace struck him and took his feet from the ground. The force of the impact of skeleton against metal brought Ryan's body bouncing onto the bonnet of David's Focus. Swerving, he moved the steering wheel from side to side quickly. But there was no need. His victim bounced over the bonnet and landed with a crushing thump, as his car slid into the grass verge.

Staring in the rear-view mirror, he saw the journalist lying motionless on the ground. Twisted, limbs pointed in unusual positions, looking like a completed jigsaw that a child had sabotaged. Hastily, he turned his car around in the narrow lane and drove slowly past Ryan. It was hard to see him but he wouldn't dare put his car lights on. Swallowing, he drove tentatively by and continued quietly down the lane, leaving his lights off for a few more seconds.

Calmly, manoeuvring like he was driving back from a pleasant Sunday lunch, David drove for a minute, hands shaking, before he pulled over. Cutting the engine, he swallowed acidic bile and gulped in air from the open window before exiting his vehicle. Quickly he removed the fake plates from the front and back of his car, before returning to the driver's seat and continuing his drive home. As he tried to regulate his breathing, David anxiously hoped he had done enough to end Ryan's life. Taking deep breaths, he thought about what had just happened, then immediately thought about his future with Emily, and a cold smile crept across his face.

Chapter 9

Ronnie sat at his country-style oak dining table sipping his second coffee of the morning. He'd been awake since 6am, his body clock forever set after being a police officer for over half of his life. Chewing on a piece of seeded toast slathered in marmalade, he flicked through the news app on his phone as he heard Caroline padding around upstairs. They went to the Cake Station, three days a week at 7am, to prepare some freshly baked goods for the day. Well, Ronnie helped rather than baked, and on the other days, their recently employed baker worked his magic.

Since retiring from Northumbria Police a year ago, Ronnie had only adjusted slightly to his change in pace and routine. The Cake Station had provided a focus, and something to share with Caroline, after she had given him and their marriage another chance following years of the force coming first. After a year apart, the old saying, 'You don't know what you've got until it's gone' had never rung truer for Ronnie and he surrendered his second love of his career, retiring early for his first and most important love: his wife.

Did he miss the lover that was Northumberland Police? Who could be seductive, satisfying, and give him the ego boost every person craved? The third wheel in his marriage who also snatched time, compromised safety, and often made him loathe the human race? Of course he missed it. He was bereft still, and it would always feel like a part of him was missing. But Caroline was a bigger part, and that year living in a rented flat alone, away from the home that had been his family's heart, well the loneliness had felt like a tumour growing in him, despite the outcomes and excitement that his mistress of Northumbria Police gave him.

When the couple were reunited, Ronnie shared the joy of anticipation with Caroline for their new adventure in the catering world, and their reignited relationship. They'd spent time together and it had cushioned the crippling void he carried, heavy in his pockets, from not having the force – no longer being Detective Sergeant Ronnie Ericson. His ties hung like sad donkey tails on the rail in his wardrobe and despite being elated to have his clothes back in the bedroom of his marital home, they felt like a tormentor, part of his identity erased.

He'd known male colleagues who had retired from the police and died within a few years. They weren't like most women who could fill their day with ideas, activities, hobbies, and friends. Men of his age, well, they just didn't really think like that. It was work, role, identity. Ronnie understood why some of his colleagues declined, withered like daffodils out of their spring prime. When he retired, he'd felt an emptiness, despite his heart being full. And it was still there, although he would never admit it to his wife. Despite knowing he would do it all again, one hundred times over, there was a piece of his personal puzzle missing.

And after seeing Polly the day before, witnessing tired eyes on her small, round face, and despite her protesting all was fine, he knew it wasn't. She hadn't talked about the case, only having fifteen minutes to spare on an ever-timed break. But Ronnie had read about the Oliver Thornton case and after years of media language he'd given himself to the press, he knew they had no strong leads.

Pulling a hand over his mouth, he thought back to those final days in the force. He had made it clear to Chief Inspector Richardson that he would be happy to help out in the future, in a civilian role. It felt too much of a break-up to say never again, although Ronnie had known – even without his marriage being given CPR that brought it back to life – that he would have less than ten years left in the force. However, he had expertise that undoubtedly came from time, knowledge development, and the hundreds of cases he had worked on.

'Call it volunteering*,' he had said to CI Richardson, chuckling but underneath being deadly serious. And even though he had his time occupied with the Cake Station and the love of an incredible woman, his mind still wandered, still needed, still craved crime-solving.

Sighing, he shook his head at his pity-me moment and continued scrolling through the news app. The usual world disharmony and climate chaos, along with local crime news, that Ronnie always kept up to date with – old habits and all that. He heard his wife coming down the stairs and stood, moving to fill the kettle to make her a morning cup of tea. Entering the kitchen like a welcome breeze on a humid day, she smiled at her husband before approaching him, kissing his cheek and wishing him good morning. Her dark, wavy hair brushed against his two-day stubble. Inhaling her fragrance, he touched her hand, as she turned and wandered to the fridge for breakfast, before a morning of baking.

Chapter 10

It was 7.10am, and McCardle stood with DC Boyd at the scene of the crime. CSIs were doing their duties: quiet, methodical, respectful. Hands rammed into the pockets of her long black coat, Polly shook her head, breathing out into the cold air.

'Drunk driver?' queried Boyd, looking at her superior.

'Could be,' McCardle said quietly as she watched one of CSIs collecting miniscule pieces of debris from the road.

The body had been taken to the mortuary, where the cause of death would be confirmed, hopefully along with identity. What they knew so far was that the deceased was an adult white male. After chatting with the CSIs, McCardle and Boyd made their way down the lane towards their cars. Uniformed police stood as the press waited. Cheetahs spotting the gazelles, ready to rush in and attack for answers to feed their tabloids and social media. The officers ducked under the police tape, a nod to their colleagues before the barrage of questions and camera flashes started on the still dark morning.

'Detective, what's going on? Can you give us an update?'

'Officer, is it a body?'

'Can you tell us what has been discovered?'

McCardle held her palms up in a stop motion. She was calm, pleasant, but assertive, and despite being petite, she was a mighty force who warranted respect from colleagues inside and outside of the force. The journalists stepped back slightly and Polly began to speak, keeping her body language neutral, professional.

'The body of a male adult was found this morning. Northumbria Police were alerted by a delivery driver. CSIs are at the scene. We will be making enquiries and will update the press when we have more information. Thank you.'

The journalists all began talking at once like a room full of parrots, but McCardle and Boyd walked through the crowd to get to their vehicles.

'See you at headquarters,' Boyd said, nodding as she walked the few steps further to her car.

Belting up, Polly drove away from the boisterous scene. Arriving at HQ, she grabbed the milk and teabags from her boot. Coffee and tea were drunk almost as quickly as emails were sent in the MIT. Walking into the office, it was quiet, the shift not yet started. Boyd was in the kitchen, picking up the kettle.

'Something in this at the moment,' she said, nodding to the running water then looking at her superior.

'You're right there,' McCardle replied, puffing out air.

And Boyd was correct. The last month had been a crime banquet in Northumberland, with a large number of incidents and organised crime escalating. The team was already small given the geography of their patch, made harder by staff sickness and DC Myers being absorbed with a current drugs operation on a local estate - where no resident was giving any information or leads. All the officers knew it was out of fear or because they were involved, but it was like asking a butcher to cook for a hall full of vegans.

After making them both a cuppa, Boyd made herself some toast as McCardle returned to her desk. Logging on to her computer, she sent an update to CI Richardson and a few to other departments about the discovery of the body in Crosley Country Park. There would be a briefing in fifteen minutes once the shift started, then Polly could attend the mortuary, with the CSI manager. After a few minutes, her colleagues began trickling in, saying a hello as they dumped bags on desks and headed to the kitchen for a hot drink

Soon, staff had their caffeine medicine in a mug and McCardle's team were in the briefing room. She sat at the front, incident boards with several different current crimes and enquiries behind her. She had received an email from the contact team with some possible progress on the body in Crosley Country Park that morning. Tucking her blonde bobbed hair behind her ears, she cleared her throat. Her small team focused on her.

'Right, folks. I know we are thin on the ground.'

'Not here, boss,' Birdy said, as he tapped his gut hanging over his trousers.

McCardle grinned and her colleagues chuckled. Banter was essential in the force and was often the glue that kept a team together. Despite training, their familiarity and normalisation of the bad, mad, and sad, they were still people before their profession. Fatigue got to everyone, and officers had to manage life and death, risk and order of the towns in their jurisdiction, as well as navigate everyday life in their own private time. Humour was one of the most important things in the job, and sometimes Polly thought it kept the team as safe as their training.

'You can walk it off in the country park, Birdy,' McCardle replied, giving DC Birdy a nod. 'So, there was what looks like a fatal hit and run overnight at one of the entrances to Crosley Country Park.'

DC Lucas raised an eyebrow. 'Crikey, there's been more bodies in our woods this last twelve months than the local cemetery.'

His colleagues chuckled again, some rolling their eyes.

'Lucas has a point and another civilian found this one as they drove a delivery van up the lane towards the onsite centre.' Turning to the incident board, there was only a tiny piece of information: a map of the vast Crosley Country Park and a pin in where the body was located.

'Boyd and I were at the site first thing with motor patrols and CSI. White, adult male is the deceased. Although not confirmed that it was a RTA, it's looking certain given some tyre marks in the road and a few fragments of what appears to be smashed headlights. The collision investigation team have taken tyre impressions from a muddy verge on the side of the road, so will update us accordingly.' McCardle looked at her small team, who were scribbling notes.

'One of the call handlers received an incoming ten minutes ago. The person said he lives with a local journalist and the journalist hadn't returned from their usual jog. They had tried to call him but with no reply and watching their Ring doorbell, the housemate saw that he had left but hadn't returned. The country park is his route. We have the victim's broken phone to run through the system, but it's looking likely – given the housemate's description – that this is our deceased. A local journo for the *Northumberland Herald*: one Ryan Mortimer.'

Taking a sip of tea, she uncrossed and re-crossed her legs. 'So, the plan for today is to check CCTV in the area, which isn't much from a council or commercial perspective. The café and visitors centre in Crosley Country Park has CCTV, but given the park is three miles in circumference, it's unlikely to highlight anything. Nonetheless, you all know the drill.' McCardle looked around at her nodding team.

'Lucas, Birdy, if you can both go to the country park and speak with staff, also do a recce on any CCTV around the entrances of the country park, including residents' possible footage. We may need it imminently, along with door-to-doors.

Once pathology come back with cause of death, we can begin quicker movement, but getting ahead of the game will be key, especially given our ever-dwindling resources.' She rubbed her collarbone, tilting her head slightly to the opposite side.

'Boyd and I will go and visit the suspected deceased's housemate once a positive ID has been made. I'll be visiting the hospital to meet pathology, then Ryan Mortimer's next of kin after the briefing. CSI will continue to look for matches and evidence.' Clapping her hands together, she rose from her seat. 'And unless authorised by me, no one is to focus on any other current incident, please. I can't haemorrhage any more staff!'

McCardle absolutely meant it, knowing that there was no money in the budget for more resources and given the size of the force area and current spate of crimes, she was aware that there would be quite a few long shifts and sleepless nights ahead. The room emptied, and closing her eyes for a second, McCardle took a deep breath.

Death never got easier. It was unpleasant to see but for Polly, it was always so much harder to tell loved ones left behind, than to see dead bodies. Obviously there were some that imprinted on your mind, like a childhood recurring nightmare that made you feel sicker than gastroenteritis. Some images lived in your brain forever. Or a smell, a sound that dug itself into your mind, taking up permanent residency. It wasn't always the ones people would expect. Sometimes, Polly was haunted by the fear on a middle-aged man's face, or the horror of a pensioner who should have been able to live their life out in peace, dying of old age and not at the hands of warped humans. Or kids, whose lives had been extinguished in a way that every parent fears.

With over a decade's experience in the force, she only had a few years on the MIT. And on the scale of depravity, danger, and degradation, the MIT had lived up to its name in those few years. The killers, drugs lords, serial sex offenders, and radicalised hadn't crawled, but dived, out of the woodwork since Ronnie Ericson retired.

Informing loved ones of those who had been snatched from the earth, never got easier. A split-second bad decision from a fellow human, or a premeditated process by a calculated killer – either way, it scraped something inside her heart that felt like a scab never allowed to heal. Exiting her vehicle at Ryan Mortimer's mother's house, she groaned. Normally, it would be a task completed in pairs, but they were so short-staffed that McCardle opted to save time, still ensuring face-to-face communication.

Walking down the driveway to the red front door, she held a bomb in her hand – an unwanted gift she would pass to Mrs Mortimer that would change her life forever in a second. Never to return to the minute beforehand, when everything was fine. Clearing her throat, she rang the doorbell, hearing it through the front door. Listening to approaching footsteps, she saw the door open, a smiling woman in her early sixties staring at the stranger on her doorstep.

Polly looked like a copper, despite the lack of uniform. Perhaps it was the long black wool coat, or the shirt, or the tailored trousers and ankle boots with small heel. The lack of obvious make-up and jewellery, and the ever-serious body language.

'Hello, Mrs Mortimer?' McCardle asked, her voice gentle.

The woman nodded. 'Yes, can I help?'

Flashing a smile, she showed her police ID. 'I'm Detective Sergeant Polly McCardle from Northumbria Police. Can I come inside please?'

She witnessed the colour dissolve from Mrs Mortimer's face,

like clouds covering the sun. The homeowner moved from the doorway to the side of the hallway, gesturing her in. Clearing her throat, Polly walked into the stranger's house silently. Passing her, she could almost hear Ryan's mother's heartbeat.

'Through there, on your left is the lounge,' her cracking voice said. 'Take a seat.' She looked at the sofa, and Polly sat. 'What is this about?'

Sitting opposite on an armchair, McCardle could sense the frantic fear. She swallowed and wished that she didn't have to say the life-altering news.

'There has been an incident. We believe it may have involved your son, Ryan.' She kept the calmness in her voice that she had trained herself to maintain over the years.

There was a little gasp as Mrs Mortimer's hand flew to her mouth. 'Ryan? Is he okay? What's happened?' She rushed the words out, eyes wide as she waited for reassurance.

Polly swallowed, her gentle eyes remaining on the woman opposite her. 'I'm afraid someone was killed, Mrs Mortimer, and we think the deceased may be your son, Ryan. I am so deeply sorry to inform you.'

There was a guttural scream that filled the neatly decorated lounge. McCardle pressed her lips together, almost absorbing the world-slashing pain coating the air.

'It can't be him. I only spoke to him yesterday,' she sobbed, shaking her head quickly.

'I'm so sorry I have had to tell you this, Mrs Mortimer. The accident was only discovered this morning.'

'What ha-hap-happened?' she stuttered after a minute, voice coated with emotion.

'There was a road traffic accident. We are trying to establish the details, but we suspect it may have been a hit and run.' She looked at the broken mother, tilting her head, keeping eye contact and trying her best to make an impossible situation less painful. Heartbreak was visible in each line on the woman's ageing face.

Covering her mouth, Mrs Mortimer shook her head. 'Who would do…' She glanced to the mantelpiece at a photograph of her son before jumping up from the sofa and rushing out of the room. A few minutes later, she returned, apologising.

'No need to apologise. I understand your heartbreak.' Of course, Polly didn't understand. She didn't have a son that had likely been killed by a hit and run. But sometimes, there was nothing else to say. 'I'm afraid that we do need you or someone else to come into police headquarters, Mrs Mortimer, to identify the body. I'm so sorry.' Polly felt like she was at a farm choosing which animals were going to the slaughterhouse.

The woman's eyes were on her interlocked hands, sat in her lap. Tears plopped down onto her pale fingers. McCardle remained silent for a few moments, giving her the time to try to comprehend the devastating words a stranger had just delivered.

'It… it can't be my boy.' She gasped and raised her eyes to the police officer in her lounge, pleading for her response to indicate it was a mistake.

'I'm so sorry,' McCardle repeated.

There was silence for twenty seconds before Ryan's mother sniffed then spoke. 'Will you be with me?'

Nodding, she replied. 'Yes, we can go together. I'll stay with you.'

She watched the woman put her head in her hands and sob. Guttural cries from information that had altered her world in an instant.

'I'll wait in the car, Mrs Mortimer, in case you need to call anyone. Take your time.'

Ryan's mother nodded silently as Polly left the room, then house, returning to her car. Sighing, she rested her head back against the head rest of the driver's seat and wondered if having kids was really worth it. Driving to North Tyneside General Hospital, Ryan's mother remained silent in the passenger's seat, apart from the odd whimper escaping her mouth. McCardle knew that there was absolutely nothing that she could say that would bring any comfort to her other than, 'It's not your son.' They soon reached the hospital and Polly gently tapped her forearm as they walked into A&E. It was a lame attempt at comfort in the devastating moment.

'This way,' she said as they walked past reception and to the lift, where she hit the basement floor on the lift keypad. Mrs Mortimer began sobbing as the doors of the lift opened and the clinical, cold environment greeted them.

'Sorry you have to do this,' was all Polly could say as she led the way, holding the door open after her as Mrs Mortimer walked through, as if she was going to hell itself.

Doctor Harris was at her laptop. She glanced up, smiled, and rose, introducing herself before explaining the process of identifying the body. McCardle watched Mrs Mortimer, her eyes frantic and watery, not registering the process. The coroner could have been an alien, talking in a language she would never understand. And really, could anyone? Having to identify the body of a loved one. A child, who developed inside them then they nurtured as they grew in the outside world. A child who they should see settle down, happy, fulfilled – not who they should outlive. Some things, you never got used to in the force – telling people their loved one was dead and watching them identify them, was up there at the top.

'I do need to advise you that there are some facial injuries where the man fell to the ground after impact.' Doctor Harris delivered the news as gently as she could but nonetheless, it added to the mother's distress. She sobbed and covered her face with her hands.

Doctor Harris, McCardle, and Mrs Mortimer walked through into the next room. A body, covered in a white sheet, lay on a stainless-steel slab. It was almost butcher-like and Polly felt nauseous. A scream burst from Ryan's mother's mouth like a lion escaping an open cage. McCardle rubbed her arm again and told her to take her time.

Stepping forward, the coroner moved towards the top of the white sheet where the body lay, a shell: cold, stiff, soulless. Mrs Mortimer's body shook as she grasped Polly's sleeve, who moved her hand down and squeezed her hand. Slowly, the pair stepped towards the stainless-steel slab. Doctor Harris peeled the sheet back and a scream was released that Polly felt would have made the birds in the Amazon jungle fly from the trees. It was a scream that symbolised everything that could ever hurt in the world, running through a human. A scream of a mother staring at her dead son. A scream that would forever haunt Polly.

Chapter 11

After ploughing into Ryan Mortimer, David headed home, feeling like he was in someone else's life; watching it as if it were a dream or a film. The heinous act he had committed, a blur. But alongside the detachment, he also felt jubilant that he was closer to Emily. Ryan was arrogant, critical, abusive almost – disrespecting Emily online, then attempting to seduce her. Men like that prick spent their lives thinking they could get what they wanted, without hard work and dedication. They could get the friends, the job, the house, and always got the girl.

While the Davids of the world were left with the scraps. Never quite getting to the front of the queue. Never quite standing out. Blending in, like a shell on the beach. But David was sick of blending in, not being seen. He had spent his life in the shadows and now it was his time. To get what he wanted, who he wanted. Destroying the barriers in his way and protecting her, showing he would do anything for her, and he knew that it would bring them together.

Ryan and Oliver's murders even had some similarities to those in her books, life imitating art to a degree. Emily should be flattered! He chuckled then scrunched his eyes together, trying to dispel the sound of the journalist's body against his car. Returning to his dark flat, he gulped whisky that had been a gift from work. Shaking, he felt nausea dancing with a sense of relief. Walking into the lounge with the bottle of alcohol and a glass, he sat on his cream armchair, placing the bottle on the maple side table. His hand trembled and he grabbed it with the other as if to scold it. Drinking more of the putrid whisky, with each mouthful he felt closer to his beloved.

The next morning David was hungover, but luckily it was his day off work. Waking, he smacked his lips together before dragging himself to the bathroom and gulping water from the tap. Groaning, he put a hand to his forehead before lifting his gaze to the mirrored bathroom cabinet. For a moment he stared, glazed over, at his own reflection. Not an unattractive man, he was distinctly average, normal, vanilla – blending in with the crowd in all areas of his life. Not exceptional, not incompetent, just average, like the man next door or the guy working in the supermarket.

The difference between David and the average guy was that he was a killer, and he had killed for love. Convinced that his actions would bring Emily Robinson closer, that one day soon, they'd be together. Not only her biggest fan, he was her protector, her love, her future husband.

Shuffling into the lounge, he scratched his head and switched the TV on, placing the remote on his sofa as he walked through to the kitchen, filled the kettle, and put it to boil. Taking a cup out of his dated kitchen cupboards, he yawned, rubbing a hand through his brown hair. Making some toast, he then carried his breakfast through to the lounge. David flicked to the local news on TV, to see if anything had come in yet about the discovery of a body in the country park. He would have to check his car for repair work, now it was daylight, knowing already that there was damage to it.

Absentmindedly, he rolled his eyes as if thinking about something as simple as spam email, and a dart of anger punctured his heart as he reflected on the lack of response to the letter he had sent Emily. After everything he was doing for her. Maybe if she knew it was him, she would have replied. Rubbing his beard, he knew he was getting the opportunity to get closer to her in real life, and when that happened the letters, the fake Facebook account, and anything else would be redundant. Sighing, he glanced at his mobile phone screensaver. It was a photograph of the pair from Emily's last library event. Big smiles decorated their faces as they both held a copy of *Persuasion.* Their bodies close. Posture matched, elbows touching. He bit his lip; they really did make a wonderful couple.

Sinking his teeth into a slice of toast, he crossed his legs and leant back into the sofa. The news showed nothing – more likely meaning it was yet to be submitted by local journalists, rather than the body hadn't been found. He chuckled to himself thinking about the irony of when one of Ryan's colleagues reported on the incident, before anxiety kicked him in the stomach. Turning off the TV, David took a sip of strong coffee. He swallowed and rested his head back into the coolness of the sofa cushion, cup in hands, warming them. He looked at the yellowing Artex ceiling and took a deep breath. Silence echoed nothing but his thoughts as he replayed the events of the last twelve hours and pondered on the next step to get closer to Emily.

Moving back into the kitchen, he wondered about the Ryan-shaped indentation on his bonnet where the prick had been thrown in the air like a dog toy and had landed, bouncing from his vehicle. There was also a smashed headlight that he had noticed when parking his car the previous night. Tutting, he then sighed. It was worth it, the inconvenience. It was all worth it for her. He would look for a car garage out of town later alongside monitoring the news, knowing the story of the discovered body in Crosley Country Park was imminent.

He also needed to catch up with Emily's Facebook page, as well as plan the next time he would see her, through a scheduled event or something he would have to arrange himself. He missed her and the need to get closer to his love was growing each time he managed to remove an obstacle in his path. And despite the bubbling fear, the end goal of Emily was worth it. Like brutal Olympic training to be awarded a medal after the gruelling effort. He wasn't an evil person, not a calculated killer. Well, he hadn't been. But all his life, David had lived in the shadows and now he had a chance to shine, his light bringing love closer to him.

As he stood in the kitchen, staring out of the window at the gloomy sky, he rubbed his chin. His eyes turned down to the communal parking below, his car wasn't in its usual spot. He'd parked it facing the bushes, in the hope it, and the dent Ryan had made, was less obvious. It was early November and the air outside looked coated in a layer of polar bear breath. David absentmindedly watched a family walking to their car, the mother rushing her two young children as they dragged school bags and water bottles, their coats hanging off their shoulders as if the material was trying to run away. A sad smile crept across his face.

Things had been denied for him. Opportunities, chances for happiness. Whilst he had to take some responsibility for not putting himself out there after the heartbreak of his only relationship ended, David knew that his adolescence with his mother and Keith – then her absorption of his energy and her narcissistic needs to keep him for herself – had meant his life had been loveless, childless, lonely, and inside there was a longing that made him feel like he was consuming poison each day.

Until he found Emily. He closed his eyes and inhaled, thinking about her perfection. Her beautiful face: round cheeks, skin smooth and flawless. Her long, golden blonde hair that made her look pre-Raphaelite. The curves of her body, womanly, inviting. He licked his lips. She would be his. Emily Robinson would be his, and his alone. Picking up his mobile phone, he scanned through his photo collection of her as the kettle re-boiled. Motivated for their future, he thought about their lives together. Going to bookshops, theatres, and museums, as a couple. Meals that he would cook for her. Places they would visit and all the hotels they would make love in. Then his current predicament jerked him back into the here and now, and he clenched his jaw, placing his fists on the kitchen countertop. He would check social media, find a garage, then go and visit his mother in the care home.

Powering up his laptop, he put it on the arm of the cracked-leather sofa. Sitting, he placed a brown cushion on his lap, resting the laptop on the cushion and logged into Facebook. Scanning Emily's page, he nodded at some comments, praising *Persuasion* and some fans mentioning recent events and signings. Of course, Emily didn't just do events and signings in the North East; she travelled all over the country, even visiting other countries. She was a big deal. *They* were a big deal. And although David knew he couldn't just eliminate everyone around her, that was fine. Because when he had Emily Robinson, when he had her as his partner, his wife, well, he would at last feel secure and know his happy-ever-after had arrived.

His bubble of future happiness was popped when he noticed a comment from Chloe Logan. She had already been disrespectful previously. A few weeks ago, she had said the DCI McCoy storyline had been exhausted. She had also made a comment a week ago stating she hadn't liked *Persuasion,* and again, stating that the series was getting boring. David had replied from his Jen Brady account, telling her to leave the group and keep her nasty opinions to herself, which had simply been responded to with a laughing emoji, enraging him.

Narrowing his eyes, he read the bitch's latest comment.

Persuasion was our last book club read. It was dreadful. No one enjoyed it and we are done with books by Robinson until she writes something that's not the same story with different characters! Do better, Emily!

Pulling a hand over his mouth and chin, David felt anger soaring inside him, ricocheting around his stomach. Who the fuck did this woman think she was? How absolutely dare she slate Emily like that, on *her own* fan page! And the 'do better' comment. Seething, he gritted his teeth, his nostrils flaring. The comment had been made last night and no one had responded. He began typing, then stopped, taking three deep breaths as if he were about to go into an interview for the job of his life.

Book club. The little bitch mentioned a book club in her bitchy comment. He clicked back onto the comment and the photo of Chloe Logan that looked like a melting clown. Her profile was still closed but he was able to view some information. She was local and co-founder of the North East Book Addicts. David's eyes widened, not remembering that information the last time he looked at her profile. He clicked on the North East Book Addicts link, and it directed him to the book club's Facebook page. His heartbeat increased. There were sixty-two members on the page. David couldn't join – it would give his identity away as he had used his Jen Bradley profile to reply to Chloe's comments on Emily's page with the forked tongue she deserved.

Taking a sip of coffee, he scrolled through the Facebook page, noting that the group had been established for several months and met the second Wednesday evening of each month at a quiet pub in the town of Morpeth. People were making the odd comment to posts and it looked like there were a few admins, including Chloe Logan. He sneered. She didn't even look like she could bloody read, never mind be able to give a valued opinion through a literary review. *She probably just went to get pissed,* he thought, moving his tongue around his mouth as if the thought of her left a bad taste.

Eager to know more, David clicked on the photos from the page and saw some of the books they must have been reviewing, as well as a few group photos of the actual book club. He studied one of the group. 'Vile tart,' he muttered, looking at the photos and recognising Chloe with all the muck and shite spread across her face. Sneering, he thought of Emily, such an organic stunner, and smiled.

Moving on to the photographs of the books, he noticed that Emily's most recent, *Persuasion,* was the group's book club read that they had met about last week, which correlated with what the spiteful cow had said in her comments on Emily's page. There was photo of the group all holding the book and a separate image of the book with comments below, that spanned a five-week timeframe. The oldest comments included people saying they were looking forward to the read. Chloe had commented saying she didn't enjoy the last in the series but was looking forward to being proved wrong.

What a bitch, David thought, shifting on the sofa. Why the hell was she a member of Emily Robinson's fan page if she was such a rubbish writer, according to Queen Emily! He jiggled his legs, becoming increasingly irritated. On the group photo, some of the members had commented with their star rating of *Persuasion,* out of a possible five stars. Some had scored three, a few fours, and one five. Then there was a two star, from Chloe.

'What is her fucking problem?' David said aloud, running a hand over his beard.

Returning to the posts on the group page, he ascertained more information about the next book club meeting, in just under three weeks' time. A comment by another admin stated that new members were welcome. Letting out a chuckle, he shook his head. If the group were inviting new people along, it would be rude not to go, wouldn't it?

Chapter 12

After the morning with Mrs Mortimer, which left Polly feeling unusually emotionally vulnerable, she was happy to have the company of DC Claire Boyd to visit Dexter Reed, Ryan Mortimer's housemate. Buckling up for the ten-minute drive, Boyd looked at McCardle and smiled.

'I'm cancelling my leave next week, boss. I'm not going anywhere, and well, I think we need as many of us as possible at the minute.'

McCardle glanced at her as she put the car in reverse. 'No, Claire, honest, don't worry. You need your time off.' In truth, Polly needed Boyd on the team and in work. Her dwindling resources couldn't take any more haemorrhaging and she already knew she would have to have a conversation with Chief Inspector Richardson, that might resemble a child begging a parent to be allowed on the school trip.

'I don't mind, boss. I really don't.'

She knew that Claire was looking out for her. All of her team were great: dedicated, competent, team players. But naturally, she had clicked more with Boyd when McCardle was a DC and that connection had remained, despite Polly's promotion. And she was grateful for that, especially when things became challenging at work.

'Thanks, Claire, I appreciate it. Have a think about it.' She smiled at her colleague as they left HQ car park, heading towards Dexter Reed's and Ryan Mortimer's former property.

It was a dull November day but pockets of sunshine chinked out of the carpet of clouds, like little shards of colour from a crystal ornament. McCardle loved her home county. It didn't have great weather, but it had the most beautiful scenery. Mile upon mile of countryside, and the stunning North East coastline that on the warmest weeks of the year felt like it could be the Mediterranean. Alongside this, Northumberland had a tapestry of history, and the castles such as Alnwick, Bamburgh, and Warkworth attracted visitors from all over the globe.

They reached the street where Dexter Reed lived and she began reversing into a parking space.

'I think this is the worst part of the job for me; telling loved ones,' Boyd said as she put her phone away.

Nodding, Polly's eyes remained on the tight space she was navigating her large car into.

'Sometimes, it's worse than you know, the dead bodies. It's as if we are stamping on the future of the person we are telling. Setting it alight with no extinguisher. I'm not sure I'll ever get used to it, boss.' Boyd rubbed a finger across her right eyebrow, released her seatbelt and began to get out of the car as her superior did the same.

'I don't think we should ever get used to it, Claire. We should never stop caring about victims. It would be like a teacher not wanting a child to learn, or a doctor not wanting to cure an illness. But I agree, it's bloody hard and I think all of us have an understanding of just how fragile life can be.'

Boyd swallowed, nodding as the pair walked up the driveway to the terraced house where Ryan Mortimer had been a resident until less than twenty-four hours ago. Where he had likely been happy in his existence, not knowing that his life would get snatched away within hours. McCardle rang the doorbell, and almost immediately the green wooden front door opened. A chubby man with glasses stood there. Pale skinned, he looked tired as a weak smile flashed over his face.

'Mr Reed?'

'Yeah, come in.'

The officers showed their IDs as Polly introduced them, walking into the hallway onto a Moroccan-style runner. They followed into the lounge, where he gestured for them to sit.

'Do you want a cup of tea or coffee?' he asked, remaining standing.

'No, we are fine thanks, Mr Reed,' McCardle said as she took a seat.

'Please, it's Dexter.' He smiled sadly, running a hand over his auburn hair before sitting on a mustard armchair.

'I'm really sorry, Dexter, that we have come with such bad news. As I mentioned on the phone, the body discovered at one of the entrances to Crosley Country Park was identified by the next of kin as being Ryan Mortimer.'

Polly saw his Adam's apple move on his pale neck as he swallowed. Boyd held a notepad and pen, remaining silent.

'We have our teams trying to establish what happened to Ryan, but we believe he was the victim of a hit and run and died from internal injuries associated with the impact of a collision with a vehicle.' McCardle kept her voice clear, gentle, and calm as Dexter lost his composure, eyes filling up.

Shaking his head, he glanced at his interlocked hands before speaking. 'What kind of bastard knocks someone over and flees the fucking scene?' He pressed his lips together and two tears plopped from his eyes onto his cheeks. 'Sorry. I'm sorry for swearing,' he glanced at the officers. 'Ryan, he's… was such a great bloke. Why would someone do such a thing?' His voice cracked.

'We are trying to establish that. It's an awful situation and we are so sorry for your loss. It's now our focus to find who did this and bring them to justice.' McCardle had a calmness and authority about her that no doubt helped people greatly in their time of need. Something Ronnie Ericson always said.

Ronnie would tell her that she seemed older than her mid-thirties age, in the very best way, as if she had lived many lives and knew on a deep level about the needs of people, their psychology, and just how to make them feel better without a patronising edge or unachievable promises. She was direct but with the empathy of a nurse, he used to say. And each time he said it, she felt five inches taller with pride. Because she knew he meant it and in more ways that she would ever fully let on to anyone, she needed to hear it.

'It just doesn't seem real. I only saw him last night before I headed off for night shift.'

McCardle put one booted foot over the other ankle and nodded. Boyd had already established that Dexter was at the *Northumberland Herald* on nightshift the evening before. He worked on the print side of the press and despite being a housemate of Ryan's, that hadn't automatically mean he wasn't involved in his death.

'We understand, Dexter, and we have lots of specialist support we can offer if you need it now or anytime in the future. We do need to ask you some questions about Ryan if that's okay and have a look in his bedroom, if you don't mind?'

Dexter's blue eyes widened, the skin under his eyes almost translucent with tiredness and his pale skin tone.

'Do you know of any enemies Ryan may have had? Any ex-partners? Any recent fallouts or anything he mentioned regarding issues with people at work or things he was reporting on?'

Rubbing a hand over his nose and mouth, he looked briefly at Boyd. 'I mean, God, I don't know. I don't think so.'

'Just take your time,' Boyd said. 'Something might come to you later, if not straight away.'

He nodded and flashed her a smile. 'Ryan had a few ex-girlfriends. He was a good-looking lad, got all the girls.' Dexter chuckled lightly then his eyebrows furrowed. 'He was a decent bloke – loyal, even though he was popular with the women. He was on speaking terms with some of his exes.'

Boyd made notes as McCardle retained eye contact with him. 'What about any fallings out with friends or family?'

He rubbed a bent finger over his top lip and shook his head slowly. 'No, not that I can think of. Ryan had a small family but they were close. He never talked about any falling outs. He was just a nice guy.' Glancing down at the striped rug in front of a log burner, his eyes glazed over momentarily.

McCardle felt the sting for him. They could have been friends for months, years, she didn't know but living with someone, well that built a bond. And it was clear that Dexter was devastated about the senseless, possibly premeditated murder of his housemate.

'What about work? Could Ryan have made any enemies? Colleagues? People he reported on?'

Dexter shook his head and bit his lip. 'I don't think so. His team was small. I know some of them, working in printing. They are a sound bunch.' He sniffed up, his nostrils flaring and he rubbed his hands together. 'He only reported on the entertainment. Film reviews, music, books. He covered the odd event, gig, play. But it's not like he was covering the exposé of pedos or scandal. He wasn't calling out abusive churches, or care homes. I don't think he could make an enemy from a local gig.' He puffed out air and grabbed the cream cushion to his right, placing it on his lap.

McCardle nodded. 'I understand. Thanks. If you do think of anything, you can give us a call.' She coughed. 'Do you mind if we have a look in his room, Dexter?'

He shook his head. 'Erm, not at all. I'll show you. I haven't been in, since, you know.' He sighed and rose from his armchair for the pair to follow him upstairs.

Thirty minutes later, the officers left Dexter Reed's home with little information. However, they had Mortimer's laptop and an old phone and Dexter had told them if he thought of anything relevant, he would contact the police. McCardle drove them back to the station. She hoped for an update from toxicology to confirm if anything was in Mortimer's system. The team briefing was in four hours, but before that McCardle needed to speak with CI Richardson, and she had a feeling it wasn't going to be the easiest of conversations.

Chapter 13

David had searched online for garages out of the county, identifying one in North Shields, around fifteen miles away. Pacing the lounge, he dialled the number. What sounded like a teenager answered the phone.

'Hello, Lawson's Garage. Can I help?'

'Hi, yes, I hope so. I hit a deer when I was driving along a country lane the night before last,' David said calmly. 'The deer scarpered, so I'm hoping it was okay. My car seemed to come off worse. I have a dent where it landed on the bonnet and a smashed headlight where one of its hooves cracked into.' He swallowed. David didn't like lying but when it was essential, well, it had to be done – like a check-up at the dentists.

'No bother at all. I'm sure we can sort that out. Let me see when we have availability.'

David heard a clicking of a mouse and he tapped his forefinger to his mouth.

'I'm afraid we can't do until Wednesday morning.' The voice was monotone, disinterested.

'Wednesday morning? Don't you have space tomorrow?' He groaned.

'I'm afraid not.'

Gritting his teeth, he thought he could look elsewhere but they might not have capacity either.

'You could bring it by last thing tomorrow and leave it in the garage, then one of the lads can do it as soon as they come in on Wednesday morning. They usually start at 7am?' the voice said.

David made a hmph noise. 'Okay, yes, I will do. Thanks.'

'Can I take your name please and is this number okay to

contact you on?'

He felt flustered as if caught coming out the works toilet after taking a massive dump. 'Erm, yes, it's Andy Palmer. Also, can I pay cash? I'm bloody useless and I've lost my bank card,' he said with a chuckle at the end.

'Yes, or you can pay with credit card at reception or online.'

'Excellent. Thanks. I'll drop the car off tomorrow.'

'See you then, Mr Palmer. Goodbye.'

David hung up, his heart racing. He hadn't even thought about protecting his identity and had panicked. He grinned at giving an old colleague's name.

The care home where David's mother resided was ten minutes' drive away. Before that, he needed to go to his allotment to check things. It was a quiet, unusually large patch that had been his late grandfather's plot. The people on his site were elderly, mainly male pensioners who frequented the place in the spring and summer, then left in the late autumn until the following year. When David's mother still lived at home, work and the allotment were his only escape. He would often cycle there and get drunk on cheap, strong lager in the shed that he had replaced and improved over time.

In the small flat he frequently felt suffocated with his mother; her health deteriorating and her inability to get over Keith's death increasingly draining by the week. The allotment could get cold, so over the years, David had improved his patch, putting money and effort into making the shed more like a summer house, with a small window, a secure front door, electricity, heating and plumbing. He even had a portable toilet in there similar to what would be in a RV or caravan, with a septic tank. Along with storage, a camping stove, a microwave, a sofa bed, and an old armchair, it had become quite the retreat at times. He was proud of it and knew his grandfather would have also been proud.

The growing of fruit and veg was a bonus and the solitude of the site – even to a degree in the summer where a few of the old guys congregated together but only usually spoke small talk to him – created an anonymity that made David feel free, calm, and safe. A few regulars had left early last month, packing away for the winter, happy with their crops that year. The odd person came all year long, monitoring their Brussels sprouts, kale, onions, and garlic over the winter, but not near to his plot.

Pulling up to the allotments, he unlocked the large communal gates. Each person had a key for the padlocked gates, that had been installed six years ago after youths drove motorbikes into the allotments and purposely destroyed the place. Pointless crime, only being cruel and spiteful. Each time David unlocked the outside gates, he thought of those little bastards and hoped they got their karma. When he drove further in and reached his plot, he always smiled. It was his place; a place of reflection, solitude, and of happy memories with his grandfather.

His crop was never large: carrots, potatoes, tomatoes, red onions, spring onions, garlic, rocket, peas, and strawberries – but for him, home-grown, and in his and his grandfather's place, well, it tasted like the best food on earth. He pulled his shoulders to his ears as he thought about cooking for Emily. A meal with ingredients grown by his own hand, nurtured with care and love, for his love. Exiting his car, he glanced around, feeling calm. Many times over the years, he would stay there all day, cooking his crop in his shed-cum-summer-house. It meant a quarterly electricity bill but he had installed solar panels to save money, and really, it was one of his few luxuries in life, so he didn't mind.

His end plot, with only one neighbour, was private due to the fence separating them, which had been used for trellising, a number of plants camouflaging it. David could sit outside on his wooden bench, seldom being disturbed, even in the summer months. The shed provided privacy, solitude, and inside, after much time, effort, and money, it was almost a home. Over the next few days, he would ensure he had all he needed there, and replenish stock, as well fit a new padlock on the lockable metal screen that covered the front door, for extra security.

Although people could see through the wooden gates, many of the sites had further security-proofed their plots following the break-in. You could never be too careful. Shutting the dark green wooden gate after himself, David walked the gravel path to the shed. The stones crunched under his walking boots and he stopped to check on the odd plant. Reaching the door to the shed, he straightened the hanging dream catcher that had twisted, its beads tied up in the chimes. It made a tinkling as he untangled it. Then he unlocked the shed and opened the door – wiping his feet on the brown coir mat that had welcome written on it – before going in.

The structure had been made out of a timber frame, packed with insulation and then plaster-boarded on the inside, before being painted to give the homely effect. The roof had been felted before solar panels were installed. There were limits on what he was allowed to do. To build the shed, he had enlisted an old neighbour who had since left home and gone to university. He'd paid him £100 to help over two days and, in all honesty, it had been nice to have the company. They had done a great job and David had been happy with the shell of his structure, continuing the work inside over a few weeks until it became the place he wanted it to be. A place his grandfather would be proud of.

Opening the double metal cabinet, he perused the shelves. Checking stock, he saw there were towels, cleaning products, toiletries, tins of food and dried supplies, candles, and matches. Walking to the sink, he checked the cupboard under it for pots and pans, crockery and cutlery. The kettle and microwave were clean and he had two plug-in radiators and a blowy heater, which ate the electricity, but was good to blast the room for ten minutes. In the ottoman, he had a quilt, blankets, a pillow, and some hot water bottles. Smiling to himself, David clasped his hands together. It was homely and it would do the job just perfectly.

Arriving at the care home, he parked his car at the far end of the car park, where most people were too lazy to walk from. He wanted to disguise the dent and cracked headlight as much as possible to avoid some nosey old blabbermouth asking questions. He would have to be careful driving round with the car until he was able to drop it off tomorrow after work. Driving with a broken headlight was an offence, and David was a good boy. Chuckling to himself, he was immediately winded with a whack of worry.

It hadn't been on the news about Ryan Mortimer this morning but despite his research and planning, there was some evidence in the form of his cracked headlight, at the least. He shook his head, certain there was no way of linking him to the area. No motive and no CCTV cameras on that estate and particular entrance to Crosley Country Park, plus he had used the fake registration plates now. He had the next step in his plan to think about and Ryan was simply the bug, buzzing around, that he had squashed. A pest in his path.

'Afternoon, Mr Creighton,' a pleasant voice said as he walked past reception. It was one of the team leaders, who always made an effort to chat with him and clearly loved her job.

'Afternoon,' he said back, a wide smile on his face.

'Your mother is in the lounge.'

He nodded as he continued to walk slowly. 'Thanks.'

Strolling along the corridor, he glanced at the dark green carpet with a beige swirl design that was likely chosen to make the place feel more homely but made him feel nauseous. As did the smell of the kitchen as he got closer to it. A mixture of powdered potato, overcooked broccoli, and some form of cheesy sauce that smelt like it had been trapped in a bag that someone had farted into. He gagged slightly, reaching the double doors of the lounge, where the nauseating carpet continued but the food smell was replaced by the odd waft of incontinence.

Spotting his mother in the corner, her head stooped and eyes closed, David sighed. She looked old and frail, despite not being old in years. There was a spare high-back armchair next to where his mother slept. Smiling at a man a few seats down, he sat next to his mother. He listened to her sleeping, seeing her body becoming something unrecognisable with each visit. She had spent years dwelling on Keith and when she wasn't in mourning, she would be encouraging, yet sabotaging David's growth. Asking why he wasn't dating then saying he didn't need anyone anyway as most girls were bitches or cheats.

'You just need your mam. The most important woman in your life,' she would say, giving him a hug before serving up his favourite meal.

He loved his mother, but since she had been in the care home, the curtains had opened on David's life. The lack of co-dependency, the freedom of movement that he now had, not quite registering the level of coercion from his mother.

Behaviours, tactics that were used on her by Keith to mould and manipulate a person. Subtle, like a slow weight gain. Until it became alarmingly obvious. Inhaling, David closed his eyes and clenched his jaw.

'Son, are you Michael?' a voice from behind him said. He turned. It was the man he had smiled at.

'No, I'm not Michael. I'm David.'

'Well, where is Michael then? He said we would go to the match.' The man's brow furrowed and he slapped his hands on the padded arms of the chair he sat in.

'I don't know, sorry.'

'You know…'

'Shut up!' said a voice from another seat.

He saw a scowl from the cross face of a tiny dot of a woman, and chuckled slightly. The two began bickering as his mother woke up. Opening her eyes, she blinked quickly and wet her lips with her tongue.

'Oh, my boy,' she said as she grabbed his hand in between hers.

David smiled as he looked at his mother and was pleased she loved him, despite their challenges over the years. But the love from a mother simply wasn't enough for him. He needed the love of a woman and that woman was called Emily Robinson.

Chapter 14

McCardle knocked on Chief Inspector Richardson's office door, consciously refraining from making her alert to the 'police officer's knock'.

'Come in,' he shouted.

Polly opened the door, the blue carpet tiles, a lot cleaner than those in the corridor. CI Richardson looked up from his desk. In his late forties – despite his job that held the responsibility heavier than the Angel of the North – he had strong shoulders and straight posture. It made McCardle straighten her own shoulders.

'Sir,' she said, smiling.

'DS McCardle. How are you?' He had a clear voice that still held the slight bounce of friendliness but Polly knew it could command a room as well as terrify a hard man.

'Good, thanks, sir. You?' McCardle moved further into the office.

'Please, sit.' CI Richardson bypassed the query on his well-being, nodding to the seats opposite him.

Clearing her throat, she sat on one of the grey padded chairs, leaning forward. After updating CI Richardson on the current case, she tapped her notepad with her thumb.

'Sir, the team, we are struggling for officers. With sickness and DC Myers involved with the Ashmouth OCG drugs racket, and others are still searching for leads on the Thornton murder.' She moved in her chair, trying to keep her posture straight, assertive.

CI Richardson nodded, then glanced at his laptop before looking back at her. He removed his glasses, folding the legs and placing them on his desk, running a hand over his black beard that was peppered with grey.

'I understand, McCardle. The budget is very tight. You know the force has had a cut in funding this financial year and well…' His hand moved back to his beard. 'We could maybe offer overtime for a week or so. I could speak with the neighbourhood team, although I know they are inundated.'

He glanced at his computer momentarily as McCardle tucked some of her blonde hair behind her ear. 'There is another option.' His eyebrow raised slightly as he interlocked his hands and laid them on the table separating them. 'We could ask Ronnie if he was interested in volunteering in a civilian role?' He said the word volunteering, making inverted commas with his fingers as he did so.

Asking Ronnie for help was something that had crossed Polly's mind many times since he had retired a year ago. She was a competent, experienced DS. But Ronnie, well he was something else. An oracle, and no matter how many years she was in the force, Polly knew she was no Ronnie Ericson. And that didn't intimidate her, because she admired him like she had never admired a man in her life, both in and out of work.

'That's if you wouldn't feel put out, Polly?' CI Richardson looked at her intently. He was being sensitive despite the desperate situation of resources.

'No, sir, I wouldn't be put out at all. The whole team respects Ericson, and he was my mentor. I owe him a great deal. I loved working with him and his expertise and approach would really help out at the moment.' She swallowed and glanced at her closed notepad, feeling uncomfortable momentarily.

'It has no reflection on your capabilities, my suggestion. You know that, don't you?'

She nodded. 'Yes, sir.'

'I know we didn't back-fill your position and you have one staff member on long-term sick. You're an exceptional DS.'

McCardle needed to hear this. Don't we all need validation sometimes? She rolled her shoulders back and nodded. 'Sir, I can't say I haven't thought about DS Ericson, Ronnie, I mean. When he left, he said to us all that he might be back in the future and although he said it in jest, I know him well enough to realise he probably meant it.'

Richardson laughed. 'Yes, you're right, McCardle. We can't ever retire from the force. It won't let us completely!'

She chuckled alongside her superior but she also thought about Ronnie's second chance at his marriage and how he'd desperately missed Caroline in the almost year they were apart. It was when Polly had just joined the MIT and she was assigned to the case involving the murder of homeless people. She had worked intensely with the then DS Ericson.

They'd clicked in a way only colleagues who know they will become friends do. As the case developed, the pair spent a lot of time together and he had opened up about Caroline, his estranged wife and mother of his daughter, Kelsie. His marriage had dissolved as his relationship with Northumbria Police dominated every aspect of his life. Ericson was so dedicated to his job that it felt like he'd almost committed adultery on his wife. She'd been stood up and let down one time too many, and their relationship broke down.

Ronnie was a man's man. The type who watched the darts and read the newspaper in print rather than online. The bloke in his late fifties whose dad had racing pigeons and whose grandma lived with them. Who didn't fancy America for a holiday, even before Trump. The man who worked hard, from the age of fifteen until his retirement. But when they began working together, in a short time, the man's man slowly opened up to Polly, and their friendship became solid.

Ericson had looked out for her. Not in a patronising, 'women-can't-do' way and she got to experience a (albeit slightly younger) father figure and a positive male role model that she hadn't seen much of in her life. And despite the promotion, her great team, and her happy home life, she missed Ronnie every day. Popping into the Cake Station once or twice a week and socialising as a foursome every so often was lovely – but seeing him every day, the synergy they had, their minds working together to become the key that fit every lock to solve crime, well, she missed that in a way that wasn't getting easier with time.

'Obviously, it will be a civilian role and unpaid, except for expenses, but he may have some capacity and interest in helping out a few days a week, under your supervision?' CI Richardson leant forward in his chair, eyes straight on McCardle. 'But only, Polly, if you feel comfortable with it. I don't want you to feel undermined or that you are not able to manage with the team. This is purely resources and lack of them, and for want of a better term, Ronnie would be a resource.'

McCardle inhaled deeply. 'Yes, sir, I agree, and he would be a very experienced resource. I wouldn't feel put out, sir. This is about the force and solving crime, protecting our community. My ego is always left at home when I put my shoes on for the day.' She smiled and Richardson mirrored it.

'And that, McCardle, is why you are an exceptional leader and an exceptional DS. Anyway, have a think, we will chat later.'

McCardle thanked Chief Inspector Richardson for his time, leaving him to get on with his non-stop stream of demands. Closing his door, she leant against the white wall to the side of his office, tilting her chin up and closing her eyes briefly. The truth was, she was struggling and the lack of resources was making her question her capabilities. Although Lisa would listen at home one hundred times over, she didn't have that listening ear at work. DC Boyd was her closest colleague but having only been in the role of DS for a short time, she didn't feel she could offload too much onto those she managed. It felt messy, undesirable, like accepting a sweet from a stranger.

There was a lot to consider, with pros and cons, and Polly hadn't even asked Ronnie yet – which was a bloody big ask, given the reason he left the force and her respect for Caroline. Dropping her head to her hand, she ran her hand over her forehead and through her hair. She needed a cigarette desperately, but a vape would have to do. Shaking her head, she took the stairs to the ground floor of HQ and went into the back yard to smoke her vape before the end of shift briefing.

'So, team, after the positive identification of her son today, we now know that the deceased discovered this morning is Ryan Mortimer, a journalist at the *Northumberland Herald*, aged thirty-nine.' McCardle turned to the photo of Ryan Mortimer supplied via his social media, then looked back to her team. 'I'll be visiting Mrs Mortimer again tomorrow to check in on her and have a conversation about any potential useful information such as associates, possible enemies, his past.' McCardle tapped her pen on the top of the table that she leant against. 'Right, team, updates from today, please? Lucas?'

DC Lucas coughed and shuffled some papers on his lap. 'Yup, boss. Me and Birdy went to Crosley Country Park and spoke to staff at the centre. It's half a mile from the crime site, but it was useful to hear about the country park and its entrances and staffing. The manager said they have CCTV cameras recording twenty-four hours a day at the centre site only. We looked at the footage for that day on vehicles arrival and leaving times. We have all registration plates to trace, if needed.'

'And just because a vehicle left, doesn't mean it didn't come back to knock Ryan Mortimer over,' added Birdy.

'Exactly. Nor does it mean a vehicle that hadn't been on site isn't our target. This is murder, manslaughter at least but also a Section 170: fleeing the scene.' McCardle glanced at her team who were nodding. 'If this wasn't targeted and was an accident, it still resulted in the death of someone and we need all the evidence we can get to find the offender. What about the person who found the deceased?' Polly took a gulp of cold tea and rolled her shoulders back, hearing the crunch as if walking over gravel.

DC Birdy shuffled in his seat. 'We spoke to the van driver, boss.' He glanced at his notes. 'He was on-site at six forty-five, taking stock to the centre. The shift manager at the centre starts at 6.30am, but she came from a different entrance, and we checked this with CCTV footage.' Birdy glanced to Lucas sitting by his left, then back to McCardle. 'Understandably, the van driver was shaken up. His statement corroborates what he said to first responders and the information he initially gave to call-handlers. There're no CCTV cameras on that entrance, so we will need to cross-reference his tyres but when we visited him, there was no smashed headlight.'

'Not to say he couldn't have dodged to a garage and got it replaced,' added Lucas.

Birdy tapped a thigh. 'Exactly. There's also possible home CCTV footage from some of the cameras in the streets leading up to and including Jeffreys Street – the one meeting the lane to get to the country park, boss.'

'Great work, lads, thank you.' McCardle smiled at them and they both leant back in their seats.

'Boyd and I visited Dexter Reed. Boyd, do you want to

update the team, please?'

She nodded. 'Yeah, so Dexter Reed works mainly opposite shifts to those Mortimer worked. Last night, he was working and this has been verified by the print shift supervisor at the *Northumberland Herald.*' Boyd uncrossed her legs. 'Reed last saw Mortimer before he went to work that evening, leaving at six-forty pm. On arriving home at seven-twenty am, Dexter drove past where the uniforms stood, guarding the lane to the country park. Once in the house, had a cup of tea and some toast, before going upstairs to bed. Mortimer's bedroom door was open and there was no sign of him. Dexter checked the bathroom and, no Ryan there either.'

DC Boyd looked at McCardle who nodded for her to continue. 'After calling his phone and no reply, it felt out of character. Dexter checked the Ring doorbell footage back. Mortimer went out jogging but didn't return. He walked to the cordoned-off road to the country park and asked uniforms, who gave little away. After claiming he thought his housemate was missing, they connected him with call handlers.'

Boyd looked at her superior. 'We searched Mortimer's room. Brought his laptop and an old phone in and what looks like a work diary. Could provide something.' She shrugged.

'We need to understand possible motives and dig into Mortimer's past for any information that could provide a lead. Who did Ryan Mortimer piss off? Who were his possible recent and long-term enemies? What were his recent movements?' Some of the team were making notes. McCardle glanced at the incident board and the photo of the crumpled body of Ryan Mortimer, that lay in an almost foetal position until it was grimly discovered.

'We need to visit the *Northumberland Herald* and speak with his colleagues, revisit his mother, review his diary and IT, and do door-to-door for possible CCTV footage. CSI will carry on with the tyre print analysis and it's likely CI Richardson and I will do a press release asking for information.' She looked at her team, just three of them sitting in the room alongside her, minus DC Myers, who was supporting with the Ashmouth drugs OCG case. Sighing, she tilted her chin up. 'I'm hoping we get some more resources, team. One way or another. But thank you, for being such diligent officers and well, for supporting me.' She pressed her lips together and swallowed.

'Anytime, boss,' Birdy said, getting up from his seat and smiling at her as they began to leave the room, ready to catch criminals.

Chapter 15

Returning home from visiting his mother, David parked along from his usual parking bay outside the flats, hoping the neighbours were too self-absorbed to notice the damage to his vehicle. The dark nights helped but he needed to minimise the rubberneckers gawping at his damaged car. Scurrying up to his flat, he was relieved to be home. His head was like the wheels of a spinning bike with thoughts of Ryan Mortimer, the police, and the next stages in his plan to win Emily's heart. He hadn't much thought of Oliver Thornton, especially as all had gone quiet over a month ago in the media. That wasn't to say that nothing was happening on the case, but there was no link to him.

After making a cup of tea, he sat on his leather sofa with a sigh. Murder hadn't been on his timeline when he first met Emily. Christ, maybe her books had brought it out in him? He'd read them so many times that he felt almost a character. And in a way, David was a character in Emily's life – her future lover, pursuing her from afar. Her hero, protecting her and not letting anything or anyone stand in their way. He smirked before sipping on his tea. In all seriousness, David wasn't sure if he meant to kill Oliver Thornton. It was impulsive and he wasn't certain that he had *wanted* to kill him. Maybe he had just needed to prove a point that he wouldn't let anyone bully or harass his woman. He was standing up for her, something he had never done for himself.

It had been different with the student, spontaneous. But it had changed him, given him a power that he hadn't felt before, but didn't realise he had needed so much. Now, he had gotten in too deep with his desire. Like playing a game of roulette and winning on black, it had felt dangerously exciting. And like with Oliver, when David killed Ryan, there was something more than Emily on his mind. Of course, she was his focus, his end goal. That's why he was doing this, to get to her and be with her. However, there was still something else. A revenge against the people who had hurt him, bullied him, dismissed and belittled him all his life. Keith, people at school, his only long-term girlfriend, who broke his heart, and his mother. It was like he had confronted them all, was being noticed – even if anonymity was crucial. And it all brought him closer to his Emily, to protect and cherish her.

The murder of Ryan had been planned, calculated, but there was something about it that David found so easy, as if he were born to be a hitman. He chuckled to himself and glanced out of the window of his sixth-floor flat. The sky was a dark blanket of deep blue, purples, grey, and black, like a gigantic bruise covering the sky. Did something inside him feel bad? Yes. He had no idea who the journalist's family were. If they were decent and loving. But a huge part of him didn't care.

He had been denied so much in life: a loving father, a mother that put him first, a relationship. For what? Now he was alone, his mother rotting in a care home, each day deteriorating like fruit going bad in the summer heat. David deserved his happiness. He'd waited over forty years for it and now he would get it, no matter what. And getting away with it had made him stronger, more in love, and more determined to get the girl.

Ryan Mortimer wasn't just rude with his reviews, he was cocky, arrogant, and a threat. He'd witnessed Ryan flirting with Emily and knew he would pursue her, regardless of his disrespect to her creativity. He would have kept going, running faster in the race, pushing David down into the dirt – laughing at him, just like his stepfather and the bullies at school had. Well, David stopped him, and he never got the prize that was Emily. She was waiting for him, and he would fight any battle for her. Resting his head on the cushion of the sofa, he closed his tired eyes briefly. The local news would be on soon, and he would find out if there had been any progress in the case. Until then, he would scroll the internet, going first to the *Northumberland Herald's* site. Despite him glugging his tea, David's mouth turned dry as he read the first article.

Cherished Family Member and Colleague Found Dead – the headline read with a large photo of Ryan Mortimer. Grabbing his mouth, he began reading the story, yet halfway through he couldn't help but smile. Ryan had sleazed all over Emily that night at the book event, and that was after he had given *Persuasion* a scathing review. The article gave little away, because of course, the media only knew so much. It summarised that there was an ongoing investigation and if members of the public had any information, they should contact the police. He would keep an eye on the local news over the next few days; it was likely the police would be interviewed at some point soon.

David was exhausted. It had been a tumultuous twenty-four hours and the pace of his day hadn't allowed for him to really process the enormity of what had happened. Muting the TV, he rested his hands on his flat stomach, feeling the material of his woollen jumper below them. Closing his eyes briefly, his thoughts travelled to another issue: Chloe Logan.

Picking up his mobile phone, he logged on to the library app and ordered the book for November's North East Book Addicts group, the date of which was in his diary. After reserving the book that he would collect tomorrow, he scrolled on social media, focusing on Emily and the North East Book Addicts page. There was nothing new from the last time he checked.

He thought about the letter to Emily. She hadn't responded and David felt he had given her ample time. He could write another but what would he say? Really, some things needed to be said face to face. The next part of his plan could provide that. Everything would come together. He just had to be patient and, luckily for him, it was one of his skills. He had been patiently waiting all his life.

The evening news came on and he stiffened in his seat. Unmuting the sound, he leant forward. It was the top story and the newsreader stared at him, face solemn as he mentioned the discovery of a body in Crosley Country Park and that the deceased was local reporter, Ryan Mortimer. He spoke in his trained monotone voice, skilled in giving no non-verbal communication away, and David watched, mesmerised. His knees began to bounce as the screen changed and two police officers appeared on his TV. On the bottom of the screen, their names and positions were written in white on a royal blue strip.

'Chief Inspector Richardson and Detective Sergeant McCardle' flashed up. The man began, explaining what had happened, reiterating some of the words the newsreader had previously said. The female copper chipped in when indicated to do so by her superior and updated the anxious public on what Northumbria Police were doing. At the end, the man spoke again, advising anyone with any information to get in touch by a variety of means and finishing the sentence with the promise that Northumbria Police would do all that they could to bring the perpetrator of this heinous crime to justice.

For a moment, David felt like the chief inspector was looking directly at him, promising him that he would be caught and punished for killing the journalist. Moving his tongue around his mouth, he swallowed, a tinge of sting in his throat.

Panic rose from his stomach, to his chest, and neck, making it flush. Then David shook his head violently, expelling the thoughts. Nothing had happened with the Oliver Thornton case and that had all gone quiet. He had been careful with Ryan and the police wouldn't link the crimes. David Creighton was a good member of the community. He had never been in any trouble and worked with the public. He would be fine and more importantly, David would get the girl!

Chapter 16

The team briefing was over and McCardle had instructed her colleagues on the next steps in the Ryan Mortimer case. Before it was home time, a press conference was scheduled with CI Richardson. It would be a short speech from them with an appeal for help. They couldn't give information but could reassure the public not to panic – always easier said than done. As they walked along the hallway to the room where the local press were waiting, CI Richardson turned his head to her.

'Polly, have you thought about what we discussed earlier regarding Ronnie?'

'Yes, sir. I think it could be great for the team. I will call him, unless of course, you would prefer to?'

Richardson shook his head. 'No, I think it's important it comes from you. You would be his superior, after all.'

She swallowed. 'Yes, sir, will do.'

They reached the room where the press conference was being held. McCardle swallowed, smoothed down her short-bobbed hair and followed her superior into the room. Thirty minutes later the journalists had left, Polly had said goodnight to Chief Inspector Richardson, and she was sitting in her car. Feeling like she was melting inside of her head, she just wanted to get home, eat some comfort food, and sit with her wife. Driving home, she thought about what she would say to Ronnie.

'Fuck it,' she said aloud, before instructing her car to call him. It rang three times before a jolly Ronnie answered.

'My favourite Polly. How you diddlin'?'

She laughed. It was something he often said, a reference to

her not-so-popular name and the fact she was the only Polly he had actually ever met. 'I'm good, thanks, boss. How are you?'

'When are you going to stop calling me boss? It's been a year,' Ronnie replied, with a secret fondness.

'You'll always be the gaffer to me,' she said seriously. 'And that's really why I'm ringing. Although, of course, it's always good to speak to you.' She was rambling and shook her head.

'Oh aye, you in bother, pet?' he said in jest, a light chuckle in his voice.

She didn't respond to the joke and went straight to the point. 'You'll have heard, Ron, about the death of Ryan Mortimer?'

'Yeah, bloody awful. I didn't recognise him from the regular journos but he was in entertainment, wasn't he?'

'Yeah, not one of our usuals. I'm working with such a depleted team, we make Tristan da Cunha look overpopulated.'

Ronnie laughed and Polly did too, although her situation felt humourless. 'We need more help, resources, expertise.' She paused. She felt cheeky asking him to work for free but she knew that his love for the force had never gone. Baking cakes hadn't sweetened the blow of leaving his life-long career, and something he was exceptional at. Ronnie Ericson was a force within the force and his colleagues far and wide admired him.

Not only had he been the best mentor to her, he had been a friend, becoming the father figure she never realised she so desperately needed. But above everything, Polly respected Ronnie Ericson in a way that could make her heart stop if she thought she was disrespecting him.

'Ron, you know what we all think of you. What *I* think of you. I don't say it a lot, but well, you're more than an old boss.' Polly pressed her lips together, feeling emotional.

'Eh, less of the old!' Ronnie chuckled. 'But I know, pet, and I feel the same. You know you're like a daughter to me. What's this all about? Just spit it out, it's okay.'

Inhaling, she nodded, despite knowing he couldn't see her. 'I spoke to Richardson and he mentioned that when you left, you said if we ever needed you, you'd be happy to come in and volunteer as a civvy. I mean, I, we, would never want you to feel like we were taking the piss, exploiting you and that, but...'

'Exploiting me? I'm not a trafficked sex worker, Poll!'

She sniggered. He always had a way with words. Sometimes, it was a bit close to the edge, but Ronnie had a heart bigger than a dartboard and even when he said the odd risky thing, it seemed to always hit the bullseye.

'You know what I mean, you silly sod. We are running on empty. The team, I, need help and someone experienced.'

There was a moment of silence and she could almost see him tapping his eyebrow down the phone, knowing he would be thinking of the right thing to say, for both of them. Polly knew she was a very capable DS, but she couldn't deny that she was still learning and even with the basis of a brilliant detective, it was ultimately experience and cases that brought knowledge, expertise, and transferable thinking in the force. And that's what Ronnie Ericson had in abundance, whilst she was still in her infancy.

'Boss?' McCardle asked, checking he was still there.

'I'm here, Poll, I'm still here,' Ronnie mumbled. 'I'll give you a call before work in the morning.' His voice was rushed and she wondered if it was the baby kicks of excitement or the nerves of knowing he would have to say no. She bit her fingernail as she drove.

'Perfect. Thanks, boss. And it would just be what time you had to give, that you could manage alongside the Cake Station and Caroline. No pressure. Just have a think.'

'I will, pet, and I'll talk with the home-boss. Then we can

catch up in the morning, first thing. Okay?'

'Yeah, great. Thanks, Ronnie.'

'You're welcome. Have a lovely night with your Lisa. Speak tomorrow.'

Polly smiled. 'Speak then.'

She instructed her car's computer to end the call and took a few deep breaths before pulling into her housing estate, knowing a relaxed night and chat with her wife would help make everything a little less foggy in her mind.

Ronnie put his mobile phone on the arm of the dark blue sofa, the satisfaction of being needed, warming his torso. When he left Northumbria Police, he had said to Chief Inspector Richardson and McCardle that he would help in the future if needed. However, Ronnie had offered, never thinking that anyone would actually want him back, for the paperwork element alone. Fighting crime was in his DNA so, of course he wanted to return. Tapping his mouth, he contemplated. It never left, that drive, that need. Like an addict in recovery, the craving was always there. And the police was Ronnie's drug, his elation, his satisfaction, but also his demise – well, in his personal life anyway.

He paced the lounge slowly. Richardson was a dark horse, never giving much away, but it felt like he had got star of the week at school knowing the big boss thought he could assist and moreover, wanted him to help. Ronnie would rush back to the MIT quicker than he gobbled a chocolate éclair, but the indigestion the force had given his marriage meant that the decision would never be his alone, and he felt queasy just thinking about the conversation he would need to have with his wife when she returned from yoga.

It was still early into take two of their marriage. Ronnie

couldn't, wouldn't jeopardise it. He knew that Caroline would want him helping, but their life this last year or so had been what it should have been for all those years together. They had been a partnership, an equal, supportive team. They had fallen in love again as they developed their business, and expanded their waistline with all the new recipes and treats that made the Cake Station a success. That missing something had never been digested in Ronnie, and although his new venture was easier to live with a million times over than not having his wife, the offer from Polly and Richardson made him starving for a taste of his old life.

After their evening meal of slow-cooked beef casserole, Caroline and Ronnie sat in the lounge, the TV on quietly in the background.

'I'll make us a cuppa, love,' he said, rising from the sofa with a groan.

He returned ten minutes later, tentatively walking into the room, frowning in concentration with a cup of tea each on a tray, alongside a plate of ginger nut biscuits. Placing the tray on the coffee table, he passed Caroline her cup of tea, then sat back down on the dark blue sofa, his body turned in slightly to face her. Cup in one hand, he reached for her hand with his spare. Her skin was soft, like cool silk, her fingers long and thin sliding into his rough, bulbous ones. Ronnie placed his cup by his feet, twisting slightly without releasing his wife's hand. Turning back, he pulled her hand to his mouth, kissing the back of it.

She chuckled. 'What are you after, Ronald Ericson?' She tilted her head, a chunk of dark hair falling across her cheek as her aquamarine eyes looked into his.

Christ, she was beautiful, he thought as he swallowed, preparing himself for what felt like a prostate examination by Edward Scissorhands.

'Love, I've been speaking with Polly.'

'Is she doing okay?' she asked nonchalantly.

Ericson scratched his head. 'Erm, yeah. Yeah, she's fine. Well, in a way she is…' He was muttering, something he did when he was nervous. The red flag waved in front of Caroline.

'Ronnie, what is it?' She took her hand away from his and he placed his hand on her leg.

'Love…'

Caroline stiffened and began shaking her head.

'Please, just hear me out.'

She pressed her lips together, and her shoulders dropped. Sipping some of her tea, she remained silent.

'They need help.'

Ronnie watched his wife's gaze drop to her lap.

'*Polly* needs help. And you know… well, you know she's like another daughter to me.'

Caroline nodded. She did know her husband loved Polly like a member of the family. She was very fond of her too. It was hard not to like Polly, but that didn't mean she wanted him to go back to working seventy-hour weeks, especially now they had the business. And more importantly, she wanted her husband to be exactly that, her husband – un-tempted by the mistress that was Northumbria Police.

'Go on,' she said, before taking a deep breath.

'She's under-resourced, her small team being spread thinner than Lurpak in a canteen. And they've got no money, love.' He rubbed his grey eyebrows with his thumb and forefinger. 'It would just be to help out one, maximum two days a week in a civilian role, so I'm not committing or anything.'

'You mean they are getting your labour for free, Ronnie!' Caroline said, eyes wide.

He cleared his throat. 'Well technically, yes, but it would only be temporary. And, love, it would be for the community.'

She rolled her eyes. 'Don't do the bleedin' guilt trip on me that some old woman will get mugged if you don't help.' She glanced across the room, away from his eye line to the TV for a few seconds. It had taken Caroline thirty years to get quality time with her husband, now her business partner. The anxiety of it all turning rotten again was etched across her furrowed brow.

Ronnie knew she was trying to convince herself that his help wasn't needed. That she and the Cake Station needed his assistance more than McCardle and Richardson. But she knew that her husband was a man of integrity, of care and justice. He wanted to make the world a better place and it was one of the reasons she fell in love with him.

Still looking away, he grabbed his wife's hand. 'It won't be like it was, Caroline. It will never be like it was.' She looked back to him and Ronnie saw a flash of nervousness on her pale face. 'It wouldn't, I promise. And if you really don't want me to, then I won't.' He looked down, swallowing. 'But the truth is, love, is that there's a need in me to help.'

He clenched his fist and tapped his heart with it as she swallowed, eyes fixed on him. 'I need to make this community better. And I'm not thinking I'm important enough to do that alone. Christ, I never have been and I've always been a tiny cog in a massive machine. But there's something, a medicine that I used to get, that makes me think what if it was you needing help, or our Kelsie. And I've missed that.'

Inhaling deeply, he took both of her hands in his, their knees almost touching. 'You, us, the Cake Station, it's my world and I'm grateful each day that you gave me, us, another shot after I know I'd neglected you for all those years. But some days I just feel inadequate, and that I'm not enough for you or anyone.'

Caroline frowned and touched his cheek. 'Ronnie, you're more than enough. You always were. I was just sick of competing in a race I could never win.'

She sniffed up as he nodded then put his palm on top of her hand. Taking their hands away from his face, he interlocked their fingers, absentmindedly spinning her wedding ring around her thin, pale finger.

'You've got the prize now, you'll never lose it.' He winked, which turned into laughter for them both.

There was silence until she spoke. 'Just a few days a week, temporarily?' she asked again, wanting reassurance.

He nodded. 'I promise.'

'Okay, but if you let me down, Ronnie, I…'

'I won't. I promise, love.' He leant in and embraced his wife.

Ronnie closed his eyes, relief coating him, and felt more excitement than when England made it to the UEFA Euro 2024 final. Pulling away, he looked into her eyes and gently tilted her face up to his before he kissed her tenderly on the lips. She nodded. They both knew he had to help and Ronnie prayed that the police wouldn't tear his marriage apart for the second time.

Chapter 17

After a restless night, Polly woke at 6am. The evening before had been made better by baked beans on toast, followed by chocolate sponge and custard, and a good chat with Lisa. As a social worker, Polly's wife had a level of empathy and understanding of how complex it was working with people and the issues that humanity created.

Lisa knew her wife had been up and down since Ronnie Ericson retired. It wasn't due to Polly not being an excellent detective; it was simply due to the nature of the work. Lack of resources, circumstances that presented almost daily that were crazier than a bus full of creepy clowns, and the fact that to understand the depths of humanity, well, it just took time, years, if ever. Polly got great outcomes and was a brilliant detective and boss, but police work was teamwork and she needed a bigger team. Now, it was just a matter of waiting for Ronnie's response. Stirring her coffee, she watched the swirl of the liquid, mesmerised momentarily.

'Morning,' Lisa said, strolling into the kitchen.

Polly turned from the wooden countertop and smiled at her wife, who came over and kissed her on the cheek.

'Just boiled,' she nodded to the kettle. 'Coffee?'

'Please,' Lisa replied, moving to the cupboard.

'How did you sleep?' She turned her head as Polly rolled her eyes.

'Badly. But today is another day!' She poured the boiling water into the cup for Lisa.

'Hopefully Ronnie will get back to you with some good news and always remember, it could be worse – you could be in a full broken-down lift with the shits!'

They both started laughing. The analogy was something they often said to try to put things into perspective. Sometimes, it didn't work, but it always made them chuckle. Thirty minutes later, breakfast had been eaten and Polly was ready to leave for the station. After the morning briefing, she planned on visiting Mrs Mortimer to ask more questions. The team had tasks to continue with, as they tried to gather intel around the hit and run.

The local radio station played in the background as she drove to the station. Five minutes into her journey, her phone rang. She saw it was Ronnie. A small patter of nerves danced in her stomach as she instructed her car computer to answer.

'Morning, boss. You okay?'

'When will this bloody boss lark end, Polly?' Ronnie said, laughing afterwards.

She smiled. Polly said it as much out of habit and respect as she did out of knowing he would appreciate it.

'Always the gaffer, Ronnie!'

'Not at home, I'm not, pet!'

She hoped his comment didn't mean that Caroline had put a halt on him helping out.

'Although saying that, I spoke with Caroline.' He sighed and Polly felt her stomach drop to the level of the pedals in her car.

'She wasn't overly keen, Poll, you know why…'

'Of course, I totally get it. I would never want her to…'

He interrupted, 'But she knows how much the force meant to me and recognises the sacrifice I made. Albeit, I should've always put her first and I'm a daft old man for not seeing that. You know what she's like. Heart bigger than a frying pan, my Caroline.'

Polly smiled to herself as she checked her speed. He was

right, Caroline was a special woman but he was a special man and like attracts like.

'We had a good talk. She understands and she said it's okay for me to help out. As long as it's not full-time and forever. I do have the business to support, after all. And cakes and bread, well they are almost as hard to get right as solving crime!'

The pair chuckled and Polly felt relief as the clouds over Northumberland began to dissipate. 'Ron, this is great news. Thank you, to you both. It'll really help and the team will be so happy to have you on board. *I'm* so happy to have you on board.' She stopped at the lights and took a huge breath.

'And I'm grateful to be asked. I can probably do up to three half days, or two full days a week in the first instance. Don't want to push my luck with the wife. Just let me know what works best for you.'

His voice was jolly with a tinge of excitement that she remembered when DS Ronnie Ericson used to approach her desk rubbing his hands together – a smile on his round face, and a cheeky glint in his grey-blue eyes – when he had some good news or a plan. She would look at him and feel every bit of his energy and enthusiasm, hoping that after thirty years in the police, she would still have that magnetic vigour for fighting crime.

After arranging for Ronnie to come in the next day, Polly pulled into the car park a few minutes later. Grabbing her backpack, she exited the car, and walked to the building that was her second home. During the morning briefing, McCardle reiterated the plans for the team that day. Before dismissing everyone, she updated them on Ericson's return.

'As you have all been aware and felt the brunt of, we've been under-resourced for some time.' There were groans and nods. She had empathy for her team who worked hard and supported each other. But it was tiring and they were all weary.

'So, CI Richardson and myself have chatted and we know we need extra help on the team. However, there's no budget.'

Her colleagues moaned. It had been the same message over the last few years. Further government cuts to policing and an increase in crime had changed the dynamics of policing across the country and the impact had rippled through communities, regions, and across England.

Tucking her hair behind her ears, she continued. 'But there is good news...' She couldn't help but smile. 'You'll all remember DS Ronnie Ericson. Well, he's coming back as a civvy to volunteer his time and expertise.'

'Get in, boss,' Lucas said, clapping his hands together.

The others cheered. Ericson was one of those bosses that everyone liked, you couldn't not. He told it how it was, supported and understood his team and importantly, for his colleagues and the community, Ronnie Ericson had integrity that was stronger than the Tyne Bridge.

'Yeah, he starts tomorrow. Only part-time, but I know he will be welcomed back to the team and will be a fantastic support.' McCardle clasped her hands together.

'As long as he can take your instruction, boss,' Boyd said, raising an eyebrow, and Polly knew it was a little nod to acknowledging that she was in charge, regardless of the past.

Polly appreciated it. She'd had a moment or two doubting her capabilities. But it wasn't about ego, this was about solving crime and right now there were two unsolved murders on her patch, along with some organised crime, none of which seemed to have many leads. And she hoped Ronnie Ericson would help the team put the pieces together.

The briefing room emptied as her diminished but diligent colleagues got to work. McCardle placed her hand to the small of her back and pushed her stomach forward, feeling the stretch. At thirty-five years old, she was fit and healthy but carried a sandbag of tension on her shoulders and back. She closed her eyes for a moment, enjoying the stretch, before opening them and turning to the incident board.

They needed information and motive. After the Thornton case had grown cold, McCardle was under pressure from CI Richardson and above to get results. Leaving the briefing room, she glanced further along at another board, where photos and little information remained plastered about Oliver Thornton. Shaking her head, she opened the office door and walked to her desk to check emails, before she visited Mrs Mortimer.

Ryan Mortimer's mother had lived in Northumberland all of her life, as had her parents and grandparents. The county and villages and towns held a history of generations of families, with few people moving away. Pit villages, farming, and fishing industry had kept men in work and as the generations changed and times moved on, industries such as offshore wind, energy, and hospitality grew in the area. For the Mortimers and so many other families, Northumberland had always been home, and with home, came the feeling of safety. However, safety had been compromised and it had resulted in the biggest tragedy for Mrs Mortimer – the murder of her son.

Polly knocked on her door for the second time in just over twenty-four hours. Ryan's mother opened it, heavy-eyed, with slow movements and a sallow complexion. Heartbreak had coated her. Her lips turned ever so slightly up and she croaked a hello. Polly knew her voice was hoarse from the anguish of pain and crying. Following her inside, McCardle felt a coldness in the air that had nothing to do with the temperature and everything to do with the chill of loss, and in this case, the frost of murder. As well as needing to advise on what the police were doing around the murder of her son, McCardle was there to ascertain information that could lead to motive.

'Would you like a cup of tea?' she said, voice shaky as they walked into the lounge.

'I tell you what, how about I make us one?' Polly smiled, her blue eyes fixed on Mrs Mortimer.

Wringing her hands together, she nodded before her bottom lip began to quiver and she started to cry. Instinctively, Polly moved and gave her a hug. The grieving mother's shoulders softened in her grasp and she let herself be comforted in her desperate time of need. McCardle could do little about her loss but she could and would bring the person to justice who had snatched Ryan Mortimer's existence away and fled the scene of the crime. Remaining silent for a minute, Polly held her as she sobbed with the pain of her child being taken – something that would result in Mrs Mortimer walking with a limp forever.

Chapter 18

David was at work and needed to get his car to the garage at the end of the day. In the meantime, he would park in a back alley, in the hope that fewer people would see his damaged vehicle. Angry with himself for not ringing another garage for a possible earlier slot, instead, he was putting himself at risk, especially with all the nosey bastards who lived in his block of flats. Tutting, he got ready for work, recalling when his mother began to deteriorate. The then next-door neighbour was helpful and supportive without interfering. She would message him with concerns and offers to help. Then she moved, after meeting a man on the internet and falling madly in love.

Rolling his eyes, he pulled on his work chinos, then a jumper over his polo shirt. Other neighbours began to say the odd comment about his mother, some helpful, but many felt judgemental, insinuating that he shouldn't be leaving her alone or she should be in a care home. What the hell did they know? They knew nothing about David or his life. The comments had pecked away at him, bits of his patience chipping off as time passed, until one day, he snapped at the man in the flat below, telling him to piss off.

People stopped commenting after that, keeping their distance, and within six months his mother had moved into the care home. Now, if he saw someone from the block of flats, they would just say hello or flash a smile, with limited small talk. He just hoped they didn't notice the large dent in his bonnet and smashed headlight on his Ford Focus.

Grabbing his packed lunch of a cheese and ham sandwich, fruit, and two boiled eggs, David left the flat. His thoughts became a reality as he saw a woman from three doors down on reaching the bottom of the communal staircase.

'Nasty bit of damage there to your car!' She widened her eyes and pointed towards his vehicle, as if he didn't know which one was his.

He grinned and nodded. 'Yeah, a bloody deer ran into it down the country lanes in Hallington.' He shook his head. 'I'm sure it'll cost a small fortune to fix.' He rushed towards his vehicle as the woman remained on the spot, clearly wanting to know more. Not looking back, David scurried to his car, clicking his central locking as he approached, and launched himself into the driver's seat.

'For fuck's sake,' he muttered, glancing in the rear-view mirror to see if she had gone. 'Nosey bitch.' He slammed his hands on the steering wheel and felt a hot sweat come over him. Work would be a good distraction today and he would be getting the book for Chloe Logan's book club. Luckily, David loved his job and it was where he first met Emily Robinson so it also felt like 'their place'. His job gave him access to meet people like Emily, a pathway to get closer, and David knew the perfect way to get her alone and begin their more intimate dialogue.

Arriving at work, he said hello to his colleague. It was a small team, and luckily he liked or could tolerate them all. Entering the kitchen, he placed his lunch bag in the fridge. His manager would be in her office, so he would make a cup of tea then go and see her to propose his idea. He had a little bounce in his step as he walked to the kettle. It had been a challenging few days but David had proven to himself how strong he was when he had a goal in mind.

Filling the kettle, he put it back on its base to boil and moved to the lockers, placing his coat and bag inside, as he ran over the proposal to his manager in his mind, the kettle beginning its quiet journey to boiling. As he popped a teabag in his Penguin book mug, the kettle clicked off and he poured the water over it, watching the clear liquid turn brown. Adding a dash of milk, he stirred his tea, dropped the spoon in the dishwasher, and lifted his cup from the bench before walking to his manager's office.

'Come in,' she said loudly after he knocked on the door.

Opening the door, he smiled. The smile was returned. 'Have you got five minutes?'

'Sure, David, come on in.'

Taking a seat after pleasantries, he began discussing his thoughts. 'So, I have an idea.'

His manager raised her eyebrows. He had proposed several good ideas previously, many of which had been successful.

'Go on,' she said, moving slightly in her chair.

'I thought for the website each month, it may be useful to interview someone to represent the broad range of activities, interests, and facilities we provide here at the library. It could then be typed up and shared on the website, social media, and so on. We could interview the resident artist, someone from the walking group, the IT support, and local authors.'

His manager interlocked her hands and placed them on her stomach. 'Yes, I like it. A bit of PR and different voices and experiences to represent our community.'

He beamed. 'I'm happy to lead on it, trial it and see how it goes? I was thinking after the event a few weeks ago, and since she's such a great local support, Emily Robinson may be interested in being interviewed as the first. She could plug her new book too.' Releasing a light chuckle, he tapped his thighs.

'Sounds great. I think Emily would go for that. Let me get her email and you can contact her on our behalf.'

His manager began clicking her computer as David watched in silence, elated that she had agreed and feeling yet another step closer to the love of his life. Leaving the office a few minutes later, he fizzed with excitement having had the green light for his plan and obtaining Emily's email address. Before logging on to the computer, he collected the book he had reserved for the North East Book Addicts group, who were meeting in less than a week. Reading the blurb, he shrugged. Scanning it out on the machine, he popped it into his bag inside his locker, before returning to his desk.

His priority was to email Emily. He had yet to write another letter to her but writing an email from himself, was a different kind of pressure. He was representing the library, as well as moving closer to her. David had always been professional, courteous, and considerate. He had never been sleazy, unlike Ryan Mortimer. He clenched his fists. Always being a perfect gentleman, Emily appreciated that, especially after her ex-husband, who David knew from the media, had cheated on her.

'Utter bastard,' he muttered under his breath. How could someone do that to her? Although, if Emily's filthy ex-husband hadn't cheated, it would make it so much more difficult for him to get close to her. For her to realise they were meant to be. He knew in his heart that when Emily and he became an item, she would appreciate the respect he had shown her by not being one of those creeps. Instead, he'd been a true gentleman. And what woman didn't want to be treated right, with honour and respect?

Smiling, he drifted into a daydream of the life they would have. He would sell his pokey flat and they would live in her cottage, somewhere in Amble, twenty miles up the coast. She would write all day as he continued to work, perhaps in one of the county's other libraries. It would only be part-time work so he could look after Emily – being her protector, agent, admin, muse! All of her ideas would be run past him and he would help her bring her genius mind alive through the day before pampering her on the evening with massages, baths, and making love to her.

They were meant to be. Already on their trajectory to love, the email and interview would provide another step in his plan. Getting to know her one-to-one would be like their first date and during it, he would ask her out to dinner. It would be perfect. And if she needed a little persuasion, well, David had a plan B.

Chapter 19

The next day, as he stood in the lounge looking in the mirror hanging above the fireplace, Ronnie couldn't help but feel a little taller. It was 7.30am and he was about to set off to police HQ. Polly had rung the evening before to talk shop. Only this shop was less dough and cake batter, and more murder and organised crime. The more he heard about the lack of resources from her strained voice, the more he knew he was doing the right thing helping.

It wasn't just about his love for solving crime, it was about helping his former team, and helping Polly. In the time that they had worked together, they had felt more than colleagues, more than friends. They were family. Ronnie buzzed at the thought of returning to his old stomping ground: police headquarters in Crosley – even for just a few hours a week on a temporary, voluntary basis. Getting ready that morning, he couldn't stop smiling, feeling like he had enough energy to propel himself into the air and fly to the station.

When the plans started eighteen months ago for him to retire, he had secured the most important thing, and essential distraction: the resurrection of his dead marriage and a new adventure with his wife. Plus, the peace of mind their daughter Kelsie had, knowing her parents were reunited and happy. However, retiring from the force had left a bad taste in his mouth that no amount of cake would ever sweeten. And even though he would do it again over and over for Caroline, the amputation of his career and the wound it left hadn't healed, nowhere near. Ericson felt like those men he had known. Those colleagues and friends who had retired, not just from the force, but from other fields: healthcare, sales, construction. Those from the same era who had ended their employment lives and deteriorated. Many not asking for help. For many the shock of fifty years graft disintegrating overnight, turning into a terminal illness.

He shuddered. Ronnie was frightened of burning his and Caroline's newfound happiness. But he knew that the Cake Station alone just wasn't enough. He loved it, his expanding gut maybe not as much, but it was an incredible business and he enjoyed interacting with customers. However, they had the baker and a part-time sales assistant and Caroline was in her element there. He acknowledged when they took on the lease that it was more for his wife, but she had wanted to fill the void the police was inevitably going to leave in his life. As well as having something for just them, after years of her feeling second best; always getting the silver medal as Northumbria Police smugly held the gold.

Kissing his wife before he left that morning, he pulled her in for an embrace, inhaling the apple scent of her long dark hair.

'I'll text you at lunchtime. Have a good day in the bakery,' he said, holding her at arm's length.

There was a nervousness in her eyes that produced a lump of guilt in his throat. 'It'll be okay, love. I promise.' His eyes locked into hers.

She pressed her lips together and nodded slightly. 'I know,' she said, rubbing his forearm. He kissed her, picked up his backpack from the bottom of the beige-carpeted stairs, and left their home. Pulling up in the small car park at Crosley Police Station fifteen minutes later, it felt like putting on an old, comfy but now slightly tight sweater. As he cut the engine of his car, Ronnie couldn't help but feel full, not from breakfast but from a serving of purpose.

He walked into the building to be greeted with cheers from those officers who knew him and smiles from a few new faces. As he entered the MIT office, Polly dashed over and he handed her a bunch of yellow roses – her favourite flowers. Putting a hand to her chest, she smiled, touched by his thoughtfulness as she looked at their sunshine colour.

'I thought they would cheer up these tatty old desks!' He chuckled. 'And these are for you all.' He held out a white box and she lifted the lid with her spare hand, breathing in the fresh sweetness of the brownies she often ordered to take away when she visited the Cake Station.

'She only wants you for your cakes!' shouted DC Lucas to a round of laughter and clapping.

McCardle blushed a little and rolled her eyes. The team had great banter, and she was sure that in many ways Ericson had missed that as much as he had missed the crime-solving.

'And here was me going to share, Lucas. You can bugger off now!' Grinning, she walked past him to the kitchen to put the kettle on. 'Cuppa, b… Ronnie?' she asked turning to him as she continued towards the kitchen.

'Abso-bloody-lutely,' he said, following her, bouncier than a playing kitten.

In the kitchen, McCardle held up the cup that Ericson had bought her when he left. She shook it gently and he nodded.

'It's nice to see you.'

'It's only been a few days!'

'You know what I mean, in this capacity. In your domain.'

She smiled, feeling a tinge of self-consciousness that she wasn't quite as good as her mentor perceived. 'I'm glad you're here, Ron. We all are. When I told the team yesterday, they were buzzing.'

After making hot drinks, all flocked to the briefing room.

Ericson went to sit amongst the crowd before McCardle caught his eye, gesturing him towards the front where she tapped a seat near the incident board. He felt a wave of discomfort. True, he was in his old stomping ground, his cosy sweater, the place where he used to spend most of his week. But he wasn't in the force anymore, no longer DS Ronnie Ericson. Not now. Now he was Ronnie Ericson, the civilian. He walked slowly to the front and sat close to Polly who stood to address her team.

He observed as she conducted the room. As soon as they had met, Ronnie had warmed to Polly McCardle. She had an empathy that wasn't extinguishable and an astute approach to detail. Full of integrity, she was also a team player. There was nothing not to like about her and it was clear respect coated the air around her.

'Right, team, I know it's like having a local celeb with us.' She turned to him and the small team began cheering and clapping.

He feigned a curtsy and the room laughed. They all needed to keep the humour up, it was often their fuel.

'We are all very pleased you're here, Ron, and appreciate you taking time out from baking and eating cakes to give us your expertise.' She held her hands together, smiling at her former boss.

'Ericson, you can bring us cakes as well, though!' DC Birdy shouted to the applause from his colleagues.

'Anytime, son, if you can get them out of the hands of this one.' He pointed at McCardle, who held her hands up in a guilty as charged motion.

'So, down to business. Ericson is going to read the case files but can we give a brief overview of where we are all at on the Ryan Mortimer case? DC Boyd, can you start please?'

Eyes moved to Boyd who nodded, glanced at the notes on

her lap and began talking. 'I visited Dexter Reed yesterday, after he called in with possible useful information. He said that he had remembered Ryan used a dating app for a few months up until the summer. He had come off it as there was a woman harassing him after they had been on a date. Apparently, he had blocked her but she kept using a different profile. Then it stopped.'

McCardle cradled her cup in her hands. 'Interesting.'

'Yeah, he didn't know her surname but he's scrolled through his texts from Mortimer and got her first name and photo. There may be some emails from around the time he was on the dating app, so we can work with the analysts to try and eliminate, then speak to the woman in question to ascertain any recent communication and alibi.' Boyd smiled and tapped her pen against her notepad.

'Great, Boyd. Thanks. Lucas? Birdy? How's the CCTV going?'

Birdy leant forward in his seat. 'We started door-to-door yesterday, in the street leading to the entrance of Crosley Country Park, where Mortimer was found. We've established that some households do have CCTV cameras and Ring doorbells. We are going back today to collect the footage for analysis.'

Lucas chipped in. 'Hall, one of the analysts, is looking through Ryan's mobile phone and laptop for any information. We should be able to trace his old dating account if needed, Boyd, and put in a request with Telecoms.' Lucas turned to his colleague who did a thumbs up in thanks.

Glancing to her left, Polly saw Ronnie making notes in what looked like a new notepad. His first job was to read the current case files and perhaps consider other approaches and leads that hadn't already been explored as well as chasing up any loose ends and being allocated current work. She fell into a pool of gratitude – having him back felt so right.

Returning her focus back to the incident board, she tapped her pen against the tyre skid marks on the road where Mortimer's body was found and a further imprint on the muddy grass verge.

'CSI are making a tyre imprint. Someone out there is driving a damaged car. They will likely be keen to get their headlight fixed as soon as possible, given it could result in being pulled over. Can someone today begin to ring garages within in a fifty-mile radius and see if there have been any vehicles booked in for a smashed headlight and other damage, please?'

'I can help with that. Or anything else,' Ronnie said, his finger up.

McCardle smiled. 'Thanks, that would be great.' She glanced at her colleagues who were nodding or sat with open body language, and knew that they too appreciated him being there. Ego often dissolved with the right team when it came to shared goals and supporting each other, and McCardle was pleased and proud that this was the mentality of her team. She took a sip of her tea before talking again.

'I visited Mortimer's mother yesterday. Understandably, she is distraught but we managed a conversation about her son and possible enemies he may have. Like mentioned previously, she referred to the fact that her son was an entertainment journo so likely didn't attract enemies that news-reporting colleagues can acquire. The worst thing he did was write bad film or book reviews!' McCardle said, shrugging. 'We talked about past partners as the deceased wasn't in a current relationship. His mother said his relationships had always ended on okay terms. He was engaged for a few years but his fiancée moved to Australia for work and their relationship didn't last.' She moved on the spot slightly, rolling her shoulders back.

'He had good friends, and Mrs Mortimer mentioned how he enjoyed living with Dexter. She really couldn't think of anyone he could have upset enough to warrant such a horrific crime. She mentioned possible mistaken identity and it's something we do need to keep in mind. Mortimer had not mentioned to anyone in his circle that he was currently getting harassed or receiving any form of grief. We need to visit the *Northumberland Herald,* as well as get and review all of his articles over the last year, including online, noting any comments and associated names. There's got to be some answers here, team, and I know we can find them.'

On that note McCardle dismissed her colleagues, including Ericson, who left the small incident room office and went to read the current open case files with the eagerness of a child leaving school on the last day of term.

Chapter 20

David signed off the email to Emily with his name, rather than the team. Despite mentioning the idea was something for the whole library and of course, her fans, he wanted her to know that he would be her point of contact. That it would be him looking after her. Getting on with his day, he had the energy of a racehorse as he put books away, ordered the newest releases and interacted with the customers. He was hardly able to keep the smile off his face, even during his lunch break, when the local news covered the death of Ryan Mortimer.

'Bloody shocking, isn't it?' his colleague said, not waiting for a response. 'No one is safe anymore. Friggin' monsters.' She tutted before shoving a forkful of cottage pie into her mouth, eyes remaining on the TV screen.

'Indeed,' he replied, a smirk spreading across his face as he thought to himself that he would remove anyone who got in his way to Emily or bad-mouthed his beloved. He was born to love her and had waited so long. Now, the time was getting closer. True love always won. However, as he listened to the news over his colleagues' tutting, the police were following leads and he wondered what they could be. No criminal mastermind, David was ordinary – until love possessed him, altering his thoughts and behaviours.

He had researched and planned methodically. But things had happened, outside of his plan. Like the headlight on his car being smashed and the dent in his bonnet. He knew that the police would have combed the area and possibly found something. A good person, a decent citizen, he wasn't on any police database and wanted to remain that way, anonymous.

Shaking his head, he tried to focus on Emily. The police were under-resourced and overstretched. The area was rife with organised crime, perverts, and drugs. Someone else would get the blame, likely deservingly so. Nodding to himself, he felt slightly comforted.

Moving to the other end of the staff room, he stared at his lunchbox and wondered if it was wise to go to the garage after work. He'd given a false name but they had his mobile number. Maybe the police were searching car garages, making enquiries? He had deliberately booked in with a garage a distance away but would that be an obvious move for experts in crime-solving?

'Shit!' he said, his knees bouncing under the table.

'You okay, Dave?' his cottage-pie munching colleague asked, twisting her head around.

He chuckled. 'Yeah, I just forgot my mayonnaise!'

Scratching his head, he needed time to think, reflect on what to do. He would have lunch, start the book for the North East Book Addicts book club, and weigh up his options that afternoon. The book club meet-up was less than a week away and he was looking forward to putting Chloe Logan in her place about Emily. The meeting location was a quiet pub in Morpeth, around ten miles from his flat.

Quiet was good, the fewer people the better, and he had decided he would shave off his usual beard and wear glasses that had a clear lens in. Precautionary of course. He would go under the name Andy Palmer, like he had used on the phone to the garage. Not following the page on Facebook, he would simply say he wasn't on social media. This wasn't about him wanting to join a book club and make friends. It was about stopping the harassment and bullying of Emily. It was about putting the nasty little troll named Chloe, back under the bridge permanently!

By the time his shift ended, David had decided that he wouldn't take his car to the garage, and instead would try to fix the headlight himself. How hard could it be? He would order the piece online that evening and YouTube how to fix it. At least then he would remain anonymous to a level. It would mean a delay in it getting fixed, but it was safer that way, and he'd look for someone mobile to repair the dent. Perhaps meet them somewhere away from home, a supermarket car park or something, saying he worked there. Checking his emails for what must have been the hundredth time, he saw there was still no reply. He read the sent email again.

Dear Emily, I hope you are having a great day. As you know, here at the library, we are all such huge fans of your work. We are grateful that you support our libraries and inspire local people through your exceptional writing. We have decided to begin a monthly feature, where we interview people of significance. The interviews will be typed and shared on our website, in our newsletter, and across our social media platforms to promote the services of the library as well as the guest interviewee.

We would love to start off the idea with an interview with yourself, Emily. I appreciate you are very busy but if you have any spare time, it would be an honour to interview you. Many thanks and warm wishes.

David Creighton, library assistant

Satisfied it was pitched in the right way, he shut down his computer and hoped she would answer overnight. After saying goodbye to his colleagues he left for home, to order his replacement headlight and research how to fit it. There was a lot involved with navigating his path to Emily, but it was all worth it. Everything was worth it for Emily Robinson.

It was lunchtime the next day when the garage got in touch. His mobile phone rang as it lay next to his Penguin book mug. Walking quickly into a quiet side room, he puffed out air, shutting the door.

'Hello,' he said, putting on a rough voice.

'Is that Mr Palmer?' asked a pleasant voice.

'Nah, this is Keith Rushworth, pal. You've got the wrong number.'

'Oh, I'm sorry. Thanks anyway. Goodbye.'

David ended the call and giggled. Maybe he could go into acting! Hopefully that would halt any possible lead to his car. Swallowing, he closed his eyes momentarily, pleased for the delay at the garage, and therefore space to think and cover his tracks. He snuck back out of the room and walked around the library floor, smiling at customers and checking the displays. Returning several books, he thought of the North East Book Addicts meeting in a few days. David had managed to read a chunk of the book of the month last night after ordering his headlight replacement and researching how to fit it. He wasn't confident but he would do a botch job and sell his car in a few months, once everything died down.

Checking his work emails, Emily had replied. He felt a rush of anticipation, like the overall body tingle of walking into the sea on a hot day. Taking a deep breath, he opened the email.

Hi David, thank you for your lovely email. You are all so supportive and welcoming at the library, it's a pleasure to do events there and I would love to be part of your interview idea. It sounds a wonderful way to celebrate the work of the library and your support to local people and creatives. When were you thinking? I'm quite hectic next week but have space a week Monday, if that works for you? With thanks and best wishes.

Emily

David pressed his lips together and read over the email three more times. This was it. His big leap further to his love, to them being together. Emily and him in a room, just the two of them, close, chatting, connecting. It would be his opportunity to have the one-to-one time that would develop their relationship. Like a date, where he could flirt and advance his move towards their future. It was his chance to show his idol that he was the man for her.

Chapter 21

Ronnie had spent the morning reading the files on the Oliver Thornton and Ryan Mortimer murders. The Thornton case was a strange one. No clear motive and seemed a bit random. Considering most homicides were perpetrated by someone known to the victim, and the lack of complexities of who Thornton was, on first impressions, Ronnie felt he could have been the victim of mistaken identity. He understood why the leads had gone cold.

Then there was the Mortimer case. The journalist had more reason to have attracted disgruntled people and acquired enemies through his work. But he was hardly on Roger Cook's level. A pissed-off local singer or mediocre actor, a local author or playwright could be involved, but the *Northumberland Herald* was no *Daily Mail*. He was visiting the newspaper office with Polly that afternoon, so perhaps something would spark an idea in him.

A cup landed on a coaster where he sat and Ronnie glanced to his left to see DC Boyd.

'Milk, no sugar,' she said, smiling as she pulled up a seat next to him.

'Thanks, pet.' He nodded. 'I'll make sure you get an extra cake at the end of the week.' He tapped the side of his nose and she laughed.

'It's good to have you back, boss.' Boyd looked down at her hands for a second before her gaze returned to him. 'She misses you. She won't mind me saying. We talk, you know, and I care about her. She's a mint boss. Better than you were in lots of ways.' She grinned and Ronnie raised his eyebrows. 'It's a woman thing. No offence.' Boyd shrugged.

'None taken. I know McCardle's the dogs. She always was. You lot, well, you're lucky. When I started out, I had a shitshow of a team and our boss made Maggie Thatcher look fluffy.' He made a pffttt sound. 'That one…' he nodded to where Polly was talking to Lucas '…she's always going to have your back and she's got more integrity than McDonald's have got fries.'

Boyd chuckled. 'You've got a way with words, Ericson, that always hits the nail on the head.' She rose from her seat, ready to go back to her own desk. Placing a hand gently on his shoulder she spoke again. 'It really is good to have you back.'

'You only want me for my cakes.' He tapped the top of her hand on his shoulder, before turning back to the case notes.

After lunch, it was time for McCardle and Ericson to head to the *Northumberland Herald*. Some of the team had been tasked with looking on social media at Ryan Mortimer's articles, posts, and comments. Whilst the team of researchers and analysts could help, they were also under-resourced and covered the force-wide area. The initial groundwork could be done by the team and the clock was ticking, with each hour adding a sprinkling of extra pressure from CI Richardson. The pair drove in Polly's car to their destination.

'How's Kelsie?' she asked as they hit the motorway.

'Yeah, good. Well, that's what she tells me. She'll graduate next year and to be honest, Poll, I hope she comes back home. She's got friends there, a part-time job, but she rents the digs and hasn't got a boyfriend.' He stared out the window.

'Maybe she will. I can imagine there's no more opportunity in Leeds than there is up here.' She flicked the indicator to come off the slip road, reducing her speed.

'We miss her. She'll always be my baby. Even when, if, she has her own babies.' He chuckled then let out a sigh. 'What about you and Lisa? She still eager for kids?'

Polly tapped the steering wheel. 'I don't know, Ronnie. She mentions it less, since she's been working in child protection. You know the score, the cases.' She shook her head and swallowed. 'Her seeing kids abused, neglected, traumatised every day. And this depravity, drip-tap of inhumane behaviour that we see as often as the sun rises…' she sighed '…it puts me off. I don't want to bring a child into this world. And that makes my heart break a little.' She glanced him, sadness in her blue eyes.

'I know, pet, I know.' He didn't know what else to say.

The pair soon arrived at the *Northumberland Gazette* office. Parking up, Ronnie groaned as he got out of the passenger side of the car and stretched, pushing his stomach out as his hand rested in the small of his back. Polly looked at him and giggled, her eyes on his stomach, which made him look ready to drop a baby himself.

'Alright! I think I can get you done for being fat-phobic or fattist, or whatever it is,' he said, winking.

'I wasn't laughing at your cake-baby gut, boss.'

She winked back and clicked the central locking as the pair began walking to the entrance of the building, where the assistant editor came to meet them. Walking through the office, they noticed there was an atmosphere of sadness and tension, eyes glancing at the officers, who although not in uniform, wore the copper second skin.

'It's been hard,' the assistant editor said.

McCardle nodded. 'Understandable.'

The three went into a small office where Polly began asking for information about Ryan Mortimer. 'I know it's a difficult question, but did Ryan have any known enemies?'

The assistant editor shook his head. 'No, honest. He was a

top bloke.' His shoulders dropped.

'What about anyone in here? Or ex-colleagues? Any competition or could he have riled anyone?' Ronnie asked, pen poised.

Again, the assistant editor shook his head. 'No one I can think of. He was a cheeky chappie, had great banter, but never anything offensive, or nasty.' He pulled a hand over his mouth. 'Sorry, it's a lot. I'm, we, are all gutted. It doesn't make sense.'

Polly nodded and flashed a gentle smile. 'Well, if you do think of anything. In the meantime, we need access to all of Ryan Mortimer's files, articles, hard drive on his desktop computer and any news pieces he was involved with, please?'

The assistant editor nodded. 'Of course, not a problem.'

They rose, Ericson and McCardle following the assistant editor to Ryan Mortimer's old desk computer.

'You can take it away, or you're welcome to look here.' He put his hand out towards his desk.

The chairs on each side of the desk were occupied and the wide-eyed solemn faces looked at the officers, giving strained smiles and weak nods.

'We'll take it away, thanks. Likely we would have to at some point anyway.'

'I'll get someone from IT to come and help and give you all the log-in details.'

'Thank you, then we can get out of your hair.'

The assistant editor exhaled deeply and nodded, before turning and walking away to find someone to assist.

The pair returned to headquarters forty minutes later. Carrying computer equipment from Polly's car, they got help from their own IT staff member to set up Mortimer's computer to begin the lengthy process of searching for information. The analysts would help, but in the first instance, the pair would have a look for any possible leads. In the meantime, the other officers were assigned tasks. It was two hours until the evening briefing and as the deceased's computer got set up, Ronnie placed cups down on their desks, whistling a tune as he did so.

'That's ready to go, ma'am.' The IT colleague nodded.

She thanked him and he left. Ericson plonked down in the still-warm seat as McCardle sat in a matching tatty blue chair, squeezed into the same desk space.

Rubbing his hands together, he spoke. 'Righto, let's see what's going on here, then.'

Polly sipped her tea, seeing the enthusiasm in her former boss. Something he always had, even in the tough times, and even after decades in the job. Professional fatigue didn't seem to happen to Ronnie Ericson. She swallowed, feeling a little inferior, through no fault of the role model to her left. He picked up his pen and tapped it on his new notepad as if to get her attention – wanting her to take the lead and begin the process of searching the files on Mortimer's computer. Clearing her throat, she moved her chair further under the seat.

Two hours later, it was time for the briefing. The team updated on the events of the day, including the online search regarding Mortimer's published articles for the *Northumberland Gazette*.

'There's a lot on social media and because they are open, a load of comments.' Lucas glanced down at his notepad, then back up to his superior. 'A lot of knackers commenting, boss, as you can imagine. Some people saying he has shit taste in music, film, books, etc. Some people commenting he's a rubbish journalist, or they can't read the articles due to pop-ups and that type of thing.' McCardle nodded and Lucas placed his pen against his mouth for a second. 'We are only a little way through. It's proving a big job. But the analysts have a little capacity. We are making notes of recurring names to cross-reference.'

'Boyd, any CCTV on houses in the street?' McCardle moved towards the incident board and pointed a pen up to the map of the area. 'Jeffreys Street, the one that leads up to the entrance of Crosley Country Park where Mortimer was found. And also, Fenwick Street, where the deceased lived.'

Boyd nodded. 'So, there are five doorbell cameras or CCTV cameras in Jeffreys Street. A number of cars are seen on the night of the hit and run and I'm currently looking at narrowing these down to within the few hours that Mortimer died. Fenwick Street has less activity as it is a one way in, one way out street. A dead end, excuse the pun, boss.'

Ericson chuckled and McCardle playfully rolled her eyes. 'Thanks, Boyd, that's great.' She turned to the incident board and tapped her pen against the enlarged photograph of the tyre-tread marks left at the scene of the crime. 'CSI have a plaster cast of the tyre found at the scene, which gives us some circumstantial evidence that will be useful if we find the suspect's car. Boyd, we can ask ANPR to support with any vehicles identified in the area on any possible match.'

Boyd nodded before scribbling something down. Polly glanced at Ronnie, who was also making notes. 'We'll continue with our tasks and catch up again tomorrow, team. Thanks, all of you, for your hard work.' McCardle gave a warm smile to her tiny team before turning her palm up and holding her arm out in the direction of where Ronnie sat. 'And thank you to Ericson, for coming in and helping us. You've been a miss.' McCardle's eyes softened as she looked at him.

'Ah, shucks, you'll make an old man blush,' he said, playfully waving her away. 'Seriously, it's nice to be back. I'm flattered to be asked and to work for such an impeccable boss…'

'Hear, hear,' shouted Boyd, to nods from the rest.

'…and such a dedicated team.' He looked around the space. 'You lot are what makes Northumbria Police great.'

'I'm feeling the love in the room,' said DC Birdy, chuckling.

They all rose, collected their empty cups and notepads, and left to pack up for the evening.

'It's good to be back, Poll,' Ronnie said, tapping her forearm.

She nodded and put her hand over his on her arm. 'It certainly is, boss.'

After washing his cup and packing up, Ronnie said goodnight to his colleagues and drove home. He wouldn't be back for a few days, despite his eagerness. Driving home, he felt purpose fizzing around his body. It was followed immediately by a karate kick of guilt for not feeling satisfied for what he had with the Cake Station and his wife. It wasn't that Ronnie wasn't grateful. Crikey, he was beyond grateful for the second chance with the love of his life. It was just that baking cakes wasn't enough. He had tasted the excitement that Northumbria Police provided once again, and now wanted a big slice of it.

He tapped the steering wheel as he drove, mentally reminding himself that he couldn't get ahead of himself, or seem too excited in front of Caroline. She would worry, naturally, that he would go back to old ways. Plus, he didn't want her to feel that their life wasn't enough, because in most ways, it was. There was just a need in Ronnie, a craving that the bakery could never satiate and only crime-fighting could.

Chapter 22

The day of the North East Book Addicts book club had arrived and David couldn't wait to meet Chloe Logan. Although slightly apprehensive as to how the night would play out, he had to stop her venomous tirade at Emily. She had made a few further comments on her Facebook page and whilst they were not as harsh as previous ones, there was an insidious, nasty intent. He was determined to find out what her problem was, and stop her abuse towards his beloved. A revolting, jealous bitch, he was quite certain – but David wanted to know why and warn her to stop. He had to protect his precious woman.

The good thing about the book club was that he hadn't needed to complete any registration. He could turn up on the night, and that was exactly what he planned to do. There was no paper trail, nothing linking him to the group, meaning he could attend, confront Chloe, and firmly tell her to stop – with force, if needed. A grin spread across his face as he thought about his role as hero. Emily's very own good guy, stopping evil in its tracks! The protective protagonist.

Adopting another personality, he had shaved off his usual short beard, would wear a pair of glasses with a clear lens that he had purchased online, had a cap to wear, and would refer to himself as Andy Palmer. It was as much as he could do to conceal his identity and manage risk. Thinking about it, he puffed out air as he sat in his cream leather armchair. His thoughts returned to Emily and the interview scheduled for Monday next week.

Closing his eyes, he felt a calmness descend on him, a warmth of the love he felt for her. Their chance to be together, to continue their relationship, moving it to the next level. He was certain there was something there from her side. The way she acknowledged him – smiling and with intense eye-contact. The way she remembered things about him and thanked him for what he did for her at all the events. She didn't do that with anyone else; he was special. David knew it and he needed to make the next move, so their romance could blossom the way it should. The way it did for DCI McCoy in Emily's own books. He sighed, then a smile crept across his face.

Yesterday, on his first day off, he had attempted to fix his headlight, after watching YouTube videos and searching for advice online for over three hours. It hadn't been as easy as he had predicted, resulting in a cut hand and lots of swearing. However, it was done and it would stop any possibility of him being pulled over by the police. He planned on getting rid of his Ford Focus as soon as he could. As for the dent, he would arrange to meet a mobile repair guy away from the flat.

Being off work that day, he planned to check in at the allotment, visit his mother, then go to the book club in the rural town of Morpeth. Finishing his cup of coffee, he rose from the armchair and walked to the kitchen. Rinsing his cup, he stared out of the flat window at the dull sky, his eyes glazed over as the temperature of the tap water slowly increased. The heat from the warming water soothed him and he felt a longing for human warmth, contact, comfort. Something that had been missing for so many years in his life.

David loved his mother but it had always been hard, strained. Mainly due to Keith and his presence in their life, both alive and dead. He had learnt over the years that his mother was one of those women who defined themselves by a man. After his birth father left, she had clung to the first man who showed her and her young son any interest. His mother had tolerated being Keith's doormat, subordinate to him, often to the detriment of her son. He had forgiven his mother, knowing she was weak. But he had never forgotten, and her weakness had meant his own ability to love was tainted – as if a virus hung around, deterring people from coming near or staying.

Steam began to rise in front of his eyes and he snapped out of his thinking, realising the water was hot and his hands were almost being burnt. Snatching them away from the cascading water, he turned the tap off and clenched his fists quickly before reaching for a tea towel. Wrapping his hands in the soft material he inhaled deeply. It was going to change. He had so much love to give. Emily would love him back and he wouldn't feel alone anymore.

After taking more supplies to the allotment and checking on the security, David was happy all was okay on his patch and left to visit his mother. Arriving at the care home, he greeted the staff and headed towards his mother's room. The door to her bedroom was open and she sat in her high-back pink armchair, tapping the armrests as music played softly from the radio by her bed. Smiling, he walked in the room and kissed his mother on the forehead. She beamed up at him.

'Hello, son. Have you been at school?'

He turned to get the visitor's chair. 'Ah, just the allotment, Mam. Sorting out the winter weeds.'

As he turned back to his mother, he was startled to see a carer behind her, having been in the bathroom.

'Was just tidying up in there,' she said, smiling and nodding towards the small bathroom.

He forced a smile.

'Allotment, eh? Sounds nice. I've always wanted to grow my own veg,' the carer continued, tapping his mother's hand.

'Oooh, he goes with his grandad, they grow all sorts,' she

said, smiling at her son.

Not knowing what to say and not wanting the conversation to continue, he looked at the carer blankly, hoping she would take the hint and leave.

'Well, have a nice time with your son, Moira,' the carer said as she looked at his mother then nodded, leaving the room.

David sat on the chair opposite his mother and retrieved some fruit and a magazine from his bag, placing the items on the plastic-coated table on wheels by her chair. His mother liked to look through magazines, but he was unsure as to whether she read the articles or not.

'How's the allotment, son?' she asked, a twinkle in her eye as she talked about something that was sentimental to her.

'Great, Mam. It's looking neat and tidy and I've added some things to the shed to make it look homely and nice.' He rubbed her hand as she smiled. 'I'm thinking about what to plant next year.'

'Your grandad can help, son,' she replied, tilting her head.

Nodding, he didn't comment.

'Or Keith could help?' She looked at him, expectant eyes, wanting him to agree.

David swallowed the words he wanted to say, that Keith was a bastard and he was pleased he was dead. Instead, he clenched his jaw as his mother turned her head, glancing out of the window. Following her gaze, he saw two birds perched on the fence outside. He smiled momentarily.

'I've got a girlfriend, Mam.'

Her eyes turned to him and she leant forward. 'Really? Who is she, son? Is she from a good family?'

He made a pfft noise as if it were his first girlfriend as a teenager. For his mother and her fading cognition, it was.

'Yes, Mam. She is from a good family. She's incredible. A

writer.' He bit his bottom lip and leant in towards his mother. 'She's so beautiful, Mam. Like a film star.'

She opened her mouth in delight and clasped her hands together.

'She's called Emily and I'm in love with her.'

His mother grabbed his hands, squeezing them. 'You must bring her home, son. I will cook for us all. I'd love to meet her and so would Keith.'

He grimaced. David would never have brought someone like Emily home for his stepfather to meet. Keith was a repellent. Like a monster under the stairs, and he had a wandering eye, making most women and girls feel uneasy. The one relationship David had when Keith was alive, failed miserably, and no doubt the uncomfortable atmosphere his stepdad created contributed to its demise. After he died, his mother never wanted her son to find love as it meant leaving her. He glanced out of the window again, not wanting the stink of Keith's memory to pollute the bubble of love and happiness he was floating in.

Back home, after a quick meal of pasta, he began getting ready for the book club at the pub in Morpeth, choosing clothes he wouldn't usually wear to try to disguise himself further: a hoody, jogging bottoms, and a cap, along with plain lens glasses. Apparently, they were a fashion thing now. Tutting, he tried them on once more before removing them. Book in hand, he left the flat to drive the distance to the rural town. The radio played as he drove in the dark night. A love song came on and David tapped the steering wheel, listening to the words as if they were a direct message to him about his love for Emily.

'Not long now, my love,' he said quietly before releasing a contented sigh, staring at the narrow, dimly-lit country road.

Fifteen minutes later, he pulled up to the pub. It was next to a village green and he noticed a church to the left, with some houses further past it. The pub was a traditional old English pub. The kind like on the film, *The Holiday,* that Americans would swoon over but were so common that they lost their appeal to British folk. Cutting the engine, he sat for a few minutes to compose himself. He was always one to blend in and it didn't come natural to him to be a charlatan. But needs must and what man didn't protect his woman? A poor one, that's who. A man like Keith. David was nothing like him and would do anything for Emily. Absolutely anything. Slamming his hands into the steering wheel, he felt rage burn in him. He would stop Chloe Logan bad-mouthing her, trolling her, and protect his love – just like any boyfriend would.

Ready to take on the persona of Andy Palmer, he cleared his throat, put on the fake glasses, got out of the car and straightened the cap that sat tightly on his head. Pushing his shoulders back, he gulped in the crisp evening air and walked to the entrance of the pub. Opening the heavy wooden door, he was greeted by the heat and smell of sizzling onions and meat. Wiping his feet on the coir mat, he tentatively strolled in, glancing around. The pub was large, with two separate sitting areas, divided by a huge bar area in the middle. It was quiet and he wasn't sure if this was a good or bad thing. It would mean fewer people to remember him but more reason for those in the pub to recall.

He shook his head; he had to just get on with his purpose, to warn Chloe Logan to leave Emily alone. No one had to get hurt, he just wanted to enforce the message that she was a bully. A nasty little bitch and she needed to shut her mouth. David would tell her and if she didn't listen, he would tell her by force.

Chapter 23

Glancing around the pub, David spotted a group of people near a roaring fire. Mismatched chairs were occupied around a huge oak table and he spotted Chloe. Of course, she only looked a little like her profile photo and odd photo he could view on her social media. The young ones applied more filters than those used in chemical processing, so without scrutiny, you couldn't be sure who the hell was who.

But David knew it was her. She radiated bitchy energy and self-entitlement that many of the arrogant young people wore. People like Oliver Thornton. Making a hmph noise, he strolled to the bar, ordering a pint of Guinness. After paying the middle-aged, smiling bartender, he walked casually to the group.

'North East Book Addicts?' he said chirpily, holding out the book of the month in his free hand.

'Yeah, that's us. Hello!' said a woman in her thirties, raising her hand.

'Take a seat,' gestured Chloe, smiling as she pointed to a chair two seats to her left.

'Thanks.' He nodded and sat, placing his pint on a coaster.

After some small talk, the group got started.

'Why don't we begin with some introductions as we have a new member.' Chloe raised an eyebrow and looked at David. The five people around the table nodded and smiled. 'I'll start,' she said confidently, clasping her hands together and placing them on the wooden table. 'I'm Chloe, co-chair of the North East Book Addicts. Trainee financial advisor by day. Book addict by night!' There were some chuckles and she moved her head from side to side, fluttering her eyelashes as if she were a model about to take the stage.

David had to use all his might to not sneer at the attention-seeking bitch. The introductions went around the table until it came to him. 'Hi, I'm Andy Palmer. Mechanic by day. I live local and I love to read. Just got back into it after a few years off looking after my late father...' Pausing, he glanced around the table. Sympathetic eyes looked back and one woman placed a hand on her chest in pity. 'Thanks for having me.'

'Thanks for coming, Andy,' said another woman.

'So, what did everyone think of the book?' asked a red-haired woman, eyes wide as she shook the book in the air.

A discussion began about the book of the month, which he had quite enjoyed. The group started talking about how the current read rated in the books that year. Chloe retrieved a notepad from a tote bag and began scanning the pages.

'This is our fifth crime book this year, Andy,' said the enthusiastic redhead.

He nodded. It was an opportunity to open up the dialogue. 'Which was the favourite and least favourite?'

'Let's see the list, Chloe?' She reached over the table. 'My favourite was this one.' She pointed to Emily's DCI McCoy book, *Persuasion.*

David smiled. He liked this woman. 'Oh, that's a brilliant book. Emily Robinson is an amazing author. So good to have such exceptional local talent.'

The red-haired woman nodded and Chloe tutted. His gaze shot to her eye line and she giggled.

'Chloe's not a fan,' she said, nudging him before her eyes returned to the list of books.

Chloe's lip curled and David kept his eyes on her, waiting for a response.

'I just think her books have been exhausted, and for me,

knowing when to end a series is a skill of a writer.' She shrugged as if she worked for Harper Collins and knew everything there was to know about books.

'I disagree. I think she keeps the suspense, action, plot, and character development going strong in each book. In fact, they seem to get better,' he said assertively, feeling his legs tense under the large table.

Another woman nodded nonchalantly.

'I don't like the storylines, they are unbelievable and well, I don't buy into her as an author. She feels fake.' Chloe raised her eyebrows and took a sip of her drink.

Feeling his temperature rising, he ran his tongue over his teeth. She had left some awful comments on Emily's fan page. Nasty, unnecessary comments that would have upset her. They had certainly upset David, and her blasé answers now were infuriating him.

'She's incredible, inspiring, and she's the nicest person you could wish to meet,' he said, shaking his head.

'Ah, Chloe, you're just jealous that she's seeing your bloke!' said a woman in a child-like voice.

His eyes darted to her as he watched the woman casually drink from her glass of wine and chuckle.

'Get lost, Sonja. It's not that!' Chloe replied, half-joking.

'It is, hon. But we understand,' the redhead added.

Swallowing what felt like a brick in his throat, he focused on trying to sound upbeat. 'Oh yeah?' he said lightly, when inside he felt the temperature of rage.

'Well, maybe just a bit, but I still don't like her books,' Chloe huffed.

'Chloe works with Emily Robinson's new squeeze,' the woman called Sonja said. 'She's a bit jealous, shall we say,' she continued, with a little laugh.

'Are you sure?' he asked, trying to mask the panic in his voice. 'I assumed she was single after her husband and that...'

'Well, she's hardly going to tell you, is she, Andy? After meeting her at an event and reading a few of her books.' Chloe sniggered.

'Now, now. Just because you're jealous that you didn't get to go on a date with Adam before he met the beautiful Emily,' one of the women said, rubbing Chloe's arm.

'Well, he'll get sick of her and her crap books and come to younger and fitter me,' Chloe said, folding her arms and pushing out her bottom lip.

The group chuckled and David tried to laugh along, when it felt as if he was trying to breathe underwater. It made sense now; why Chloe was so unpleasant in her comments on Facebook. She was jealous of Emily's relationship with this Adam – whoever the fuck he was. Dissolving inside, he needed to know, to intervene, stop it. Stop him.

Just under an hour later, the book club finished and everyone began getting ready to leave, having selected their book choice for the next month. David could only think about Emily and Adam and his desperate need to know more. Taking his opportunity, he approached Chloe as the group began exiting the pub.

'Can I just ask a few questions about the Facebook page, please?' he queried, looking at her as the group left the pub, holding the door for one another.

'Erm, yeah.'

As the others said goodnight, David felt sweaty. He let the heavy wooden door of the pub close behind him and looked back at its barrier between them and the warm inside. Swallowing, he tried to think on the spot, but his thoughts were so consumed with Emily and this possible boyfriend. Leaning down for a few seconds, he pretended to scratch his ankle, delaying the conversation and allowing the others to dissipate. He raised his eyes back to Chloe, and she tilted her chin up, impatient with his hesitation.

'So, I'm not on Facebook. Is there any other way to keep up to date with the chat?' He watched the others head to their cars. Turning his eyes back to Chloe, he saw her mouth was downturned as she hugged her dark coat around her body.

'Not at the moment, but we did mention a WhatsApp group, so we will probably sort that out.'

She began walking in the direction of her car. He quickly followed. 'And do you always meet here?'

Pausing on the spot, she nodded. 'Yeah, it seems pretty central for people.'

'Where did you say you worked again?'

Chloe glanced at him. 'Poland & Hardy's, the financial advisors.'

David swallowed. 'With Adam, Adam …?'

'Swinton. Why are you so interested in Emily?' She almost spat out the words and he wanted to pull her tongue out.

'Because… I think she's a really nice woman and deserves a nice man.' He didn't know what else to say.

They had reached Chloe's car. She tipped her head back and laughed. 'What, like you? Newsflash, mate, people like her don't know we exist. They don't give a damn and she doesn't deserve someone as lovely as Adam…' Gritting her teeth, she dipped her hand in her bag to find her car keys. 'He's the type of man no woman ever wants to give up. And that slag…'

'Don't you dare call her a slag!'

Her eyes jerked up to his. 'What the hell is your problem, you weirdo? She is a slag and a shit writer.'

Opening her handbag wider, she turned her eyes down to

look inside for her keys, the poor lighting from the street not assisting with her vision. In that moment, David felt saturated with loathing and despair. His Emily, she couldn't have a boyfriend. She wouldn't do that. She was *his*. And this little bitch was targeting her because of it.

'You like Adam, don't you? You're jealous he's with Em-Emily?' His voice shook as a wave of sickness consumed him.

Glaring at him, her eyes narrowed. 'So what if I am? She doesn't deserve him. I do! I deserve him. And I'd have him if it wasn't for her. She was all over him when she came into the firm looking for a new accountant. And she was disgusting, fake. And he fell for it.' Tutting, she rolled her eyes

Shaking his head slowly, he attempted to take it all in.

Chloe began laughing. 'And you seem weirdly obsessed with her! I mean *really* obsessed!' She clapped her hands together. 'Well, at least I have a chance with Adam. You've got as much chance with her as my brother has with Dua Lipa!' She grimaced, looking him up and down. 'Deluded, much?'

Chloe Logan really was a nasty piece of work, he thought, standing a metre away as she mocked him. Laughing at him, laughing at Emily, and laughing at the love he had for her. As he glared at her, cackles of amusement trickling out of her mouth at his expense, his internal temperature rose rapidly, boiling, bubbling, exploding. In the dark street, dimly lit by sporadic lampposts, her face swirled into a mass of pink and peach with darkness where her open mouth was, like one of those spinning coloured circles at the funfair or on a baby's play mat. Her features almost melted into one another as his vision changed, only seeing rage and hearing her mocking snigger.

Bolting his arms out in front, his large hands clasped around her neck. The laughter stopped and Chloe's hand shot up to where his now lay, tightly held around her neck, gripping her throat as if squeezing a sponge in a bath filled with bubbles. David's grasp became firmer, stronger, as she held her hands to his and tried to pull them off her neck, struggling against his strength and the fuel of his anger. His eyes glazed over, unblinking, muttering something incoherent as she gasped and grabbed, eyes bulging with terror and pressure.

Her legs began to give way and his hands followed, holding her neck, restricting her airways like he was sitting on a whoopee cushion. Not letting go, he lowered to the ground with her. All he could see was something else that someone was trying to take from him. A precious thing: his Emily. Then, a beam took him out of his trance. The brightness was from an approaching bus. Freezing briefly, he glanced down at Chloe, now passed out. Releasing his grip, he cursed, looked up at the bus a hundred metres away and slid in between the cars, like a snake through the bushes.

David ran to his car, shaking his head. Starting his engine, he sped off in the opposite direction. Looking in his rear-view mirror, he noticed the bus didn't seem to be stopping, likely unaware of what had happened and that a woman lay on the ground in between two cars. Unsure as to whether Chloe Logan was alive or dead, he heaved and sick filled his mouth. Opening the window, he spat out the rancid vomit as sweat trickled down his brow and he wondered if what he had just done could be the end of him.

His journey home was a blur. Panic blinded him as he thought about Chloe and what he had done, or not quite managed to do. Exiting his vehicle, he rushed across the car park to the block of flats, feeling nauseous and wondering if his fate was sealed. If Chloe was dead, he could be implicated. If she was alive, he would also be implicated. Entering his flat, he slammed the door and slid to the ground, releasing a yelp.

David had simply wanted to warn Chloe at the book club that evening. He'd thought about killing her but it wasn't going to be a reality – just a warning. All he wanted to do was to protect his Emily. Having never been impulsive before in his life until the last few months, he didn't recognise himself. And didn't know who or what he was becoming. Sitting on the hallway mat, he dropped his head into his hands.

Love had changed him. It had become a growth in him that had blossomed into something special, a goal, a desire. But he wondered if the growth was planted in toxic soil and that instead of continuing to grow into a thing of beauty, it was becoming poisonous, dangerous, and would never look the way he wanted it to. Now it was a case of waiting to see if there would be any news on Chloe. Either way, he would have to cover his steps.

'Fuck!' he shouted into an empty vortex before grabbing his brown hair with his hands, short nails digging into his scalp. Regardless of the outcome of his attack against Chloe, his plan would have to escalate. He had to get to Emily, convince her that he was the one for her. Not this fucking Adam character, who sounded like a player and show-off. Placing a hand on his chest, he took a few deep breaths. His heart hurt from what he had discovered tonight. Shock that Emily had begun dating someone and the pain of rejection.

David knew that his beloved had been destroyed in the past by her vile ex-husband who had cheated on her. Tutting aloud, he closed his eyes momentarily. Her ex-husband's betrayal had created the pathway for Emily to reach her real love, him. And now some flashy accountant, who probably played rugby on a weekend and drank red wine, was sabotaging it. Forcing him off the road. But he wouldn't have it – not when he had come this far. No, he wouldn't lie back and let his woman get away.

His plan was the only way Emily would see their destiny.

Waking the next morning, David felt like he had been at an all-night rave. Not that he had ever experienced such debauchery, but it was what he imagined a night of insanely loud, repetitive, bass-heavy music, along with flashing lights and consuming numerous shots of sweet alcohol would feel like.

At work that day, he would need to maintain his professional persona. Too much rested on it, including his interview with Emily that would become the next step in his plan for them to be together. Nodding to himself in approval, he rose from his double bed. Straightening the blue bedding that was faded from being washed too many times, he walked across his flat beige carpet and entered the shower, trying to wake himself a little.

As he began getting ready for work, David put the TV on in the lounge, switching to the local news. Although likely far too early for anything to come in around Chloe Logan, he listened, unsure what he wanted to hear. His life was becoming a mess. Like a child's scribble on a piece of once clean, crisp white paper. Now it was looking rather unsightly. Certain he could turn things around with Emily's love, he had to execute the next part of his plan with precision and continue to avoid suspicion.

The police hadn't linked the crimes so far, well, they hadn't indicated anything of the sort in the press conferences or media. He felt sure that they would have suspects elsewhere. Likely known criminals, of which there were plenty in Crosley and the neighbouring towns of Ashmouth and Hallington.

Letting out an, 'Aghh,' he poured boiling water over his instant coffee. Nostrils flaring, he was angry with Chloe Logan, and Ryan Mortimer, and bloody Oliver Thornton. Why couldn't they have just left Emily alone? The thing was, that if he would have thought about it without the volcano of emotion inside of him bubbling up and erupting, he would have seen that Chloe Logan could have assisted him. She could have helped to sabotage the early-stage relationship of Adam Swinton and Emily Robinson. Instead, he was so consumed by rage and jealousy that her comment, highlighting his inferiority, made him accelerate with anger.

He had to think about the future and his interview with her the following Monday. Until then, he would do some research on Adam Swinton, the accountant from Poland & Hardy's. They couldn't have been together long and surely it was just a fling. A bit of attention for her before David made his move, romantically seducing her and Emily realising what real love was. A love that would never cheat on her, never disrespect her, always adore her, and never hurt her – well, not intentionally anyway.

Chapter 24

'So, what's it like having him back?' asked Lisa as she scooped vegetable casserole from the slow cooker into bowls for their evening meal.

Polly tilted her head, carrying a plate of sliced crusty bread to the dining table. 'It's like he's never been gone, Lees.' She paused for a moment, putting the plate down and keeping her back to her wife who was gathering cutlery for their meal. 'And he's like my comfy coat.'

'What, a bit too tight and needs a good wash?' Lisa laughed, looking in her direction.

Polly spun around, a playful scowl on her face.

'Aw, he's just such a good guy, isn't he. Like Baloo from *The Jungle Book* and you're his Mowgli!'

'What are you on tonight? It's like you've been on shift with Ricky Gervais.'

Lisa raised an eyebrow and giggled. 'Seriously, I'm pleased he's back. Your team is as under-resourced as mine and well, as long as you're okay with it, Ronnie can only make life easier. And that's the name of the game, darling.'

She winked and Polly smiled, taking her seat as Lisa handed her a steaming bowl. She inhaled the warm richness of the casserole: hints of sweet carrots, earthy mushrooms, and rosemary. Having dinner together always felt precious. It was the simple things in life that she appreciated. Dinner with her wife, a walk on a Sunday, a few ginger nut biscuits dipped in a cup of tea that someone else had made, clean bedding, her comfy coat. It all helped after a day at Northumbria Police.

The troops gathered for the afternoon briefing the following day. Without Ronnie's presence, McCardle and the team had continued their work. Crime, harm, death, it was their bread and butter, but it didn't mean it was easy to digest. In addition to the cases coming into Crosley Police Headquarters, she was keeping a close eye on the neighbouring teams and even Central and Southern Command, in case of any possible links.

Cup of tea in hand, Polly tucked her notepad under her arm and placed a pen in her mouth as she walked to the briefing room. The air inside was stale and she scrunched her nose before wedging the door open, against health and safety advice, to try to circulate the lingering scent. Soon, her small team trundled in and sat.

'You look tired,' Boyd said gently as she passed her superior.

Nodding, she spoke. 'These unsolved cases, Claire, they keep me awake.' She smiled weakly, and Boyd tapped her arm.

'Hopefully not unsolved for long.'

The meeting commenced and the team shared progress from evidence scrutiny, conversations, and research that day.

'After narrowing the time frame down for the approximate time of death of Ryan Mortimer, we identified ten cars driving on Jeffreys Street. Some of the registration plates are not fully clear from the house CCTV camera footage that shows the best angle of the street but we are working on them through the ANPR and should have a clearer idea soon,' DC Boyd said, tapping a pen against her notepad.

'Brilliant work. Any update on social media?' She looked at DC Birdy and DC Lucas.

Birdy put his cup on the floor and cleared his throat. 'So, there are a few names that we've collated by cross-referencing social media post comments associated with Ryan Mortimer. A list of around fifteen names that have recurred, mainly with trolling comments. Today, we've been looking into the profiles of the list of people, gathering more info and put an application in with the Telecoms Unit to request information from Meta. It'll provide the email address of any accounts and hopefully an IP address, unless a VPN has been used.'

Lucas clicked his pen on and off. 'Should have a complete list of possible people to eliminate from early tomorrow, boss. Then, we'll submit the request to Telecoms.'

Clasping her hands together, McCardle smiled. 'Excellent work, team.'

After five more minutes of discussion, the briefing was over, and another day at the office had come to an end for Polly, despite knowing that her brain would continue its shift late into the night.

The next day, Polly pulled up at headquarters fifteen minutes early. Cutting her car engine and leaning her head back, she closed her eyes, taking a few deep breaths. A braying on her car window startled her out of her mindful trance.

'For fuc…'

A smirking Ronnie peered into her window.

She laughed, shaking her head as she opened the driver's door. 'I nearly shit myself, Ron!'

'Sleeping on the job already, Poll,' he joked, nudging her as she tried to get out of the car.

She couldn't help but laugh again; he was like a big kid at times. They walked into the station, dumping their bags and coats, and mechanically headed to the kitchen for a cuppa.

'You miss us yesterday?' she asked, grinning, before taking the kettle from its base and filling it with water.

He tilted his head from side to side. 'Actually, I did, but the bakery world can be dark and depraved as well, you know!'

Raising an eyebrow, she carried the kettle back.

'The exploitative costs of flour and little old dears who take one free sample too many.' He rubbed his hands together as he tried to keep a straight face.

'Criminal!' she replied, getting cups from the draining board.

'Precisely! I've brought some tiffin in, though. The old dears didn't snaffle that.'

Ten minutes later, they had finished their cups of tea and a piece of tiffin, and McCardle had updated him on the small progress yesterday.

'It's frustrating, Ronnie. Slow.'

'But you're getting the detail, pet, and that can be missed when everyone barges in with their size sixes and elevens. At least it's not gone cold.'

Sighing, she nodded, knowing he was right. But still, she wanted to solve this case, prove herself to CI Richardson in some high-school kind of way. 'You're right, and the team are amazing. We just need more resources. Time is passing and well, it's critical, as you know.'

'That's why I'm here, boss, to help out. So, tell me, what do you need me to do today?' Ericson straightened his back and turned his palms up.

She smiled and pointed to the computer screen in front of them. 'We need to get some car details from ANPR. Claire is on the case but could do with some help to try and identify owners, and possibly our suspect. And you can continue the enquiries with garages in the area, please. I don't think anyone had capacity to pick it up yesterday.' Grimacing slightly, she shrugged. 'A shit job, I know, Ron, but it could be a lead.'

'Abso-bloody-lutely. Consider it done.' He clapped his hands and she rose, gently tapping his shoulder. 'I'll make another cuppa.'

Ronnie lifted his glasses to his head and scrunched his grey-blue eyes before rubbing a hand over them. Leaning back into the office chair, he stretched his arms above his head and yawned. After spending five hours at the desk, he had managed to complete a list of local garages. None had a repair booked in matching that of the vehicle used in the hit and run, but all agreed to make contact if such a job came in. He hoped they would be competent, but didn't hold out too much faith.

Despite the throbbing at the base of his spine, Ericson was coated in the warm feeling of purpose. *It's good to be back*, he thought to himself, as he glanced over his notes to take into the briefing. After a period away from the job he loved and hated equally at times, Northumbria Police felt like the missing ingredient in his life. Guilt for Caroline, for his promises, and a fear that he would screw up again, lingered. However, she had noticed the energy around him from the few shifts back at headquarters. He had played it down, but Ronnie stood taller, beamed a little brighter, and felt needed – something he hadn't realised was important to him until it was too late.

Polly loved having Ronnie back and the extra set of hands were a bonus, but she couldn't shift the feeling of inadequacy and frustration that felt like a Great Dane on her shoulders. Pressing her lips together as she drove the coastal route home, she knew she was being harsh on herself but old habits die hard. Years of self-loathing and blame tarnished her confidence like metal oxidised over time. Swallowing, she tried to stop her spiralling thoughts, but they had their own will.

Growing up with no father on the scene, Polly's mother to this day, had never given any explanation about her father – who he was, or where he went. Nothing about their relationship other than claiming he was a one-night stand and he didn't want to know when she announced her pregnancy. Polly's mother, on the few occasions she had asked as a teenager, had commented that she was too embarrassed to talk about it in any more detail. Did Polly believe her? No. Instead of feeling her mother was protecting her daughter, it had just left her thinking she wasn't worthy of having a father. That she was nothing more than an insignificant night, an error in someone's life that he had been erased and forgotten about.

And she carried that unimportance, that insignificance to the present day. Achieving at school and university, then sailing through her police training and exams, she wasn't short of dedication and determination. However, putting her all into something meant that when it didn't work out, those haunting feelings of inadequacy felt like she was wrapping a towel full of needles around her body. Inhaling, she shook her head. She didn't even want to start thinking about the battles she had around her sexuality in her teens. Turning the radio up, she hoped it would silence her internal audio, and drove the remainder of the journey home focusing on what she would have for dinner.

The following morning, the troops rounded up for the briefing. McCardle would share Ericson's update from yesterday, but before that, she gave an overview of crimes reported in the last few days from other teams, across the force. Northumbria Police spanned a vast geographical area. Northern Command consisted of the large county of Northumberland and the small borough of North Tyneside. Central Command covered the nearest city, Newcastle, and neighbouring Gateshead. Finally, Southern Command accounted for the borough of South Tyneside and the city of Sunderland. Each team within came under the Northumbria Police umbrella, named when the area was historically referred to as Northumbria.

'Several notable logs force-wide on the NICHE system.' McCardle glanced at her notes then back to her engaged team. 'A suspected hit and run in Sunderland – deceased is a young man. A possible murder in South Tyneside – victim is a middle-aged man in his home, and a possible attempted murder up the road in Morpeth – victim, a young woman, found by her car. I've actioned the analysts to run a daily report on all suspicious deaths.' The team nodded at their superior. 'Yesterday, Ronnie made progress with car repair garages across the area. No leads but garages are aware in case a job comes in. Any update, Birdy and Lucas?'

The two officers nodded and Lucas began to share their progress. 'We're waiting on access from Meta for the Facebook account info.' Birdy rolled his eyes. The team were used to the slow wait for the Telecoms Unit to get access from Meta, and even then, it was limited in the information that they could obtain. 'We are keeping an eye on the pages for any further activity, in the meantime.'

'Great stuff. It's coming together, thanks. Boyd, anything on the ANPR update?' McCardle rubbed the back of her neck as she sat on the worn office chair.

'We have a list of cars in the area from a house CCTV camera during the night of Mortimer's murder. Registrations are being checked, some are back. So, homes to be visited, and alibis confirmed, or not. One has come up already as a fake plate, so that will be the priority, with ANPR looking for it in the area. It's not clear on the house CCTV as to whether the car has damage. It's a dark colour.' She glanced at her notes then back to her superior. 'A black or very dark blue Focus or Astra. We need to look at other nearby CCTV, in case of more footage.'

McCardle nodded and stood. 'Brilliant, that's something to work on for sure. Everyone clear on their actions for today?'

The team chorused a yes and stood to continue their search for justice. McCardle would go with Boyd to interview the drivers of the vehicles whose details had come back from ANPR. Likely a process of elimination, given the car with fake plates, but still essential. Then she would have an update meeting with CI Richardson, who was clinging on for progress to pass up the chain and placate the press.

Two hours later, the pair got into McCardle's car and clicked their seatbelts into place. Polly sighed. 'Well at least we can scratch off a good proportion of those in the area!'

Boyd nodded. 'The net is slowly closing in.' A smile flashed on her face as she tried to reassure her superior.

McCardle was aware it should be the other way around, but she also knew, that out of everyone in her team, bar Ronnie, she could be a little of herself with DC Claire Boyd.

'I know it's hard, boss, after the Thornton case went cold. It's not your fault though. We all tried our best, you especially. I've never known anyone as dedicated to their job as you.'

Polly tapped Claire's forearm, before starting her engine and driving away from the house of a person of interest, who was now in the clear.

'Thanks. It means a lot. You're right, Claire. We'll get them. I believe in us. You, you're all amazing...' She decided to leave it there. Not one for opening up, she had to remember that she was the authority, and even with the people she trusted, sometimes showing weakness could bite you in the backside.

They drove back to headquarters in silence, both officers ruminating in their thoughts and hoping their leads would continue, no matter how slow they seemed to be.

The next morning, as she sat stuck in traffic on the motorway, Polly clenched her jaw before scolding herself in case the influx of traffic was due to a vehicle collision. There was a Northern Command meeting that morning at Crosley Headquarters, and Polly had wanted to get in early to make sure the briefing room didn't look and smell like student digs.

Arriving at her home-from-home twenty minutes later, she grabbed her bag and exited her car quickly, dashing across the carpark as rain drizzled. After flashing a smile and saying good morning to the front desk staff, she took the stairs to the first floor and entered her office. It was empty, the crew not due in for another forty minutes, giving her time to prepare for her guests, have a cup of tea, and check her emails.

Switching the kettle to boil, she took her cup from the cupboard, putting the dry ones from the draining board away as she did. Rings of dirt were visible on the stainless-steel. Puffing out air, she reached over to the sink and picked up the dishcloth. A waft of unpleasantness shot up her nostrils. Sniffing the dishcloth, she grimaced. Holding the offending item out like it was a soiled nappy, she shook her head. 'Scruffy bastards.' Turning the hot water on, she reached for some disinfectant from under the sink. Her team were great officers, but their cleanliness left *Stig of the Dump* looking immaculate.

Three hours later, the meeting came to a close. Senior officers began leaving as she gathered her paperwork.

'DS McCardle, can I have a word?' asked DS Munro, a detective on the neighbourhood team covering Morpeth.

'Of course,' she replied, moving her hands from the table and turning fully to him.

He nodded. 'It's a bit sensitive. You would have heard about the Chloe Logan case.'

McCardle looked up momentarily, trying to recall the name.

'The attempted murder case in Morpeth?' She had been made aware of it following the analysts' daily search of suspicious cases in the area, for any leads that could help tighten the net on the Mortimer case.

'That's the one.' He glanced at the floor, shaking his head, before his gaze returned to her. 'Terrible situation. Hopefully, Chloe will recover from the attack. But I was wondering if you or a trusted colleague could keep an eye out down here? The victim is from Hallington, so your patch, even though the crime happened on mine. However, the victim is the niece of one of my officers – so, it's a bit closer to home than usual.'

McCardle nodded. 'I see, that's dreadful. Absolutely, Daniel, I'll get someone onto it and send you a name to liaise with. Anything we can do locally, we will.'

DS Munro tapped her forearm. 'Appreciated, Polly.'

They walked out together and after saying goodbye, she returned to her desk to see the smiling face of Ronnie on the next chair along.

'Morning, my favourite Polly. How are you diddlin'?' A wide grin stretched across his jowly face.

'All the better for seeing you, boss,' she replied, looking into the white bakery box he held out with one hand. 'God, I'm going to be one big sugar doughnut by the end of the year with you here!'

'It'll only add to your sweetness, pet.' He winked and McCardle playfully rolled her eyes.

'Ron, I've just had a word with DS Munro from the Morpeth neighbourhood team.'

'Ah, good old Danny. Is he okay?'

'Yeah, yeah, he's good. Erm, one of his team is the relative of the young woman who was attacked a few days ago in Morpeth. The attempted murder, Chloe Logan.'

Ronnie rubbed his mouth. 'Oh aye, I read about it. Another mad bastard walking the streets.' He shook his head.

'Yeah, hopefully, she'll wake from the coma and be okay. Anyway, she's from Hallington, so our patch. Munro asked if we can help out with enquiries if anything comes in, to ease the emotional pressure for his officer and team? Can you help if needed, please?'

'Of course. We used to do that a lot, share cases. It's the way it should be, even across the water with our Mackem friends.' He grinned, referencing the ancient local football rivalry.

'Thanks, Ronnie. That's a great help. I'll put the kettle on.' She lifted his empty cup, hers still in her hand, and glanced again at the doughnuts before raising an eyebrow and turning to make them both a hot drink. It was just like old times, but with cakes instead of breakfast sandwiches. Ericson being at headquarters definitely made the day sweeter.

Chapter 25

The attack on Chloe Logan had been on the news the evening after David had left her for dead in Morpeth. As the serpent of worry grew inside of him, he had listened to the monotone news reporter stating that the police were treating the incident as suspicious and the victim remained in a coma, having being found unconscious by a member of the public.

He berated himself for letting his anger dominate him. Knowing that Chloe had to pay for what she had written about Emily, he hadn't necessarily planned to harm her. But love makes us do extreme things, and love had become the driving force behind the majority of his recent actions. As he made his dinner that evening, he contemplated the last few months. David Creighton, a quiet, middle-aged, single man with a good job. Who worked hard, caused no trouble, looked after his dementia-riddled mother. Who had fallen in love with Emily Robinson. She was his drug, he was addicted, and it had become deadly.

And now, there was no going back. After everything that had happened, there was no way he would not get the prize: his Emily. The interview at the library was in a few days' time and he was looking forward to not only seeing his beloved, but also producing the first newsletter for the library. Having read the email from her over and over, he knew each word, each intent, and felt it in his heart – that she would feel the same about him. Adam Swinton would be a distant memory and the prick would move on to someone else. *Perhaps not Chloe Logan,* he thought, sniggering as he poured baked beans over golden toasted bread.

In a flash, it wasn't so funny. Chloe could wake from her

coma and tell the police what he had done. He had used a false name, disguised himself slightly, but this didn't mean he wouldn't be found. They could already be looking for him. Shaking his head, he tried to disperse the thoughts, focusing on Emily. It was only two days until Monday, the day of the interview, and David needed to rehearse his questions, rehearse his schedule to advance their relationship, and account for what he hoped he wouldn't need: his plan B.

Monday arrived, after a tense weekend for David, unsure as to Chloe Logan's condition and looking over his shoulder the two times he left the flat. However, he had an injection of positivity, as it was the day he would interview his future wife at the library. His chance to move their relationship from professional and friendship, to love. Biting back his anger, he felt that the excitement and build-up had been ruined, like a graffitied mural, due to Chloe Logan.

The interview wasn't until 6pm, after the library closed to the public at 5.30pm. As a key holder, he had locking up responsibilities and his colleague would finish around 6pm, leaving David to conduct the interview with Emily and make the building secure after they left.

Eating breakfast, he tried to shift Chloe from his mind, focusing on the way the evening with Emily would play out. Yet the little bitch returned to his thoughts, like mould on the ceiling in the winter. He had seen the story on the local news, solemn-faced family members crying into the camera. Police saying they were making enquiries and treating it as attempted murder. He'd swallowed down nerves with glugs of beer, then the next day, there had been reports in the news that the police were conducting interviews with people she had seen the evening and day of the attack on the, 'popular young woman'.

He sneered. Chloe Logan was a nasty piece of work. Spiteful, jealous, and a bully. Why did the press always make out like victims were saints? If anything, David was a victim. A victim of years of abuse from his bastard stepfather and selfish mother. He had never been given the chance to be *popular* like Chloe. He wasn't handed opportunities to find friends, love, a life – too busy following the cruel orders and regime inflicted on him by Keith, then when the bastard died, becoming trapped by his emotionally weak mother before her illness started to seep into her mind, like an ink blot spreading.

And now it was his chance. He had travelled to the depths of depravity to ensure it. Was he proud? Certainly not. Did he regret hurting Oliver Thornton, Ryan Mortimer, and Chloe Logan? No. Because they hurt Emily, and she was all that really mattered to him, the only woman he had a future with. Aware the police might be tracing him following witness interviews, he felt that he had disguised himself enough that night and eliminated any way of being traced through the comments he dropped into conversation.

Physically, David didn't stand out. He wasn't memorably good-looking, not noticeably large or small. He didn't have distinctive features that someone would remember, and the little props he wore and amendments he'd made to his style and appearance would keep the witnesses off the scent for a while. Fake glasses, clean-shaven, casual clothes, and a cap that he never took off during the meeting.

Shaking his head, he gritted his teeth. Ruminating wouldn't stop anything, except for his enjoyment of the day. It would be their anniversary; the day he and Emily Robinson got together. She would see that he was the one for her, not that prick Adam Swinton. No one could love her like he did and would. David would show Emily Robinson this evening that they were meant to be.

Library staff wore a uniform but since he would be interviewing Emily after the library closed, he wanted to make an effort. Changing his clothes from his work wear of navy-blue chinos and polo top, to a smart shirt, would make the interview feel more like the date it was intended to be. He'd carefully hung a light blue shirt on a hanger and placed it in his car, putting it straight in his locker on his arrival at work. A toiletry bag with a toothbrush, toothpaste, deodorant, and aftershave accompanied the shirt. At the bottom of his backpack lay plastic sandwich bag. Pushing the toiletries slightly to the left, the bag peeked out. Pressing his lips together, he looked around to ensure no one was in the staff room then pulled the transparent bag out, checking its contents before returning it and locking away his belongings.

He tried to act normal for his shift. Not that the staff really knew him anyway. Pleasantries, a Christmas meal out, that was as far as it went with David and his team. Interactions were always friendly, but not overly personal. He didn't really care what part someone's brat was playing in the Nativity, or where so-and-so was going on their holidays. Not noticing if someone had a new hairstyle or caring why someone was on the sick. It was irrelevant to him. He did his job and was happy to be there, doing his best, and being part of a team in the way he needed to be. Professional, not overly personal, and that suited him just fine.

The afternoon dragged as he began panicking that perhaps Emily wouldn't turn up. He hadn't emailed her since the initial reply to her accepting the invitation for interview. Should he have emailed to remind her? A message telling her he was looking forward to it?

'Shit,' he said quietly, clicking into his emails. There was nothing from her in his inbox, and with less than three hours until the interview was scheduled, it seemed a bit silly emailing her now. Plus, she'd likely be busy working, not sitting by her emails. Puffing out air, David rose from his chair. Back straight, he walked into the library area to check on customers and tidy a little, hoping it would distract his racing mind.

Two hours later, the library was empty of readers and people using the IT suite. The manager and his colleague on shift said goodbye, leaving him in the quiet sanctuary. The domestics attended early each morning, rather than after the library closed to people, so there would be no disturbances. Rushing to the small room where he would interview Emily, he glanced around. It contained a sofa and an armchair, and a small table in between them which sat on a striped rug. Leaning over, he picked up the cushions on the sofa attempting to plump them up. They were flat and tired, a donation from a member of staff who no longer wanted them. He wedged the door open for some fresh air to circulate in the windowless room.

Going to the bathroom, he brushed his teeth before changing into his pale blue shirt, spraying aftershave around his neck. As he looked at himself in the mirror, a strained smile crept onto his face. David wasn't an unattractive man. No model, he was average and his mother always told him he had a nice smile. Practising in the mirror, he smiled again. His teeth showed in the gap as his lips curled up, a splattering of brown on his chin and around his mouth as the hairs of his former beard began piercing his skin to escape. But cold eyes and a reflection of anger stared back at him. Inhaling, his nostrils flared and he shook his head, washing his hands before drying them on paper towels.

This was his time, his chance. And nothing would stand in his way. Glancing at his watch, he saw it was less than fifteen minutes until Emily was due. Perhaps he should stand at the entrance of the library. Most of the lights in the building had been turned off, to indicate the facility was closed to the public. He had intended on locking the main front door once she arrived and they would leave together through the back entrance of the library after the interview. *Hopefully, holding hands,* he thought, biting his lower lip.

Deciding he would put the kettle on to boil for her arrival, he took two clean cups from the cupboard and checked for any biscuits. He scorned himself for not being better prepared and buying some luxury biscuits or chocolates for her. Although he had remembered flowers, the most romantic of gifts. Rooting through the cupboard, he found a tub of chocolates. Inside, a few were scattered on the bottom, individually wrapped. They would have to do. He poured the chocolates into a small bowl and left the kitchen to stand at the entrance, waiting for his future wife to approach.

The dim light from behind illuminated his silhouette as he stood by the entrance. It was raining lightly, but mild for the end of November. Standing, he observed three teenagers cycle past on the footpath, without lights on their bike, and shook his head at the irresponsibility of some people. David's thoughts drifted to the next few hours and he swallowed, not wanting to contemplate the evening going wrong. If she said she loved Adam, wanted to be with him, then…

He realised he had tensed his body, his hands in tight fists by his side. He wouldn't let Adam Swinton block his path to Emily. Not after he had come this far. She couldn't, wouldn't reject him. Not now. Not when he had put everything on the line for her, for them, their future. Scrunching his eyes shut he inhaled violently. She wouldn't let him down, he wouldn't allow her to. Tilting his head back for a few seconds, he sighed.

Hearing the automatic doors slide open, he whipped his head up. Emily dashed into the library, out of the drizzle. It was like she brought the sunshine in with her as she beamed with radiant beauty. His face melted into a big smile.

'Hi, David, how are you? It's so dreary out there!' She let out a wonderfully bouncy giggle as she moved towards him.

'Oh, hello, Emily. It's so lovely to see you.' He cleared his throat. 'And yes, typical North East weather, eh?' Rolling his eyes, he chuckled. 'I'm so pleased you could make it. I've been looking forward to your visit all day and our readers will be so excited when the interview comes out.' He clapped his hands together, before releasing them and gesturing for Emily to walk through the dimly lit library. 'I'll just lock up.' He travelled past her and promptly locked the entrance doors, before pressing a button for the automatic shutters to lower.

She watched before he turned back and moved towards her. 'I'm really grateful for the opportunity, David. You, the library team, you are all so supportive and it really does mean so much.'

As she held her hand to her chest, he quivered inside. She felt it, she knew he would cherish her, give her the world. He was certain of that. 'Anything for you, Emily.' He tilted his chin up, feeling his confidence rising.

They walked for a minute across the library, illuminated by low lighting.

'Did you get parked okay? I should have told you to park in the staff car park.' He glanced at her, and she nodded.

'I've just parked where I normally do on Lenton Street, so it's no bother.'

David nodded and swallowed down his flickering nerves. He had parked his own car in the back lane around the side of the library that day. The lane ran along the rear gardens of a row of terraced houses and flats, most with tall walls or garage doors to help make his vehicle less conspicuous. A few cars were often parked there, likely households with multiple cars who couldn't get parked on the road out the front. David had to ensure a plan B, but hoped it wouldn't get that far.

There were no CCTV cameras to the rear of the library. A warehouse faced the building that had provided clear CCTV coverage of the library. Becoming vacant six months ago, all internal and external equipment had been relocated and the library had yet to install their own camera to cover the now blind spot. Luckily for David, the lack of risk management by his employer had helped him create his plan B.

'Just in here,' he said, as they reached the small room, the door still wedged open and an atmospheric lamp switched on.

'Lovely. Nice and cosy.'

Was she flirting? he wondered.

Emily took off her long black coat, revealing a floral tea dress and thick black tights covering her shapely legs. Her beautiful long golden hair cascaded over her shoulders and rested on her chest. He wanted to touch it. Touch her.

'Take a seat.' He pointed to the sofa. 'I'll make us a cuppa. You like tea, don't you? Milk, no sugar?'

She smiled. 'How did you know?'

'I remembered from making you a drink at the event here last month.'

She giggled lightly, her sparkling eyes on him. 'What a magnificent memory you have, David.'

He stared at her for a few seconds, in awe of her presence. If perfection were an image, it would be Emily Robinson. She sat on the sofa and he clicked out of his trance, feeling his cheeks blush slightly.

'Okay, cuppa coming up!' Leaving Emily in the room, he rushed to the staff kitchen and flicked the kettle to re-boil.

Glancing at his locker, he tapped a spoon on the countertop, thinking about what was inside. Certain that he wouldn't need it but just in case. Once the kettle had boiled, David made the cups of tea and carried them back to the room where Emily waited, the small bowl of chocolates wedged in the crease of his arm.

She was sitting cross-legged, glamorous and ladylike on the sofa. David imagined her in their future home, him by her side, in love. Holding hands as they sat, cosy, watching TV or talking about books. He zoned out momentarily, standing, holding the cups. She cleared her throat, jolting him out of his trance. Shaking his head slightly, he placed the cups on the table, followed by the chocolates.

'Sweets for the sweetest author there is.' He flashed a shy smile, taking a seat in the grey armchair opposite the sofa.

'Oh, that's so kind. Although, I guess the topics of my books aren't all that sweet.' She chuckled and he joined in.

'I think you are the most amazing, talented author I've ever come across, Emily. And I work in a library, so I come across many!' He turned his palms up and shrugged.

'You're very generous and supportive. You must really love your job.' She tucked a thick lock of hair behind her ear as she leant over to take her cup.

Nodding, he took a sip of his tea. 'I do. Books, they are so important.'

Emily nodded back.

She's engaged and really cares about what I say, he thought.

'Growing up, books were my friends. I didn't have many friends at school. The few I had were never allowed to our house because my stepfather was a brute.' His gaze dropped to his hands then returned to her. She held a sadness in her eyes that he knew was for him. She truly cared. She cared about him.

'In a book, we can make friends and travel the world. They are wonderful companions who never judge us.' Emily leant forward towards him.

She was looking into his eyes and he wanted to kiss her; hold her forever, and never let her go. She was the woman of his dreams who he never thought existed and now he had her, they had to be together.

He coughed. 'And authors, they allow that. Creating the worlds that bring us comfort and joy, entertainment and knowledge.' Leaning for his notepad, David wanted to make notes for the interview but wanted to steer the conversation to more than writing. He wanted to talk about them. After asking a few general questions that readers would want to know such as how she got into writing, her inspiration, and favourite books and authors, he began steering the conversation to her personal life so he could approach talking about them.

'Do you read much at home, Emily? I guess you don't get a lot time with writing?' He glanced up, resting his pen on his lap.

'I try. Reading has always helped me relax, but so does writing – although not editing!' She giggled.

He nodded. 'I bet. I guess that sometimes takes as long as writing the book.'

'It certainly does and an author could go on forever, changing, fixing, amending a book. You need to know when to stop. It's all-consuming and it will never be perfect.'

Frowning, he spoke. 'Respectfully, Emily, I beg to differ. *All* of your books are perfect. Just like you.' He flashed a goofy smile and she touched the back of her neck.

'You're too kind, David. I wish everyone felt like you do about my books.' She tilted her head.

'They should. However, I am your number one fan!' He beamed at her.

Emily pressed her lips together. 'And the most wonderful fan you are!'

'I would love to do more. Support you in further ways. Promote your books, assist with launches. Anything that would help.'

Emily moved slightly on the sofa and rubbed her fingers with her other hand.

'Maybe we could go for dinner one night this week and talk about how I could help you?' He leant forward, his legs bouncing slowly with both excitement and nerves.

She smiled but remained silent.

'I think we would make an excellent team, Emily. I know your books like I wrote them myself.' He chuckled, clapping his hands together as his pulse increased. 'And well, I think you are the most incredible woman.' He sighed and the air was filled with silence for a few seconds.

As she smoothed her dress down, an awkward smile appeared on Emily's face. 'You really are too kind,' she said quietly, a light laugh at the end.

Nodding, he tapped his pen on the notepad resting on his knee. She hadn't answered the question about going for dinner. He would have to bring it up again. He felt disappointment soak him and the flare of anger ignite. *Bloody Adam Swinton.* He needed to try to steer the conversation to find out for sure if Emily was seeing him and how serious their relationship was. Adam needed to be erased from the picture.

'We've talked about your books and future books, which all sound incredible.' He straightened his back, trying to appear more confident than he was. 'So, do you have anyone who reads the first drafts, apart from your editor?'

'Great question,' she began, leaning back on the sofa. 'I have a friend who always supports with my first drafts. She gets a mention in the back of each book and I really value her feedback and friendship.'

David bit back his frustration. 'Great friend. If you ever need another first draft reader…' He pointed at himself.

'I'll make a note of that. Thank you.' She tapped her head.

He tried to ask more questions to get her to talk about any intimate relationship but he knew he was starting to go off topic. Emily looked at her watch and David felt she was ready to wrap up the interview, which was fine, he would ask her questions as they got ready to leave, and mention going for dinner again. After thanking her for her time, he slowly began to get ready for them to leave, talking as he moved to keep her engaged.

'So, perhaps we could go for dinner then?' he commented as he collected the empty cups, trying to sound casual when he felt dizzy with emotion.

She swallowed and nodded slightly. 'Erm, yeah, I think dinner would be nice. Perhaps the team can come, after all the support everyone has given me.'

He clenched his jaw. Did she not understand what he was saying? He wanted her alone. A date. Not with the bloody people he spent all day with. 'Or maybe just you and I. We can talk books again. I'd love to hear more.'

Smiling weakly, she remained silent as she moved from foot to foot gently on the spot. No answer was forthcoming and David cleared his throat. 'I'll pop these in the kitchen then we can leave.' Exiting the room, he felt wobbly before a gust of desperation soared through him. He marched to the kitchen, thinking he would give her one more chance before he would have to take things further, make her see.

Removing his backpack from his locker, he quickly opened it, removed the sandwich bag and placed the contents on the countertop. Glancing at the door, he then returned his focus to the items: a vial of Diprivan sedative, purchased from a local undesirable, along with a needle and syringe. Having researched what he needed to do, David still felt the cold sweat of panic. Swallowing, he filled the syringe with the sedative before carefully placing it in the front pocket of his backpack. Exhaling, he quickly shut his bag and scooped it over his shoulder.

'Right, all sorted. Let's go,' he said in a chirpy voice.

They walked to the back of the library and after flicking the lights off, moved through the door, travelling the stairs to the rear exit, used only by staff. Feeling tense, David rushed ahead. Turning to Emily, she half smiled, eyes wide. Reaching the back door, he set the alarm and the pair left.

'Oh shoot, I forgot, I have a thank you for you in my car. It's just this way.' He pointed to the direction and began to walk, not waiting for her to respond.

She followed, clearing her throat. 'Oh, there was no need for that. I'm always happy to do anything for the libraries.'

As he walked, his heart raced. His back was clammy and David knew that the next minute would determine their future.

'I'm just parked here.'

Emily smoothed her hair down with one hand, as her other hand gripped her jacket around her. She looked at him then his boot as he placed his backpack by his feet and leant to unzip the front part, taking the syringe out and carefully concealing it in the palm of his hand. He rose and tapped his pocket.

'They're here.' Rolling his eyes at his pretence of not knowing where his keys were located, he removed them from his pocket and clicked to unlock the boot of his Ford Focus, being careful with his hand containing the sedative. He brought a bunch of red roses out of the boot. The flowers of love, he had thought when purchasing them. Smiling, she looked at the pretty flowers.

'A bunch of beauty for a beauty.' He held them out.

'Oh, they are stunning, David.' She gazed at the flowers momentarily, lost in their striking deep colour, before her eyes lifted. 'Really, there was no need, but thank you.'

He leant in towards her to kiss her lips. She moved and his mouth landed on her cheek.

'David, erm, I don't think...' Emily stepped back.

'I really like you, Emily. And I think we have a special connection.' His voice wavered but it was his last chance.

She let out a nervous chuckle. 'Sorry, David, I think you're lovely. But, I'm... I'm in a relationship.'

He swallowed fury. In a fucking relationship? And she laughed at him. Perhaps a nervous laugh of shock or not knowing what to say, but he perceived it as insulting, making him feel inferior. How could she laugh at him?

'But we, us. He, he means nothing...' David leant in towards her again and she stepped back once more. Apprehension glimmered in her eyes on the dimly-lit lane.

'I have to go, sorry.'

She turned to walk and he flared his nostrils as anger and heartbreak ripped him apart like the jaw of a shark. Following Emily the few steps she had walked, he held the syringe, the tip of the needle poking out between his thumb and forefinger.

'Emily, please, you don't understand. I love you.'

She glanced around, brow furrowed, fear dancing in her eyes, and turned back quickly, speeding her step. David rushed, reaching his free hand out and grabbed her arm. Stretching her head and neck the other way, Emily let out a yelp, as David stepped forward and jabbed the needle into her neck. Her hand dropped the flowers in almost slow motion and travelled up to her neck, her eyes staring at him in shock for a few seconds as it registered what he had done. Mouth open, she managed to croak a, 'Help!' before she dropped to the floor, next to where the flowers lay.

Letting out a gasp, he looked around quickly. The back lane was silent and dark. What had happened in the last two minutes felt like he was being kicked in the heart. Her reaction to his heartfelt confession. Shock, rejection, walking away. And what he had just done to the woman he loved. Feeling dizzy, he covered his mouth, stifling a scream of pain and anger. Clicking the central locking to open his car, he put the empty syringe in his jacket pocket and quickly grabbed Emily under her arms. David was average in strength for a healthy male of his age and size, but she felt a heavy weight, despite being slim.

Part lifting, part dragging, he brought Emily to the back of his car. Flashes of Oliver Thornton appeared in his vision and he shook his head abruptly. She would be passed out for at least two hours, by his calculations. Opening the door to the back seats, he frantically looked around again, before lifting Emily and pushing her unconscious body into the car, expelling a groan as he did so.

'Fuck!' he said quietly, as he shut the door on her and rushed into the driver's seat. Momentarily he held his hands to his head, digging his short fingernails into his scalp. Starting the engine, he turned his side lights on to be a little more discreet and began driving down the lane. In his rear-view mirror, he saw the beautiful bunch of blood-red roses, lying in the road, looking bleak.

Chapter 26

Polly kept her eyes shut for a few minutes, willing herself to fall back to sleep. Hearing the slightest noise during the night seemed to be her superpower, and one she didn't want. A leaf blowing off the ground, an animal in the garden, a car in the distance – would all wake her and the instant she woke, her mind began its firework display in her head. It never slowed down and her inability to relax, although great for Northumbria Police, proved debilitating out of work.

Scrunching her eyes tight, she knew it was no use. The party had started in her mind and thoughts were dancing. Looking at her watch, it was 4.47am. Mouth dry, she licked her lips and swallowed. Turning onto her back, she tried to breathe deep and relax for ten minutes, without success, before giving up and quietly getting out of bed. Sliding her feet into her slippers, she moved towards the bedroom door, gently pushing the handle down and exiting the room into the dark landing. Softly closing the door on a peacefully-sleeping Lisa, she mechanically moved down the stairs of their terraced home.

Traipsing into the kitchen, Polly filled the kettle, and switched it to boil. After making a cup of tea, she went into the lounge and sat on the enveloping olive-green velvet sofa. Tipping her head back to the cushion, she rested the warm cup on her lap and closed her eyes. The unsolved cases were teasing her, and although the team had some great leads, it was taking too long and not producing enough for her liking. Something felt missing; part of the engine that prevented movement. She inhaled and sipped her tea, enjoying the quiet lounge.

Feeling chilly, she placed her cup on the side table and leant forward to the basket that sat under it, where they kept a fleece blanket. As she pulled out the cream softness, her eye caught a glittery gift bag lying by the side. Lisa's sister's birthday gift. She pulled the bag closer, nosing in to see what Lisa had bought her older sibling. Polly smiled on seeing the yet to be wrapped gift – three hardback books. Having a quick sift through, she knew, as an avid reader, that her sister-in-law would appreciate them. Then she paused, still, soundless, apart from a screaming voice in her head telling her this could be it.

She placed her hands to her mouth in a prayer motion, and her heart raced. 'Fuck!' she said, eyes wide, no longer feeling the weariness from lack of sleep. She picked up her mobile phone and clicked on the BBC News app. Going to the local section, she scrolled through to the article she had read about Chloe Logan two days ago. She knew the answer to the questions in her mind, but not being able to log in to the police MIS from her home, BBC News was the next best thing.

The headline of the latest story on the Logan case told her that the twenty-three-year-old had been in a coma for six days following the attack after an evening out in Morpeth. Scrolling through the article, it talked about Chloe as a fun-loving woman, adored by her family and friends, who worked at a local accountancy firm. On the evening of the attack, she had been at the monthly book club for the group she co-established, the North East Book Addicts. Nodding, she glanced at the gift bag still by her feet. Chloe Logan ran a book club and was attacked the night the group met. Ryan Mortimer was an entertainment journalist, specialising in reviews of books, films, and plays. And Oliver Thornton had been to a library event the night he died: a place surrounded by books.

'Shit!' she said, getting up and beginning to pace the lounge as she ran a hand through her blonde bob. Three unsolved crimes. Murder times two and attempted murder. All with a link to books or reading. It could be nothing, but Polly was like a loaded spring and knew she needed to run it past someone immediately. She glanced at the retro wall clock. It was just gone 5.30am. Turning her eyes down to the geometric-style rug, she tapped two fingers to her teeth. Too early to call Ronnie and she wouldn't call CI Richardson, not until she had got her possible theory less convoluted in her head. Coincidence? Perhaps. Motive? Possible.

Moving to the kitchen-diner, Polly reached into the junk drawer and pulled out a tatty notepad and pen. She put the kettle back on to boil, made herself another cup of tea and began to make notes. After she'd been scrawling for twenty minutes, it was almost 6am. Polly showered, got ready, and kissed a still sleeping Lisa goodbye, before driving to headquarters.

Arriving to an empty office, she logged on to the NICHE system that recorded incidents and cases. Unlocking her drawers, she took out her notepad, placing it alongside the notepad from home. Polly clicked to access current files, including ones that were open with limited activity. The murder of Oliver Thornton fell into this category after no new leads in a few months.

Scanning the data and case notes, she tapped a pen to her mouth, leaning into the screen. There it was, information from the night Thornton was last seen, as he visited a local library for an event, then went to a bar afterwards with a friend. Library staff had been spoken to but were unable to help with much, other than to confirm he had attended the library. The actual event wasn't noted in the case file. McCardle made a note to speak with the library to ascertain which event it was – it could provide further leads.

She would also task the team with revisiting Mortimer's recent reviews, focusing on the book reviews in particular. They had been working on the social media side of things, analysing comments from the public on Facebook and Instagram to see if there were any names recurring. They were waiting for imminent Meta access following a request by the Telecoms Unit. This would highlight the email addresses of the accounts needing investigated, alongside the IP address where the sites had been accessed – as long as no VPN had been used.

Additionally, Polly wanted to establish the books read so far by Chloe Logan's book club, North East Crime Addicts. Nothing might come from it, but it could be significant. In the meantime, she would read over all the case notes for the Logan attack. The young woman remained in a coma, but the Morpeth Neighbourhood Team had been investigating and interviewing people who were there the night of the incident, as well as chatting with her family.

McCardle rose from her blue office chair, that squeaked each time it moved on the castors. Walking to the kitchen for a cup of tea, she looked at her watch. It was 7.10am, he would be awake by now; the police alarm clock never stopped. Putting the kettle to boil, she walked back to her desk and picked up her mobile phone. The screensaver of her and Lisa flashed up and she smiled, before unlocking it and going to her call log. The call was answered within three rings.

'Alright, Poll?' came the voice she loved to hear.

'Hi, Ronnie, sorry for ringing early.'

'Not to worry, pet, I was awake. I'm coming in for 8.30, is everything okay?'

Polly heard crockery chinking in the background and walked back to the kitchen, to make her own drink.

'I think I might have something, Ron.'

'Aw, aye, like one of those STDs?' He chuckled.

McCardle rolled her eyes. 'That's very men down the social club. You used to be so professional!'

They both laughed. 'Sorry, and it's only seven o' clock! Go on.'

'The Ryan Mortimer case. And possibly the Chloe Logan case, and Oliver Thornton case.' She lowered her ear to her shoulder, trapping her mobile phone as she poured boiling water over a teabag in her mug, the steam rising near her face.

'Crikey. That would be something.'

She squashed her teabag with a spoon. 'It could be nothing, Ron, but I want to run it past you. I know you've helped out a little on the Logan case for DS Munro.'

'Give me fifteen minutes, I'll get there for half seven.'

She bit her bottom lip before answering. 'Thanks. See you soon.'

Hanging up, Polly put her mobile phone on the beige countertop and pulled her hand over her mouth. It was still almost eerily silent in the office but she appreciated the brain space. After adding milk to her tea, she returned to her desk, and replied to a text message from Lisa checking all was okay. Clicking on the Logan case, she saw there were many entries and attachments. They would take a few hours to go through. After taking a gulp of tea, she moved her arms and pushed out her chest, creating a small stretch in the arch of her back. It was going to be a long day but she felt positive that something might come of her thinking. Returning her hands to her desk, she looked at the mass of scribbled words on her notepads, hoping that it would be the key that unlocked the current unmovable doors on the unsolved crimes.

Fifteen minutes later, Ronnie rushed into the office like a gust of winter wind – only much more welcome than the cold,

North East weather. Approaching her desk with ruddy cheeks and a smile on his face, he held out a paper bag.

'Bacon sarnie. Thought you wouldn't have had time for brekkie.' He placed the bag on her desk.

She smiled. 'You thought right. Thanks.'

He nodded, content to be looking after her in some way. It was the little things that had always made a difference in their friendship. The small gestures and kind, encouraging words. The genuine care that is rarer than we realise. The times that they asked how each other was, and it wasn't out of pleasantry or habit of dialogue; it was because they were concerned, cared, and truly wanted to check on their friend's well-being. Ronnie wasn't just a colleague, a literal partner in crime. The cups of tea and coffee, biscuits, cakes, sandwiches. The silly memes after a shit day. Those things felt more precious than a jeweller's counter to Polly, and they made her feel cared for in a way that no man had ever made her feel.

Over the next fifteen minutes, before the team began to slowly arrive for the working day, McCardle shared her thoughts and notes about the three currently unsolved cases with Ericson, to much head nodding, eye-widening, eyebrow raising and several statements of, 'Bloody hell.' After she'd summarised, Ronnie leant back in the chair and exhaled deeply. His tie flopping to the side, showing a tomato sauce slop from the bacon sandwich he had only just eaten.

'Well, that certainly makes sense when you say it like that. And that feeling, in your gut...' He made a fist with his hand and hovered it over his stomach. 'If it's there, it means something. I've always told you that.'

She nodded. He had, and he was always right.

Drinks in hand, everyone strolled into the briefing room, talking about the latest Netflix show or the football the night before. McCardle's mind was a cyclone of actions but she needed the update on any developments, even if it meant going over things that had been said in the briefing the previous day. Glancing at the incident board to her left, she saw that details of Ryan Mortimer's life and death were displayed like sad artwork. The board would need filling with the returning photographic evidence of Oliver Thornton and evidence surrounding Chloe Logan, if her gut proved to be right.

Stifling a yawn, she took a seat and began addressing her team. 'Morning, folks. So, can we share where we are all at with the Mortimer case, then there will be a few new actions. Boyd, can you update first, please?'

'Yes, boss. So, there are still a few car owners to interview from the home CCTV footage. However, the focus is on the dark vehicle with fake registration plates. It's likely a Ford Focus…' she glanced at her notes, 'a 2010-2013 model. ANPR are looking at CCTV in the area for possible matching vehicles with damage, the night of Mortimer's murder and since.' DC Boyd scanned the small team, who nodded. 'I went back to the houses on the street for door-to-door with an image of the vehicle yesterday and will finish that today. Just in case anyone saw the car outside, walked past with a dog, and so on.' She clicked her pen.

'Great, thanks, Claire. Birdy, Lucas, are there any updates on social media associated with Mortimer's articles or personal accounts?'

Lucas began. 'We've received some Meta data, boss. The analysts are going to hopefully assist today in checking email sign-ups and IP addresses for accounts.'

Birdy chipped in. 'Of the accounts of interest, a few have no profile picture or an AI-looking image. Two profiles are unlocked and we've been able to search through. They are of less interest but all will be investigated.'

'Brilliant. We are getting there, team.' McCardle smiled at her colleagues. 'And any update on the car garages, Ericson?'

Shifting his body slightly in the uncomfortable chairs to face her a little more, he spoke. 'All garages in a forty mile-radius have been liaised with. No jobs have come in matching the damage on the suspect's car but all garages have advised they will make contact if a car matching comes in. Now I have a list and emails, I can send an email to all with the likely description of the vehicle. And thanks for your help, Boyd.' He glanced to his colleague, who smiled.

'I'll help again today, boss,' she said, before blushing slightly, addressing him in his old role.

'Perfect, thanks, everyone.' McCardle rubbed a hand over her mouth, contemplating whether to tell the team her current thought process about the cases being linked. It wasn't that she didn't trust her thinking, or at least thought it was worth pursuing. For Polly, it was more about the thought of being wrong and it being known publicly amongst her colleagues. She had enormous shoes to fill once Ronnie had left, and the shadow of inadequacy clung to her skin and clothes.

Inhaling deeply, she stood. 'Team, I think there may be a possible link between the Ryan Mortimer case and two other current investigations.' Glancing around the room, she saw raised eyebrows in anticipation of what she was about to say. 'The Oliver Thornton case. And the recent attempted murder of Chloe Logan in Morpeth. And this case, Ryan Mortimer.' She glanced at the incident board. 'There is something that links them all. Books or reading. And I think this link may lead us to our killer.'

For the next ten minutes, McCardle explained her thinking. The officers made notes, asked questions, and documented actions, before she dismissed them, each knowing the next steps and their role – which involved searching Mortimer's book reviews over the last twelve months, ascertaining what books the North East Crime Addicts read over the same time period, revisiting Crosley Library about the night Oliver Thornton was last seen, and cross-referencing any of the names shortlisted by Birdy and Lucas, to see if they followed any book pages or author pages. Her colleagues exited the briefing room, all eager to get working on existing and possible new leads.

'They got it,' Ronnie said, pushing his chair under a table.

She nodded. 'Yeah, they did. I just hope it brings home the goods.'

'We can but try, pet. I'll make you a cuppa before you get cracking on those case notes, eh?'

She smiled. 'Thanks, boss.'

Returning to her desk, McCardle saw an email from CI Richardson, requesting a short meeting that afternoon for case updates. She grimaced a little, unsure how to approach her recent theory with him. 'Books link the killings', sounded a bit lame. She would use the morning to go through the case notes of the Chloe Logan incident, which would include last movements, CCTV and dashcam footage, interviews with witnesses, and any possible suspect descriptions. After speaking with CI Richardson, she would seek authorisation to share anything that could become a lead with DS Munro from the Morpeth Neighbourhood Team. Wringing her hands together, she inhaled, before a cup appeared in her eye line and Ronnie plonked himself on the seat to her left.

Two hours later, McCardle had some notes and requests ready for her meeting with CI Richardson that afternoon. From the Logan case, all witnesses bar one had been interviewed. The final witness had not been traced so far: a new member called

Andy Palmer. Witnesses stated he hadn't been active in the social media group. However, one witness mentioned that they thought Chloe might have left the pub with him. A photo e-fit of Andy Palmer, now the suspect, had been created when interviewing witnesses. The pub staff had been interviewed and CCTV footage obtained. It wasn't great quality and the possible suspect had been wearing a baseball cap.

McCardle needed authorisation to proceed with the cross-area cases. It was 11am, and despite the bacon sandwich Ronnie had brought in, she was hungry. Deciding to visit the canteen for a cheese toastie, she turned to him to ask if he wanted something to eat. Her desk phone rang, indicating an internal call. Clearing her throat, she picked up the receiver.

'DS McCardle.'

'Hi, DS McCardle, it's reception. There's a man here wanting to speak with a senior officer about a possible missing person.'

Chapter 27

Putting the phone down, Polly clicked her neck before walking through the office and down the stairs. Reaching the bottom, she pushed open the double doors to a corridor leading to reception. When she arrived in the foyer, the officer nodded towards a man standing, head stooped as he looked at the mobile phone in his hand. Over six foot tall, athletic, with brown hair, he lifted his head, showing a chiselled jawline, and a furrowed brow. Stepping forward, she put a hand out.

'I'm Detective Sergeant Polly McCardle. I believe you requested to speak with someone?'

The man nodded and swallowed. 'Yeah, please. I'm Adam Swinton. I think my girlfriend may be missing and I think it could be linked to some recent murders.'

Her eyes widened. This she wasn't expecting when she came into work that morning, but immediately the train of thought that had been building speed in her mind since early morning, set off again.

'Okay, let's go and find a room.' McCardle turned back to the door she had come from, pushed it open and walked through, holding it for Adam Swinton to follow. Scanning the corridor, she opened a door second on the left and ushered him inside. 'Are you're alright in here? Would you like a cup of tea or coffee?'

'Water would be great, thanks.' He raised a hand to his head.

'If you can just give me two minutes, Mr Swinton, then I will have a chat with you. And what is your girlfriend's name?' She smiled and pointed to a chair.

He took a seat and swallowed. 'It's Emily. Emily Robinson.

She's a local author.'

Polly could feel the colour almost drain from her face. Flaring her nostrils, she tried to take in some air and act normally. 'Okay, thanks. I'll be two minutes.' Leaving the room and shutting the door, she closed her eyes and muttered, 'Friggin' hell,' to herself. Feeling clammy, she dashed back to the MIT office, travelling up the stairs two at a time, her heartbeat increasing with each step. She wanted Ronnie to hear this.

She walked into the office to see him sitting next to Boyd. Polly smiled momentarily. He looked at home and it made her happy. The pair had their eyes on Boyd's screen, as she scrolled data and spoke. Polly cleared her throat as she approached, and he looked around.

'Alright, pet'? A smile spread across his slightly jowly jaw. Then he saw the serious look in her eyes.

She scratched her head. 'Can you come and sit in an interview, Ron? I've got a bloke downstairs whose girlfriend may be missing...'

'Of course.' Rising from his seat, he tapped Boyd on the shoulder, who smiled and continued with her work.

The pair began to walk towards reception. 'You won't believe this...'

'I have a feeling I already know. Is she an author?'

McCardle nodded and clasped a hand to her mouth. 'Fuck, Ronnie, they *are* linked. They have to be now.'

He pushed through the doors to the stairs as she scrolled on her mobile phone looking for Emily Robinson events. A page with upcoming events flashed up.

'Careful, Poll,' Ronnie said, hand out towards her as they took the stairs, her eyes fixed on her phone.

Nodding, she watched her footing before tapping in past

events into her search for Emily Robinson.

'Fuck!'

Ronnie turned to her, holding the door open to the corridor.

'It was her, that night. The 29th September, when Oliver Thornton was last seen. The event he attended was an event with Emily Robinson.' She ran a hand through her hair. They were less than twenty seconds' walk from where the author's boyfriend sat, wondering where his partner was.

'Can you get some water, please, Ron? We are in interview room 2.'

Nodding, he dashed off to the kitchen as she continued down the corridor to Adam Swinton, cursing herself for not connecting the dots sooner. Opening the door to the interview room, she flashed Adam a smile.

'Sorry about that, Mr Swinton. Thank you for your patience.'

'No bother,' he replied, rubbing his jawline.

McCardle placed her notepad and pen on the table that separated her and Adam, pulled out a chair and sat. She heard glasses chinking off one another outside the door, as Ronnie tried to open it with full hands. Standing, she opened it and he entered with a jug of water and three glasses. Placing the water on the table, he poured Adam a glass before taking a seat, the chair leg catching slightly on the coarse carpet tiles.

'This is retired DS Ronnie Ericson, who is now helping the team as a civilian.'

Ericson smiled and Adam nodded as his legs bounced.

'Can you tell us what has happened, Adam?'

Ericson turned to a blank page in his notepad, ready to make notes as Adam's brow furrowed in frantic concern.

'So, my girlfriend, Emily Robinson.'

'The author?' McCardle clarified.

Ericson glanced up. He actually knew Emily's work. She

wrote crime books, and most of the time, she got the police procedural side pretty spot-on from the few he had read.

Adam nodded. 'Yes. She had some sort of event or meeting or something early yesterday evening. She's always out and about with her work but we had planned to possibly see each other, depending on the time she finished.' He pulled a hand over his mouth. 'It's an early relationship, you know and the plans weren't definite. But, well...' He scratched his head and took a gulp of water before placing the glass back on the white plastic-coated table. 'I didn't hear from her and sent a few texts before I went to sleep. Usually, we would text or call before bed.' Running a hand over his forehead, he exhaled deeply. 'I was shattered from work and fell asleep around eleven.' He licked his lips and swallowed.

McCardle could see the anxiety plastered on his face as he rubbed his eyebrow, thoughts bombing around his mind.

'This morning, I woke up at six and she hadn't texted or called.' He looked at them both. 'I work at Poland & Hardy's, the financial advisors, and today is meant to be my late shift, so I wasn't due in until twelve.' Adam took a breath, almost a gasp. 'I texted Emily at six, thinking she would be awake within thirty minutes. She's an early riser, writing first thing.' He smiled and Polly returned it. 'I emailed her, in case she had lost her phone. It happens, doesn't it?'

McCardle nodded. 'It does, yes.'

'Anyway, she still hadn't texted or returned the email by 8.30, so I called and her mobile was off. I racked my brain, thinking had I pissed her off? Done something wrong? We've not been together long, but we really like each other and well, we are both in our mid-thirties, so no energy for games.' He let out a sad laugh and glanced at Ronnie, who tilted his head from side to side.

'I had this sinking feeling in there.' He touched his stomach. 'So, after leaving a voicemail, I decided to drive to hers since I wasn't in work until midday. I thought if she wasn't there, I'd call her mum and friends, in case she was at someone else's house and I was panicking for nothing.' He wrung his hands together and shook his head.

'At nine, I drove to her house. Her blinds were shut, and her car wasn't there. Then I thought, is she out? But if she lost her phone, she would have emailed me, surely? We aren't in each other's pockets, but we keep in touch throughout the day.' He glanced at them both and then grabbed his scalp with his hands.

Ronnie side-eyed Polly and wondered if she thought Adam Swinton could be hiding something himself.

'I called Emily's mother and her mate, Ainsley. They hadn't heard from her either and her mother said she must be busy but she would let me know if Emily made contact. Ainsley said she would check her Facebook as I'm not on there. I kept trying to contact her until half an hour ago, when I decided to come here.' Tilting his head back, he gulped in air and let out a short yelp. 'I don't mean to come across as dramatic but it's out of character.' He pulled a hand over his mouth. 'Something feels wrong. Driving back home from hers – I live in Ashmouth – I was trying to piece things together.' He dropped his head and muttered a quiet, 'Fuck.'

'Take your time, Adam, it's okay,' Ericson said gently.

Adam's gaze rose and he smiled weakly at Ronnie. Tears filled his eyes. 'I remembered a conversation we had about five nights ago over dinner. It was after Chloe Logan was attacked in Morpeth. I'd mentioned it the day before when it was on the news because Chloe works at Poland & Hardy's on my floor.' He took a gulp of water and placed his hands on his lap. 'She's a lovely lass and we were all upset. I talked about it to Emily and she said the name sounded familiar but couldn't place where from. The next day she said that Chloe had been trolling her a little online for the last few months.'

McCardle leant forward, listening intently.

'I'd said surely not. Chloe's a nice lass, friendly and popular. Then she showed me the comments and it bloody was her. Nothing too vile but comments about her books being rubbish on Emily's Facebook page. Some a little personal, nasty, you know? And I had thought, well to be honest, there are a load of these arseholes around who spread nastiness online. It always says more about them than the person they are trolling, right? But it was nothing like the Chloe I know.'

McCardle nodded.

'Emily shrugged it off and said maybe Chloe had a crush on me, saw her as competition. It made sense, I suppose. But then she said that she also knew the journalist who had been killed in that hit and run recently. Again, I guess at the time and 'cos of her work, it wasn't a big link.' He swallowed and exhaled deeply. 'Emily knows lots of people. But she said he had asked her out on a date, flirted a bit at one of her events, and made it clear he fancied her.' Adam paused and dropped his forehead into his hands.

Ronnie pushed his glasses onto the top of his head and raised his eyebrows at Polly.

Lifting his eye line again, he continued. 'She's not one to exaggerate that type of thing or say it to make me jealous. I know Emily from school and well, I really like her.' His voice was swimming with emotion.

'Mr Swinton, we will help how we can,' Ericson said and Adam nodded.

'That journalist, Ryan, he had reviewed her latest book,

Persuasion, a few weeks before he died and he had been emailing her about upcoming events, telling her he would be going and suggesting they had a catch-up. Then he was killed. Emily had mentioned it briefly at the time and I was shocked. I'd seen it, seen you...' he glanced at McCardle 'on the news. It was sounding a bit weird, unnerving, when she mentioned it last week, after Chloe. And now, I don't know where the hell she is.' He dropped his head into his hands.

McCardle glanced at Ericson. Both knew what the other was thinking. She had already worked out the link, and Adam Swinton was bringing more to the table, including a possible abduction.

'Do you need a break, Adam? Some fresh air?' she asked as he sobbed.

He shook his head and slumped back in his seat, placing his hands on the table in front of him.

'You've done the right thing coming here, Mr Swinton,' Ronnie said, also putting his hands on the table.

'It's just all so weird and you can understand my worry, can't you? Some mad stalker could have taken her.' Inhaling, his nostrils flared slightly as he opened the top button on his pale blue shirt that had fresh sweat rings under the armpit. He glanced with desperate eyes between the two officers, who nodded in agreement.

'We understand your concern, Adam. We need to ask a few questions to ascertain more information. Is that alright?' McCardle asked.

Adam nodded and she began confirming information he had shared and asking several questions.

'Did Emily mention any other cases recently that she thought may have a link? Even in a perhaps jokey way that they might be linked?'

Adam straightened his back. 'Emily wouldn't joke about harm to people.' His voice was defensive and distressed.

'Sorry, I haven't worded that right. I don't mean making light of anyone coming to harm. I'm trying to determine if Emily perhaps had even a small inkling that other cases could be linked to her job, her writing, or anything that her books had a connection to.'

He rubbed the back of his neck. 'I don't know. Nothing that comes to mind. My head is scrambled. I just want her found, safe.'

Polly tilted her head. 'We understand. Does the name Oliver Thornton ring a bell, Adam? Did Emily mention him?'

Pressing his lips together, he shook his head slowly. 'No, I don't think so. My nephew is called Oliver, so I would have probably remembered if she mentioned that name.'

'Okay, thank you. I think we have enough information to assist us at this stage.' McCardle passed Adam one of her business cards. 'If you hear from Emily, or think of anything else, please get in touch. We have your number now and will let you know how our enquiries proceed.'

Adam began to rise slowly from the chair, reluctant to leave the place where he felt the mystery of his missing girlfriend could be solved. After seeing him out, McCardle popped her head back into the interview room, where Ericson was gathering the jug of water and glasses.

'Fresh air break?'

He nodded. 'I'll pop these in the kitchen and see you out there.'

As Ronnie entered the back yard of the police station, his colleague was sucking on a vape as if it needed mouth-to-mouth resuscitation.

'Crikey! What's in those things these days?' he chuckled, as she let out a breath.

'Not enough,' she replied, leaning back against the wall of the building. 'Shit, Ronnie, he's got her, hasn't he?'

He grimaced slightly. 'Possibly, pet. But he could also be a she. We know only too well not to make gender assumptions in this game!'

McCardle nodded. He was right, albeit men tended to make up around ninety percent of murderers in the UK. The pair stood in silence for a moment and Ronnie knew exactly what his partner was thinking. A few seconds later, she said it aloud.

'If only I would have realised sooner. Maybe she wouldn't have been taken?'

'Poll, we don't know if she has.' He tapped her forearm but her furrowed eyebrows didn't alter. 'And bloody hell, you're the only one who has come up with a probable link. How many of us have been working on these cases, some of your team for months. *You've* found the link and that's going to be the biggest lead so far.'

Her gaze dropped to the floor.

'And there are descriptions of the suspect from Logan's book club. You've seen that in the case notes this morning. We can go back to the pub Thornton visited with more of an idea, and surely we still have the CCTV footage from that night?'

She nodded weakly.

'The team have social media leads for Mortimer. They are looking at reviews. You orchestrated all this, boss.'

'But...'

'No buts, Poll. I won't have you minimising your skills. You found those leads and you've instructed the team to actions. Now, let's get inside and keep going. I'll make us a cuppa.' With that, his assertiveness softened and a smile spread across his chubby cheeks.

Looking up, she swallowed. 'Thank you.'

'Put that weapon of mass destruction away.' He pointed to her vape. 'Let's get inside.'

And off he strolled, Polly watching him for a second before following. And despite the heaviness in her stomach that made her feel like her guts were an anchor sinking into the sea bed, she was extremely grateful Ronnie Ericson was by her side.

Chapter 28

Emily woke, her head pounding. The room was almost dark, only shards of light peeping through the sides of a blackout blind against a small window – as if they shouldn't be there but boldly wanted in. *Where the hell am I?* she thought. Swallowing, she felt the inside of her mouth was dry as something stuck to her lips. She was unsure if she was dreaming, her head cloudy. She tried to part her lips and stick her tongue out but there was something over her mouth. Material? Tape? Emily wasn't sure but it was thick and she couldn't breathe through it.

Flaring her nostrils to inhale as much air as possible, she felt her shoulder throbbing and attempted to touch it. Wincing, she was unable to reach with her hand; her wrists were tied together and her arms couldn't move freely. Her head pulsated, as if it were the tarmac one hundred soldiers were marching on. As she tried to see in the dark, panic ricocheted around her mind. Moving her hip slightly, she lay, foetal position, on a sofa bed. Her hands, with what looked like a thick cable tie around her wrists, restricted her movement. Her bottom hand, unable to move more than a few centimetres, was tied to the frame of the sofa bed with a handcuff. What was going on? Was she having some unnerving nightmare?

Attempting to control her rapid breathing – that was already constrained due to her mouth being covered – Emily inhaled long, slow breaths through her nose. Scrunching her eyes several times in an attempt to wake from what she hoped was a nightmare, she let out a muffled yelp. Unable to identify her surroundings from the sprinkling of dim light coming through a tiny window, she couldn't distinguish the time of day or where the hell she was. Panic engulfed her as she began to realise it wasn't a dream. Sweat gathered on the back of her neck as her shoulder pulsated. She was feeling thirsty, her head throbbing as she tried to determine what was going on. Then the library and David Creighton flew into her mind. It couldn't be! He wouldn't do this to her, surely?

Emily felt vomit rise in her throat and grimacing, she had no choice but to swallow it back down, feeling the vile burn. Breathing deeply in and out through her nose, she retraced her steps. She had gone to the library for the interview with David, who had told her that the write-up would go in a newsletter. It had been an honour to be asked. She loved the local libraries and was grateful for the support. After meeting with her editor until 5.15, she had driven straight to Crosley Library for the interview, looking forward to it. David was a polite, middle-aged man who always had a smile on his face. He had been working and helpful at all of her library events in Crosley and he had attended others locally, showing support. Emily saw the pair of them as colleagues in the world of literature.

When she arrived at the library, he had been happy to see her, welcoming her in. Just the two of them alone caused no alarm. Emily felt she knew him, trusted him. The interview was in a small, cosy room. They had chatted lots during events, and he was a kind, considerate support. She thought back to when he had intervened when Ryan Mortimer had been coming on to her a little. Her heart began to race. *Ryan. Shit!* Did the librarian have something to do with Ryan's death? Surely not. Shaking her head, she instantly regretted it, with the throb of a bowling ball banging around in it.

Emily closed her eyes and tried to focus. David had been a little odd, intense. But he took his job and books seriously. He had made a few comments. She was used to compliments about her work or her appearance. She'd thanked him but they had continued through the interview, including references to them making a good team.

Letting out a groan, she pulled her knees into her chest as much as she could. Her ankles were tied together with the same offensive contraption her wrists were, and locked to the sofa bed frame. Her feet were still in her thick black tights and she wore her floral dress. For a moment, Emily felt relief that she didn't think, or more, she didn't feel, that David had sexually assaulted her. Two tears fell and she tried to scream. Only a muffled, low noise came out of her mouth, trapped in the thick, sticky silencer.

Scrunching her eyes again, she attempted to go back to the library and the chain of events in her mind. They'd had good conversations about her books and future plans, despite some slightly awkward flirty comments coming from the librarian. She had been diplomatic, kind, changing the subject subtly and ensuring she used language and thanks aimed at the whole library team, which included David, but was not directed at him alone. He likely had a crush on her, that was fine. Sometimes, people were in awe of an achievement. It wasn't always even a sexual thing. It could be admiration, a role model. And if people were attracted to her, well as long as she didn't lead anyone on and no party were unpleasant, that was manageable.

They had come to the end of the interview and he had explained to her what would happen with the newsletter before they got ready to leave. David had mentioned going for dinner, for the second time and she had felt awkward, easing the rejection by suggesting a meal with the whole of the Crosley Library team. He'd referred to just the two of them again, and Emily had kept quiet, a half-smile on her face, unsure what to say to get the message across.

The librarian had gone to the kitchen and she had felt relieved and a little embarrassed by his crush. David was attractive in a way, but she had never and would never see him as more than a colleague. Plus, she had Adam. Thinking of Adam, she began to cry. He could be wondering where she was, although Emily had no idea how long she had been tied to the sofa bed. She hadn't soiled herself and wasn't desperate for the toilet, so she estimated that it hadn't been more than ten hours.

The pair had left the library through the back door and he had mentioned having a gift for her in his car. An image of the red roses flashed in her mind and she instinctively smiled at the flowers, only to yelp and realise they were likely a trick to get her to follow him. *Shit!* He had told her he wanted to be with her. Had he said he loved her? Emily wasn't sure, but the words were rattling around her mind.

She had turned to leave. Thanking him for the flowers but wanting out of the situation and away from him. It had become awkward and there was a creepiness about the librarian that felt unnerving. *Christ, it was fucking unnerving.* Emily swallowed then released a whimper. He had pulled her arm. She couldn't reach it but felt a tenderness to the skin on her neck. The monster had injected her with something. It had knocked her out and he had tied her up here in his house or wherever the hell she was.

Shuddering, she was cold and desperately needed some water. Not being able to see much in the room made it worse and her heart almost stopped beating for a moment. What if he was in there with her, watching from the darkness? Silent, like an assassin? Keeping as still as possible, Emily listened for a minute. She couldn't hear anything – just her own heartbeat and thoughts screaming in her ears. Certain she was alone, Emily sobbed and sobbed until she eventually fell into uncomfortable slumber.

Chapter 29

David sat on his tatty leather sofa, staring at Emily's switched-off mobile phone that lay on his coffee table. His hands were red and sore from lifting and moving her, then tightening the restraints around her hands and feet. He'd not slept all night. Adrenaline, sadness, fear, determination, and guilt were all blaring inside him, competing to be the loudest. It had gone wrong and he had implemented plan B, something he hadn't wanted to do but had proven necessary.

Love had rendered him unable to control his actions. His pursuit of Emily had become a beast of its own, dictating, controlling, and driving him. David was no longer behind the wheel, instead a passenger, sometimes willing, sometimes not so much. And now he would have to deal with the aftermath of what he had done. *It isn't too late for her to see?* For Emily to change her mind and for them to be together? Maybe she would realise the lengths he had gone to for love?

Slamming his head into the softness of the sofa cushion, he groaned. He needed to visit the allotment and check on her. Perhaps take some red roses to make up for the ones she dropped last night. Smiling, he drifted momentarily to a place of comfort where they would be together, before reality sucker-punched him. Clenching his jaw, he closed his eyes. Last night, in the darkness, he had taken her to the allotment. Driving as far to his plot as he could, then carrying Emily inside. She hadn't stirred – he had injected her with enough sedative to knock her out for a bit.

Gently, respectfully, he had placed her on the sofa bed and made her comfortable. Ensuring she had nothing in her coat pockets, he had left it on her. Removing her shoes, he had bound her feet and hands. Rolling her onto her side and securing her wrists and ankles to the frame of the sofa bed, David had been pleased he'd purchased a decent one and not a flimsy alternative. Thick plastic cable ties and handcuffs were used. Emily had lain on the sofa bed looking like an angel, her blonde hair spread around where her head rested, halo-like. He had smiled, mesmerised by her.

'My angel,' he had whispered, as he kissed her warm, plump lips. Sparks of arousal had travelled through him as he watched her. But David was a gentleman and there was plenty of time to move their relationship to the next stage once they could talk about their future seriously. He had cut a piece from the roll of industrial-strength masking tape, placing it over Emily's mouth as his eyes glazed over. He didn't like gagging her, but it would only be temporary until they could talk, plan their future.

'Sleep well, my love,' he had said as he turned off the small lamp and left the shed-cum-summer-house, locking it and clicking the extra padlock shut before glancing around and dashing back to his car. Arriving home, he had parked as far away as possible, reducing his noise, and crept to his flat. Inside, he had showered and made a cup of hot chocolate, taking it to bed. However, sleep wasn't forthcoming and instead, he had battled between panic and joy about his future with his beloved.

Now it was 5am, and David had been sitting on his sofa for an hour. He wasn't at work today, which was a blessing and meant he had all day to speak with Emily and get their future sorted. Hoping she would understand, he had gone to extremes last night because he loved her. Everything he had done was because he loved her and he would explain, make her see.

It was 5.45am by the time David pulled up at the allotments, having gone to the supermarket to collect some flowers. Given it was December, the place was desolate. It was a chilly morning and he hoped that she had been warm enough. With a few blankets in the shed, he should have covered her up but his mind had been racing like Pac Man when he brought her there. Now, as he approached the shed he had built with love on the space where he had some of his favourite memories with his late grandfather, David felt nervous to see Emily – as if it were their first date. But like a first date, he felt the rush of excitement for their future.

Glancing at the red roses in his hand, he smiled. Everything would work out. She would see. They would be happy together and look back on this as a misunderstanding. Inhaling, he nodded. Yes, everything would work out, he had waited long enough for his happy-ever-after. Life owed him that and now it was his time. As he walked towards his end-plot, the sky was turning blue and yellow from black, the dark curtains of the night opening. Shuddering in the chill, he reached the shed.

When building it, David had gone for the best quality, making it more than a basic shed. Of course, he didn't have the plan that had escalated last night in mind when he was constructing it, more of a sanctuary for himself. However, he was pleased that it was secure, strong, and safe from trespassers. The wooden door with a key lock entry was an old house door that had been secured to the entrance. In front of that, a padlocked metal-mesh gate.

The security was perhaps a little extreme, but other plot-owners had duplicated similar precautions after the spate of break-ins previously. David unlocked the padlock and opened the metal gate before placing his key in the lock of the door. He turned the key tentatively, nervous and excited to see his love, and hoping she was okay. Opening the wooden door, he saw the room was in almost darkness, as he had prepared. Wisps of light snuck in through the tiny shed window that was covered by a blackout blind. Once it was fully daylight, he was sure the shut blind would still provide a light for Emily to not feel frightened.

Quietly he entered the shed, quickly bolting the door on the inside and placing the keys in his jeans pocket. He swung around to see her lying on the sofa bed, foetal position, her back to him. She seemed to be asleep. The room was cold and he felt a stabbing of guilt for not covering her in the blankets. Moving closer, he was as silent as possible. A floorboard under the lino and rug creaked slightly and Emily turned her head as much as her body allowed. Even in the dim light, he could see terror in the watery glint of her eyes. She started making muffled noises, eyes wide, a frown on her pretty face as hair fell across her forehead.

'Shhh, it's okay,' David said as if talking to a child who had woken from a nightmare. He switched on a lamp by the sink, her eyes following his every move. 'I've brought you some flowers.' He held them out, smiling, before he turned and walked to the sink area. Grabbing a jug from a shelf, he filled it with water, placing the roses inside, still in their wrapper. He put the jug on a side table and clasped his hands together. 'There you go. Beautiful red roses for my Emily. To make up for last night.'

The look in her eyes unnerved him. He didn't want his beloved to be frightened of him and he needed her to see his actions were for *her*. For *them*. She began making noises again.

'It's okay, calm down,' David said quietly as he took a plastic glass from the cupboard below the sink and turned on the tap, filling the vessel. She watched, silently, as he placed it on a side table and moved towards her. She began the muffled noises again, fretting under the thick tape silencer that clung to her mouth.

'Shhh, it's okay,' he repeated. David moved closer to the sofa bed where she lay. Leaning over her, he pushed his neck out. 'I'm going to take the tape off your mouth, Emily. Do you promise not to scream?' *Not that anyone is around to hear her,* he thought as he looked at his beauty.

She nodded frantically, eyes intense on him. *Even now, she still looks beautiful,* thought David as he glared at her, his body still.

'This might hurt a little. I'm sorry,' he said, voice gentle, filled with concern, as he slowly removed the tape from her mouth.

Wincing, she scrunched her eyes for a second as the tape began to lift. Fine hairs around her mouth ripped out and her dry lips felt as if they might split open.

'Don't scream,' he said, leaning further forward.

She nodded again, gasping, and he moved the plastic glass of water to her lips. Emily greedily gulped it in one go.

'Dav-David,' she began, tears welling in her eyes. 'Wh-what are you do-doing?' she stammered before licking the skin around her sore mouth. 'This, it-it must be a mistake?' She tilted her head, her green eyes focused on him.

He swallowed. Why hadn't she just done what he wanted her to? Why had she fucked it all up? After everything he had done for her. He felt a crash of anger and clenched his fists.

'Emily, I'm sorry. You left me with no choice.' He spoke assertively, stepping back and taking a seat in the brown armchair opposite where she lay.

Shaking her head slightly, she looked at him with pleading eyes. 'I don't understand.'

Rising from the armchair, he put his hands to the back of his head. 'Us, Emily, us!' His gaze fixed on her, before he began pacing, feeling frustration marching inside of him. 'I've loved you from afar for so long and it was my time. *Our* time. And you ruined it. You gave me no choice.' He slowly pulled a hand over his mouth and chin. Looking her straight in the eyes he was silent for a moment. Staring, unblinking, he spoke again. 'And now, you have to do as I say, or more people will get hurt.'

Chapter 30

McCardle and Ericson sat side by side looking at the notepad, digesting the interview with Adam Swinton. Two untouched cups of tea sat on coasters, growing cool as the pair re-read the notes Ronnie had made in interview room 2. Polly looked around at her small team, all working away on actions allocated only a few hours ago.

'Keep them here, will you. I'm going to call DI Richardson, get the green light to liaise with DS Munro and get the team out to re-interview and corroborate statements from the book club members. And we need to get to the library.'

As she rose from her chair, he nodded. She looked pale, eyes heavy. It was a look and feeling Ericson had worn often over his years in the force. She walked to the privacy of the briefing room, mobile phone in hand. Ending the call with DI Richardson ten minutes later, Polly groaned and glanced at the incident board, which was not yet updated with her early-morning hunches that she had shared with the team. Now, she had more evidence and time was critical. Having been given the green light by her superior, she needed to update DS Munro from the Morpeth Neighbourhood Team, then share new priorities with her colleagues.

He answered after three rings. 'DS McCardle, how are you?'

'Yeah, good thanks, DS Munro. You?'

'Not bad for a Tuesday afternoon,' he said, chuckling afterwards.

'I'm calling about the Logan case. I've got some possible leads and further potential victims.'

Munro listened intently as McCardle explained the new

information and possible link between recent crimes, before asking questions and commenting he had colleagues available to assist that day.

'Bloody good work, Polly,' he said as she paced the room.

She was beating herself up for not seeing it earlier, and now another person was at risk. She wouldn't see anything as good work until the perpetrator was caught, Chloe Logan came out of her coma, and Emily Robinson was found safe and well. However, McCardle appreciated the support from DS Munro, whilst the weight of responsibility covered her like snow falling off a roof.

Ending the call with the promise from Munro of two officers heading over in the next hour, Polly closed her eyes, took a deep breath and opened the incident room door.

'Team, emergency briefing, please.'

Her colleagues followed instruction and gathered in the room. McCardle gestured to a seat next to her for Ericson, who obediently sat. Sighing, she glanced once more at the notepads and began talking.

'A critical update from the discussions and actions this morning, team. Ronnie and I have just interviewed a local man, Adam Swinton. He is a colleague of Chloe Logan at the accountancy firm where they work. He is also the partner of local author, Emily Robinson. He came into the station to report her as possibly missing.'

DC Birdy ran a hand over his bald head, eyes wide.

'Fuck,' DC Lucas said.

'Fuck indeed, Lucas,' she replied. 'Emily Robinson could be our fourth victim. A serial killer on our hands.'

Boyd rubbed her mouth and leant forward.

Inhaling, McCardle clicked her pen. 'We need to get to the book club members and re-interview them. CSI have an e-fit for the possible suspect. I've contacted them for an update and image as priority. DS Munro is sending over a few officers who have already spoken to the book club members. Ericson has met two of them, but they require speaking to again as soon as possible, in case of any further information.' She looked at each officer on her small team. 'We need to establish Emily's movements yesterday. Her partner said she had a meeting or event but didn't know the details. However, she had been with her editor beforehand. Adam Swinton has been instructed to update us with any news. And we need officers to visit Poland & Hardy's.'

The team made notes and nodded.

'Lucas, Birdy, if you can pass the social media work on to the analysts to continue with when we are all out interviewing witnesses, please. DI Richardson has authorised it as a priority, so they can pause other case work.'

'Understood, boss,' Lucas replied.

'Okay, thanks. Anything to add, Ericson?' McCardle glanced to her left where he sat.

He shook his head. 'I think you've covered it, boss.'

She rubbed her hands together. 'Let's get going.'

The team left, all clear on next steps. Officers would contact the North East Crime Addicts book club members whilst they waited for the imminent arrival of their colleagues. Any of the members available there and now would be visited by Ronnie, who was familiar with the case, and another officer, until the Morpeth team arrived. Others would go to the accountancy firm where Chloe Logan and Adam Swinton worked, to speak to Chloe's colleagues and try to identify possible links, as well as visiting Crosley Library.

Returning to her desk with a robust plan, Polly began to feel more in control. She searched Google for Emily Robinson's publisher and after reading two articles, the third online link provided the information she needed. They would be able to give the details of her editor, and hopefully that would lead to information on Emily's schedule yesterday. Writing the number of Mellor Publishing Limited on a piece of paper, she then called it from her mobile. After a few rings a pleasant voice answered.

'Mellor Publishing Limited. Emma speaking. How may I help?'

'Hi, Emma. My name is Detective Sergeant Polly McCardle. I'm calling from Northumbria Police Headquarters, Crosley.'

'Oh, hello,' she said quickly.

'I'm wondering if you can help me. I need the contact details for Emily Robinson's editor, please?'

'Erm. Is everything okay?'

'I'm not at liberty to discuss that, I'm afraid. I will give you the number of Crosley Police Station. If you can please source Miss Robinson's editor's contact number and ring the station, asking to be put through to me – just so you can be reassured I'm who I say I am,' McCardle said clearly.

'Okay. Sorry, what was your name again?'

'Detective Sergeant Polly McCardle.'

There was quiet and she assumed the receptionist was jotting her name down before Polly gave her the number for the front desk at headquarters. Ten minutes later, McCardle's desk phone rang.

'Hello, DS McCardle.'

'Hi, Detective Sergeant. I have Emma Minazza from Mellor Publishing on the phone.'

'Thanks. Put her through.'

After she'd been provided with details for Emily Robinson's editor, McCardle ended the call and rang the number given.

There was no answer and she was directed to voicemail, leaving a message requesting the editor ring Crosley Station. People naturally thought the worst when they received a message from the police and she didn't like to inflict that on someone, but needs must, and all Polly could think about was that with a missing person, the first forty-eight hours were critical. They had to find Emily Robinson before it was too late.

Boyd and Ericson were heading to Sonja Charters' residence, one of the North East Book Addicts' homes. Boyd drove, Ronnie sitting in the passenger seat.

'How's the bairns, Claire?'

'Expensive!' she said, laughing.

He nodded. 'Tell me about it. Our Kelsie is still costing us a fortune and she's lived away from home for almost three years.' He chuckled, a smile remaining on his face afterwards, as he proudly thought of his daughter.

'Do you worry, pet? About the world they are growing up in? Your two, they must only be eight? Ten?'

Boyd kept her eyes on the road. 'Seven and nine, both going on eighteen. And yeah, I do, boss. It's not like when I was a kid. Of course, things get better. But Christ, so much is worse.' She shook her head. 'Kids are killing kids these days, Ronnie, and it's as if it's not a shock anymore, it happens so often.'

He placed a hand on his cheek. 'Sadly, you're right pet.'

'When I was young, we never heard of any of this madness. The scary, gut-wrenching tragedy that comes in, day in day out. It happened, I know that, and my dad, he was in the force.'

Ronnie nodded. He remembered Boyd's father who was a DI in Newcastle.

She continued. 'But now, it's almost expected. It sickens me and it never gets any easier,' she said.

'It's cos you care. Sadly, we exist in a society that is selfish, with many people out for themselves: criminals and law-abiders. I've seen the shift over the years. Neighbours not knowing each other anymore. People no longer talking to strangers at the bus stop. Or if they do, there is an air of wariness.'

Boyd shook her head, as the car approached a housing estate.

'Don't get me wrong, there are still kind folk, but...' He shrugged. 'So, keep that empathy, pet. Your dad always had bucket-loads of it.'

'Thanks, Ronnie. You're a wise old copper.' She laughed.

'Less of the old, you cheeky bugger.' Ronnie chuckled back.

There was a beep to Boyd's mobile phone. 'Check that, will you, boss?'

He took her mobile from the car phone holder. Tapping in the passcode she gave, he opened the email. It was from McCardle and contained the photo e-fit from CSI.

'Suspect e-fit.' His gaze remained on the screen. 'Looks very average, no real distinguishing features. Good timing for the interview, though.' His eyes rose. 'It's the next left, then left again.' He scanned his notepad. 'Number 34.'

Pulling up, the officers got out of the car and Boyd looked at the suspect e-fit before the pair walked down the driveway to Sonja Charters' semi-detached house. Knocking on the door, Ronnie glanced back up the drive to a ginger cat, strolling by like it owned the street. The door was opened by a middle-aged woman, a smile flashing on her face.

Recognising Ericson, she spoke. 'Hello again. Come on in.' Sonja moved to the left, inviting the officers in.

'Hello again, Mrs Charters,' he said as they walked in and wiped their feet on the grey hallway runner.

'Thanks. I'm DC Claire Boyd and you've met my colleague, Ronnie Ericson.' Boyd flashed her identity card.

The three sat in her lounge. 'I take it the police haven't found Andy yet?' She looked at Ronnie.

Following the interviews last week, all members of the North East Book Addicts had been spoken to, apart from the new member, a man calling himself Andy Palmer, the main suspect.

'No, Sonja, we haven't been able to trace him and that's why we're here today, to gather any more information you may have and ask further questions.' Boyd opened the email from McCardle, containing the photo of the suspect. 'You gave a description of the man, Andy Palmer, from the book club to the police last week. I know the officers did the e-fit with you there and then. Can you confirm still that the man calling himself Andy looked like this?' Boyd passed the phone to Sonja, the photo of the suspect filling the screen.

She looked at it for a few seconds, focusing on the image. 'Yes, that's him. That's how I remember him. Like I said last week,' her eyes moved to Ronnie, 'I thought it a bit strange he kept his baseball cap on. I know the young 'uns would wear them indoors. But older people, middle-aged men like him. Maybe it's my old-fashioned thinking. Now I believe he did it to disguise himself. Else why hasn't he come forward?'

She was right and the man calling himself Andy Palmer was the number one suspect. After ten more minutes, Boyd and Ericson thanked Sonja for her time and left, with confirmation that the e-fit was still a strong resemblance and a request for Mrs Charters to get in touch, if she thought of anything else that might be useful. However, Chloe Logan was still in a coma, and as the only current living victim that they knew of, she was their most precious lead.

Chapter 31

Pouring boiling water over noodles, David glanced back at Emily. She was watching his every move, with pained, startled eyes. He swallowed and stabbed a fork into the noodles. David didn't want her to be frightened; it was a terrible way to start their relationship. He wouldn't hurt her, couldn't hurt her. She just had to see, understand, then they could have a normal relationship. Clenching his jaw, he turned with the noodles and put them on the floor by the sofa bed Emily was chained to – the plastic fork already bent from being jabbed into the hard noodles like a kid's sword into a tree.

'You need to eat and drink.' He placed a plastic beaker filled with water by the noodles. She nodded, remaining silent. 'I'm going to release one of your arms, Emily, so you can eat.' David spoke mechanically, coldly, his eyes unblinking on her. She nodded again.

Taking a Stanley knife, he cut through the thick cable tie connecting Emily's wrist as she winced, worried the knife would penetrate her skin. Once her wrists were separated, she rubbed her freed wrist as much as possible with her other wrist handcuffed to the frame of the sofa bed.

'David, you can't keep me like this,' she said slowly, softly, looking at him with watery eyes.

'Eat your food, Emily.' His eyes darted to the floor then back to her.

Sitting up, she moved as much as the restraints allowed, reaching for the carton of noodles. Resting them on the sofa bed against her chest, she carefully used her free hand to eat.

Gazing off, he spoke. 'You're safe here. There's no one

around. No one visits this time of year and you left me with no choice.' Sitting in the brown armchair, he wrung his hands together before grabbing the material of his grey sweatshirt. 'Why did you have to spoil everything?' His voice cracked as his gaze turned down towards his lap.

Emily swallowed the noodles quickly. Despite having zero appetite, she knew she had to eat and try to keep her strength up. There were no clues as to what might happen whilst she was a prisoner of this unhinged madman. Eating the curry-flavoured carbs, she was utterly perplexed about everything that had spouted from the librarian's mouth. All she could think about were his chilling words, 'Do as I say, or more people will get hurt.'

One thing was for sure, she wouldn't give up without a fight, and this maniac – who could have committed the most heinous crimes – wouldn't get away with it. Returning the empty carton to the floor, Emily reached for the water and gulped it down in one, wary that he could take them away at any time. He was unpredictable and disturbed. She almost chuckled at how absolutely insane the situation was. This seemingly quiet, hard-working, supportive librarian who had flipped into an obsessed psychopath. Then Emily chastised herself. David Creighton was exactly what a psychopath was like. Someone who blended in, a no one in many ways. A person who hid in the shadows of others, viewing their success from the darkness. Career, love, family, happiness. Somewhere along the lines, he had lost these things, or perhaps never experienced them. And instead, ironically just like some of the characters in her own books, he had decided to take what he wanted, and taken it by force.

Watching him, head down, almost in a trance, Emily had to think quickly. She needed to approach this as the hostage she was but also as someone who she knew David Creighton had an unhealthy obsession with. A lust, love, desire, infatuation. She needed to keep safe and away from his touch. Shuddering, she thought of what he might do to her. What this monster in disguise could do, had done. He had potentially already gone to horrendous extremes to get to her. 'Do as I say, or more people will get hurt.' The words echoed in her ears.

Emily swallowed and her teeth began chattering. She breathed deeply, needing to take control. Christ, she wrote about these types of scenes, it could be straight from one of her books. Grimacing at the irony, she glanced to the red roses plonked in a jug.

'David,' she said quietly.

His eyes lifted and he smiled like he did as she entered the library the evening before. Emily was terrified, her body felt like it was being pulled by the tide as she tried to control her breathing and racing heartbeat.

'David, talk to me. Tell me how we got to this?' Her eyes softened on him. Tilting her head, she forced a smile. If she could get him to talk, try to reassure him, maybe she would get out of here safe. Alive. Just maybe.

Sitting back in the armchair, David crossed one foot over the other, immaculate white trainers almost shining in the dimly lit room. Emily had no idea of time but the room was lighter, streaks coming through the gaps in the blind. Given it was early December, she predicted it was at least 8am.

'I've cared for you for so long, Emily.'

She immediately winced at his choice of words.

'Patiently, I've waited for you. Supporting you. Advocating you. Waiting. Waiting. Waiting.' He shook his head, as if disappointed with a train delay.

'But we were friends, surely?' She tried to control the nerves in her voice and used her energy to retain eye contact with her captor.

Nodding, he continued. 'We were friends. I supported you, encouraged you, adored your books and you. But I loved you from the start, Emily.' Sighing, he ran a hand over his jaw. 'And as my love grew, I knew…' He flared his nostrils, looking away momentarily towards the small kitchen area. 'Emily, you began to feel it too. Our connection. The way you smiled at me. The way you touched your hair.' He closed his eyes, pressing his lips together. 'The way you spoke to me. You felt it. You fucking felt it. I know you did.'

Slamming his fists into the arms of the brown chair, he jumped up, stepping onto a grey rug and moved towards her, as she tried to shrink herself, cowering on the sofa bed. Pulling his hands over his face, David let out a strange laugh.

'I did it all for you. All of it. I protected you from the trolls and bastards like Ryan Mortimer.' He tutted then snarled.

Emily swallowed, confusion swimming against the tide in her mind. She knew so little about David Creighton and this seemed preposterous. What did he mean, Ryan Mortimer? She inhaled rapidly through her nose, desperate for air and feeling certain she would faint. *God, had he fucking killed Ryan?* The harmless journalist who was all banter, but had a good heart.

The night of an event at Crosley Library flashed into her head. David had snapped, thinking Ryan was trying it on with her. That he was flirting a bit too much and perhaps harassing her. The librarian had been protective, if a little too assertive and out of character. And Ryan had reacted in a cheeky, childish manner. A 'whose balls are bigger' moment. Had that been the point where David Creighton decided he would kill him?

Her whole body shook. Watching this monster tower over her as he kept her captive was like something out of one of her books. But this time, Emily had no idea of the plot that had got her to this point and no idea how it would end.

Staring at her as he stood, he began speaking again. 'And you still didn't choose me. You picked him. Adam fucking Swinton. After everything I've done for you.'

Standing over her, there was a blackness in his eyes. A vacancy, a void that unnerved her more than any horror film ever could. She was shaking, her body feeling it was melting into the uncomfortable foam that held her.

'I-I'm so-sorry, David,' she stammered, looking up to her captor who felt like a giant beast looming over her.

His eyes turned towards the low ceiling and he exhaled, running a hand through his brown hair. 'I know you're sorry, Emily. I believe you because I know who you are. What you stand for.' Smiling, he continued. 'We are actually very alike and that's why we would be perfect as husband and wife.' Stepping back again, he returned to the brown armchair.

Emily tensed her jaw as she moved slightly on the firm padding of the sofa bed. *Quite alike?* This monster was delusional. *Husband and wife?* Emily had always been polite, kind, and genuinely grateful to David and the team at the library. She was absolutely certain she had in no way treated him differently to his colleagues. Never flirted with him or said anything that she believed would be open to misinterpretation. Emily felt no attraction to the librarian, and after the hell she had experienced with her ex, it had taken her years to want a man in her life again.

Adam had been an old school friend. They had reconnected when she visited his company for a new accountant. How could she have not realised that David had a crush on her? Emily swallowed, her throat feeling sore and dry. Last night she had realised, he had been forward, creepy, and she had been diplomatic. And look where she was now: tied to a fucking sofa bed with a lovesick and mind-sick man spouting nonsense to her. Worst of all, she wasn't just in a room with a man who was infatuated with her, who had tied her up and was going to do God knows what to her – Emily's prison guard was a potential murderer.

'We can change all this though.' He absentmindedly wafted a hand in the air, as if drugging and kidnapping a person then holding them captive was as easily rectified as replacing an overdone steak in a restaurant. 'We can repair this hole in our relationship and maybe it will be something we laugh about in years to come.' He grinned at her. 'Of course, Adam will have to go. I'm not anyone's bit on the side.' David chuckled a menacing laugh and then glanced at his watch. 'I have to go now, to see your future mother-in-law.'

That grin decorated his face again and Emily's heart began pounding in her ears.

'Now, I'm sorry, my love, but I'll have to cover your mouth again and tie your wrists. I can't have you screaming or trying to leave. Not that anyone would likely hear.' Shrugging, he opened the lid of a storage basket on the floor and took out the cable ties and the sticky, sweaty tape Emily had covering her mouth when she woke.

'Please, David, I'll keep quiet,' she said, voice bouncing with panic.

He shook his head, raising his eyebrows. 'Trust is earned, Emily, and you had mine, then broke it by getting with Adam. Now do as I say and things will be easier.'

Terrified, she nodded and he re-tied her free hand to her cuffed wrist before placing the oppressive thick tape across her mouth, making her nostrils flare immediately to inhale the stale air.

'See you soon, my precious love,' he said before touching

her hair and tenderly kissing the top of her head.

Emily felt her insides drop. She closed her eyes and the monster left, whistling as he went, before the door shut and locks were turned. Lying on her side, she began sobbing, worrying about what would happen to her and terrified by David's chilling statement, 'Adam will have to go.'

Chapter 32

The desk phone rang and Polly answered, accepting the external call. 'Detective Sergeant Polly McCardle speaking.'

It was Emily Robinson's editor, and after a ten-minute chat, she established that yesterday, Emily had met with her editor to discuss her next novel in her current crime series. They had met at a quiet café in Hexham and had spent around two and a half hours together. The author had been well, chatty, her usual self. The editor had left around 5pm, and Emily had stated she was going for a meeting at Crosley Library.

McCardle had called the library immediately after putting the phone down to the editor. Speaking to the deputy manager, she found there were no events last night on the event planner but she had been off for over a week, so perhaps a last-minute activity had been scheduled. With the manager on her days off, McCardle advised that she would be visiting the library in the next thirty minutes and requested the manager's attendance.

Tucking her blonde hair behind her ear, Polly puffed out air, her thoughts rocketing. She needed to get to the library. She dashed to the toilet, and returned a few minutes later to see Ericson and Boyd coming in.

'A few more possible snippets of info from one witness, boss. And they still felt the e-fit matched,' Boyd said, placing her bag on her desk.

McCardle nodded. 'Excellent. Any update from DS Munro on the other witnesses?'

'Not yet but he's asked me to visit Logan's parents then the hospital with another officer.'

'Can I borrow you, Ronnie? I need to go to the library.

There's a lead and it's pretty urgent.'

He looked at Boyd. 'I don't need you, Ron. In the nicest way, of course.'

'Aye, none taken,' joked Ronnie as he put his coat back on and followed his superior.

'Great work, Claire,' McCardle shouted over her shoulder as they walked briskly to the office exit.

In her car, the pair belted up and Polly started the engine, talking as she did. 'I rang Robinson's publishing house, Mellor Publishing. Eventually got through to the editor she had met yesterday. Turns out Emily was going for an interview of some sort at Crosley Library after their meeting.' She shook her head as Ericson began nodding, reading her mind. 'Shit, Ronnie, it's a member of the library staff, isn't it?'

He made a pfft sound. 'Pet, I think you're right.'

'The assistant manager was totally clueless after being on annual leave. I asked her to ring the manager, get her in from their day off, urgently.' She glanced at him then back to the road, indicating left at a junction and manoeuvring.

Ronnie sniffed. 'We may need back-up, Poll.'

'I know. As soon as we get an answer at the library. I'll update Richardson. He's on standby and knows we might need assistance. Armed response has been alerted that officers might be required at immediate notice.'

Pushing his back into the passenger seat, he smiled at how astute his colleague was. Of course, he knew she was brilliant. However, piecing things together and mobilising action weren't skills that most people had, even some in the force!

Five minutes later, the officers parked in a lane close to Crosley Library and walked promptly to the building. On entering the spacious library, with welcoming seats and a rainbow display of books everywhere the eye travelled, they walked to the reception desk.

'Hi, I'm DS Polly McCardle and this is my colleague, Ronnie Ericson.' Polly flashed her police ID card. 'I called earlier and spoke with the assistant manager.'

The woman nodded, 'Yes, erm, she's just in her office. I'll show you the way.' She gestured towards the back of the library and began walking, the pair following in silence.

After knocking on a door and being instructed to enter, the library worker opened the door and the officers stepped into the small room. Two women rose from their chairs and introduced themselves as the assistant manager and manager before all four sat down.

'Thanks, and thank you for coming in,' McCardle said, making eye-contact with the manager. 'This is a very sensitive visit and I need to remind you that it is confidential.' They nodded back, eyes wide.

'We are looking to speak to a man who we believe may be involved with the library. Possibly a member of staff.'

'Oh, okay. Yes, we'll help in any way we can,' the manager said, shuffling in her seat.

McCardle took her phone from her pocket and clicked on the e-fit of the suspect. 'Is this man familiar?' She passed the phone to the manager who narrowed her eyes then began nodding after a second and showed her colleague, who raised her eyebrows.

The manager cleared her throat. 'The glasses and cap skew it slightly, but, yes. That looks like David, David Creighton, who works here. He's not in today but I'm sure he would be happy to help you.'

McCardle glanced at Ronnie who was making notes. 'Can I ask, was David Creighton working yesterday and if so, what time did he leave?'

The manager nodded again. 'He was interviewing a local author last night, so he locked up afterwards. He's a key holder. A responsible, professional member of staff.'

Ronnie kept his eyes on his notepad, otherwise he was certain his expression would give away his thinking that the crackerjack librarian sounds like the male version of Annie from *Misery*. He had lost the ability to keep as neutral as he did for years in the force.

McCardle kept cooler than the North Sea. 'Thank you and who was the author David was interviewing?'

The manager smiled as if about to show a photo of her grandchildren. 'It was the brilliant Emily Robinson.'

'Okay, thanks. We are going to need your CCTV footage from last night and can you give me a copy of David Creighton's work photo ID, home address, and phone number, please?'

Touching her lips momentarily, as if she had said something she shouldn't have, the manager swallowed. 'Erm, yes, of course. I'll get them now.' She glanced at her colleague who seemed equally baffled, before clicking her laptop several times.

'Is there a private room I can use to make a call?'

The assistant manager said a shaky yes, directing Polly to the staff room.

'I'll not be a moment.' McCardle excused herself, rising from the chair and nodding to Ericson. Entering the staff room, she puffed out air before calling CI Richardson and updating him on the case progress.

'Okay. Armed response is on alert, DS McCardle. Once you have the address, instruct them for back-up. The suspect may have killed several people and could have weapons.'

Polly replied, advising her superior she would follow instructions. Her body charged, as adrenaline soared through her. *This could be it.* Saying goodbye to Richardson, she returned to retrieve Creighton's contact details and photograph from his work ID. Ronnie passed the information to Polly, who looked at the photo of David Creighton – an ordinary middle-aged man – as her colleague thanked the shell-shocked library managers.

'He's due in work tomorrow, if he's not at home,' the manager said.

'We will be hoping to speak with him today. But if we can't, we have your details and will let you know. If we don't trace David Creighton today, we will need you to call us immediately when he arrives on shift tomorrow, discreetly, keeping everything confidential.' Ronnie looked over his glasses slightly and the two managers who were clearly unnerved by the last twenty minutes.

'Absolutely. We understand.' The manager glanced at her colleague who echoed her comprehension.

Thanking the library staff, the officers left in silence before exiting the library.

'Bloody hell! Richardson authorised a home visit with back-up?' he asked as they walked to Polly's car.

'Yeah, I'll ring armed response once we are in the car.'

'One step closer to catching the bastard, pet,' he said, giving a wink.

After a phone call to their expectant colleagues, the officers agreed to meet at Creighton's property in twenty minutes. As the pair were in an unmarked car and not in uniform, they would go to the address and wait for armed back-up. Polly began driving to David Creighton's property, around ten minutes' drive away.

'Just like old times,' Ronnie said.

Glancing at him, she saw a glint in his eye, partly the

excitement of getting closer to solving a crime but with a little sadness of longing. Identity was what made us, regardless of what that identity might be. Whether it be DS, teacher, shopkeeper, child, or parent. Ronnie had lost part of his when he retired from the force. And Polly couldn't help but think that if his hand hadn't been slightly forced by the need to revive his marriage, he would have a different look in his eyes.

Being back on the team had given him an energy that she hadn't seen in the year since he had retired. Sure, he had a lightness in his face, a stress that dissolved when Ronnie Ericson became responsible for cakes and pastries rather than the whole community of Crosley and beyond. But there was that curiosity in his eyes, an eagerness to always talk about the force, to know what was happening and offer advice. And his advice was the best in the business, despite many being in a higher command than DS Ericson had been.

As the pair drove, silent in their own thoughts, Polly wasn't thinking about David Creighton and what lay ahead at his property. She was thinking of her own identity and how much she loved working with Ronnie again. Pulling up at a block of flats, she looked at her sat nav.

'This is it, one in that block.'

Their eyes travelled to a 1960s block of flats. At around fifteen storeys high, the structure resembled a giant, less enticing mint humbug with its thick beige and cream vertical stripes covering the accommodation. The tired tower loomed over the car park, where they remained in their vehicle.

'What number is the suspect's?'

McCardle kept her gaze on the accommodation as Ronnie glanced at his notepad. 'Number 67.'

Both sets of eyes turned up before Polly checked her watch. She radioed in to Crosley Neighbourhood Team advising of their whereabouts and reiterating the flat number. As she tapped her mouth, Ronnie lifted his glasses onto his head and wiped his thumb and forefinger down his nose. They turned to one another.

'You're thinking the same, aren't you?' McCardle said, tucking hair behind her ear.

He nodded. 'She won't be in there. Well, unless he's kept her unconscious or she's dead.'

'Too many people, witnesses.' She shook her head before picking off a fallen hair that lay on her blue jumper. 'He could be in there though. Unhinged prick.'

Ronnie snorted. 'Aye, he is that. I mean, he could be innocent.'

She raised an eyebrow.

'But my gut…' he tapped his stomach, 'tells me he ain't.'

'Likewise,' she replied, glancing out the window to see two panda cars and a van approaching in the distance.

A minute later, they pulled up near to her car, hidden enough from view of the flat windows. McCardle and Ericson left their vehicle and walked to their colleagues. The details were finalised and every officer knew their role and was armed.

'Let's go get our suspect,' she said, as they began walking in the direction of Creighton's flat.

The police team took the stairs of the flats to the sixth floor, where Creighton lived. Armed officers would go in front of and behind McCardle and Ericson, ensuring that they were protected, like a herd of elephants shielding their young. An armed officer waited at the rear exit to the block of flats, another to the front. Their colleagues silently travelled up the concrete staircase that stank of piss and bins, using hand and head gestures to communicate. It was another language, developed over years of police operations to protect one another and identify risk.

Officers from armed response wore helmets and ballistic vests, carrying Glocks, and Heckler & Koch G36 rifles, along with a chainsaw to cut through the front door of the suspect's flat. The risk to life meant no messing about standing on a doorstep for ten minutes knocking gently like someone selling double glazing. Reaching the sixth floor, an officer went first, checking the landing, which was an outside walkway. Waving his arm, he indicated silently that all was okay. Unless leaving their flat or looking out of the window, the residents of the tower block would never know there was about to be a police raid. The team were well-versed in the process and were as silent as a couple with a newborn baby sleeping.

Reaching number 67, two officers with a chainsaw moved to the side, ready to use it once directed. The front door was the only entry and exit point to the flat. An officer pressed David Creighton's doorbell, whilst everyone remained silent, frozen. The door was white UPVC with no glass panel or spy hole. The resident would have the chance to answer, where officers would barge in to a hopefully, unsuspecting suspect.

After ten seconds, the officer looked at McCardle for instruction. She nodded and he rang again before lifting and dropping the letterbox twice. Again, ten or so seconds passed, before he dropped down to look through the letterbox, silently. Standing up, he shook his head indicating nothing was visible, before trying the door handle in case the UPVC door was unlocked. The handle moved slightly, but the front door was most definitely locked. He leant down again, and lifted the letterbox.

'Police! Police! Open up!'

'What's the friggin' racket?' said a voice from three flats down, as a head popped out of the front door.

The resident's eye widened as he registered the number of police officers on the landing. One of the officers towards the back ushered him back inside with an abrupt arm wave and he sloped back into his flat, locking his front door. McCardle glanced at Ericson, who nodded, before she turned to the officers with the chainsaw and indicated for them to saw through the door. It was always a last resort, but knowing that a possible serial killer could be in the property, as well as a possible victim, the need to preserve life meant it was essential.

The area around David Creighton's front door was cleared and the officers began their practised procedure, promptly breaking through the front door – freeing it for them to enter the suspect's accommodation. Moving in, two front officers shouted, 'Police!' as they aimed their weapons and looked around, protecting McCardle and Ericson behind them. As they cleared each doorway and subsequent room, the small flat was running out of hiding places for Creighton. Within a few minutes, it was obvious that he wasn't there.

'Shit!' said McCardle, looking at the officers who shared the disappointment.

'We will secure the site and remain here, ma'am,' one of them said.

'Thanks. And thank you all for your help. Better luck next time, eh?' She feigned a smile.

The officers conducted a more thorough search for clues of the whereabouts of David Creighton and Emily Robinson, seizing a laptop, a passport, and an older model iPhone, along with some notepads and items of clothing. Polly hoped they would find something amongst the belongings. His flat would be secured by the officers, who would remain on site, and another would wait at the entrance to the floor of Creighton's flat, for his return. From the photofit and information from the library, they most definitely had enough evidence to arrest and detain him for questioning. Until they located and arrested the suspect, they would keep cover on his home and pray he returned soon, for Emily Robinson's sake.

Chapter 33

Smiling as he walked past a carer, David made his way along the corridor to his mother's room. The heat was welcome after a few hours with Emily in the shed. The chill hung around, despite using the plug-in heaters. Plus, her lack of positivity and understanding had dropped the temperature to lower than the Arctic. He'd felt overwhelming frustration and desperation, and hoped the few hours away whilst he visited his mother would give his beloved time to think about his reasoning.

Things needed to be smoothed out between them for their future – the alarm would begin to ring on her whereabouts at some point. No doubt it would be that bastard Adam, but the pieces would start to come together and David would be implicated. He needed to coerce her into siding with him, understanding he did all this out of love. And if she would have just let herself feel and not worry about bloody Adam, then he would not have had to go to extremes. This was her fault and she needed to see it, take responsibility for it. Wringing his hands together, he swallowed. Yes, she'd see, he was certain.

Opening the door to his mother's room, she was sitting in her hospital-style chair. Seeing him, a smile danced across her face and he smiled back. She was recognising him less and less these days, but those flashes of her that came through were comforting. There was a stark difference between him and his mother. David was the punch bag for his late stepfather, and the tissue for the selfish tears his mother cried for the years after Keith died, to the detriment of his own life progressing. However, David never played the victim.

His mother had been weak in a relationship and weak in

grief. He had got on with it, even when it hurt to keep going, like running on a sprained ankle. His mother, on the other hand, had worn victimhood like a fluffy robe, keeping it close to her, depending on it. And David had become stronger in many ways. If he wanted something, he would get it – at all costs. As he kissed his mother on the top of her dark short hair, he felt proud of himself for going after what he wanted, what he deserved.

Two hours later, he said goodbye to her and headed back to the allotment, where he hoped Emily had reflected and changed her attitude a bit. Tutting about her ingratitude as he drove, he thought about Adam Swinton and that he wished he would have found Chloe Logan as attractive as she clearly thought she was. Then he rolled his eyes. Why would any man choose a cheap tart like her when they could have the most stunning portrait of Emily Robinson.

He swallowed, trying to push down thoughts of Chloe. She was still unconscious as far as he was aware and well, no one had come knocking for him. If she survived, she might not even remember. If she did, he would simply have to deal with that if and when. Chuckling slightly, he shrugged. He hadn't been discovered yet and everything had gone quiet in the media. Too many other crimes daily, and no police resources. The library had been told exactly that after some pissed arsehole had come in a few months back and smashed up three of the computers.

Making a hmph noise, David had reached the allotments. It was after 2pm, and as usual, the place was deserted. Getting out to unlock the entrance gates, he was excited to see Emily. He needed to be braver, bolder in expressing his feelings. Then she would understand and feel adored. He didn't have endless hours, unable to keep her there forever, and no doubt the police would sniff around at some point. Sniggering, he hoped the police would blame Emily's vile ex for her disappearance – karma for the prick. The police always looked at partners and family as suspects. Adam would also be ideal to frame, then he'd be out of the picture, no longer competition. However, there was another way that David could deal with Adam Swinton; a way of obliterating him forever.

Unlocking the padlock on the mesh gate, he then unlocked the Yale lock and opened the shed door. Emily's head jolted back and up, trying to see who was entering as light streamed in. As he shut the door, the room became dark again. David turned on the small table lamp and moved towards Emily. Her eyes were red and the bed was wet. He felt a jolt of guilt that a lady like her had soiled herself. It was his fault for not thinking about her need to go to the toilet. When he reached towards her to remove her mouth tape, she jerked back, frightened of him, and he felt the assault of rejection bulldoze into him. As he removed the tape, she yelped a little then gasped in air, as if breaking through the water's surface.

'How are you?' he said, tilting his head, eyes soft on the woman he loved.

She nodded slowly, reluctantly.

'I'm so sorry about that,' he pointed to the wet sofa bed. 'I should have asked if you needed the toilet.' David scratched his head. He took a towel from a wicker storage ottoman. 'Here, let's put this underneath.'

Emily shifted her body as much as she could with the restraints, as David placed a towel on the sofa bed, smiling awkwardly. She tried to move to feel more comfortable but her hip felt sore from being in the same position for hours. On top of that, she had wet underwear and her skin was soaked in urine.

Where was help? Surely, she had been reported as missing by now? She and Adam were always in contact, first thing in the morning and all day through to evening, when not together. There had been no disagreements, no reason for her to give him the silent treatment. And there were other ways they had communicated. Email, WhatsApp from their laptops. If he assumed her phone was broken, he would reach out another way, and still get no reply. She prayed that her abductor had arrived to let her go, to apologise and grant her her freedom. Of course, it was wishful thinking and Emily was almost certain of what he had done to poor Ryan. In cruel reality, that likely meant she was going nowhere. Tears plopped down her stinging face.

Noticing, he leant in towards here. 'C'mon, it's okay. I'm sorry, Emily, I never wanted to hurt you.' He turned around rapidly, his hands travelling to his head. 'Fuck!' he said angrily through gritted teeth. Turning back, he removed his hands from his head and held them in fists by the side of his sweatshirt, as if about to box.

Emily was frightened to speak, frightened to move. Her eyes fixed on him as she teetered on the edge of a panic attack. Moving to the sink, David turned the tap and filled the plastic beaker for her. Picking up the Stanley knife, he cut through the cable tie bonding her wrists together and handed her the water.

'Thank you,' she said, holding the mint green beaker.

He slumped into the brown armchair, eyes fixed on her. They looked sad, heavy, and for a split second, she felt sorry for him. What had happened to make the quiet librarian with a pleasant smile turn into this unhinged monster?

He brought his hands to his mouth in a prayer motion. 'Emily, I love you. I've loved you since you first came into Crosley Library twelve months ago. I've read all your books, attended your events, followed you on social media. I have even written to you under my middle name, William.' He let out a sad laugh and looked down at the grey rug his feet rested on.

'I've waited all my life for you, my dream woman. All of my forty-six years, they were preparing me to meet you.' Shaking his head, he looked at her, eyes pooling with water. 'And I thought I could reach you, get to you. That you maybe felt the same or you would, in time, realising we were meant to be. I could, I can give you it all. I would adore you, treat you like the queen you are, especially after what your bastard ex did to you.' David clenched and unclenched his fists as his vision moved, staring into a window of his mind.

Emily felt faint. The trauma she had experienced in what felt like days but in reality, she knew was less then twenty-four hours, was too much to absorb. This virtual stranger's confession of love was incomprehensible. Letter writing? And social media? She couldn't remember seeing his name, although she didn't even check it frequently. David and his team had arranged events at the library and he had attended events outside of the library, but so had many people. She had dedicated, local supporters and was genuinely grateful to all of them. It would never have occurred to her to perceive it as strange or creepy.

Taking a sip of water, she didn't know what to say to her captor but she knew she had to try. To attempt some level of negotiation, anything to potentially save her life. After all, she was convinced that the man in the room was a murderer. Shuffling slightly on the sofa bed, trying to avoid the dampness from wetting herself, she began speaking.

'David, I'm so sorry. I honestly never knew you felt like that. I'm flattered. You're a wonderful man.' He smiled, unblinking. Gawping, like he was in a trance. It made her shiver but she kept talking. 'I really had no idea. Sometimes, I'm so nervous and focused on the event, I don't pick up on things like that.

It's a weakness of mine and I'm sorry.' Emily kept her gaze on him as he leant back slightly in the armchair opposite her. Swallowing, her mouth felt dry and her voice shaky. 'You've always been such an amazing support, David, the best, in fact.'

He smiled again, his eyes widening at the compliment.

'I don't think I have ever met a library worker as helpful and kind as you. You really care about local authors and books.' She tilted her head, trying to soften him and show interest.

He nodded enthusiastically, leaning closer to her. 'Yes, I do. Books were my friends when I was younger. The library, my second home.' A sad laugh escaped his mouth. 'I'd go to the library at weekends to get out of the house, away from my stepfather. Or go after school to feel free for a little longer. My library card was one of my most prized possessions.' He made a hmph noise. 'Pretty sad for a teenage boy.'

She shook her head quickly. 'Not at all. I loved the library too. Reading took me on many adventures, to so many places.'

He clapped his hands together, his legs bouncing lightly where he sat. 'Yes, you're right. We're connected on so many levels.' He smiled at her, clasping his hands together and for a moment, Emily saw the David she had thought she knew. Polite, professional, supportive.

'When I got a job at the library, it was a dream come true. I guess like you and your writing. Getting that book deal must have been your lottery ticket. That's what I felt when I worked at Hallington Library before moving to Crosley Library.' Glancing up to the ceiling, he smiled, reminiscing. 'Being around books all day, it was bliss. And all the events, activities. Authors coming to talk and inspire. Well, it was magnificent. Then I met you and life became even better.' Gaze fixed, he stared past her. 'And here we are, at a crossroads. I just want you to see that we are meant to be. Adam, he's not the one for you. He's a poser, a player. Chloe Logan made that obvious.'

Emily felt her blood turn to ice. She frowned, terror coating her whilst she recalled comments that she had made to Adam just last week, after he mentioned the girl at work who had been assaulted and was subsequently in a coma. Chloe Logan who worked with him and had trolled Emily over the last few months. What had the psycho done to the young woman? More truth was about to emerge. Likely horrifying truth that wasn't her embellished imagination, as if writing a new book.

Almost too scared to ask, Emily knew she needed to find out if David had been involved with the attack – after all, it could determine her future, or lack of it. She would have to play dumb. Query who Chloe Logan was.

'Chloe Logan?' Emily tilted her head.

'Has lover boy not mentioned her?' he asked snarkily.

Emily shook her head slowly as if trying to recall. 'The name is familiar. Who is she, David?' She tried with all her energy to keep her voice from quivering.

He sniggered, getting up from the armchair and switching the kettle on. 'She's familiar, alright. She was leaving malicious comments on your Facebook page for months.' Spinning around from where the kettle began to boil, he saw her eyebrows rise.

Emily pressed her sore lips together then winced at the pain. She closed her eyes for a second and swallowed her fear. 'I get unpleasant comments from time to time. They aren't nice to read but not everyone is going to love my books.' She released a nervous laugh, her green, tired eyes fixed on him.

He frowned, running a hand lightly over his chest. 'But that's not okay, Emily. To say nasty things, on a public forum. It's not acceptable.' He walked to the small kitchen area where the kettle had clicked off from boiling. Back to her, he lifted his hands to the countertop and slammed them down onto the surface. 'It's not fucking acceptable.'

She retracted on the sofa bed as much as possible. Christ, had he assaulted Chloe Logan, leaving her for dead over a few bitchy comments about her books? Cold sweat covered the back of her neck. She didn't know how to handle this, handle him. Back remaining to her, David made a cup of tea in silence. After tapping the spoon on the side of the cup, he turned, that menacing smile on his face again.

'Do you want a cup of tea, Emily? Milk no sugar?'

Bile rose in her throat as the question took her back to the library and him asking if she wanted a hot drink, already knowing her preference and how she took it.

'I-I don't wa-want to need the toilet,' she stammered.

He coughed and removed his mobile phone from his pocket, manoeuvring his fingers around the screen. 'Here you go, that bitch Chloe Logan said this about the DCI Paul McCoy series, "*Well, I think they are all rubbish and she's exhausted this storyline*". I mean, how rude!' Glancing up at Emily, David tutted. 'There are many others. Bitchy, spiteful comments from the vile tart.' His lips curled as he placed his mobile phone back in his jeans pocket.

'Of course, I always defended you. I won't let anyone speak to you like that and I commented back. You even liked some of my comments.' David chuckled lightly and saw the look of confusion on her tired face. 'It wasn't under my name. It was Jen Bradley.' He chuckled again as if telling a brilliantly funny joke.

She brought her fingers to her cracked lips. *Jen Bradley?* The name wasn't familiar but there were lots of people on her writer's page and well, she didn't have the time to scan each comment, despite liking to interact with readers.

He continued. 'So, I wanted to meet this bitch who was dragging your name through the mud. I wanted to warn her, protect you, my love.' His eyes softened as he sighed, glancing at the red roses on the side table, then back to her.

She felt breathless at the thought of what the psychopath in front of her had done. In truth, she had hard skin. You had to in the industry, and she actually didn't really care too much if people didn't like her writing. A lock of her blonde hair, now matted and dirty, flopped into her face as she continued to observe her captor on his rant. Rising from his seat, he perched on the edge of the sofa bed. Touching her forehead, he gently wiped her hair from her face. Emily screamed inside, her internal alarm shrieking as she shuddered at his touch. His brow furrowed, she had angered him. He reached for her hand and she used all her strength to not react, fearful of punishment for her revulsion and fear.

'Shhh,' he said, as if soothing a baby, but there was nothing comforting about David Creighton and the words and his body language were bone-chilling. His eyes glazed over again.

'I researched the book club that she's a co-founder of. Likely another way for her to seek attention.' He sneered. 'I got the book of the month out of Crosley Library. It was a decent book, in all honesty. Nowhere near as good as yours.' David spoke the last sentence quickly, raising his hand in defence before returning it back to hers. 'When we met up, I despised her more than I thought. She was everything that's unattractive in a woman, false through and through with an ego bigger than a football field. Worst of all, she was a disrespectful little bitch.'

Emily felt faint with fear about what the maniac would say and do next. As he touched her and sat close, she could smell aftershave on him – the same one he wore at the library.

His lip curled. 'I steered the conversation to other books.

Ones they had liked or disliked. Yours came up and that gobshite began spouting nonsense again.' Shaking his head, he glared at her. 'I had to defend you. You can see that, can't you?' David leant forward, intensely staring, inches away from her. She nodded, terror rising inside of her.

Springing from the sofa bed, he began pacing. 'One of the other book club members mentioned that the tart worked with *your boyfriend!*' David sneered. 'Well, that was news to me. Can you imagine how shocked I was? How disappointed I was to hear that, my love?' He leant towards her, remaining standing. Pushing her body against the wall where the sofa bed rested, she was unsure as to whether he would lunge at her.

She licked her dry lips. 'I'm sorry, David.'

He tilted his head, accepting her answer then continued. 'Well, it was a revelation and I found out all about your man, Adam Swinton. How fucking dreamy he is and how *everyone* thinks he's great.' Plonking back into the armchair, Emily felt the storm of fear subside slightly as she watched his head shake and his legs bounce.

'We left not long after and I didn't know what to do. You have to understand, Emily. You have to understand that the news of your cheating was completely unexpected. It shook me and I felt an avalanche of emotions.' Briefly, he dropped his head into his hands.

Cheating? Emily felt that wave of sickness once more. The crazed librarian was dangerously delusional. He had proven that and she had only scratched the surface of what he had done and his capabilities. What the hell was he going to do to her?

'I was distraught, not sure what I was going to do. I asked the nasty bitch about Adam as we left.' He narrowed his gaze, his mouth straightened and he glared at her with dark, wicked eyes, as if expecting an apology. 'The smug cow made a derogatory comment and laughed at me. How fucking dare she? Not only had she insulted you, but she made me feel this big.' His nostrils flared as he pinched his forefinger and thumb together, leaving a tiny gap. He looked away. 'So, I snapped and well, she got what she deserved – just like the others did.'

Emily pressed her sore lips together trying to superglue them shut and prevent the scream from escaping. Others? She held her breath, every cell in her body turning icy cold, until she felt dizziness threatening to overcome her. Taking quick, shallow breaths, she watched the maniac a few metres away from her as he stared towards the tiny window.

He had tried to murder a young girl for making comments about Emily on social media then insulting him? It was ludicrous. More than that, it was evil and this bastard was psychopathic. Her eyes remained on him, despite his glare being elsewhere. She recalled her conversation with Adam having seen the local news article that the young woman had been attacked. Attempted murder, they were saying, and she was in a coma as family and loved ones rushed round, hoping Chloe would recover.

The evil man in front of her had caused it. And what else had he done? She thought about Ryan Mortimer. David had killed him, she was certain. But he had referred to others. As she convinced herself her hours alive were numbered, Emily was sure the shock of the truth would kill her faster than David Creighton would.

Chapter 34

David felt emotionally drained. Things were not going the way he planned, the way he had rehearsed in his mind over and over. That Emily would reveal her fond feelings for him, seeing him for the decent man he was. A man who would cherish her, and handle her with care like a jewel-encrusted necklace. For her to acknowledge that he had made sacrifices for her. To *protect* her. No, it wasn't going to plan and he needed to think about his next steps.

He had sat with her for a few hours. After he'd revealed what happened with Chloe, she needed time to absorb, to reflect and understand his intentions before they could plan their future. Witnessing the flickers of fear on his beloved's face had broken his heart. She needed to digest his truth and begin to see that it was for her. Instead of sharing more, he wanted to care for Emily, so he untied her, allowing her to go to the camping toilet in the corner of the room.

Both locked in the shed, he trusted she wouldn't try to escape. She hadn't screamed when her mouth was uncovered. Emily was a good girl and David hoped that she was actually enjoying his company and coming around to the idea of them. Moving her back onto the sofa bed, he had chained her again, apologising as her eyes pleaded.

'Just for now, okay?' He had smiled faintly and she had nodded meekly, like a child told it was bedtime. Leaving her hands free, he'd made her some toast and a cup of tea.

Feeling nauseous from a cocktail of fear, shock, and discomfort, Emily ate the food knowing she would need her strength. Nibbling on the toast, sickness coated her stomach as she questioned how this would end. As her captor sat watching her, she wondered what was going through his sick head. Surely he knew that people would be looking for her? Tracing her steps? Crosley Library had CCTV. And although he'd led her to the back lane to attack her, surely the cameras would have seen them leaving the rear exit of the library? She prayed help was on the way.

It must have been after 5pm, as the light had stopped seeping through the cracks in the blind at the small window. Only the low lamp offered eerie shadows of her prison and prison guard. Emily watched him bite his fingernail, wondering what was going on in his sick mind. She didn't know how to act, what to say – even though her art had ironically become life. Knowing in hostage situations that the captured is meant to try to build a relationship, show an interest in the captor – this was easy enough to say when you weren't tied to a bed in a shed somewhere hearing confessions of murder. However, she had to do something, and working out his moves and showing interest in him might work.

Clearing her throat, she spoke. 'So, are you back at work tomorrow?' She feigned a smile.

Nodding, he replied. 'Yes. But I'll call in sick and come and see you instead. We have things to discuss, things to work on for our relationship.'

He rose from the chair and approached her. Emily's legs began shaking and she hoped he wouldn't notice. His gaze was fixed on her. Bending down, David grabbed her hand, again. She flinched, involuntarily and scorn spread across his face.

'Sorry, sorry, I-I'm cold.'

He sniffed up. 'I'll get you another blanket.'

David sat holding her hand, gazing into her green eyes that felt like burning coal from lack of sleep, crying, and straining in the dark of the lair she was trapped in.

'We'll get through this, my love. I promise. Everything will work out and we will have our happy-ever-after.' As he leant over her, Emily's world paused with fear before he kissed her cheek, then rose to get another blanket. David reached for the tape, before applying the thick silencer across her mouth, his eyes unblinking. He kissed the top of her head then stoked her blonde hair.

'I love you, Emily. I'll be back soon.'

Then he walked towards the door, unlocked it and left, leaving her in her dark prison once more.

Deciding he would spend the following day with Emily rather than go into work, David wanted to go home and gather some belongings. He should have done it early that morning when he couldn't sleep. Instead, he was angry with himself for wasting time and being lackadaisical. Taking Emily had left a trail that would have the police sniffing around soon, if not already, eventually leading to him – he had to act fast. After going home to collect some belongings, he would go to the supermarket for supplies, including a blow-up mattress, and would return to the shed, so they could be together.

No one knew about the allotment. Well, that wasn't strictly true. Obviously, his mother knew but she was an unreliable witness, if ever he saw one. Colleagues at Crosley Library knew, but they weren't aware of where the allotment was based, and in Northumberland, given the vast rural landscape, it would take a while to find – that's if they even remembered he had an allotment or took any notice. They were always so busy consumed with their own mundane lives.

Rolling his eyes, David got into his car and started the engine. When he needed a shower, he would simply go to his mother's. Like the allotment, no one was aware of the care home she was in. It would be safe. All would work out fine. He just had to batten down the hatches, literally, and wait until the enemy had gone. In the meantime, he would get Emily to forgive him, to understand. And in time, she would fall in love with him. Pulling his shoulders to his neck, he smiled at the thought of their future as he began the journey to his flat.

Driving, he contemplated his plan of action. It was raining and the winter darkness and precipitation made it feel later than the 6.20pm it was. On top of that, David was exhausted from lack of sleep and anxiety. He yawned, thinking he would make the shed cosy, romantic for the lovers. Perhaps they could even share a bottle of wine. Satisfied, he smiled as he pulled into the estate where the tower block of flats was situated.

Slowly, he turned into the car park. It wasn't well lit but something reflective caught his eye. He kept driving, not slowing down nor speeding up, just observing. There it was, slightly obscured by a car in front, but unmistakably a police vehicle. With no lights on, he was unsure as to whether anyone was in the car. However, the fizzing in his stomach told him they weren't there checking for graffiti. Without speeding up and trying to look like a regular driver, David began to turn his vehicle to head back out of the residents' car park. The lights on the police car illuminated, its engine starting. Panic soaked him and he put his foot down on the accelerator.

'Fuck!' he shouted, looking in the rear-view mirrors as the police car started following him. Pressing his foot further down to the floor, he increased his speed and exited the car park, travelling along the way he came and thinking about how he would shake off the law enforcement tailing him. The siren from the police vehicle began blaring and David gripped the steering wheel of his Ford Focus, accelerating to double the limit in the residential area. He had never so much as received a speeding fine or points on his licence, but now the chase was on, and as the net around him got smaller, he had to get away, for him and Emily. Passing cars, he overtook as horns tooted and the shrill siren filled the air.

'Fuck! Fuck! Fuck!' he screamed, holding on tight to the steering wheel as his speed increased. Swallowing, he let out a yelp as sweat gathered at the base of his spine. Moving onto a dual carriage-way, he sped past vehicles, weaving in and out like a skilled getaway driver. He let out a chuckle, certain he would get away as the police car got smaller in his rear-view vision.

No one could stop him and Emily being together. No one and nothing. He released a menacing laugh and blinked, staring out of the rain-soaked windscreen. There was a lorry in front and he tooted like crazy, trying to get it to move, but it wouldn't. Instead, he boosted the wipers to clear his vision and took a chance, overtaking on the dark road, desperate to put distance between him and the law chasing him.

Only the lorry was longer than David predicted and after two seconds, he saw headlights coming towards him. On full-beam, they were blinding him and he couldn't see his route of travel. Squinting his eyes to try to focus, he swerved, attempting to make space on the road. Then he felt an intense force pushing the vehicle he was cocooned in and the car felt like it was flying, not touching the tarmacked road beneath its wheels. Floating in almost slow motion to a place he didn't know and couldn't see due to the blare of full beams and the large droplets of water that gathered on his windscreen like blobs of cream on a cake. And for a moment the horror turned to a grin on David's face, until everything went dark and still.

Chapter 35

After spending a few hours going through the items collected at David Creighton's home with CSI Manager Malcolm and the analysts, Polly had been home fifteen minutes. Creighton's laptop had shown activity under a pseudonym, Jen Bradley, which had correlated with one of the names shortlisted from social media being investigated by DC Birdy and DC Lucas.

Jen Bradley had been posting on Robinson's Facebook page and had defended her against comments that appeared slightly critical right through to trolling, including some unpleasant posts from Chloe Logan. Officers were working through the comments as evidence, along with posts on the *Northumberland Herald's* Facebook page and Ryan Mortimer's page. Boyd and Ericson were working together, focusing on Creighton's emails and liaising with the library. The pair were also looking over electoral registers and census data to try to establish family members, after the search on the suspect's property did not uncover a great deal of useful information.

'Roasted veg and fish or bean burger on buns and wedges?' Lisa shouted, as Polly folded clean laundry in the lounge.

'Ooh, bean burger please, with gherkins on the bun!' She folded the last item and began walking into the kitchen, when her work mobile phone rang. Taking it from her pocket, she headed back into the lounge as she answered the call.

'DS McCardle.'

'Hi, DS McCardle. It's Detective Leeanne Rooney, from Armed Response.'

'Oh hi, Detective Rooney. How are you?'

'Good, thanks. I wanted to update you on the Creighton

case. The suspect returned to the car park of Blyth Court this evening at 1827 hours. Officers spotted someone who we think is Creighton, but the suspect drove off.'

Shit, thought Polly, pacing the lounge as she listened to her colleague's update.

'A chase ensued and the suspect crashed his Ford Focus car. Police pursuing called for emergency service assistance and the suspect is currently in transit to NSEC Hospital.'

Placing a hand on her forehead, she closed her eyes for a second. 'Thank you, Detective Rooney. I appreciate the update. I don't suppose you know the suspect's condition?'

'Sorry, McCardle, I haven't had that information yet.'

'Understood. Thank you.'

The officers said goodbye and Polly sheepishly walked into the kitchen. 'Can that bean burger be put on hold?'

Lisa tutted then smiled. 'Of course. You okay?'

'Yeah. I've got to go to the hospital, though. I'll be back as soon as possible.' She shrugged, holding her palms up.

Her wife opened the cupboard and took out a chocolate bar. 'Take this then. And keep in touch.' Kissing her goodbye, she left the kitchen and exited their home to travel to the hospital, hoping David Creighton was still alive.

On her arrival at the hospital, Polly parked in one of the few free spaces. Getting out of her car, she rushed towards A&E, managing to step in minimal puddles, but still enough to splash over her black ankle boots and almost seep inside. Walking to the reception desk of A&E, she passed dozens of poorly people. *What a job,* she thought, shaking her head before the immediate realisation that people thought the exact same about the police. Leaning into the reception desk to be as discreet as possible, she flashed her police ID, and mentioned a man who had just arrived from a RTC with the police. The receptionist nodded, giving instruction on where the patient and police would likely be. Thanking the receptionist, she followed the signs to locate Creighton, or if not him, some other toe-rag with a warrant out for their arrest.

Walking the corridor that led to ICU, McCardle saw a colleague sitting on a row of seats part way down the corridor.

'Alright, ma'am?' he said, tilting his head up slightly.

'Yes, thanks. Was it you in pursuit, officer?'

He nodded. 'Yeah, me and then DC Sheenan behind.'

'Good work. I'm assuming it's David Creighton. What's his condition?'

'If not him, his doppelgänger! They haven't confirmed, and this is as far as we are allowed.' He rolled his eyes. 'Said they'd let me know in time.' His eyes moved to a set of double doors ten metres down the corridor.

Polly shook her head, knowing she wouldn't be able to get any information from the medical staff easily.

'The suspect was unconscious at the scene. His car ploughed through the barrier on the spine road onto the verge and rolled down. He was doing some speed. I'm not sure of the impact.'

She rubbed her neck. 'Thanks. I'll hang around. What time are you on shift until?'

'I'm twelve 'til eight, so still a bit to go.' He chuckled.

'I'll get us a cuppa then.' McCardle smiled and turned to walk to the nearest coffee machine, phone in hand to update CI Richardson, before she would call Ronnie.

Ronnie was drying the last of the dishes as Caroline enjoyed a bath. Singing along to Alexa playing rock ballads, he felt his mobile phone vibrate in his pocket.

'Alexa, stop,' he commanded. She ignored him as usual, and he repeated his instruction with more force. It silenced her and he answered the call. 'Poll, you alright?'

'Sorry to call late, Ronnie.'

'No bother at all. Is everything okay, pet?' He slung the damp tea towel over his shoulder and leant against the kitchen countertop.

'It's Creighton. He came back to Blyth Towers and fled the scene. Officers gave chase and Creighton's car crashed on the spine road. I'm at NSEC now. He's in ICU, but no updates.'

'Flippin' hell. Are the team okay?'

'Yeah, everyone is fine. Only Creighton was injured. Luckily, no other drivers needed hospital treatment. Just a little shook up, by all accounts.'

'I see. Do you want me to come up there?'

'No need, thanks. They aren't telling us anything, you know what it's like. I just wanted to keep you in the loop.'

He smiled. 'I appreciate that. Please let me know if you need me and keep me updated, Polly. The apprentice is in the bakery tomorrow, she's a whizz with the cakes and customers, so I'll come to HQ.' He let out a light chuckle.

'Perfect. Thanks. Now the focus is finding Emily Robinson. I'll update you on any changes and see you in the morning.'

'You will that.'

'And, Ronnie…'

'Yes, Poll?'

'Thanks. I couldn't have done this without you.'

'You could have, DS McCardle. You absolutely could have, but I'm never one to turn down a compliment.'

The call ended and Ronnie tapped his mobile phone to his mouth. Was it a win? Partly. However, the clock was ticking for Emily Robinson and although longer officially employed by Northumbria Police, former DS Ronnie Ericson would do all that he could to find the missing woman.

At 9pm Polly was still at the hospital. The doctors updated her on the suspect's condition. David Creighton had suffered a spinal cord injury, a head injury, neck injury and broken bones. By all accounts, had he been driving much faster, he would have likely died on impact. Now, he was unconscious and would be monitored overnight for any internal bleeds or urgency to operate. After the medical staff update, she left the hospital. Puffing out air, Polly got into her car. The rain had turned to drizzle and the car park was significantly emptier than it had been a few hours previous. Letting out a yawn, she rubbed her hands through her blonde hair and scrunched her eyes, before starting the engine and returning home. They were getting closer to finding Emily Robinson, Polly knew that. She just hoped it wasn't too late.

The next morning, McCardle rounded up her small team for the briefing. Ronnie stifled a yawn as he passed around a box of caramel shortcake to enthusiastic colleagues. Feeling a pang of guilt, Polly hoped he wasn't feeling that she and the force were taking the piss out of him. After going over the updates from yesterday, she wanted to inform the team on the chase and subsequent RTA involving David Creighton.

'As you all know, the suspect's property was raided yesterday. You all did great working on the items recovered, thank you. At 1827 hours yesterday, the suspect returned to the car park of Blyth Towers, in his Ford Focus. A chase ensued and Creighton crashed on the spine road. The RTA was significant and he is in ICU in NSEC Hospital with multiple injuries. I've left a message with ward staff for an update. The suspect's mobile phone has been seized for the analysts to investigate and the vehicle is with CSI.'

Clasping her hands together, McCardle looked around her

team, who were silent. No doubt thinking about what would happen if Creighton didn't pull through from his injuries sustained during the RTA. There was something about people evading justice in the force, and suspects dying, in many ways, was worse than never being found. There were multiple cases in Northumbria Police and throughout forces countrywide, where offenders never made it to punishment – not through the legal system anyway. And regardless of anyone's personal beliefs about heaven and hell, for the force, justice was only ever served in the courtroom. And for the MIT, this wasn't just about apprehending a suspect. This was also about potentially saving a victim.

Rising from her seat, she turned to the incident board, decorated with a range of photos and evidence from four cases: Oliver Thornton, Ryan Mortimer, Chloe Logan, and Emily Robinson, along with evidence and information about David Creighton. Her gaze returned to her colleagues as she placed a hand on the small of her back, her petite frame moving on the spot.

'It's back to the actions from yesterday with a briefing this afternoon to share findings. We can do it. Let's find Emily Robinson.' McCardle clapped her team and they answered,

'Yes, boss,' in unison.

As they left the room, Ronnie smiled at Polly and placed his hand on her narrow shoulder. 'You've got this, Poll, you've got this. We'll find her. I feel it in here.' He made his hand into a ball and tapped his stomach.

McCardle couldn't even feign a smile. This time, Ericson's gut instinct simply didn't feel enough.

Chapter 36

Struggling with a full bladder, Emily let out a muffled yelp under the thickness of the tape over her mouth. David hadn't returned and she guessed it had been a good few hours, although time certainly didn't fly whilst she was chained to a sofa bed, imprisoned by an unhinged librarian. It had, however, reached the point where Emily wasn't sure if she preferred him being there with her. Despite the abhorrent crime he had admitted to and the others she suspected – that made her feel like she was suffocating with sadness – being alone felt gutturally dark.

He had done this to her, made her feel reliant on him. And she was. Emily was dependent on that monster. The wolf in sheep's clothing who had duped her and was going to do Christ knows what to her. Stockholm syndrome, that's what it was called. She began crying. Her eyes stung as if birds had been pecking at them all day – raw, hot, and with her skin feeling grazed. Her underwear had just about dried from wetting herself and now she needed to go again. In the foetal position, she wondered if she could wriggle enough to move her tights down her body, reducing the wetness to her skin. Perhaps she could push her hips back and prop herself over the side of the sofa bed, to urinate onto the floor.

Sobbing, Emily couldn't believe that this nightmare was her reality. For around twenty-four hours, she had been in this prison. Life had completely changed by an innocent decision she made to let lovely librarian David Creighton interview her. She hated herself for being so fucking gullible. So fucking nice. So fucking stupid. Where was the help?

Her head pounded like she had been on an all-day bender. When David had allowed her to sit up that day, freeing her hands and mouth, she had looked around, sussing out her surroundings for a possible escape. But there was only a tiny window, that she doubted she would fit through, and a locked door.

Plus, there were no weapons. Nothing of great weight that she could lift and use to smash the window or break down the structure of the shed, even if she were to get off the bastard sofa bed she was chained to. Tears stung her cheeks like cigarettes being put out on them as she shook her head. It was pointless, redundant. She couldn't escape. Instead, Emily had to hope, to pray like she had never prayed in her life, that someone would find her. That Adam had alerted the police and they were looking for her, aware she hadn't returned from the library. And she had to pray that help would find her and that she wouldn't die, here, at the hands of a crazed murderous fan.

Emily had eventually fallen asleep, exhausted from panic and tears. She had soiled herself again, unable to hold her urine in and unable to slide her thick tights down that now clung to her skin, itching and stinging her flesh. Tilting her head back, she saw that daylight flashed through the covered window. David hadn't been back, at least not that she knew of. Certain that she would have woken from any noise due to her complete lack of comfort, she hadn't heard him. Instead, she had woken several times gasping for breath, feeling as if she was underwater, drowning, trapped and being pulled down further. Thirty-six hours. It had to be about that length of time that she had been there – that she had been missing.

Had Adam texted her on Monday evening, expecting a reply when she finished work for the day? Had he rung, concerned she hadn't responded? Then in the morning, attempted contact again? Perhaps getting more worried; it would have been unlike her to not be in contact. Had he tried other ways to get in touch then after so many hours, contacted her family and friends? Getting no answer, had he gone to the police? Emily closed her swollen eyes. She desperately hoped he had. Her life depended on it.

And where was David? Christ, he could be digging a shallow grave somewhere for her. She let out a yelp under the sticky gag. *Maybe he's been found, caught, arrested.* For a moment, she felt hope trampoline in her stomach. But then, if he didn't tell them where she was, she would die there in her wooden cell. Emily sobbed until exhaustion won the battle and she fell back into restless sleep.

Chapter 37

As the team got to work, McCardle couldn't help but focus on time, and the critical first forty-eight hours for leads. It had been just under twenty-four hours since Adam Swinton had come into the police station. However, Emily Robinson had been missing close to forty hours, and going on the history of the suspect, who was now in ICU in an induced coma, she could have been killed pretty instantly. She shuddered in her seat.

Ericson glanced over and shook his empty cup, asking her if she wanted one. She grinned and he rose from his chair, walking silently to the kitchen. Bringing two cups of tea back five minutes later, he placed them down on the desks and looked at his police-issued laptop.

'The neighbourhood team have found Emily Robinson's car. Four streets away from the library. They've broken into the boot and found nothing suspicious but it will get towed to the station for further analysis.'

'Great, thanks, Ron.' She groaned and stretched back in her office chair, only her tiptoes on the ground given her shortness.

The desk phone rang and her hand bolted to pick up the receiver. 'DS McCardle... Yes, put them through, thanks...' Her eyes widened and she shrugged.

'Hello? DS Polly McCardle speaking. Yes, that's right.' There was a pause. 'Okay, I understand.' Shaking her head, she looked at Ronnie. 'That's helpful. Yes, please keep me updated. Thank you.' She placed the phone back into its cradle. 'Shit! No change for Creighton. They're monitoring his vitals and will look at his condition tomorrow. We'll have to keep ringing to check.'

He shook his head. 'Bloody ironic, isn't it. He's in there in a coma and the poor young lass he tried to kill is also in there in a coma. What a bastard.' He inhaled and curled his top lip.

'Yeah, and he's still in control, even in a friggin' coma. If we don't find Robinson soon, the chances of survival will drop significantly.'

She tucked some blonde hair behind her ear and placed her hand on her jaw. Ericson took his glasses off and rubbed his blue, tired eyes. Their next task was to look over records relating to occupants at 67 Blyth Towers. It would show if David Creighton lived there with anyone at some time and any police involvement with occupants. The neighbourhood team would be conducting door-to-door interviews with residents of the flats, but they still needed a paper trail, and whichever lead came in first would be acted on.

Ronnie began searching the police database relating to the property for any incidents logged on the NICHE system. This was always easier than external requests, which could take a matter of minutes to hours, depending on who you spoke to in organisations. He typed Creighton 67 Blyth Towers into the police search, but nothing came up. He rubbed his jaw.

'Hey, Polly, didn't some of the tower blocks in Crosley used to have different names?'

She looked at him, eyebrows furrowed, clueless as to what he was talking about.

'Before your adult time, kidda. When the regeneration happened in the early 2000s, they started building those new housing estates along by the beach. The big apartment complexes, they called them...' He scratched his head before clapping his hands together. 'North and South Towers to highlight which end of Crosley Beach they were at.' Tapping a pen to his mouth, he took a second. 'That one, Creighton's block and another at the opposite end of town. They were renamed as the council got a backhander for so-called regeneration of the area. That one, became Blyth Towers and the other, Newsham Towers.'

He clicked his fingers in the air and tapped in 67 South Towers into the system. 'Bloody bingo!'

McCardle laughed as she moved her chair closer to him, giving her a vision of his laptop screen, that he tilted slightly her way. There were two entries from the property, going back almost thirty years. Categorised as domestics, with the perpetrator being a Mr Keith Rushworth and the injured party, a Mrs Moira Rushworth. Present at the scene, uninjured was a teenage child: David Creighton.

'There's our mother, Moira Rushworth.'

She felt a bubble of relief travel up inside of her. A lead. A precious lead. She typed Moira Rushworth into the system. Nothing else came up.

'I'll contact the council to check council tax records for 67 Blyth Towers and run a check on Moira Rushworth.' Polly picked up her mobile phone and after getting through to their regular contact, had some information within ten minutes.

'Suspect lives in Blyth Towers alone. Has done for a few years after his mother moved into supported living. Moira Rushworth: resident of Beachside Care Home in Hallington.'

Ericson Googled the number and called the care home from the desk phone. 'Oh hello, yes, I'm hoping you can help. My name is Ronnie Ericson and I'm calling from Crosley Police Headquarters. I'm wanting to ascertain if someone still resides there. A Moira Rushworth. You can call me back on...' He looked over his glasses at McCardle. 'Thank you, that's great. Myself and my superior, DS Polly McCardle will be there in the next thirty or forty minutes. Thanks for your help. Bye.'

He replaced the phone and pushed his chair slightly out from the desk, spreading his feet across the blue hard-wearing carpet. 'Well, that was easy. She wasn't even interested in calling back, just blurted out a yes!' He chuckled and interlocked his hands, placing them on his round stomach.

'Helpful! Let's go then.' She downed her lukewarm tea before they headed out of the door for Beachside Care Home, where they hoped another piece of the puzzle would fit into place.

As they drove towards the coast, Polly sighed. 'Did you have many, Ron, during your time? Abductions?'

He rubbed his forefinger over his top lip. 'More than what people often expect, sadly. Mainly kids. Most of the time taken by a bitter ex, or in some cases, groomed by perverts.'

She remained looking forward on the road. 'And the success rate, of them coming back alive?'

'Reasonable, yeah. With the young ones. It was all action stations, the community getting involved, press, all hands on deck. There was less of this confidentiality, cloak and dagger approach which as you know, pet, I think can actually be a hindrance in the force at times.'

'And the adults?'

He looked out the window, turning from her. 'Not so good success rates. Usually, less than half returned safe, in my experience. Nine times out of ten, it was drugs related, a partner, an ex-partner, or stalker. They never got took seriously then. They still aren't to a degree, but changes in the law helped.' He ran a hand through his silvery hair. 'As you know too well, Poll, the law will never stop some. Never. And some poor bastard will always suffer.'

They drove the rest of the journey in silence and Polly felt an overwhelming sadness. Perhaps it was exhaustion. Maybe it was that Emily was her age. Perhaps it was guilt that had she found Oliver Thornton's killer, it would have prevented Ryan Mortimer's death and the attempted murder of Chloe Logan. Maybe it was all of those things and the sad fact that Ronnie was right, the law would never stop some people.

Pulling up at the residential care home, they parked and exited the car.

'Nice place,' said Ronnie, glancing to the seafront.

As they walked to the entrance, automatic double doors opened for them, followed by another set of doors with an intercom. After pressing the button and explaining who they were, they were buzzed in. A middle-aged woman with rosy cheeks popped out of a room and introduced herself as the deputy manager.

'We're here to see Mrs Moira Rushworth, please? She won't be expecting us.' McCardle went on to explain the purpose of their visit on a need-to-know basis, emphasising confidentiality.

The deputy manager nodded. 'Moira has dementia, some days she's more lucid than others. She can get overwhelmed with new faces. I'll lock the office and take you to her room.'

Polly had thought about a vulnerable adult alert to social services regarding David Creighton on the journey to Beachview Care Home. He only seemed a risk to people involved with Emily Robinson. Still, she would speak with her contact at adult services and the care home might want to implement their own safeguarding.

The officers followed along a few corridors, Ronnie glancing around. Someone was pushed past in a wheelchair. He nudged Polly. 'That'll be me in a few years.'

She shook her head and rolled her eyes. 'Has Moira lived here long?'

The deputy manager, walking a few steps in front, turned.

'About two years, after it was no longer safe for her to stay at home.'

'She lived with her son, David. Yes?'

'Yes. Lovely man, he visits every few days.'

Ronnie pulled a face and mouthed, 'Lovely,' eyes agog.

'Here we are,' said the deputy manager after another minute. She knocked on the ajar door and glanced in. 'Moira. There are some visitors to see you.' Her voice was jolly and comforting as she pushed open the door, revealing a woman less aged than Polly was expecting, sitting in a high-back pink armchair.

McCardle and Ericson followed in, introducing themselves.

'Oooh, the cop-shop. Has David been wagging school again?' She chuckled and leant forward in her seat as Polly perched on the single bed and Ronnie sat in the corner, on a plastic chair, notepad in hand.

Putting on an act to try to discover where Creighton could have hid Emily Robinson, Polly omitted the fact that they knew that he was in hospital. Instead, she played clueless to his mother.

'Mrs Rushworth, we are here about David. Have you seen him recently?' she asked softly, leaning towards her.

Moira scratched her head. 'I saw him yesterday or maybe the day before.' She smiled then glanced out of the window.

'We really need to speak with him. Have you any idea where he could be?'

She turned her eyes back. 'What was that, darling?'

McCardle repeated what she had said.

'Well, isn't he at school? His stepdad will go mad if he isn't. The bloody toe-rag!'

McCardle smiled at the deputy manager, asking for help.

'Moira love, David was here yesterday, wasn't he? I had a nice chat with him and he brought you some new bed socks.'

She looked down to her feet, encased in slippers. 'Can you remember how he was?'

Clasping her hands together, she smiled. 'He's a good lad, you know.' Her eyes moved across to everyone in the room. 'He sticks in at school, normally. A clever bairn. Not like his useless father. Nor me, for that!' She chuckled at the end.

Polly rubbed her mouth. This was pointless.

'She's having a bad day,' the deputy manager said, grimacing.

'Aye, he's a good lad, our David. Sticks in. Not one for the girls, mind!'

Ronnie stared at his partner, who straightened up slightly.

'Well, there's plenty of time for relationships, isn't there? Although he did mention seeing a girl. He better not bring her home pregnant. I'll kill him and so will Keith!' She shook her head, eyes wide, and McCardle nodded enthusiastically. 'Stick in at school, I say to him. Girls will wait.'

'Can you remember her name, Moira? David's girlfriend?'

Moira puffed out air. 'Ah, no, I can't. Hopefully, she's just a phase. He's too young for all that carry on and love can be painful.' She glanced out of the window again and McCardle clenched her jaw, fearing they had lost the train of conversation.

Her gaze remained on the window. 'I said to him, you stick in at school, son, and instead of chasing girls, help your grandad on the allotment.'

The hairs on Polly's neck stood up and she flashed a glance at Ronnie, who raised his eyebrows.

'Sounds a good idea, Moira. And where is the allotment that he helps his grandad?'

Moira turned, her eyes fixed on the detective. 'Well, it's in Crosley of course, behind the old pit site.'

'Thank you, Mrs Rushworth. You've been really helpful.'

The three of them left the room. Turning to the deputy

manager, Polly spoke. 'We'll be in touch. How long is your CCTV footage saved for?'

'Sixty days. Anything you need, just let me know.'

After saying their goodbyes, the pair rushed out of the exit of Beachside Care Home to the car.

'Allotments! The bloody allotments. She's got to be there.'

Getting into the vehicle, Polly started the engine. Putting her mobile phone in its holder, she rang armed response.

'Hello, DS Rooney.'

'Hello, Leeanne, it's DS Polly McCardle. There's been a development in one of our cases, the missing person, Emily Robinson, the David Creighton case.'

'Oh, yes,' DS Rooney replied.

'We'll need back-up please, Leeanne? At the allotments behind Crosley Old Pit, now if possible. We think the victim is there.'

'Okay, DS McCardle. I can get the team ready to meet you there. What's your ETA?

'Fifteen minutes. Thanks, Leeanne.' Ending the call, she let out a mammoth sigh.

Ericson shook his head. 'That poor woman's failing brain could just have given us the million-dollar answer, pet.'

'Here's hoping, Ron. Here's hoping.'

The officers arrived at the allotments in Crosley, to armed response vehicles.

'The cavalry,' said Ronnie as he got out of the car, and the pair walked towards the armed response team, standing by the entrance to the allotments.

'It's locked. Padlock, ma'am.'

She glanced towards the gate. The officer turned to his colleague with the bolt cutters and chainsaw and McCardle nodded. 'Great. Thanks.'

The other officers walked over, checking their holsters as they did. She updated the team on the meeting at Beachview Care Home to nods.

'So, we don't know which plot is Creighton's. Ericson has emailed and rung the council, leaving a message with reception requesting the information ASAP. Hopefully it will come through before we have to start tearing into some of these immaculately-maintained structures.' McCardle turned her head, as did the others, scanning the allotment site that housed approximately fifty plots. 'Go in pairs. Risk is minimised with Creighton being in hospital. However, we can't be certain he worked alone and we don't know what we may discover.'

Officers cut through the locked entry gates, allowing the teams inside before Polly reiterated the approach and all began the search. She would update the team when they heard back from the council regarding Creighton's plot number and a map of the site. For now, to reduce possible wasted time, they would get started on the search – including a ground search as well as entering any sheds and storage units, by force where needed.

Ericson and McCardle worked separately, with an armed officer, operating with precision as a team. These situations reminded her how each department, each separate station across the force-wide area, made up Northumbria Police. No team was ever alone – all one big troop. A camaraderie that made her warm with pride. Ten minutes in, the officers were searching and nothing had been called out from any of the team. McCardle's phone rang with an unknown number flashing on the screen.

'Hello, DS McCardle, Northumbria Police.'

It was the allotment site manager from Crosley Council. He explained he would send a map straight over by email and that David Creighton's site was number 19. Thanking him, she ended the call.

She radioed across the site. Officers stopped and looked, then began to walk over. As all began to gather around, her phone beeped. Quickly opening the email from the allotment manager, she saw the map of the numbered plots was attached. Turning her phone to horizontal, she glanced around the site then back to her phone before passing it to Ronnie, to view the map. The remaining officers arrived in the group.

'Right, team, we have a plot number for the suspect: number 19. And a map from the council. By the looks of it, it is the end plot on the second row in. Is that right, Ericson?' She glanced at Ronnie, who nodded.

'Yes, boss.'

'Of course, it doesn't mean Robinson's there. Can I have six officers, the bolt cutters and chainsaw, please? Let's go.' She looked at Ronnie, and the pair began walking to the site, four armed officers in front of them, and two to follow behind.

Plot number 19 was on the end, a larger plot with a longer path leading to an immaculate-looking robust shed. It was the poshest shed she had seen in Crosley. More like a summer house, with a small window. Officers tentatively walked up the path in front of McCardle and Ericson. A small water butt stood to the left and there was a rusty fire pit to the right. Lines of string wafted in the wind between garden canes pierced into rows of soil. Raised planters housed more soil. Polly saw Ronnie eyeing them and knew their thoughts were aligned. Officers reached the entrance to the shed, with a metal mesh gate padlocked and a wooden door behind it.

A bit much for a shed, unless it's hiding something, she thought, as the officer mechanically chopped through the metal with the bolt cutters. The padlock dropped to the ground. Underneath, the shed door had a Yale lock installed. The officer turned to

McCardle.

'Police! Stand back!' one shouted before she nodded and they took to the door with the chainsaw, making it split.

Light sprinkled into the dark shed as the structure of the door collapsed, allowing the police to see inside. An armed officer stepped in first and ensured no risk to McCardle and Ericson. A woman lay on a sofa bed, restrained and mouth covered, with terror in her eyes. The officer glanced at her but his priority was clearing the site of any danger. A minute later he turned to his superior and Polly moved forward, entering the shed followed by Ronnie.

The inside of the shed was like one of those tiny homes, minus a bathroom. A kitchenette, furniture, and a sofa bed where the woman lay, foetal position, chained up. Hair matted, skin pale. Muffled yelps came frantically from under a covering of thick tape. Yelps of distress or gratitude, McCardle wasn't sure. However, she was sure it was Emily Robinson. They had found her, alive, and she had a fear in her eyes that Polly knew she would never forget.

Chapter 38

McCardle stepped forward to Emily Robinson, who looked like a wounded animal – wide-eyes surrounded by red rings of skin on her otherwise snow-pale face. Her naturally wavy blonde hair was clumped around her shoulders and neck. Polly softly touched her cold hand that lay tied on top of the other. She made noises under her gag as tears fell from her swollen eyes.

'Emily, I'm Detective Sergeant Polly McCardle. It's okay, you're safe now. I'm going to remove the tape on your mouth then we will get you untied and out of here.' Polly looked at her with gentle eyes.

The author moved her head weakly, tilting her chin slightly as McCardle slowly released the tape gag. When she pulled it off, a nasty red strip of skin and raw, bleeding lips showed. Emily gulped in air before dropping her head and sobbing, her mouth open as drool and pain flowed out. Polly placed an arm around her, letting her cry like a child as one of the officers cut her ankles then wrists free. She moved her arms slowly, as if they didn't belong to her until they reached McCardle. Hanging on to her rescuer, she sobbed and yelped as the last forty-three hours of trauma began to be released.

Just the two of them in the shed, Ronnie had called an ambulance and gone to tell colleagues that Robinson had been found safe. It meant they could return to the station for the never-ending list of responses and investigations.

'Thanks, Ronnie. And it's bloody good to see you,' said Detective Rooney.

'Thanks, Leeanne. It's bloody good to be back.'

Twenty minutes later, McCardle exited David Creighton's shed, closely followed by two paramedics, helping Emily Robinson to walk. She had no visible injuries on first inspection but would be taken straight to NSEC Hospital for admission and monitoring, ironically where Creighton and another of his victims were receiving treatment. As they slowly walked to the car, Emily, assisted by the medical staff, held her face up to the sun that was cracking through the light grey clouds. It stung her eyes, but she couldn't move them away from something she had been unsure she would ever feel again.

After supporting Emily into A&E, Polly and Ronnie took a brief statement, that would be added to once she had been health-checked again. They updated her on Creighton, that he was in hospital unconscious, and she was safe. Understandably she didn't feel safe, so ward staff advised police could stay with her. Psychologically, it would be a long road to recovery for the author and the officers needed to be gentle.

'We'll return in the morning, Emily. You'll be staying here overnight to monitor your vitals, treat any injuries, rehydrate you, and make sure you're okay. You'll have an officer just outside the room at all times.'

Emily placed her hands on the bedsheet, her eyes still soaked in water. 'Thank you. What about my family and Adam?' She began crying again. Ericson passed her a tissue and she dabbed her eyes, wincing at the sting of the material touching her damaged skin.

'We have their details and will call them. They'll be able to visit anytime.' McCardle glanced at the doctor who nodded, indicating that was fine.

A tiny smile flashed on her face. 'Thank you.'

'Righto, we will let the docs work their magic and will see you in the morning.' Ericson turned to Emily and they said goodbye, leaving the room.

'Christ on a bike,' he said, before shaking his head.

'Yup, and a stolen bike at that in Crosley.'

They looked at each other and smiled before both laughing. As they walked back to the car, the sun painted the pavement and McCardle felt the raincloud she was in dissipate. They now had to tie the evidence they had together for the CPS. It would meet the threshold but there were still some outstanding issues. First, Chloe Logan's future given she was still in a coma and unable to corroborate, and second, the fact David Creighton was also in ICU. However, for now, McCardle would update her team at the afternoon briefing, knowing that Emily Robinson was safe and a murderer was off the streets.

Ronnie and Polly sat opposite one another in the canteen. It was a few hours until the briefing and the team had been updated on Emily Robinson's safe return. Looking around, he smiled; nothing had changed at all in his year away. The staff, still the same, the scratched plastic blue chairs, unchanged. Even the menu was identical. And that familiarity, that uniform, was comforting and part of his history. Munching on a fish finger, he swallowed, his eyes on Polly opposite as she bit into a cheese and onion toastie, trying to not dribble the melted cheese as her teeth pulled away from the crisp bread.

He held his fork from his plate. 'You know, pet, I've learnt over the years what love does to people. The good and the bad. The extremes.'

She nodded. 'Ain't that the truth.'

'The beauty and the horror. And the number one reason why people commit crimes. Snatched love, desperate love, abusive love.'

She swallowed before chipping in. 'Cheating, unrequited

love, true love. We all have a motivator. It just doesn't turn us all to crime.'

He shrugged. 'You're right. But the number of times at dinner parties where people would ask me what I would do if someone hurt Kelsie or Caroline. And the truth is, we all have a limit. Over three decades in the force make me hope I wouldn't retaliate and let the justice system dish out the punishment.' He stopped for a moment, and inhaled, his nostrils flaring. 'But you know what, Poll, I'm not sure sometimes. And well, the law, the retribution for doing wrong, is it even a deterrent anymore with the prisons bursting and sentencing shambolic?' He looked at his colleague shaking her head.

'You're right, Ron. It's a shitshow at times. But it's our job to keep going, foot soldiers in an eternal battle.' She crunched into her toastie again and he smiled.

She was a good egg, Polly McCardle, and Northumbria Police were lucky to have her. *He* was lucky to have her in his life. They sat in silence for a minute or so. Polly had rung Robinson's parents and Adam Swinton, informing them that Emily had been found safe and advising they could visit her at the hospital. She had also updated CI Richardson and there would be a press conference after the briefing. Until then, there was more evidence to collate, and next-step instructions to action the team with.

The team gathered in the briefing room, cuppas in hand and notepads at the ready. Everyone had worked extra hours over the last week or so and the effort showed on the weary faces of her team, as well as in the outcomes they had achieved collectively.

'Okay, let's get to it. There's a lot to cover this afternoon but the great news, as you all know, is that Emily Robinson has been found safe and well.'

They cheered and clapped, and McCardle and Ericson joined in. It had been a team effort and despite being small in numbers, the MIT were most definitely mighty.

'Looks like there are no significant injuries except for the psychological impact of her ordeal. We have a brief statement from the victim, which will go to the CPS with the other evidence, and we will add to it over the following days. It includes the suspect confessing to Robinson that he assaulted Chloe Logan. Not enough on its own, but we have pieces of the jigsaw coming together.' McCardle clicked her neck and glanced at the incident board. Putting her pen to the photo e-fit and copy of Creighton's work ID photo, she continued.

'Suspect remains in ICU. He's been brought out of an induced coma. The hospital is providing progress updates, so we can go in as soon as a doctor authorises. We need to do hourly condition checks. I'll start a log, so if people can just take it in turns to call the hospital and document the outcome.'

The team agreed, along with a few groans of lacking sympathy for David Creighton's medical condition and instead, wanting justice. She understood, sometimes feelings and moral compasses were challenged in law enforcement. However, she had the added layer of having met Moira Rushworth and seeing the sparkle in her eyes when she talked about her son.

'Until we can arrest Creighton, there's updates and actions to share. DC Lucas?'

Lucas swallowed. 'I visited Crosley Library this morning, before we knew where Robinson was. The staff didn't have anything else to add but I got the records from the event that Oliver Thornton attended the night of his murder and the records of the event Ryan Mortimer attended, that matched with the days around the review of Robinson's latest book.

David Creighton worked both events. Also, the book chosen by Logan's book club on the night she was attacked was withdrawn by the suspect on his library card before the monthly book club meeting and returned the following day. So, it's something.' He shrugged.

'Most certainly, Lucas. Thank you. DC Birdy?'

Birdy clicked his pen and began. 'So, the IP address for a Jen Bradley on Facebook is logged at 67 Blyth Towers, Creighton's address. Going back over the comments he had made as Jen, there are numerous on Robinson's Facebook page, as well as Mortimer's Facebook journalist page and the *Northumberland Herald's* Facebook page. On Robinson's, they were of a very supportive nature, defending her against any critical comments or trolling. With Mortimer and the *Herald,* comments were of a trolling nature and only present on articles and reviews of Robinson's books. Surprise, surprise!'

Ericson tutted and McCardle nodded to Birdy, who glanced at his notepad before raising his eyes back to his superior.

'There's also search history on his browser for Chloe Logan, the North East Book Addicts, Adam Swinton, and, no prizes for guessing, Oliver Thornton.' Birdy took a sip of water.

'Excellent, thanks. All of these things are perfect for the CPS file. Boyd, do you have any update, please?'

'Yes, boss. I've gone over the CCTV footage from the bar Thornton was in the night he died. There were two men who I thought were a possible match for Creighton. The camera is a little grainy. I visited the bar and spoke to one member of staff who was working that evening. The manager checked the old rota and another member of staff on shift, is on holiday until Friday, so I have her contact details for when she is back in the country.' She tapped her pen to her mouth. 'Anyway, the guy on shift I spoke to said he wasn't sure about Creighton. That perhaps he was familiar but he couldn't be certain. So not of much use. But there's still the other worker to speak with.'

McCardle leant on the table near to the incident boards and rubbed her neck.

'Then we did some door-to-doors around the streets at Crosley Library. Someone said they were holding their baby by the window of a bedroom and saw two people passing down the lane. Their vision was only for a few seconds as there are high walls and garages on the back lane. When I showed her the photo of Creighton, she wasn't quite sure as it was dark, but said the people were male and female and the female had long hair. Not enough to use, but…'

Polly stood straight. 'Thanks, Boyd. I've heard back from the analyst team. They've been searching Creighton's phone, seized after the RTA. The phone was smashed but the SIM card has provided some evidence and more evidence has been found on his laptop. CSI will be analysing his car for any DNA from the victims. Mainly with a focus on Thornton, as we know he must have been transported to the woods.'

She looked at the incident board, to the photo of Emily Robinson, which was very different to the traumatised woman the team had discovered a few hours earlier.

'Hundreds of images of Robinson have been recovered. Files on his laptop. Images from the mobile SIM card. There is also eBay and Amazon accounts that Telecoms have requested purchase history for and bank statements to cross-reference.' McCardle pointed to the tyre tracks left at the scene of crime in the Mortimer hit and run. 'Suspect's tyres from his Ford Focus match the imprint left at the scene. We have enough evidence to meet the threshold for Robinson, and likely Mortimer. For Logan, we have the e-fit that the witnesses all agreed looked like their newest book club member, going by the name Andy

Palmer.' McCardle glanced at her notepad then back to the team. 'DS Munro from the Morpeth team confirmed that the staff in the bar also recognised the e-fit as the man with the book club. Statements have been taken by all and we can do a line-up ID if needed.'

She returned to her seat, tucking her hair behind her ear. 'Hopefully Chloe Logan pulls through and provides even more evidence. I'll be getting the okay from CI Richardson then sending the file to the CPS as it stands. The library have provided a list of the people who attended Emily Robinson's event the night Oliver Thornton was killed. His friend who was with him before he was killed, will need to be asked about the e-fit. Birdy, Lucas, if you can work on that, please?'

'Yes, boss,' they said in unison.

'Boyd, if you can keep on top of the analysts and check the online shopping platforms once the accounts are accessible. These are the priorities. There are still loose ends behind the scenes, but for now, this is all building a very strong case for at least three charges. Amazing work, team. Get home and get some rest and I'll see you all in the morning.'

Her colleagues clapped and began to chatter as they left the briefing room. McCardle stifled a yawn.

'You need an early night too. Maybe your Lisa will cook for you?'

She sniggered. 'Yeah, maybe the bean burger she offered me last night before the psycho crashed his car.'

'Might be a bit overcooked by now!' Ronnie laughed at his own joke as he reached for his empty cup. 'I can come in tomorrow if you want me to?'

There was a slight longing in his tired grey-blue eyes that Polly knew was purpose and pride. As much as she wanted him there every day, she also didn't want to fracture his and

Caroline's relationship or business.

'No, you're okay, Ronnie. Thanks though. You need a day squishing dough. It's all in hand here and I'll call. But maybe come in Thursday or Friday for a bit if you can?' She smiled at him and he clapped his hands together.

'Perfect, will do. Hopefully, they'll let Emily go tomorrow. Poor bugger. Mind you, she's got some bloody good new material for her books, hasn't she.' He ran a hand through his grey hair.

'She certainly has, and they say, write about what you know!'

'Fancy a walk?' Polly asked, arriving home an hour later.

Lisa was emptying a bag, having gone to the supermarket from work. 'Yeah, sounds nice.'

The pair got their winter coats on and headed out. Living in Whitley Bay had the benefits of the beautiful North East coastline all year round, and whilst there were many more cold days than hot in their part of the world, the coastline always seemed to look like a magnificent painting. Linking arms as they walked, they both looked out to the North Sea. Inky black, its rough waves slammed onto the rocks. Deadly yet desirable.

'Shall we have dinner out?' Polly asked. 'My treat?'

Lisa raised an eyebrow; they hardly ever ate out. Not only because the cost of pub grub and restaurant food had skyrocketed, but after eating on the go much of the time at work, or cramming food in at her desk, Polly liked the intimacy of the pair sitting at their dining table, their talking as the only noise.

'Yeah, lovely.' Lisa's stomach rumbled as if knowing.

She pushed some windblown chunks of long brown hair from her face, and the pair continued walking, discussing where they would go for dinner, hoping to switch off for the evening.

Polly slept surprisingly well that night. From knowing Emily Robinson was safe, David Creighton was under hospital watch, and from the comfort of being with her favourite person in the world. She remembered when her wife embarked on a career in social work and people, practitioners, even lecturers, talking about burn-out. That many people only practised for a few years before becoming too frazzled to function, as professional fatigue nibbled at them until it began to rip chunks off them.

The police were no different and Polly was pretty sure that a lot of the longer-suffering coppers just stayed because the pension was one of the best in any industry. It saddened her that life had such little balance and the retirement age kept creeping up like weeds in the pavement. Social work, the police, the medical profession, they were different worlds to so many jobs and for the vast majority of people, they would never have a clue what it was like to work even one shift in those roles.

Yet they all got scapegoated. Blamed for bad parenting, self-neglect, and abuse against others. Constantly told they hadn't done enough, there wasn't enough of them, and the wait for help was too long. It was thankless and brutal at times being a police officer. But on days like today, with a life saved and a perpetrator who would face justice, Polly McCardle knew she was born for the police. And when so many people in the world didn't give a damn, she vowed to never stop trying to achieve justice, never stop wanting to protect people, and to never stop caring.

Chapter 39

Driving to HQ the next day, Polly hoped the bright sky was symbolic of the day ahead. There was still a lot of work to do, she was under no illusion about that, but the leads had materialised, with a hefty weight to them. The press conference last night had been positive and would reassure the public. CI Richardson was happy with the team's performance, praising Polly. She had taken it with thanks, ensuring she made it clear that the whole of the MIT had been the scaffolding keeping everything stable, and that included Ronnie Ericson.

The morning's task was to send the file to the CPS for consideration. She knew it passed the threshold. Creighton would be arrested, charged and remanded, and a trial date would likely, and unfortunately, be no time soon. Another monster off the street, even though they walk amongst us in plain sight. As usual, she was the first into the office. Dumping her bag and coat, she walked to the kitchen.

Filling the kettle and switching it to boil, Polly tutted at the empty cake box someone had left on the countertop. Another Cake Station offering. The regular treats had become an addiction for the team and it wasn't going to help anyone's waistline or the canteen profits. After placing the empty box in the bin, she leant against the sink, thinking about how much she had enjoyed Ronnie being around.

They'd been through a lot in the eighteen months that they worked together before he retired. Some complex and frankly shocking cases. Polly grieved when DS Ronnie Ericson left. No one else brought her a KitKat or called her 'pet' – a comforting term of endearment that she'd always had from her late grandmother. Ronnie was a one-off and despite having him in her life outside of the force, he had become a comfort blanket inside work that she didn't want to give up.

Her inner monologue worrying that colleagues would think less of her, respect her less, and believe she wasn't competent, had all been in her own insecure head. Instead, they had seen her glow, become more assertive, and frown a little less as she had her sidekick back. Maybe she hadn't been ready to move up the ranks when he retired. Perhaps she still wasn't ready, but as the kettle clicked and steam poured from its spout, Polly felt that with Ronnie by her side she could take on anything.

Twenty minutes later, the troops began arriving, refreshed and chirpy with the success of the last few days. DC Lucas came in singing and McCardle turned, smiling at him, which encouraged some air guitar. Shaking her head playfully, she returned her view to the computer, as she checked the evidence folder for the CPS. After submitting the file two hours later, she ensured all were clear on their tasks for that day before heading to Emily Robinson's home.

The hospital had called at 9am and advised her that the author would be discharged within the hour. Adam Swinton was collecting her and McCardle would go to Emily's home to take an official statement. David Creighton was stable. He had communicated lucidly overnight and his obs were improving. However, he was showing signs of confusion and would not be released imminently. Signs of confusion translated to playing dumb to Polly. The scumbag would know the net was tightening to the point of strangulation, and no doubt he would try every delaying tactic, lie, excuse, and mitigating circumstance going.

For now, she would concentrate on Emily Robinson's well-being and getting that more in-depth statement. Not a nice thing for Emily to relive, but the sooner the better evidence-wise, and both the police and the medical teams at the hospital could refer her to therapy for her trauma. When McCardle arrived at the author's house, Adam Swinton opened the blue wooden front door. It looked like he hadn't slept much over the last few days, his eyes heavy, dark circles surrounding them. Polly walked through the door, stepping onto a grey hallway runner that lay on top of Victorian-style floor tiles. Adam hugged her. It was unexpected, but not unpleasant. Pulling away, he looked at her, his eyes watery.

'Thank you. Thank you so much. You saved her. That bastard…' He wiped the back of his hand across his nose and sniffed. 'If you hadn't found her…' Covering his mouth with his hand, he shook his head slowly, eyes wide.

McCardle tapped his arm. 'It's okay, she'll be okay. It may take time, but she's safe, and she has you.' She smiled at him, and he nodded.

'She's in here.' He turned, tilting his head as she followed.

Ninety minutes later, McCardle left Emily's home and sat in her car trying to process the interview. She would update the team at the briefing that afternoon but decided to call Ronnie before she set off for the journey back to headquarters.

'Alright, Poll?' he said, answering after a few rings.

'Half left,' she joked, copying one of his many dad-sayings.

He chuckled.

'Robinson is home. I've just been to take another statement. Sat outside of her house now, contemplating a drive-through cappuccino on the way back to HQ.'

'As long as you don't get any cakes from any competitors!'

'Never!' She laughed. 'So, Emily, she's fine physically. Psychologically, I can imagine it's going to be a long time. She jumped at noises whilst I was there, and was understandably extremely emotional.'

He sighed.

'Her statement has bulked out but mainly the same as the initial. Creighton appeared to be obsessed with her. He'd concocted some future for them as husband and wife. They were meant to be, all that stalker-like shit. He didn't hurt her after the initial attack, or touch her sexually, but showed flashes of anger and frustration.' McCardle looked down at the notes on her lap. 'Glazed over at times, is what she mentioned. And zoned out, as if he were two people.'

'Any more about the other crimes?' Ronnie asked as Polly heard the sound of crockery being moved in the background.

'No. Just reiterating that he assaulted Logan and talking about why. She mentioned Creighton referred to others. And she suspected he had killed Mortimer, especially after sharing an incident at the library where Creighton got agitated by Mortimer flirting with Robinson.'

'Ahh, interesting. Nothing about Thornton?'

'Nothing. I mentioned him and she became extremely distressed but said Creighton spoke of no other names. I didn't push it.' She glanced out her car window to the tranquil cottage Emily Robinson lived in and knew that in the short term she would struggle to feel safe, even at home. 'The file's gone off to the CPS. We'll get the charges, it's just then the conviction.'

'We'll get it, Poll. I'm certain we will.'

'Let me guess, you feel it in your gut?' McCardle mocked and heard him laughing down the phone.

'You're not wrong there!'

An hour later, McCardle was at her desk. Placing the phone back in its cradle, she groaned.

'No change?' Boyd said, collecting her boss's empty cup to make a refill.

She shook her head. 'I get it. Their primary need is to protect health but we need to arrest him.'

Boyd tilted her head. 'Hopefully soon?'

Polly tapped her pen against the desk. 'Yeah, hopefully. And fingers crossed, that young woman will come out of her coma too.'

Following the afternoon briefing, there was little to report and actions were minimal. Along with the update from Boyd, more information had been acquired to progress the suspect's online accounts. This included Creighton's Amazon and eBay purchase history, evidencing he had bought fake registration plates matching the one found on CCTV footage obtained from a house in the street where Mortimer was killed.

The online accounts also showed a purchase history of a headlight replacement. The next step was the arrest and questioning of David Creighton, currently on hold given his health condition. And the hoped-for questioning of Chloe Logan at some point. Officers would speak with the returning staff at the bar where Oliver Thornton was the night of his death, and his friend had been re-interviewed and asked about Creighton – claiming she couldn't be certain if she had seen him or not. McCardle updated DI Richardson on the slow progress of the day before her shift was over. She left work hoping that over the next few days, they could get to Creighton and arrest him.

Chapter 40

The next morning, Polly called the hospital on hands-free as she drove to work. Creighton was no longer unconscious and was stable but the doctor deemed him not quite ready for a police visit. She could hardly hold him in the cells when he was hooked up to monitoring machines, but she wanted him to know that they had the bastard by the ball sack. Before reaching the station, she called Ronnie and told him not to come in today. There was little to do on the case and officers were working on the never-ending incoming offences.

Luckily, McCardle was kept busy with other cases and knew that they were doing as much as possible with the Creighton case. DC Boyd had attended the bar where Oliver Thornton was last seen and returned with a bounce over to her desk.

'Good news, boss. The bar staff who had been on holiday recognised Creighton from the e-fit and library photo.' She sniggered before continuing. 'She said she remembered him as he had, "A face like an arse"!'

McCardle rolled her eyes. 'We always remember those. That's brilliant. Did you get a full statement?'

Boyd nodded. 'I'll scan it over for the CPS file.'

'Thanks, Claire.'

After having had early consultation with the CPS about the crimes, McCardle had the authority to charge Creighton pre-interview for the attempted murder of Chloe Logan, the murder of Ryan Mortimer, and the kidnap/false imprisonment of Emily Robinson. The CPS decided that Creighton would not be charged for the murder of Oliver Thornton, unless more evidence was submitted, which Polly hoped was imminent from

CSI, who were working on his car.

McCardle had the evidence obtained by DC Boyd that had been scanned over for the CPS to review, but she knew it wasn't as strong as she would like. For now, the arrest would be enough. As it stood, it meant that once the doctors at NSEC Hospital gave the green light, she could arrest Creighton, even if he couldn't leave his hospital bed. Do you have any idea when he will be fit enough for questioning?' she asked the ward manager the next day.

'Perhaps this afternoon, Detective Sergeant. The patient has been quite lucid this morning and had some solid food for the first time. In many ways, he has been a model patient.'

McCardle gritted her teeth, unsure if the nurse was being facetious and was angry at the comment, given two people were dead because of the man.

'Psychopaths usually are, that's how they groom victims.'

There was silence on the end of the phone for a moment before the nurse replied. 'Indeed. Erm, well, we will see you this afternoon. Please call before you will be attending so I can make shift staff aware.'

Putting the phone down, she ran a hand over her blonde hair. Ronnie would want to know and would likely want to accompany her to the arrest. Polly had to get the balance right and not push any of her team's noses out of joint. However, the MIT loved him, and weren't precious about roles and mucking in when needed. They knew they were all valued and respected.

'Fancy arresting Creighton with me this afternoon, Ron?' Polly was driving to a meeting, stuck in traffic. She didn't mind, it was along the coastal route and the scenery provided a palate cleanser to the stop-start movement of the vehicles.

'Too bloody right I do! What did the CPS say?'

She updated him on the charges authorised and that Creighton would be medically fit for arrest later that day.

'And the lassie?' he asked, referring to Chloe Logan.

'No change. Her parents are grateful for the FLO. As are Mortimer's and Thornton's families. Only it's not so positive in their case.'

'Great, I'll be in for two. And, Poll, brilliant work.'

She smiled before they said goodbye and hoped, for the sake of the victims, the good news would continue.

McCardle heard a kerfuffle and cursing as Ronnie entered the office. Struggling with the door, his hands were full of paper bags and boxes and his backpack had fallen down his arm, pushing a box to the ground. Placing the bags on the nearest desk and dropping his backpack, he turned and retrieved the fallen box, glaring into it as he lifted it from the ground.

'No casualties,' he said, grinning at Polly.

'Crikey, we are all going to need Mounjaro by the time this investigation is over.'

Ronnie chuckled. 'Sharing is caring, pet.'

After a cup of tea, some flapjack, and McCardle providing the update, they were ready to go and arrest David Creighton. Calling NSEC Hospital, she spoke with the ward manager, before the pair headed to the car park and drove to the hospital. As they walked down the clinical corridors, the only noise was the small heels of Polly's boots. There was a satisfaction in arresting someone. Also, a frustration to ensure a charge followed amongst all of the denial, lies, and blame that suspects often orchestrated. Controlling emotions was a superpower of the police at times, and she had perfected an expressionless face after hearing it all from the mouth of bullshitters. At times, people were wrongly arrested, wrongly charged, and wrongly convicted. But the vast majority of the time the police got it right, and they sure as hell had it right with David Creighton.

The officers moved through the first set of double doors to an intercom, which Polly pressed and they were granted access. As the pair walked to the ward reception desk, two nurses were milling about. They introduced themselves, one stating she was the ward manager. The pair followed her into a small, warm room with dated but soft seats, where they each discussed the next steps regarding the patient and offender.

'Okay, the nurses know you are here and the reason. We'll be outside if you need us.'

The three left the room and Polly and Ronnie walked to the side room where Creighton was. Greeting the officer waiting outside, McCardle thanked him before knocking on the door and entering. David Creighton's head turned to the open door. Although not in uniform, and one of them retired, the copper-look almost beamed out of them. On seeing his visitors, he swallowed. He was pale, and appeared thin as his body lay tucked into the clinical cradle.

'David Creighton?'

He nodded weakly. Of course, they knew who he was – Polly had seen the e-fit and photo of this man what seemed like one hundred times. Seeing him in reality felt different. Although he would never stand out in a crowd, for some reason, she expected to see something in Creighton. A defiance, a power that he had misused. Instead, he looked scrawny, meek, and pathetic as his eyes flitted from her to Ronnie. The officers moved forward. She stood a metre or so from Creighton's bed, Ronnie a few feet to her left.

'I'm Detective Sergeant McCardle from Crosley Police Headquarters.' Purposely keeping her gaze on Creighton, she tilted her head to the left quickly. 'And this is my colleague,

Ronnie Ericson.'

David Creighton flashed a glance at Ericson then returned his gaze to McCardle. He coughed. 'I'm not well enough to talk to the police.'

She kept her face straight. 'You are, David. And you're certainly well enough to listen. Now you've moved out of ICU, an officer will be outside your room twenty-four-seven until you're discharged.' Her gaze remained fixed on him as she spoke. 'David William Creighton, I am arresting you on suspicion of the murder of Oliver Thornton, the murder of Ryan Mortimer, and the attempted murder of Chloe Anne Logan. I am also arresting you on the kidnap and false imprisonment of Emily Jane Robinson. You do not have to say anything, but it may harm your defence if you do not mention when questioned something which you later rely on in court. Anything you do say may be given in evidence. Do you understand?'

He remained silent. Closing his eyes, he opened them a second later but his retribution was still in the room.

'Do you understand, Mr Creighton?' she said firmly.

Creighton nodded slowly. 'Yes.'

'You'll remain under police observation until you are ready for hospital discharge. Then you will be escorted to Crosley Police Headquarters where you will be interviewed. You will be entitled to have a solicitor present, either through your own solicitor or a duty solicitor. Do you understand?'

After saying yes again, he turned his head away from the officers. McCardle glanced at Ericson who nodded, and the pair walked to the door of David Creighton's room, the sound of quiet sobs reaching their ears as they left.

Chapter 41

It was a further two days until McCardle had the opportunity to question David Creighton at HQ. The team had been briefed and DC Lucas would be accompanying McCardle during the interview. Ericson would be sitting on the other side of the one-way glass, observing. Creighton arrived at the station on crutches, his broken ankle in a moonboot and his head and neck supported with a neck collar. He had been checked as being fit to be detained. Un-cuffed because of his injuries, he was presented at the front desk by two officers.

McCardle stood, shoulders back and stared into his cold eyes. 'David William Creighton, I am charging you with the murder of Ryan Mortimer and the attempted murder of Chloe Anne Logan. You are also being charged with the kidnap and false imprisonment of Emily Jane Robinson. You do not have to say anything, but it may harm your defence if you do not mention now something which you later rely on in court. Anything you do say may be given in evidence. Do you understand?' she said calmly.

David Creighton's eyes dropped to the lino flooring of reception as he said yes, before he was taken to an interview room. He sat, back straight, grey-skinned under the room's harsh strip lighting on a padded chair. The hard plastic seats, designed for discomfort, had been replaced due to his injuries. With no windows, the bright lighting bounced off the white, slightly scuffed walls. Creighton's solicitor arrived and they conducted their private consultation after McCardle gave the solicitor disclosure, then the police officers entered the room to question the suspect.

A plastic beaker of water was given to him before McCardle switched on the recording device and made introductions, then explained what would happen.

'This is your first interview under charge, Mr Creighton. You will be asked a series of questions relating to your charges and further questions relating to the murder of Oliver Thornton.'

He flashed a glance at his solicitor who was busy drinking from a take-out coffee cup.

'After questioning today, you will be remanded at HMP Durham, awaiting a trial date.'

McCardle crossed her hands and placed them on the table separating the officers from Creighton and his solicitor.

'I-I can't. I've got my-my mother to look after,' David stammered, turning his neck awkwardly in its restraint and looking to his solicitor for a life raft.

'I'm afraid that's not of my concern, Mr Creighton. You will be held in prison for the offences you have been accused of committing and you will have a right to a fair trial. Now, on with the questioning.'

DC Lucas balanced a notepad on his leg. Ericson was watching from the other side of the one-way glass, observing David Creighton's serious expression, wincing as he moved his recovering body.

'You like books, don't you, David?' McCardle began, going in gently.

'Yes, of course I do. I work in a library.' He let out a patronising pfft and McCardle raised her eyebrows slightly.

'And you like authors too. Love them in fact. And one in particular, Emily Robinson, you were infatuated with. Is that correct?'

He pressed his lips together and didn't answer.

McCardle continued. 'So much so that you lured her to

Crosley Library on 24th November, and after she rejected your advances, you drugged her and kidnapped her. Isn't that right?' The solicitor went to speak and she interrupted. 'Then you falsely imprisoned Emily Robinson at your allotment. Address: plot 19, Crosley Allotments, Homer Road. Is that what you did, David?'

Flaring his nostrils, he inhaled. 'No comment.'

'We have a statement. Actually, we have many statements David, from numerous people in relation to the crimes you have been charged with. You're in love with Emily, aren't you?'

Moving position in the chair, he shifted his leg encased in the support and took a sip of water. His solicitor remained quiet, shirt stretching across his stomach.

'You love Emily and you stalked her. Followed her every move and stopped anyone who got in your way to reach her. You are infatuated, obsessed with her, and thought you could have her. Take her, like you took books off the library shelf.'

Ronnie smiled behind the one-way glass. 'Nice one, Poll!' He clapped his hands together.

David remained silent.

'Is that true, Mr Creighton?' she said more forcefully, leaning forward.

'No! No, it's not. I cared about her, supported her.' He sneered then turned his head away, eyes unblinking.

'You did care about her and you supported her. Then you became obsessed, thought she was yours. And you pursued her behind the scenes, harming and killing people who got in your way. That's what you did to Ryan Mortimer and Chloe Logan. And I think that's exactly what you did to Oliver Thornton.'

'There is no charge against my client for Oliver Thornton, detective,' the solicitor said smugly.

'You're right, there isn't. Yet. However, evidence has just

been submitted to the CPS, so it's looking imminent.' McCardle grinned then took a sip of water. 'Why do you love her, David? What is it about Emily that you adore?'

His vision returned to her, eyes flicking momentarily to DC Lucas. 'I adore everything about Emily. She's magnificent.'

She nodded. 'And a great writer. I've read her books. Really good.'

A smile flashed on David's face at hearing from another fan.

'But this went further than admiration, didn't it? This became an obsession and you kidnapped Emily Robinson. Took her and held her in your shed. We know that. We have a statement from her and witnesses from the area around the library, as well as statements from your colleagues. We know that you did that.'

His eyes dropped to his hands in his lap as he wrung them together.

Polly side-eyed DC Lucas, who nodded. 'And we know you didn't hurt Emily in your shed, she told us that. You didn't touch her intimately.'

David's head lifted. 'I would never do that.' He frowned then inhaled quickly as if out of breath.

'We know. She told us that you had been kind to her in the past. Supportive when she had events in and out of the library.'

He smiled as his gaze went somewhere out of the interview room.

'However, David, we also know that you harassed, pursued, attacked, and killed people who were a threat to you or people who were unkind to Emily. We think you thought you were protecting her. Is that right?'

He nodded, not making eye contact.

'For the purpose of the tape, the suspect is nodding. You thought you were protecting her from nasty comments on social media. Trolls on her Facebook page who were saying hurtful comments. So, you defended her, using the alias, Jen Bradley. Isn't that right, David?

'No comment.'

'We have proof from your laptop. As Jen Bradley you responded to Chloe Logan. And Ryan Mortimer, who had left a less than perfect review of Emily's book.'

He jerked his head back and then winced with the pain. 'It was a scathing review! He was trying to sabotage her career.' David let out a low laugh. 'Yet he was still trying to fuck her.'

McCardle nodded. He was breaking. Emotion was breaking him. 'And that's why you killed him, isn't it, David? You killed Ryan Mortimer on 8th November as he was getting in your way and because you thought you were protecting Emily?'

David scrunched his eyes. 'No comment.'

'Young Chloe Logan, who had left negative comments on Emily's Facebook page. You found her book club, the North East Crime Addicts and you joined, under another alias, Andy Palmer. You went to Abbott's Inn in Morpeth on 19th November for their monthly book club, where you planned to confront her, make her pay for being nasty to the woman you loved.'

He shook his head and tutted. Polly wasn't going to take her foot off the brakes, she was just getting started.

'You discovered Emily was in a relationship with a man Chloe Logan worked with, Adam Swinton. That discovery made you really angry, didn't it, David? So angry that you strangled Chloe Logan outside of her car and left her for dead.'

Neither David Creighton nor his solicitor said anything.

'Only she's not dead, David. In fact, I was told by the hospital this morning that she is out of her coma and will recover. So, she'll be able to tell us herself.' This wasn't true but

McCardle was prepared to risk it.

His eyes widened and he rubbed a hand over his brown hair.

'And we have statements from the book club members who identify you as pretending to be Andy Palmer. You see, David, it's all there, all the evidence and witnesses.' She leant back in her chair, remaining silent for a moment in the hope David Creighton would realise he was screwed and start talking the truth. 'And we have a very clear witness in Emily Robinson. So, what do you think of all of that, Mr Creighton?'

He coughed. 'No comment.'

'I think we could do with a ten-minute break, Detective Sergeant,' said the solicitor, glancing at David who didn't make eye contact.

'Okay, that's fine.' She stopped the tape and DC Lucas rose.

Both left the room, allowing David Creighton and his solicitor to talk. Ronnie met his colleagues outside of the interview room and they headed to the vending machines.

'Hey, you've got more power than all the tools in Screwfix!' he said, shaking his head in amazement.

Lucas laughed and McCardle rolled her eyes playfully.

'Learnt from the best, didn't I?' She winked.

'He's got no comeback, the evidence is there,' said Lucas, shaking his head.

'Delaying tactics, nothing more. He'll crumble. Don't know when but he will...' Ronnie put his hand towards his stomach as Polly interrupted.

'Don't tell us, Ron, you feel it in here?' She made a fist with her hand and tapped her stomach, grinning as she did.

The three laughed as they reached the vending machine for a just about drinkable cup of coffee, before returning to the interview room. David Creighton was visibly uncomfortable on the padded chair in his body braces and unseen bruising. The image of Emily Robinson, handcuffed and restrained on the sofa bed in his dark, cold shed, flashed into her mind. The author's terrified eyes that had entered Polly's dreams more than once over the last five nights. Monsters like David Creighton walked amongst us, but at least there was now one less in the community.

'Okay, David. I want to talk about Ryan Mortimer. Crosley Library were hosting an event for Emily Robinson and her recent book release on 27th October. You were working and supported the event. A witness statement claims that you interjected in a flirtatious conversation from Ryan Mortimer aimed at Emily Robinson. It was alleged it was protective in nature but over the top and not requested. Added to this were a number of social media comments you made under the guise of Jen Bradley on both Ryan Mortimer's journalist page and the *Northumberland Herald's* page relating to Mortimer's articles.'

Lucas slid a cardboard file across the desk to McCardle, who opened it and sifted through a few sheets of paper. 'Here we go. On a review of *Persuasion* by Emily Robinson on the *Northumberland Herald's* Facebook page, dated 28th October, you, under the alias of Jen Bradley commented the following: "A terrible write-up and review by an amateur journalist who knows nothing about literature. Stick to writing about trashy films".'

McCardle glanced up at the suspect, who glared at her. 'And another the following day: "When are you going to sack this creep who knows nothing about anything? He makes your newspaper look like *The Sun*".'

David sniggered slightly in his chair before his face turned stony again.

'We also have a number of comments on Ryan Mortimer's journalist page. Here is one following a post about *Persuasion*:

"You are wrong. This book is a masterpiece. Just because she doesn't fancy you, you criticise her book. Very childish". Again, from Jen Bradley.'

David tutted and looked away from her.

'And another here: "Go and crawl back under whichever stone you came from before someone makes you". Have you got anything to say about any of these examples, Mr Creighton?' Shutting the paper file, she interlocked her hands, placing them on the plastic-coated table separating them.

'No comment.'

'After these incidents of trolling, Ryan Mortimer's body was found at the Jeffreys Street entrance to Crosley Country Park on the early morning of 8th November. He was the victim of a brutal hit and run. Do you know anything about that, David?'

He swallowed and remained silent.

'Tyre imprints were found at the scene that match the tyres of your Ford Focus. There were fragments of a car headlight cover found at the scene where the car struck the victim. We have records of you purchasing a headlight cover from your Amazon account.'

David began looking at the ceiling like a disinterested teenager. McCardle banged her fists onto the table and he flinched before looking at her.

'Mr Creighton, I suggest you listen carefully to what I am saying and consider your answers before replying. With the evidence we have so far against you, you are likely to never see a world outside of prison again. And more evidence is coming in as we speak. The less you co-operate, the worse this will be for you. I'm sure your solicitor would reiterate that.'

She glanced at the solicitor who held a palm up. 'My client will tell the truth, Detective Sergeant. Do not put words into his mouth.'

'Okay. Let's put it simply. David Creighton, did you kill Ryan Mortimer?'

'No comment.'

'Did you knock Ryan Mortimer over on the Jeffreys Street entrance to Crosley Country Park and flee the scene?'

'No comment.'

McCardle was keeping her cool when inside she wanted to karate chop his sore neck.

'What about Oliver Thornton?'

Lucas opened the cardboard file and took out an image of Oliver.

'This is Oliver Thornton. He was aged just twenty-one when he was murdered, the night of an event at Crosley Library on 29th September. And guess what, Mr Creighton? That event included a talk by Emily Robinson and you were on shift at the library.'

Creighton glared at McCardle and she stared back, refusing to blink. The pair held a gaze that could have set a pile of driftwood on fire. Not prepared to back down, she kept focused, unblinking, until he whipped his head away, wincing at the pain it produced to his neck. She grinned.

'The night Oliver Thornton was killed, he visited a bar with his friend after the library event. Bar staff recognise that you were in the bar, Leigh's Place, and have made statements confirming this. We also have CCTV footage identifying you.'

It wasn't exactly untrue, the footage was just very grainy but the image still looked like Creighton, and crikey, everyone and the sniffer dogs knew it was him.

'We believe that you followed Oliver Thornton and stoved his head in with a blunt instrument before transporting him to Ashmouth Woods, where you buried him in a shallow grave. Is that what you did, David?'

'No comment.' He sipped some water.

'Crime scene investigators have ripped your car to bits for DNA matching Oliver Thornton. The results are imminent and I am certain they will find it. So, I'll ask again, did you kill Oliver Thornton?'

'No comment,' he drawled, rolling his eyes.

This psychopathic bastard had killed two people, attempted to murder another, and had kidnapped and imprisoned another, yet he sat there, speaking as if someone was asking him to answer the door when he'd just sat down to watch a film. McCardle vowed she would do everything she could to ensure he joined the seventy-plus male prisoners in the UK serving whole-life sentences.

'Well, David, I can see that we are boring you, so DC Lucas and I will give you once last chance to answer four questions before we end this interview and you will be transported to HMP Durham.'

David shot a panicked eye to his solicitor, who shrugged then cleared his throat.

'David William Creighton, did you murder Oliver Thornton on 29th September?'

'No comment,' he said quickly, panic beginning to seep into his voice at the thought of the big, bad prison.

It made McCardle want to smile, but she held it together, like she always did. 'David William Creighton, did you murder Ryan Mortimer on 8th November?'

'No comment.'

'David William Creighton, did you attempt to murder Chloe Anne Logan on 19th November?'

He swallowed. 'No comment.'

'David William Creighton, did you kidnap and falsely imprison Emily Jane Robinson on 25th November?'

'No comment.'

'Okay, Mr Creighton. That's all of our questions.' She looked at her watch. 'Interview terminated at 1427 hours.' Leaning over to stop the tape, she glanced at Lucas, who rose and left the room. 'Mr Creighton, you will be placed in a cell then transferred to HMP Durham. Do you understand?'

He nodded, looking at his solicitor, who gestured for him to stand. Leaning against the table, he took his crutches with shaky hands. Officers entered the interview room to assist Creighton to the holding cell. Leaving the room quietly, he didn't look at McCardle but her eyes remained burning into him.

Polly wanted a cigarette, even her vape wouldn't do right now. However, cake from the Cake Station was the best alternative. Ericson, Lucas, and McCardle walked in silence back up the stairs to their office.

'I'll make the cuppas, boss,' Lucas said as the other two walked towards the briefing room. 'And I'll bring some of that ginger cake, if there's any left.' He raised an eyebrow.

For the next twenty minutes, the team went over the interview with David Creighton. There was nothing more they could do right now. The CPS would receive further evidence, including the hopefully imminent DNA match of Thornton from Creighton's car. The accused would be held in prison, on remand awaiting trial. He would get a chance to submit a plea within a few weeks of being on remand and a trial date would be announced. Until then, the team's hands were tied.

CI Richardson popped into the office before the team briefing and thanked everyone for their great work. Taking Ronnie to one side, Richardson thanked him personally for coming in and supporting the team.

'You know, Ericson, you're always welcome back, in a paid role.'

Ronnie chuckled.

'I mean it, under the retire and return scheme. Your pension would remain protected. Something to consider, perhaps.' Richardson tapped him on the shoulder and exited the office, leaving Ronnie thinking about the pulls in his life.

The small team entered the briefing room, all full of pride and cake. After reiterating the last few hours interviewing David Creighton, McCardle turned to the incident board plastered with the suspect, the victims, and evidence.

'What went wrong with David Creighton?' she asked, glancing at the mug shot of a distinctly average man. And that was the problem. The librarian turned killer was markedly average. He didn't stand out, wasn't exceptional or concerning enough to warrant interest. He didn't look like the weirdo or pervert that would gain attention. He was an average man to the outside world, living an average life, and performing an average job with colleagues who liked him.

Sitting down, Polly began. 'David Creighton held an obsession that he thought gave him the solution to the problem he always had: the need for love from a woman. The need to have something for himself that made him feel like a man. After years of being bullied and controlled by his stepfather, then mother. Lack of friends, intimate relationships, and despite a decent job, he had little else on his list of achievements. He saw an answer in Emily Robinson. Her mind, her work, her as a person. He became a character himself, thinking he was her hero, her happy-ever-after, and that the object of his affection would admire his efforts and see he did it all for her. However, he was a monster, a villain of the worst kind.'

Taking a deep breath, she glanced back at his mugshot. 'Warped? Undoubtedly. But he needed something. A purpose. To feel loved and love. She was an easy target. Beautiful, talented, generous in her community engagement and grateful for her support at the local library. A genuine thank you and smile from Robinson, made Creighton think he was special. That she wanted more, wanted him, and he wanted to impress her.' Pressing her lips together, she leant back in her chair and the room remained silent for a few seconds.

'Jesus, he could have tried conventional methods, boss. "Fancy a meal one time?" Rather than going on a murder and kidnap rampage!' Boyd said, shaking her head.

'Absolutely, Boyd. But then that's not in the psychopath's handbook. So now, we hope Chloe Logan pulls through and perhaps that Creighton confesses.'

Lucas made a hmph noise.

'Each of you has done a sterling job.' She looked around every MIT member, including her old boss and dear friend Ronnie Ericson. 'Thank you. You've all been phenomenal and I couldn't be prouder.'

'And you played a blinder too, boss,' said Ericson, before the room erupted into applause.

It was the end of the working day and everyone packed up, grateful to be heading home to loved ones. Polly and Ronnie walked out together.

'So, Richardson mentioned the retire and return scheme. That maybe I could come back, part-time, paid and that.'

Polly's eyes lit up. 'And?' she said eagerly, wondering what he had said.

'What would you think about it?'

She frowned. 'You know what I think, Ron.' She bit her lip, feeling embarrassed about what she was about to say but knowing she had to. 'I've missed you every day since you left.'

He pulled her in sideways and embraced her lightly.

'I've missed you too, pet. You're the extra daughter I never wanted.' He winked, knowing she knew that Ronnie would have loved to have been Polly's father.

'So will you? Come back?'

'I'll think about it, pet. It would only be part time, if I do.'

'They probably can't afford any more than that. And crikey, our waistlines can't afford for you to be feeding us sugar and cream five days a week!'

He chuckled. 'You reckon Emily Robinson will be okay?'

'Yeah, I think she will. She's a strong woman.' Polly took her car keys from her pocket and clicked the central locking.

'Just like someone I know.' He smiled at her. 'Well, if nothing else, she's certainly got some material for a new book.' He puffed out air and shook his head. 'Perhaps she could call it *Number One Fan!*'

The following day, DNA evidence of a positive match to Oliver Thorton came back from Creighton's car. It had been expected, and although it took longer than McCardle hoped, it meant another charge against David Creighton. It also meant certain justice for the Thornton family. Polly had thought about the young lad almost daily since the case came in a few months ago. Now, with clear evidence, she felt the balance of sadness lift a little with the prospect of justice.

The next week, Chloe Logan woke from her coma. During the following days, she was confused and in and out of consciousness. It was a critical time to monitor any permanent damage from the attack and attempted murder by David Creighton. However, as the days passed, Chloe grew stronger, much to the relief of her desperate parents, family, and friends. Slowly, memories of the night came back and she was able to give a robust statement, implicating Creighton as well as identifying him from the photographs.

It was a key piece of evidence that McCardle needed, but more importantly, Chloe Logan had survived. Along with Emily Robinson, she could live her life and help put a murderer behind bars. New evidence had been submitted to the CPS and a trial date set for just under ten months' time. A long pause for the victims and the bereaved families who had to put a peeling plaster over their lives – until they knew the outcome and possible small gain of justice in an otherwise life-changing, heart-breaking situation.

Creighton would go to prison for a long time, likely life. Trials were torturous for families and David Creighton had refused to enter a plea, meaning the witnesses and families would have to relive their nightmare in court.

As the days passed, cases continued to come in whilst the team waited for the trial date, along with so many other trial dates. Six weeks after David Creighton was sent to HMP Durham on remand, there was a call on her desk phone. McCardle cleared her throat and reached for the handset, lifting it and speaking.

'DS McCardle?'

'Hi, DS McCardle, we have a manager from the CPS on the phone.'

'Thanks.' The call came through. 'DS McCardle speaking.'

'Hi, DS McCardle. It's Phil Smith from the CPS. I've got an update on one of your cases: David Creighton.'

Polly held her breath momentarily as she tapped her pen against the open notepad on her desk. She swallowed. 'Okay.'

'There will be no witnesses required, DS McCardle. David Creighton has changed his plea.'

Acknowledgements

Writing a book takes a team, and I'm eternally grateful for the support I receive to write and create mine. This support comes from someone who likes one of my posts on social media through to those closest to me, who champion my every endeavour.

The biggest thanks to Paul, my partner in love and life, who encourages me, supports me, and carries me when I feel weak. Thank you to my parents and whole family, who always ask and support. And a huge thanks to Carl, Jarmila, and Julia for your expertise.

An eternal thanks to you, reader, for choosing this book when there are so many books out there. Readers will always be my fuel to keep writing, and I'm forever thankful to each person who reads my work. I value each of you and if you ever want a name in a book, get in touch! A special thank you to the readers who diligently support me by reading each book I publish, regardless of genre. I take a risk by writing in different genres, but I guess I have a lot to say and many characters fighting to be heard!

If you enjoyed the book, please do leave a review and tell people about it — this is the ultimate thank you to an author and really helps books to be seen.

For more information and updates on my other publications and releases, please follow my website/socials and those of Write on the Tyne (CIC).

www.writeonthetyne.com
www.helenaitchisonwrites.com
Instagram: @helen.aitchison_writes
Twitter / X: @aitchisonwrites
Facebook: @Helen Aitchison Writes
Instagram: @writeonethetyne
Facebook: @Write on the Tyne

Other books by Helen Aitchison:

The Dinner Club
The Life and Love (Attempts) of Kitty Cook
The 31 Days of May
Somebody's Nobody: Book 1 in the Ericson and McCardle crime series
Broken Boundaries
A Home for Every Cat
Veterans' Voices
In the Footsteps of Walker Women
Recovery Voices
Changing Futures
Tales from Low Newton Jail
Ramblings